J T SERIES
Krueger, Jim
Tomo. The Argon deception

WITHDRAWN

091409

ZONDERVAN®

The Argon Deception
Copyright © 2008 by Funnypages Productions, LLC

Requests for information should be addressed to:
Zondervan, Grand Rapids, Michigan 49530

CIP applied for
ISBN: 978-0-310-71303-6

This book published in conjunction with Funnypages Productions, LLC, 106 Mission Court, Suite 704, Franklin, TN 37067

Series Editor: Bud Rogers
Managing Art Director: Merit Alderink

Printed in the United States of America
08 09 10 11 • 5 4 3 2 1

THE ARGON DECEPTION

SERIES EDITOR
BUD ROGERS

STORY BY
JIM KRUEGER

ART BY
ARIEL PADILLA

CREATED BY
TOM BANCROFT AND **ROB CORLEY**

funnypages
PRODUCTIONS

ZONDERVAN®
ZONDERVAN.com/
AUTHORTRACKER
follow your favorite authors

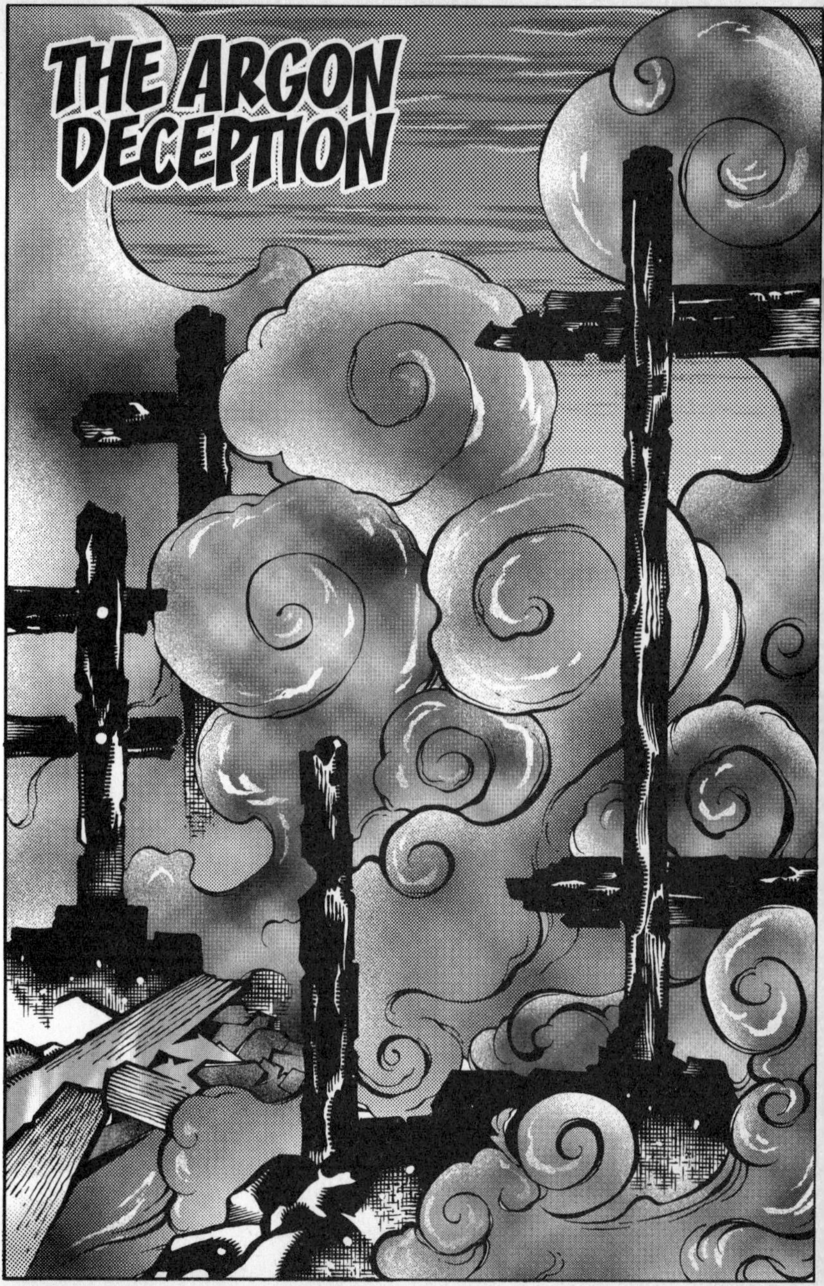
THE ARGON DECEPTION

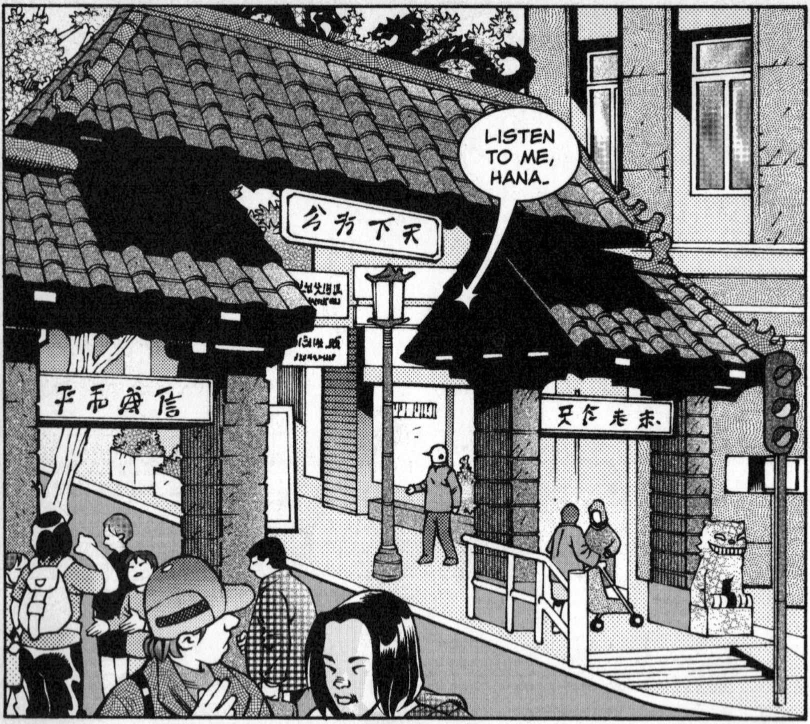
LISTEN TO ME, HANA.

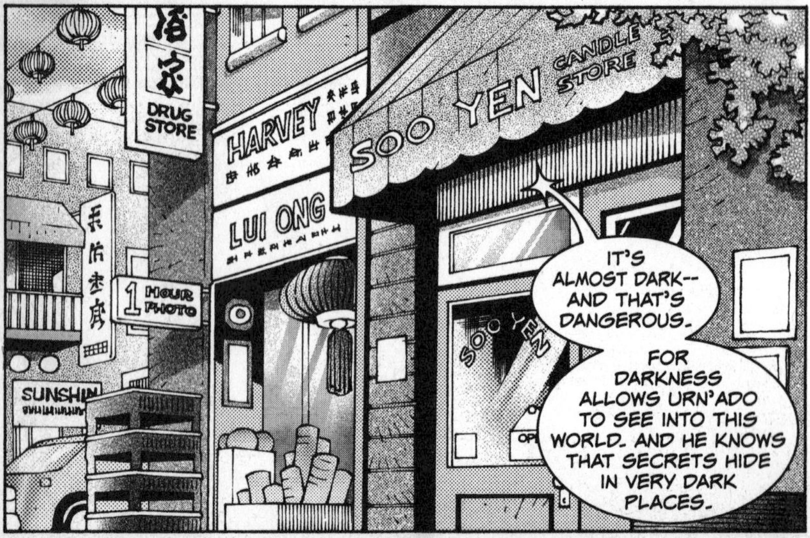
DRUG STORE
HARVEY
SOO YEN CANDLE STORE
LUI ONG
1 HOUR PHOTO
SOO YEN
IT'S ALMOST DARK-- AND THAT'S DANGEROUS.
FOR DARKNESS ALLOWS URN'ADO TO SEE INTO THIS WORLD. AND HE KNOWS THAT SECRETS HIDE IN VERY DARK PLACES.

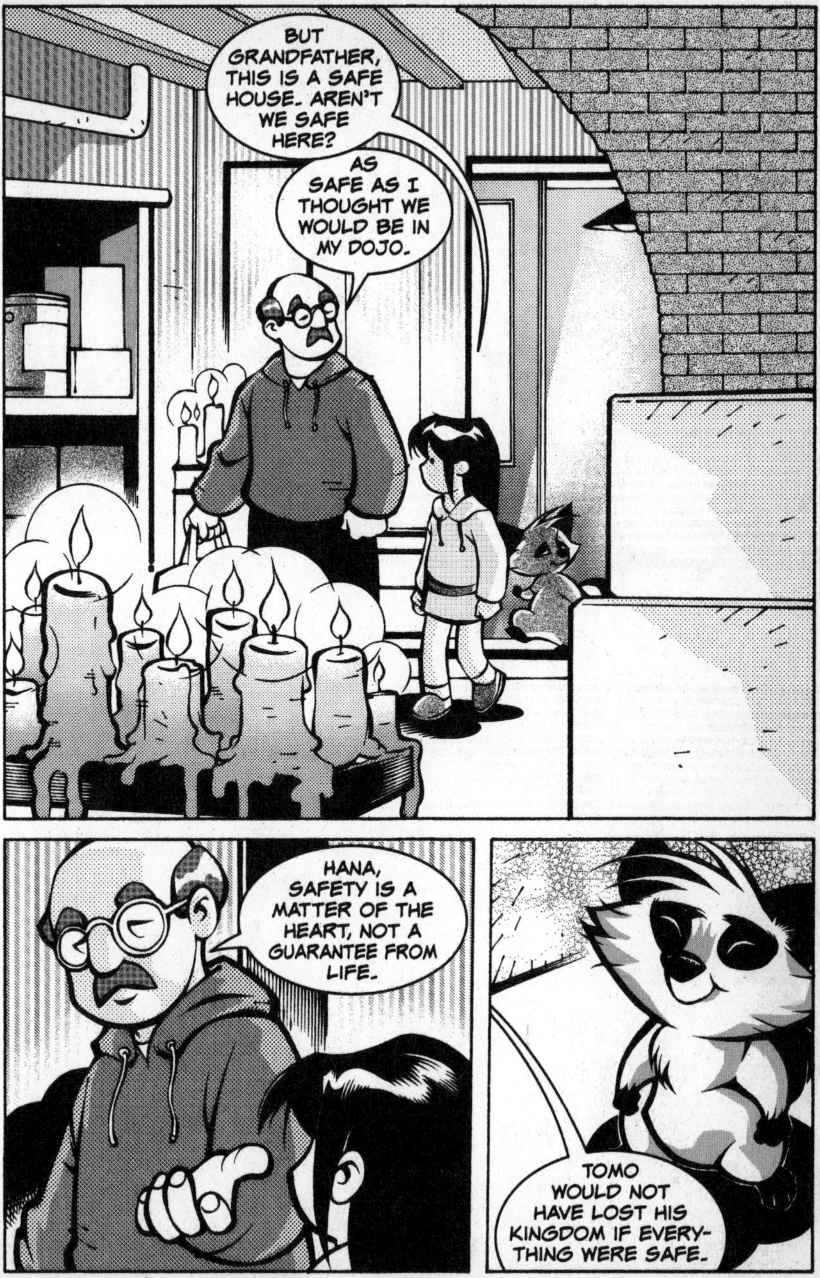
BUT GRANDFATHER, THIS IS A SAFE HOUSE. AREN'T WE SAFE HERE?
AS SAFE AS I THOUGHT WE WOULD BE IN MY DOJO.
HANA, SAFETY IS A MATTER OF THE HEART, NOT A GUARANTEE FROM LIFE.
TOMO WOULD NOT HAVE LOST HIS KINGDOM IF EVERY-THING WERE SAFE.

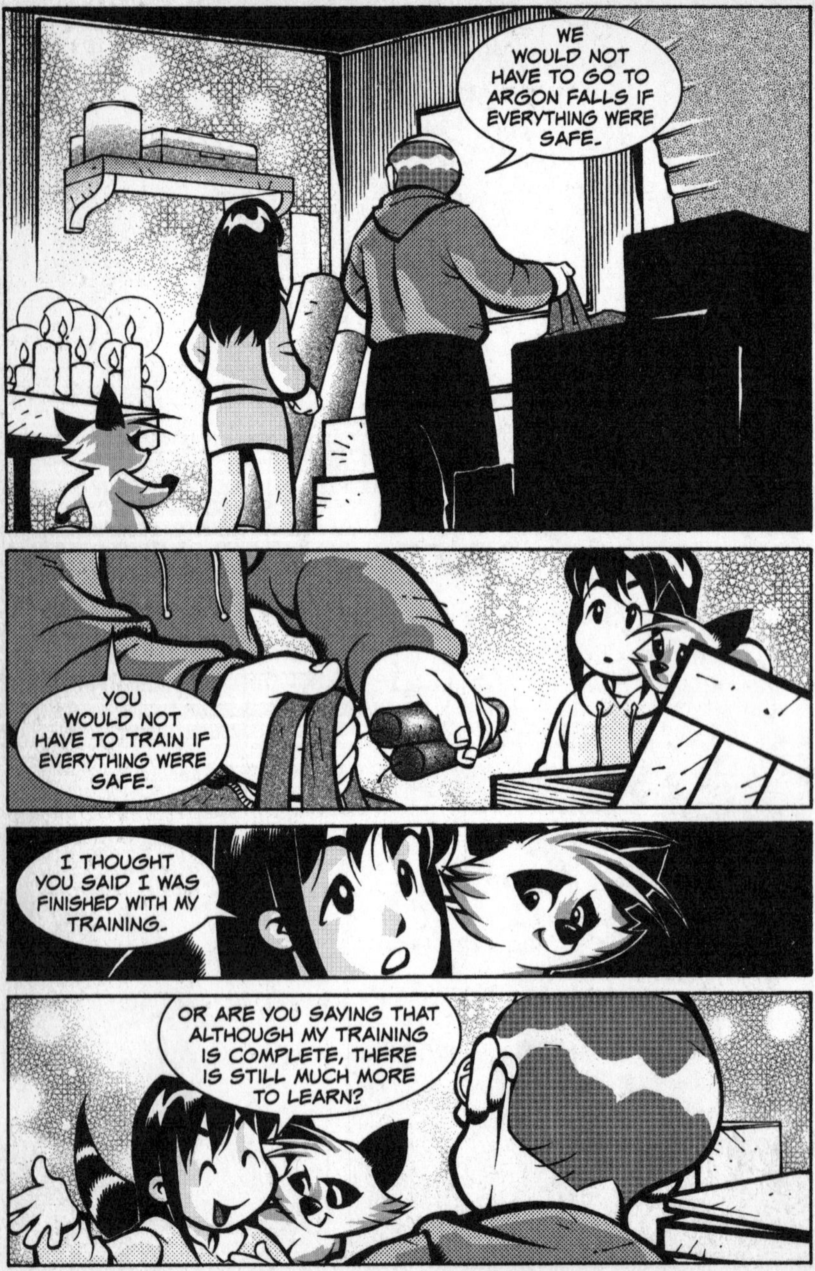
WE WOULD NOT HAVE TO GO TO ARGON FALLS IF EVERYTHING WERE SAFE.
YOU WOULD NOT HAVE TO TRAIN IF EVERYTHING WERE SAFE.
I THOUGHT YOU SAID I WAS FINISHED WITH MY TRAINING.
OR ARE YOU SAYING THAT ALTHOUGH MY TRAINING IS COMPLETE, THERE IS STILL MUCH MORE TO LEARN?

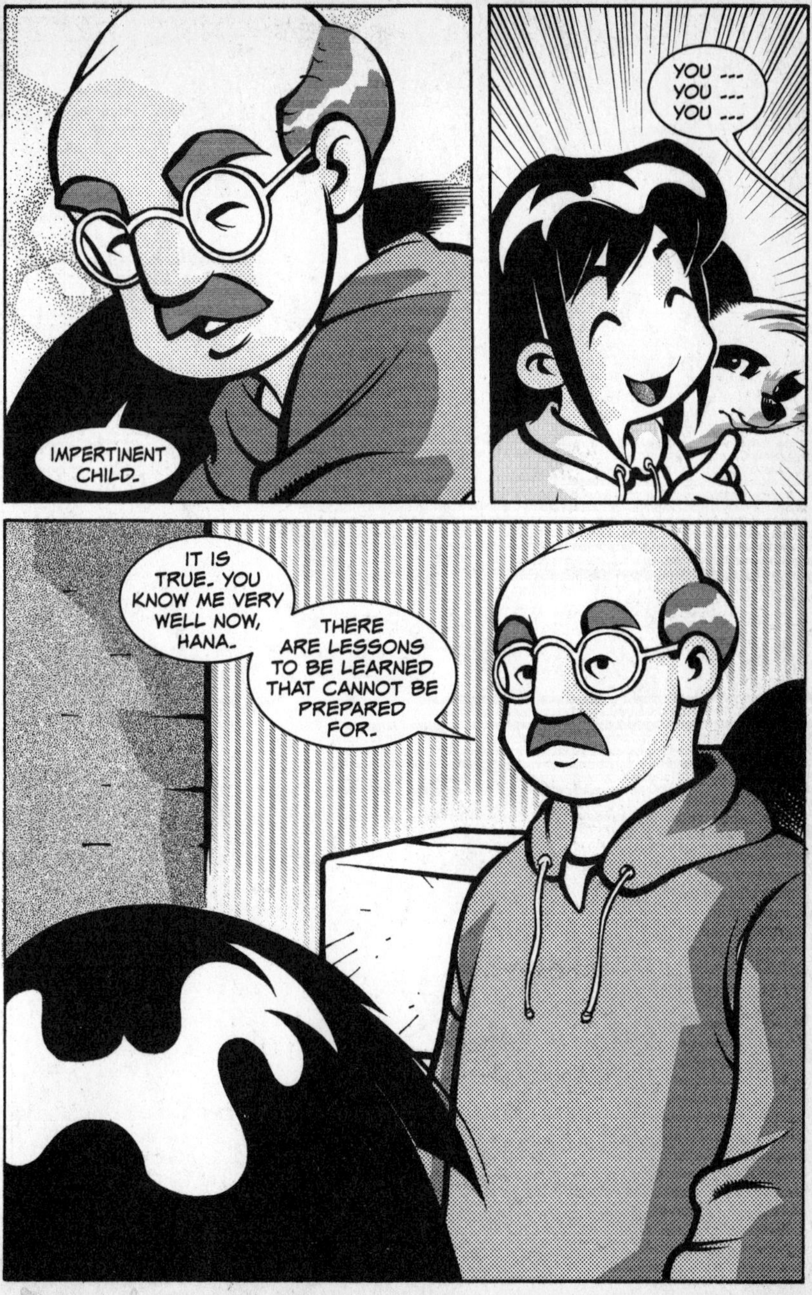
IMPERTINENT CHILD.
YOU --- YOU --- YOU ---
IT IS TRUE. YOU KNOW ME VERY WELL NOW, HANA.
THERE ARE LESSONS TO BE LEARNED THAT CANNOT BE PREPARED FOR.

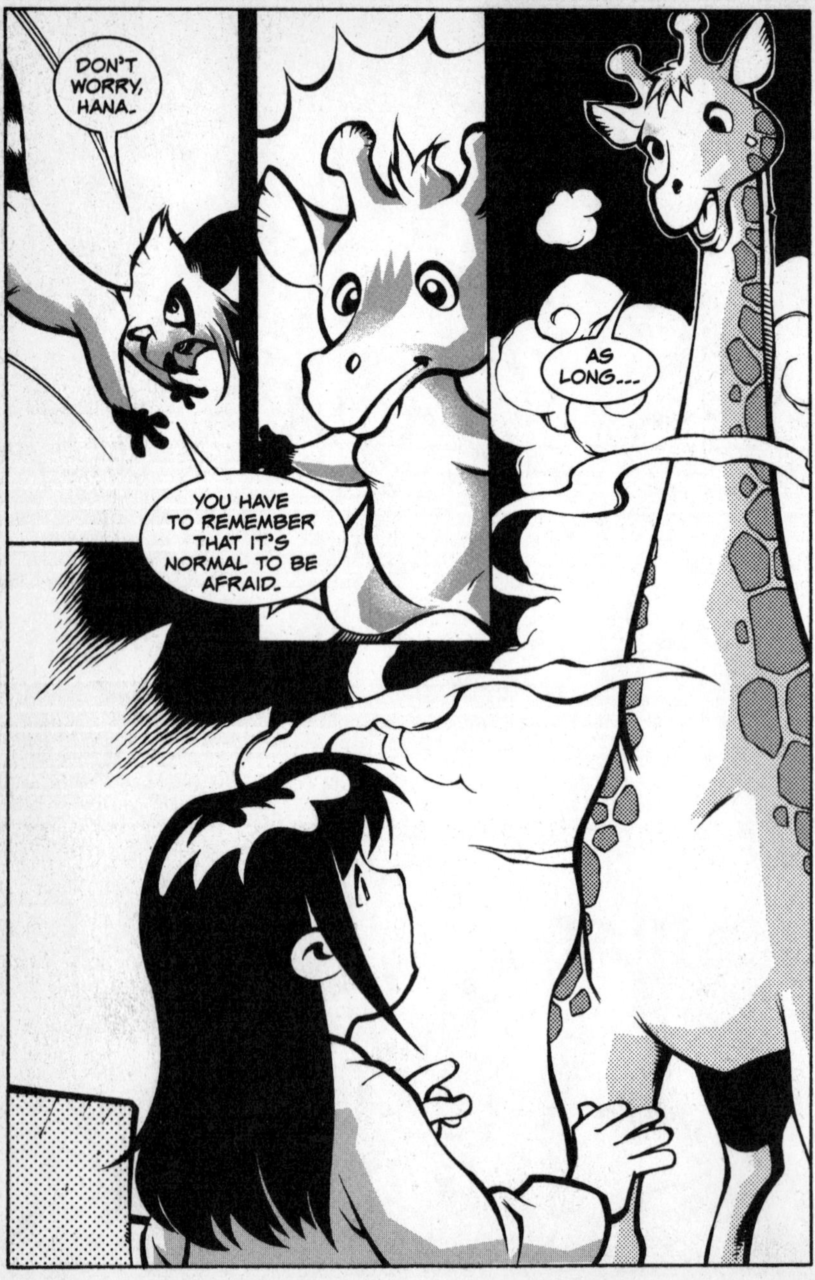
DON'T WORRY, HANA.
YOU HAVE TO REMEMBER THAT IT'S NORMAL TO BE AFRAID.
AS LONG...

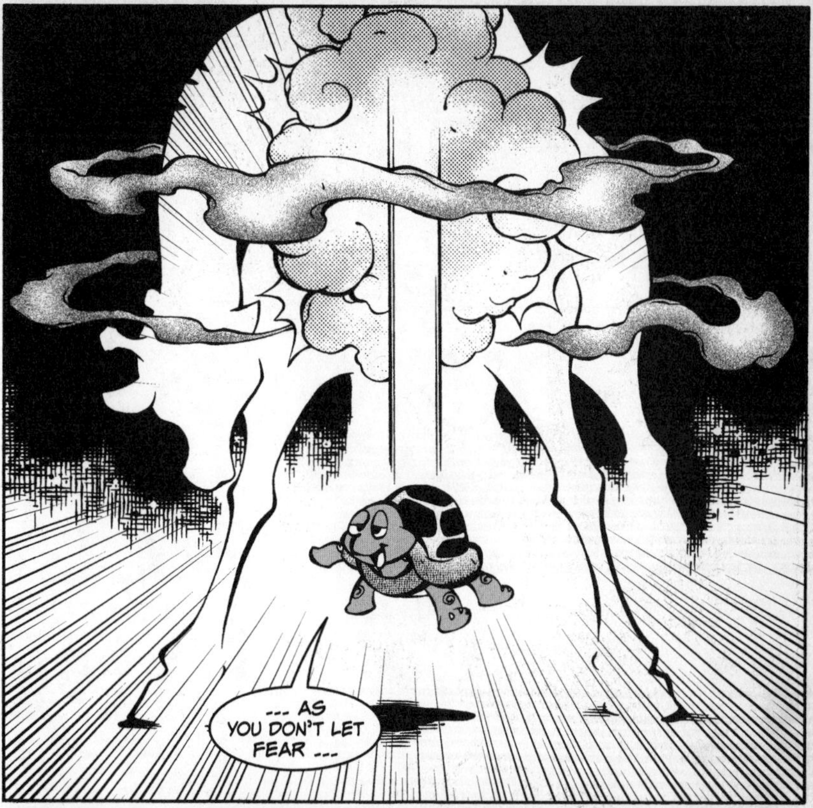
--- AS YOU DON'T LET FEAR ---

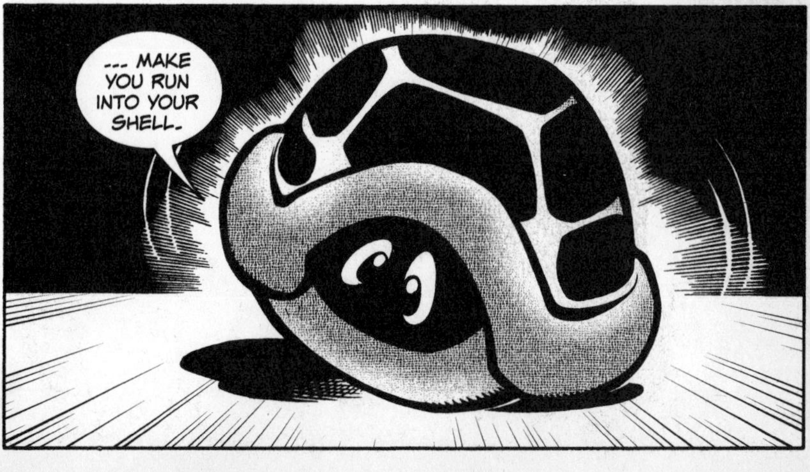
--- MAKE YOU RUN INTO YOUR SHELL.

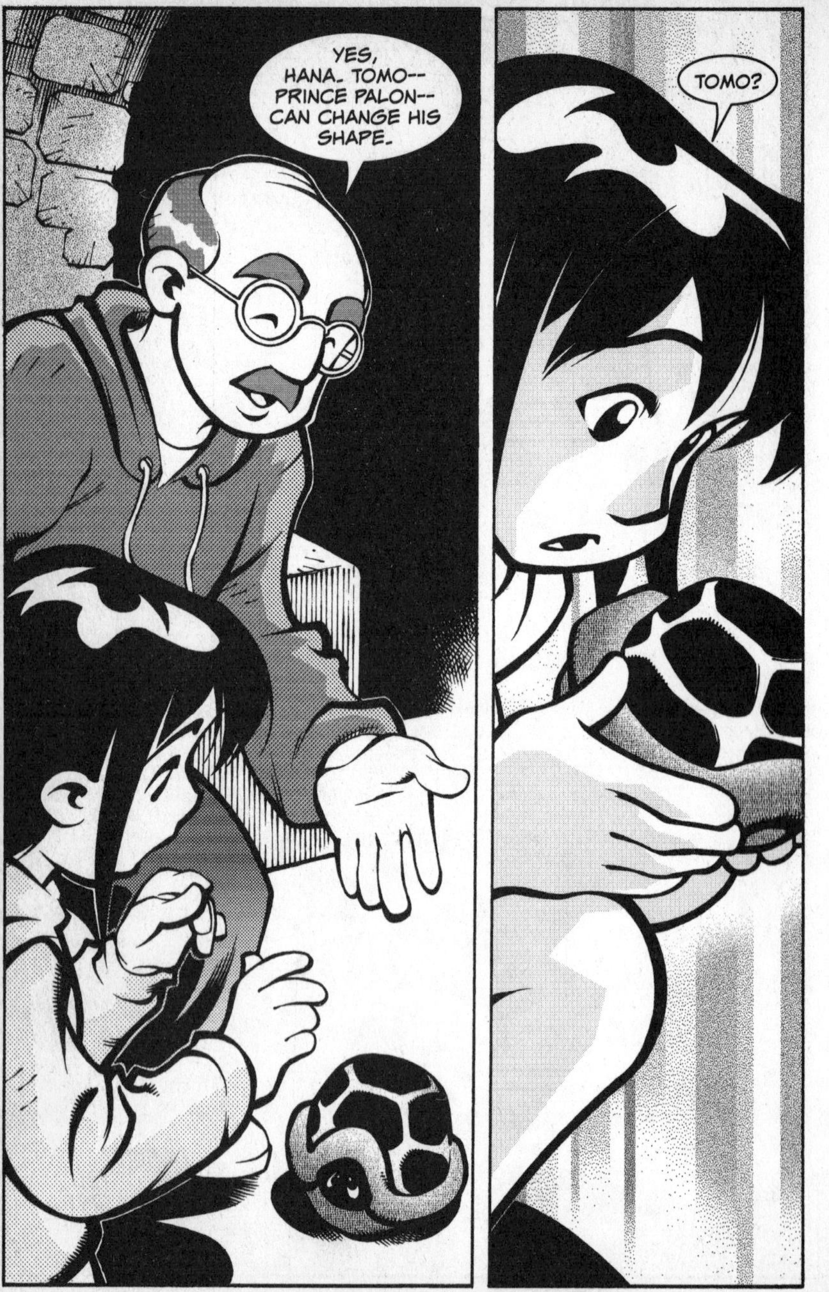
YES, HANA. TOMO-- PRINCE PALON-- CAN CHANGE HIS SHAPE.
TOMO?

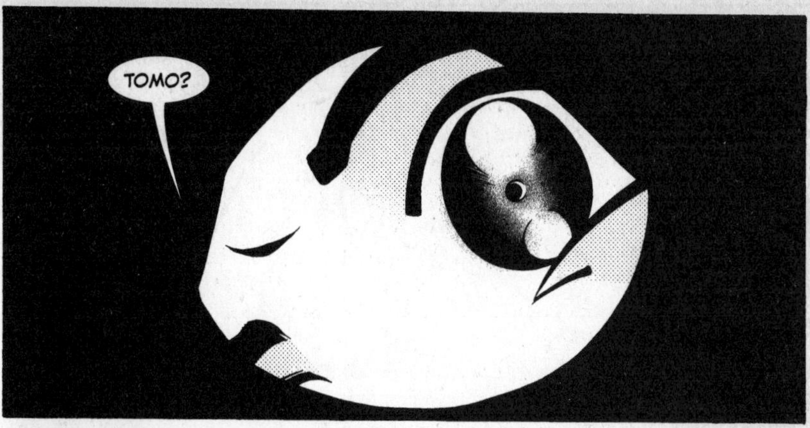
TOMO?

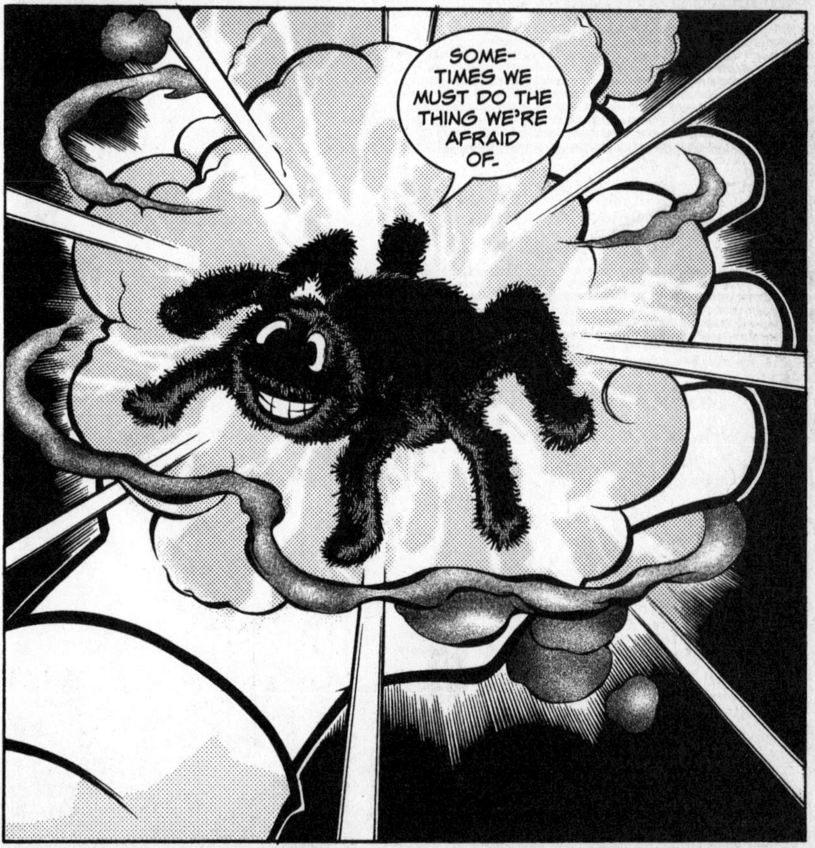
SOME-TIMES WE MUST DO THE THING WE'RE AFRAID OF.

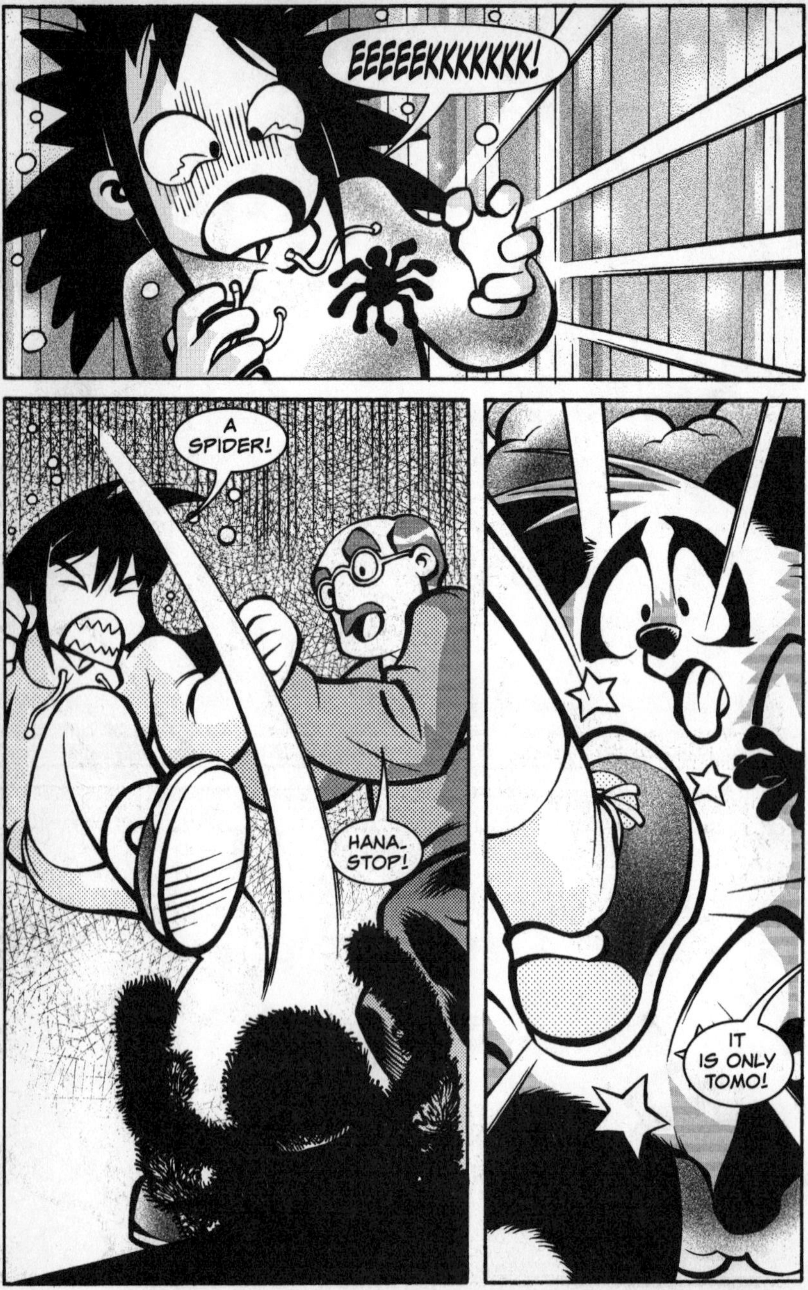
EEEEEKKKKKK!
A SPIDER!
HANA, STOP!
IT IS ONLY TOMO!

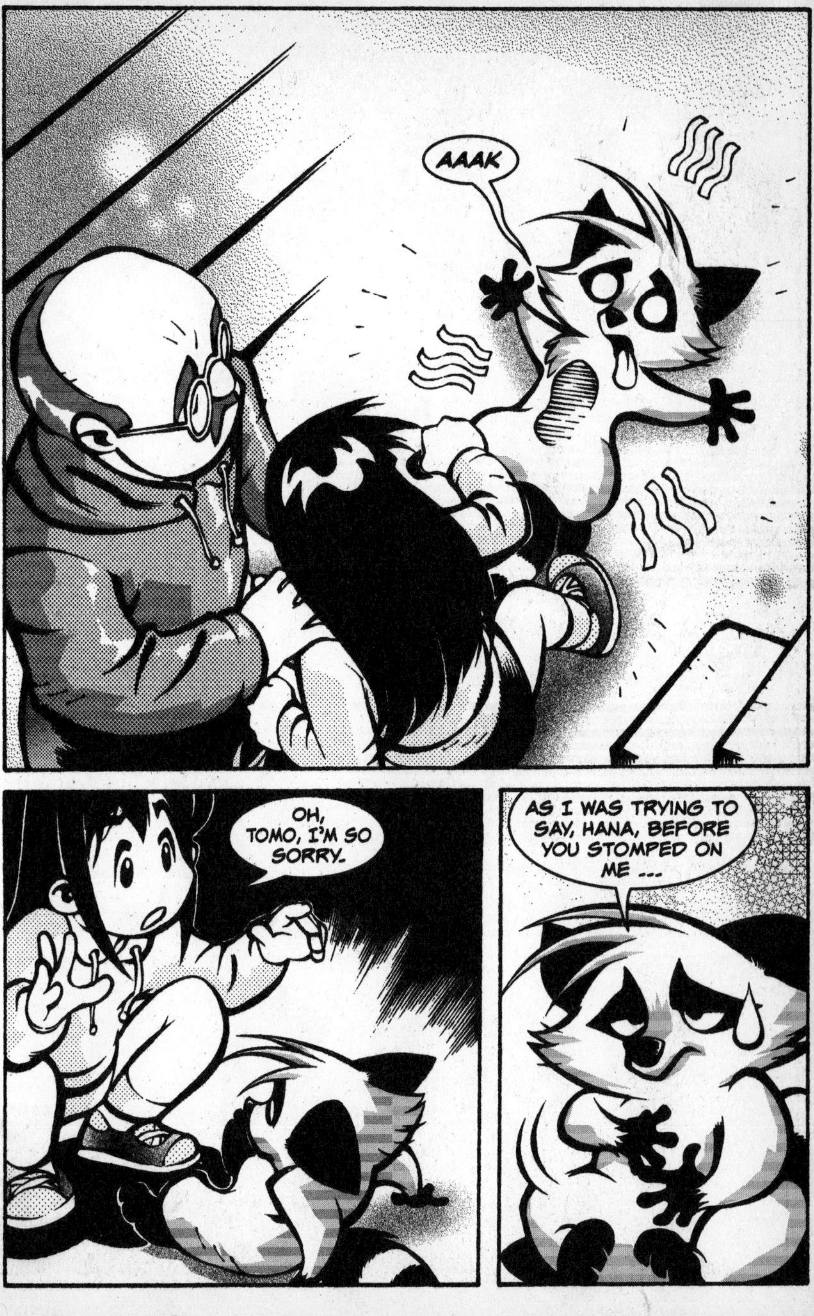
AAAK
OH, TOMO, I'M SO SORRY.
AS I WAS TRYING TO SAY, HANA, BEFORE YOU STOMPED ON ME ...

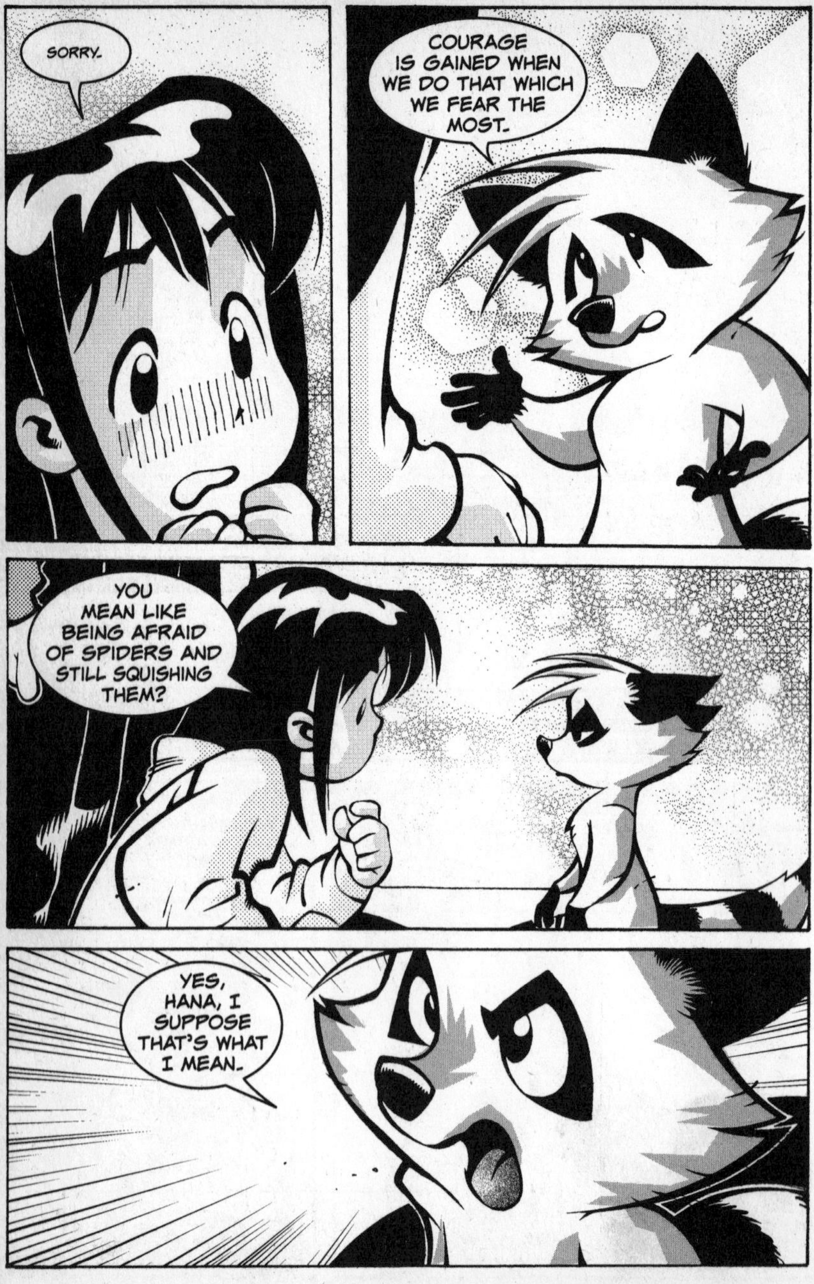
SORRY.
COURAGE IS GAINED WHEN WE DO THAT WHICH WE FEAR THE MOST.
YOU MEAN LIKE BEING AFRAID OF SPIDERS AND STILL SQUISHING THEM?
YES, HANA, I SUPPOSE THAT'S WHAT I MEAN.

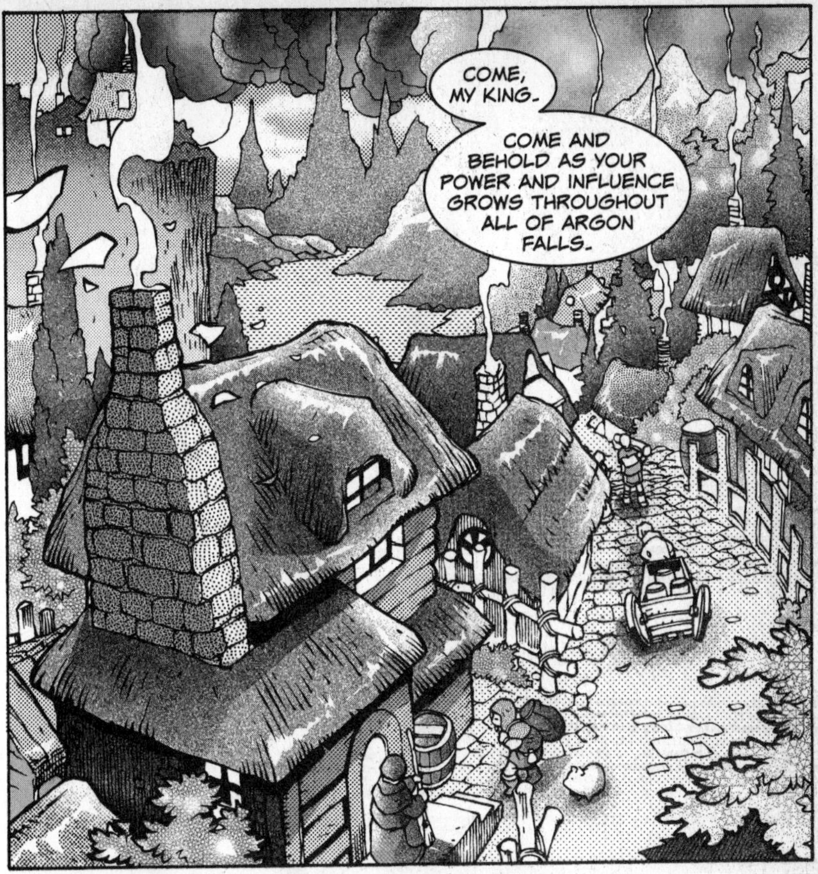
COME, MY KING.
COME AND BEHOLD AS YOUR POWER AND INFLUENCE GROWS THROUGHOUT ALL OF ARGON FALLS.
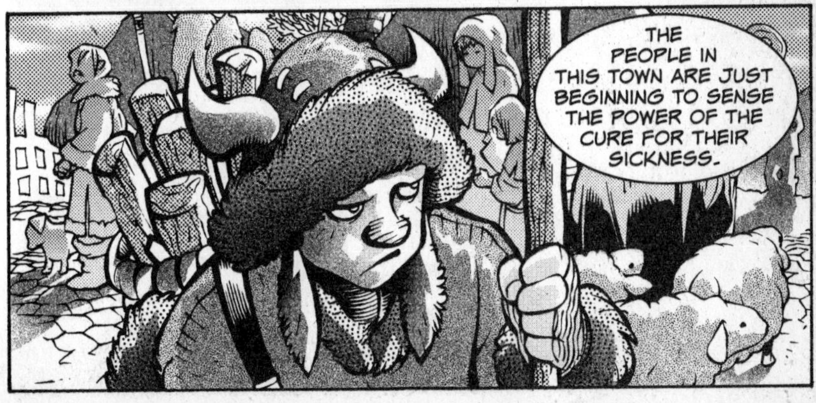
THE PEOPLE IN THIS TOWN ARE JUST BEGINNING TO SENSE THE POWER OF THE CURE FOR THEIR SICKNESS.

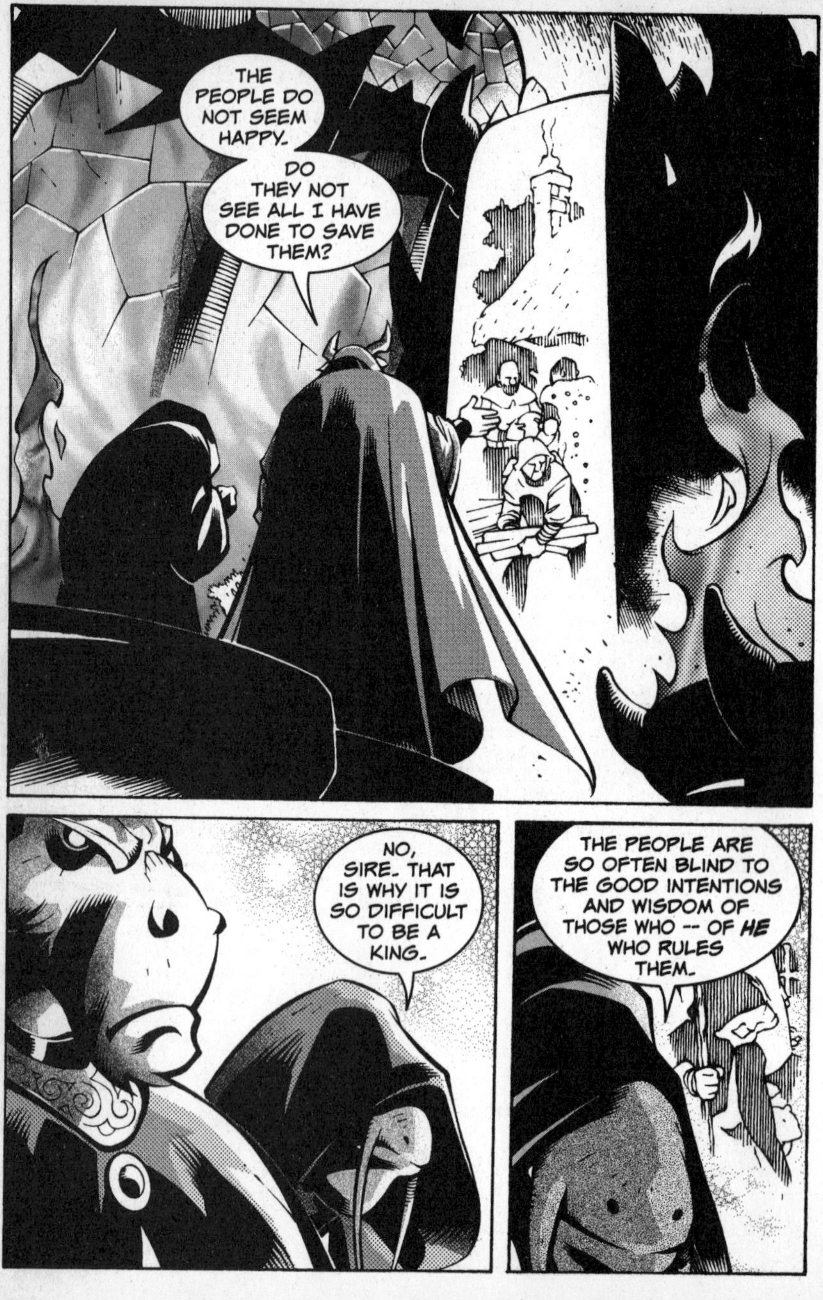
THE PEOPLE DO NOT SEEM HAPPY.
DO THEY NOT SEE ALL I HAVE DONE TO SAVE THEM?
NO, SIRE. THAT IS WHY IT IS SO DIFFICULT TO BE A KING.
THE PEOPLE ARE SO OFTEN BLIND TO THE GOOD INTENTIONS AND WISDOM OF THOSE WHO -- OF *HE* WHO RULES THEM.

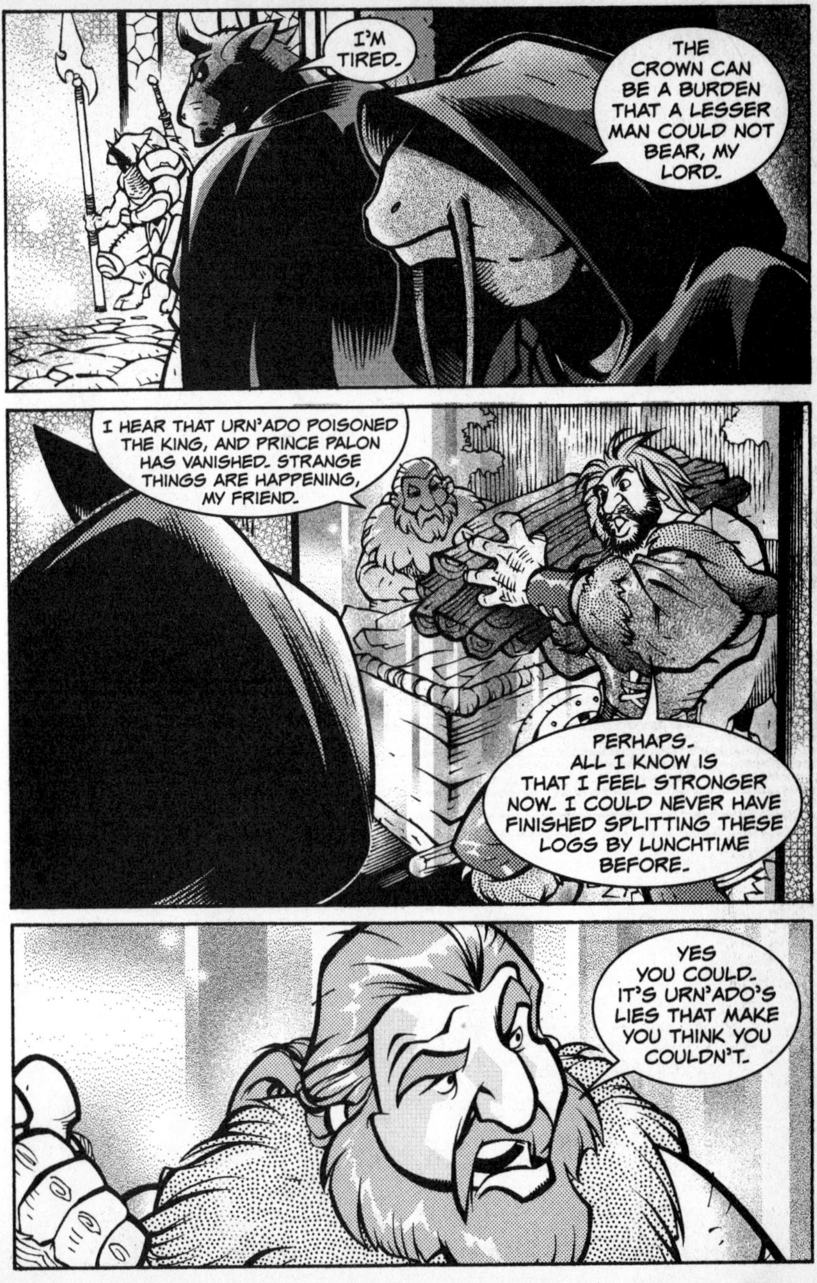
I'M TIRED.
THE CROWN CAN BE A BURDEN THAT A LESSER MAN COULD NOT BEAR, MY LORD.
I HEAR THAT URN'ADO POISONED THE KING, AND PRINCE PALON HAS VANISHED. STRANGE THINGS ARE HAPPENING, MY FRIEND.
PERHAPS. ALL I KNOW IS THAT I FEEL STRONGER NOW. I COULD NEVER HAVE FINISHED SPLITTING THESE LOGS BY LUNCHTIME BEFORE.
YES YOU COULD. IT'S URN'ADO'S LIES THAT MAKE YOU THINK YOU COULDN'T.

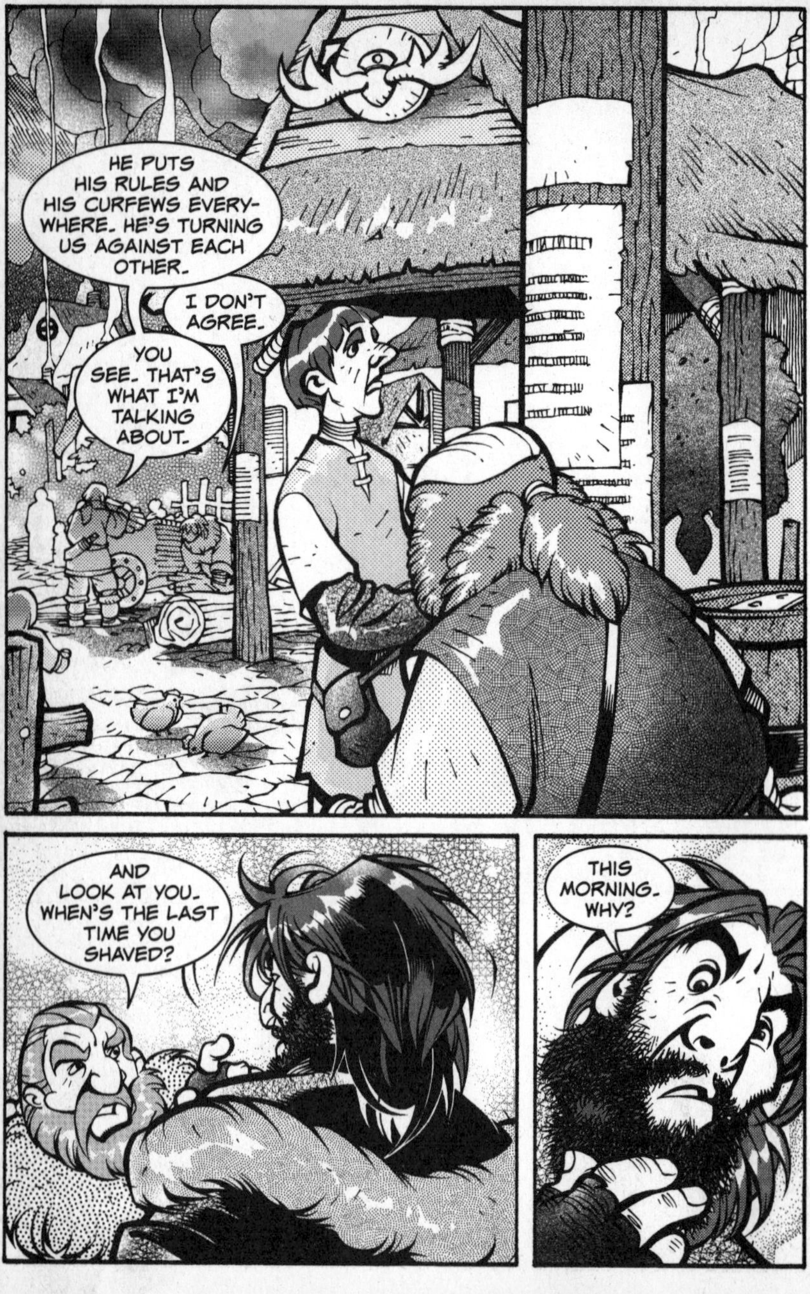
HE PUTS HIS RULES AND HIS CURFEWS EVERY-WHERE. HE'S TURNING US AGAINST EACH OTHER.
I DON'T AGREE.
YOU SEE. THAT'S WHAT I'M TALKING ABOUT.
AND LOOK AT YOU. WHEN'S THE LAST TIME YOU SHAVED?
THIS MORNING. WHY?

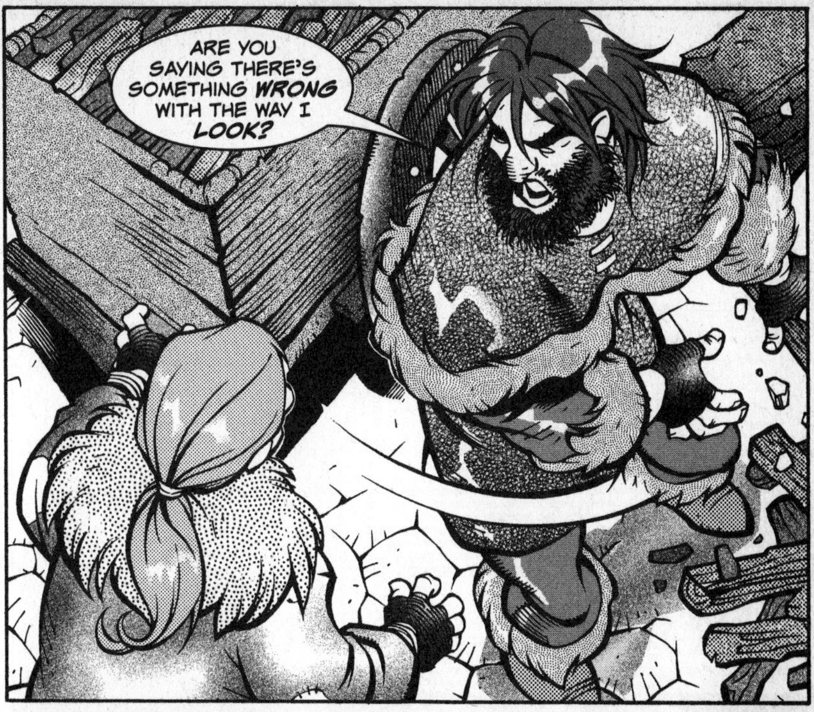
ARE YOU SAYING THERE'S SOMETHING WRONG WITH THE WAY I LOOK?
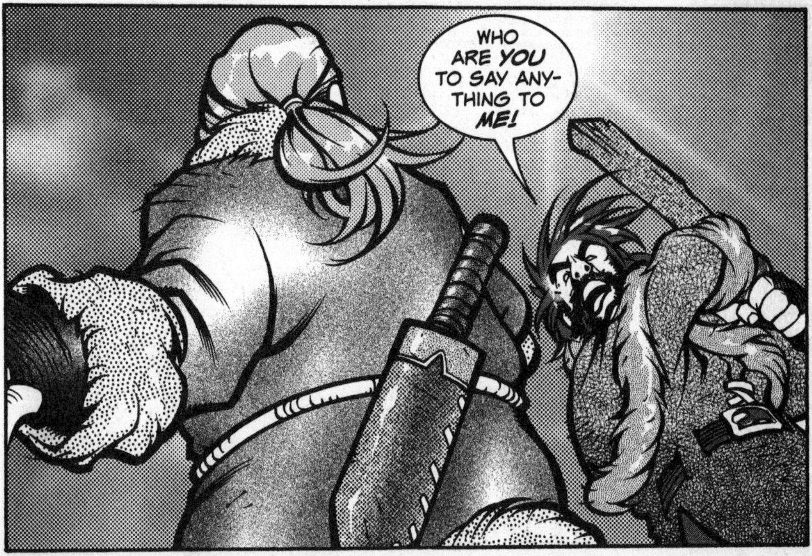
WHO ARE YOU TO SAY ANY-THING TO ME!

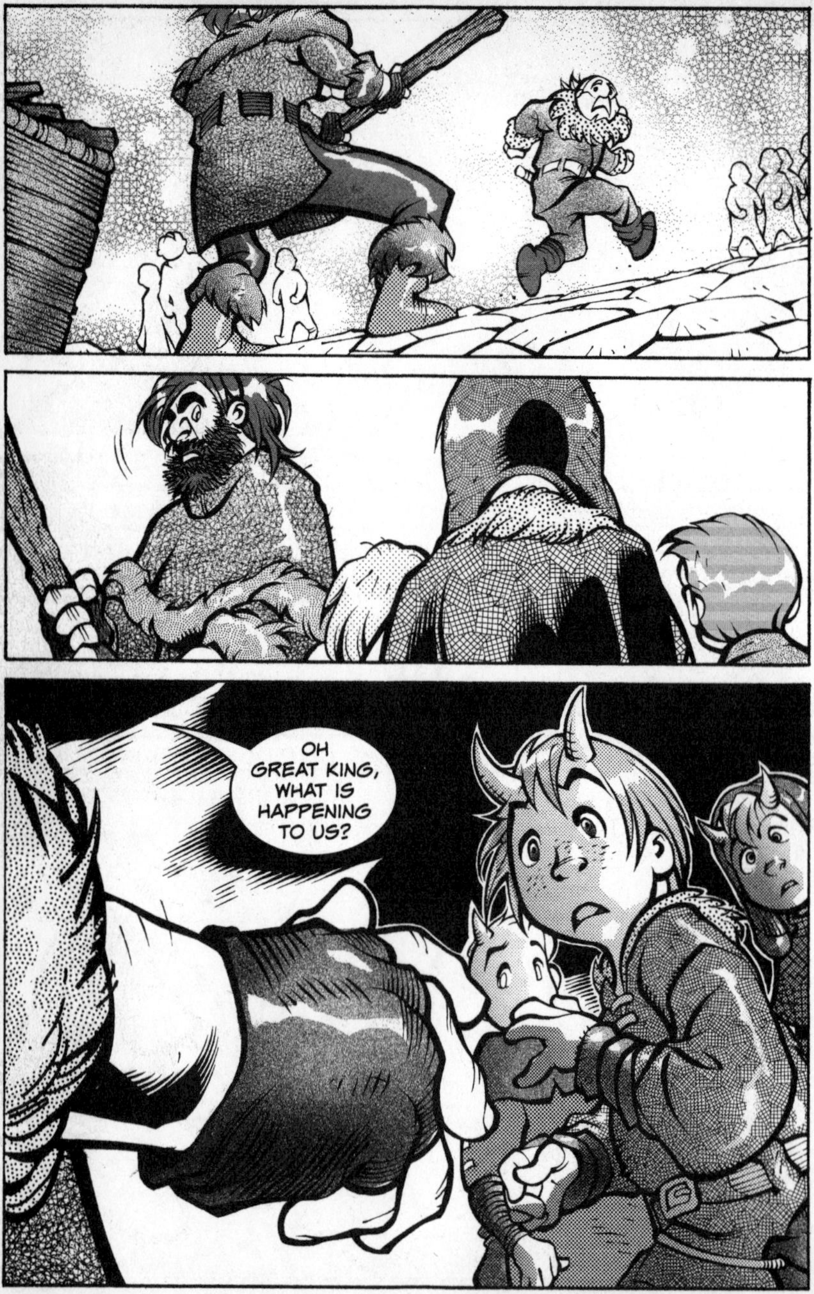
OH GREAT KING, WHAT IS HAPPENING TO US?

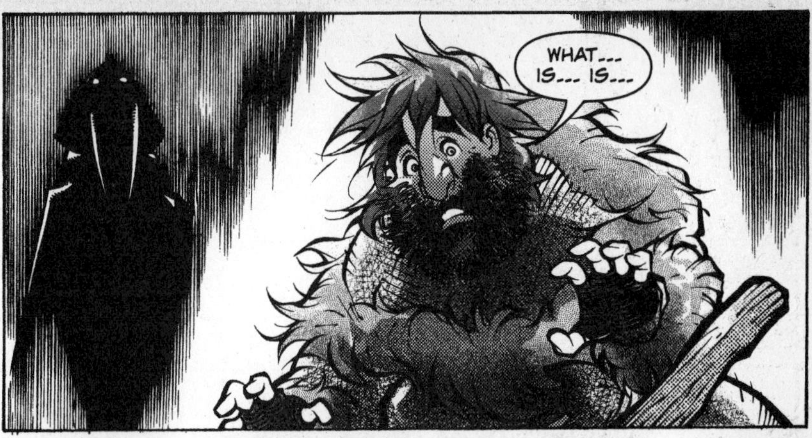
WHAT... IS... IS...
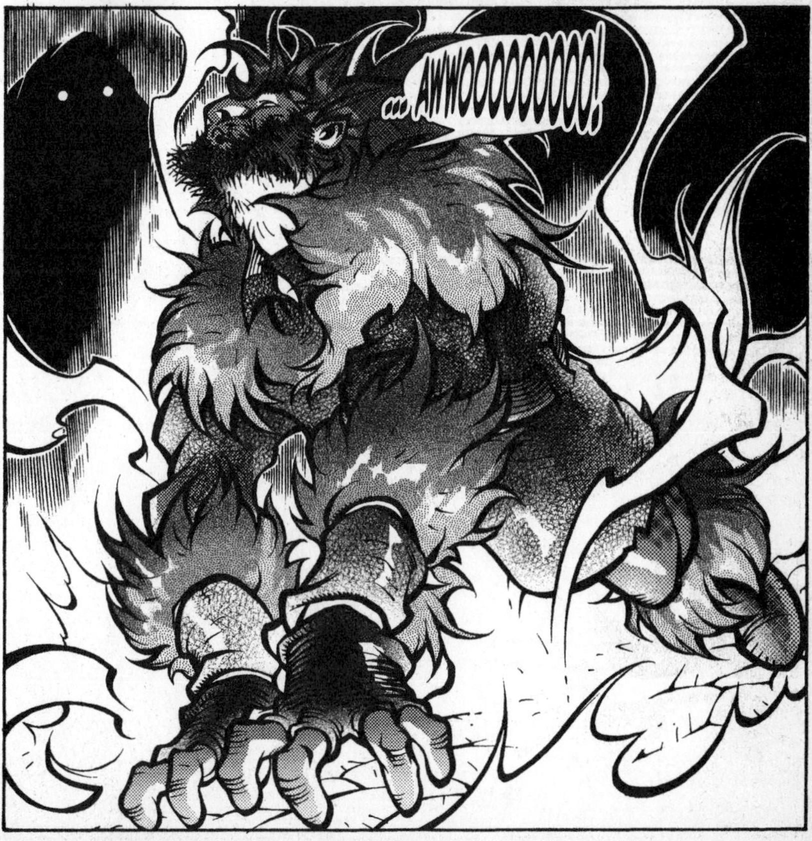
...AWWOOOOOOOOOO!

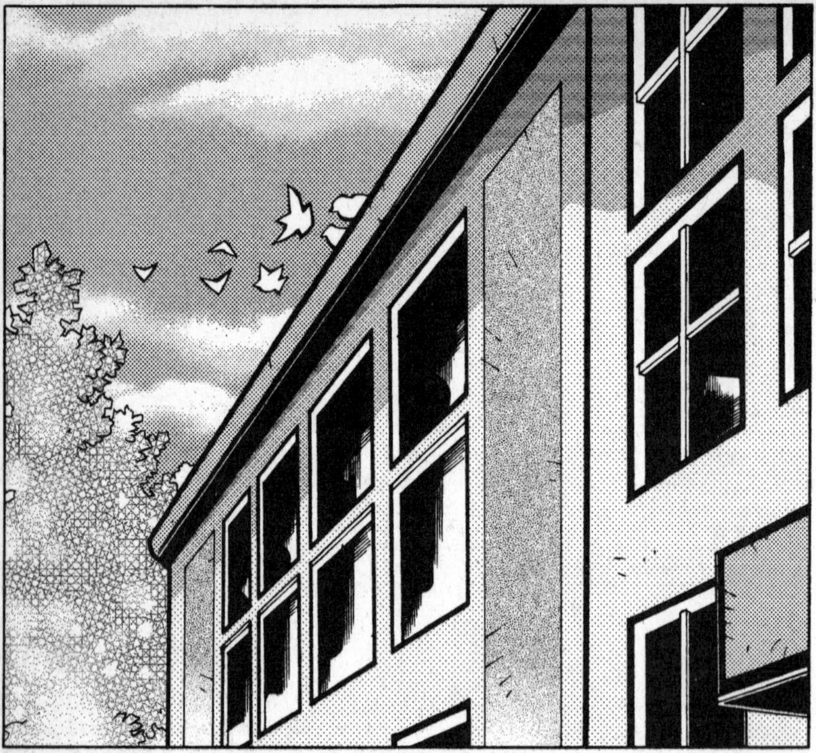

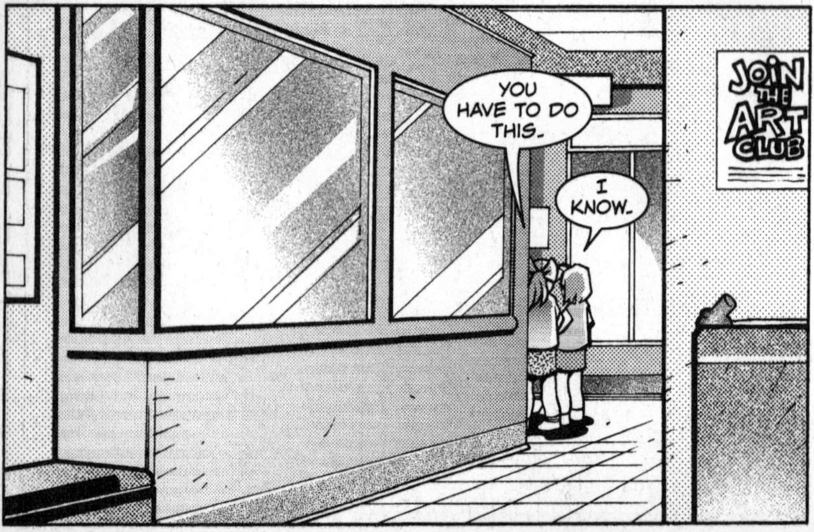
YOU HAVE TO DO THIS_
I KNOW_
JOIN THE ART CLUB

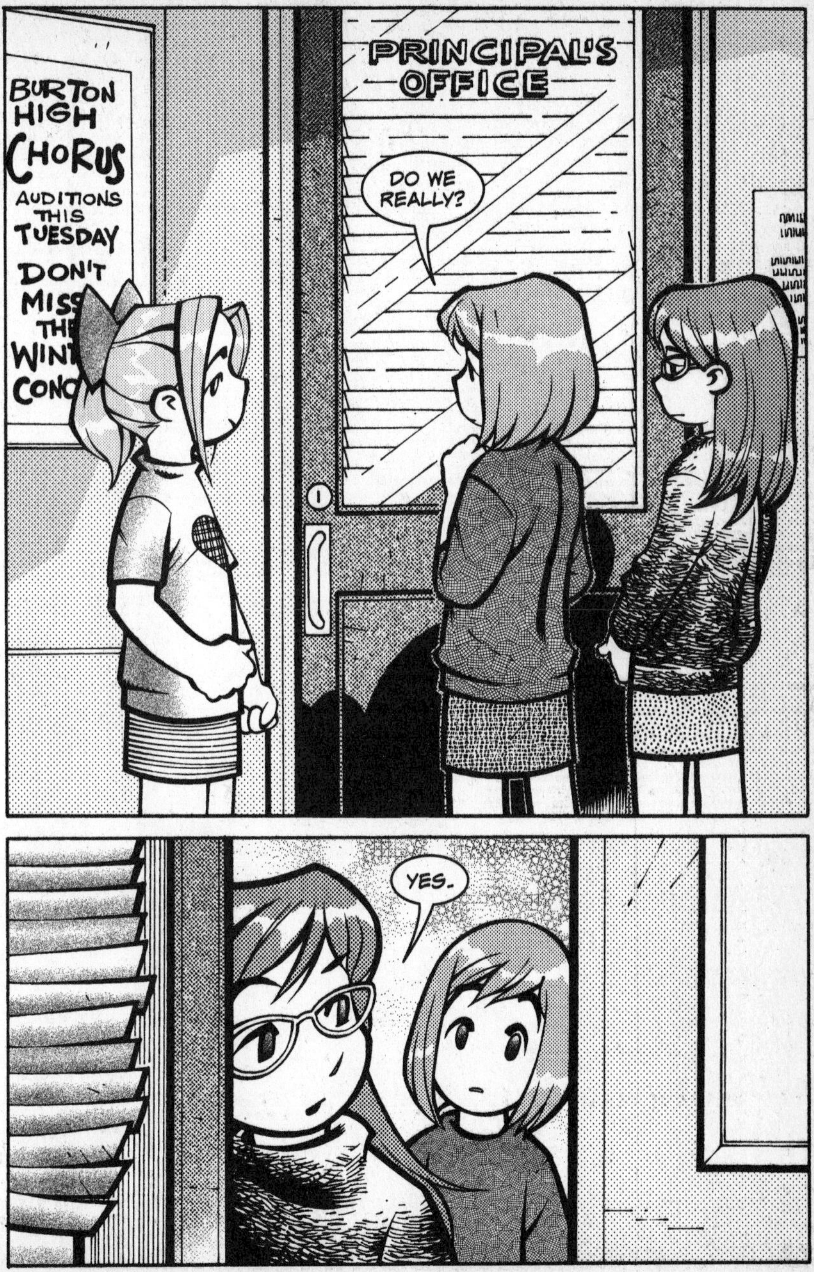
BURTON HIGH CHORUS
AUDITIONS THIS TUESDAY
DON'T
PRINCIPAL'S OFFICE
DO WE REALLY?
YES.

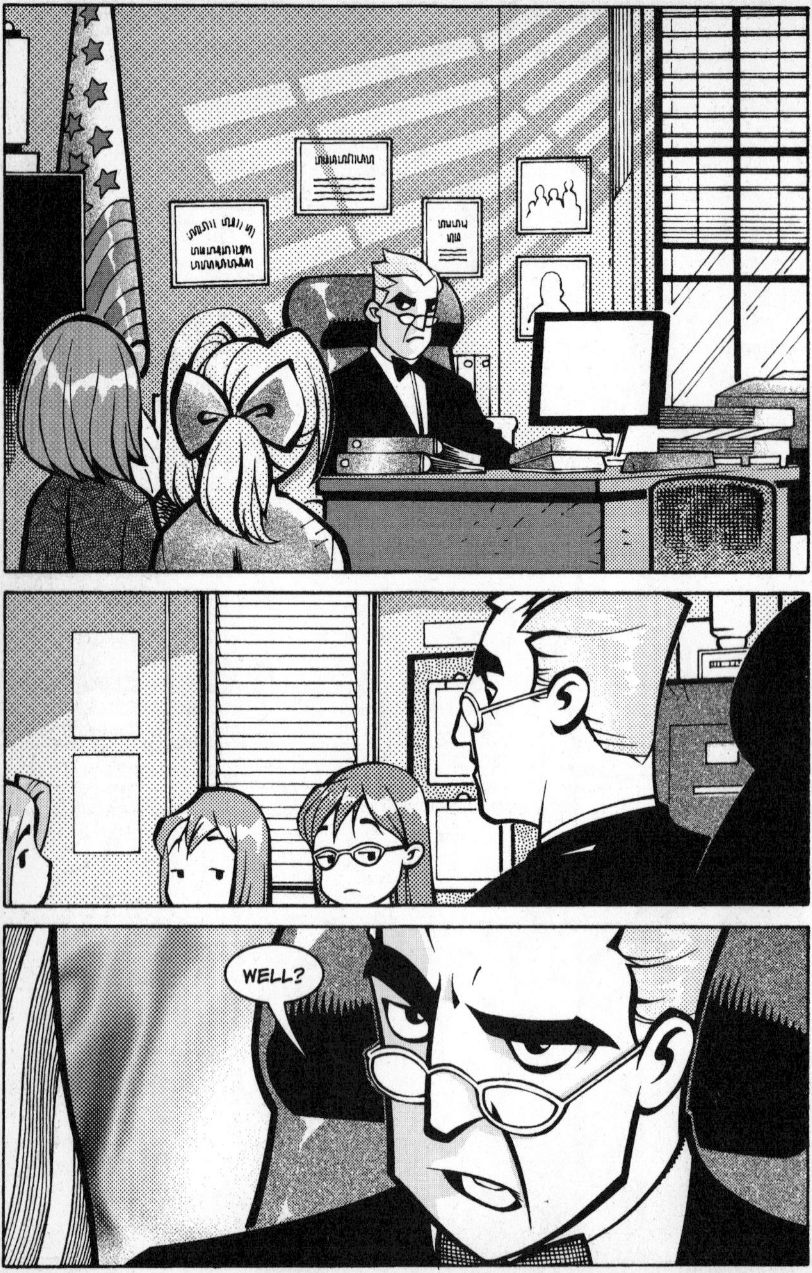
WELL?

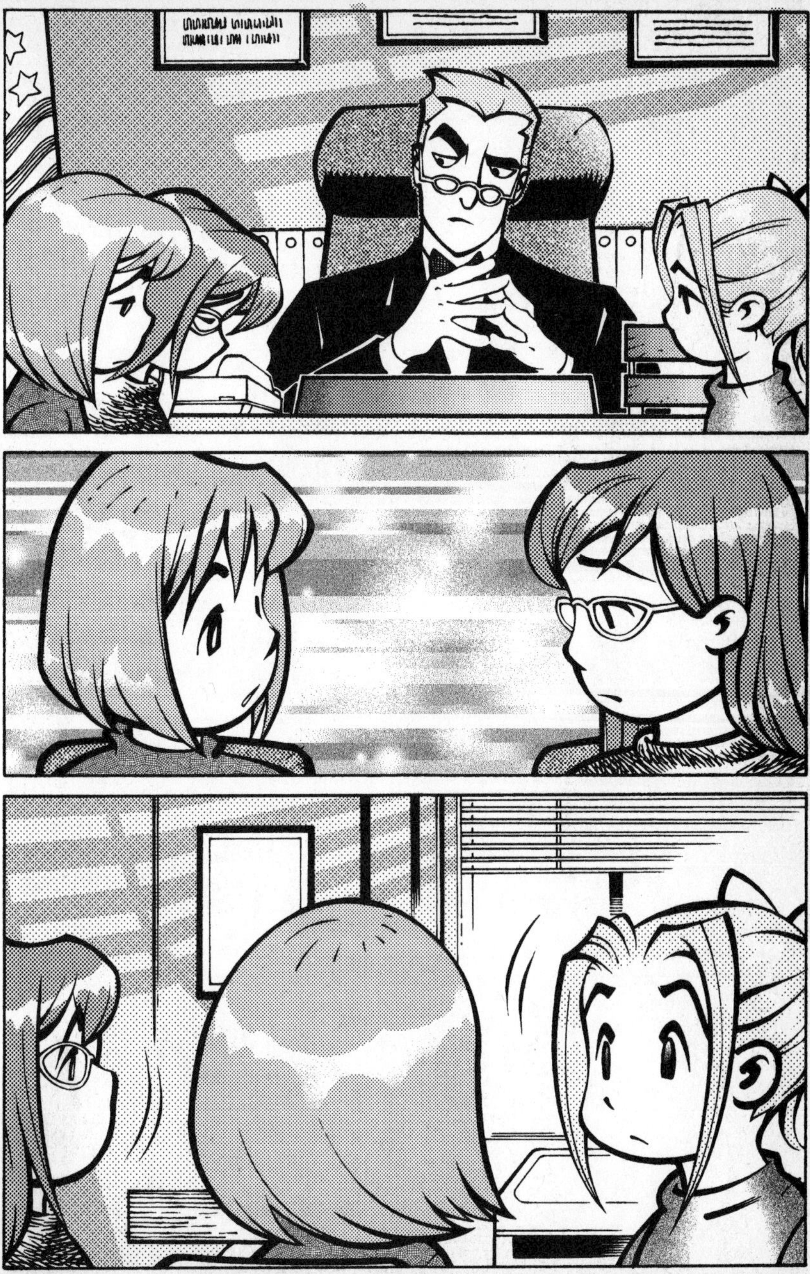

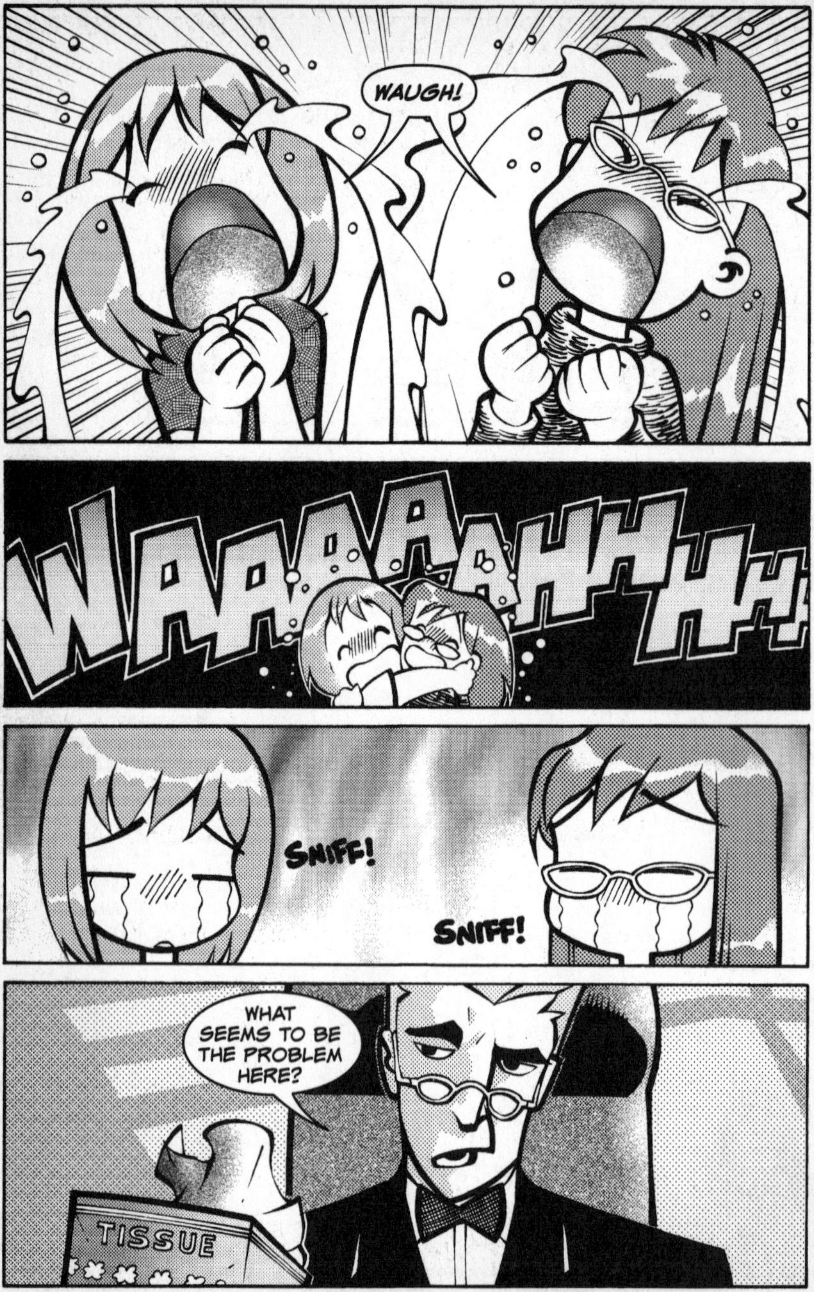
WAUGH!
WAAAAAHHHHH
SNIFF!
SNIFF!
WHAT SEEMS TO BE THE PROBLEM HERE?
TISSUE

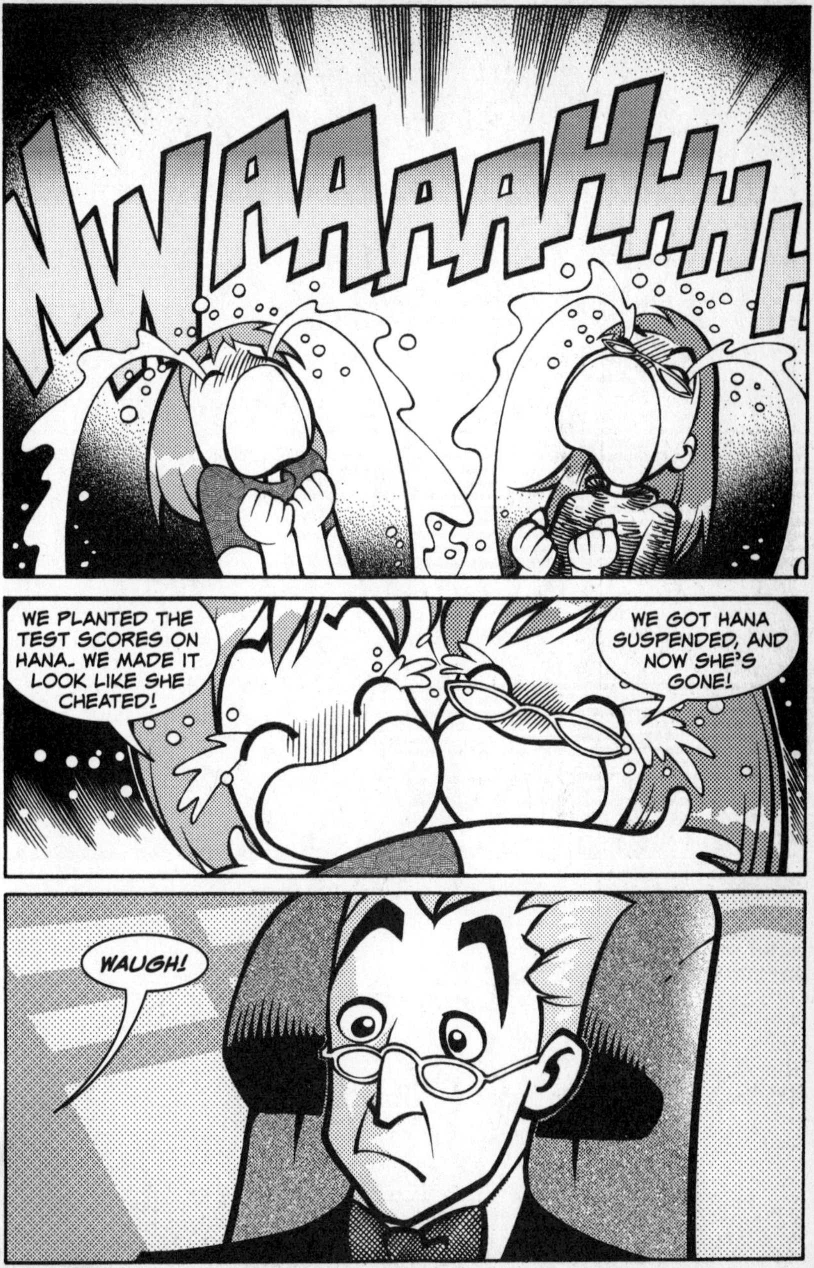
NWAAAAHHHH
WE PLANTED THE TEST SCORES ON HANA. WE MADE IT LOOK LIKE SHE CHEATED!
WE GOT HANA SUSPENDED, AND NOW SHE'S GONE!
WAUGH!

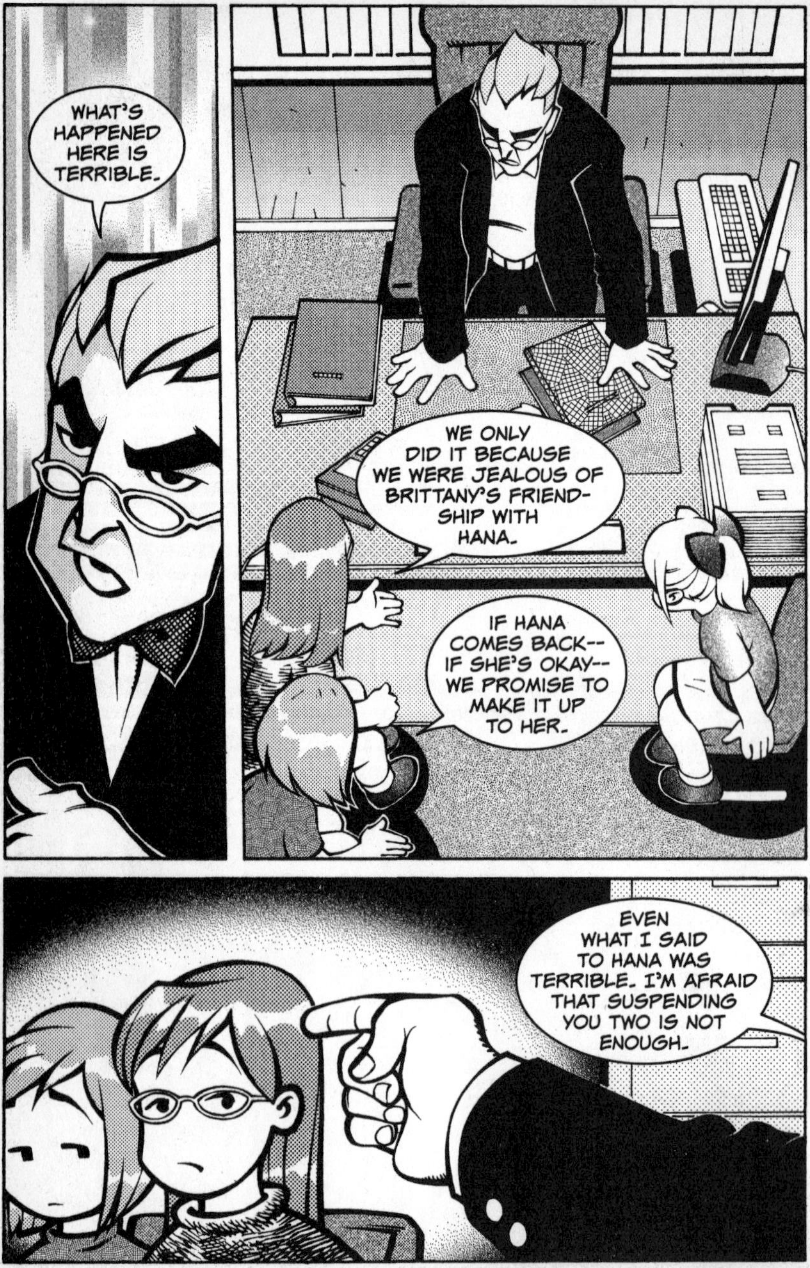
WHAT'S HAPPENED HERE IS TERRIBLE.
WE ONLY DID IT BECAUSE WE WERE JEALOUS OF BRITTANY'S FRIEND-SHIP WITH HANA.
IF HANA COMES BACK-- IF SHE'S OKAY-- WE PROMISE TO MAKE IT UP TO HER.
EVEN WHAT I SAID TO HANA WAS TERRIBLE. I'M AFRAID THAT SUSPENDING YOU TWO IS NOT ENOUGH.

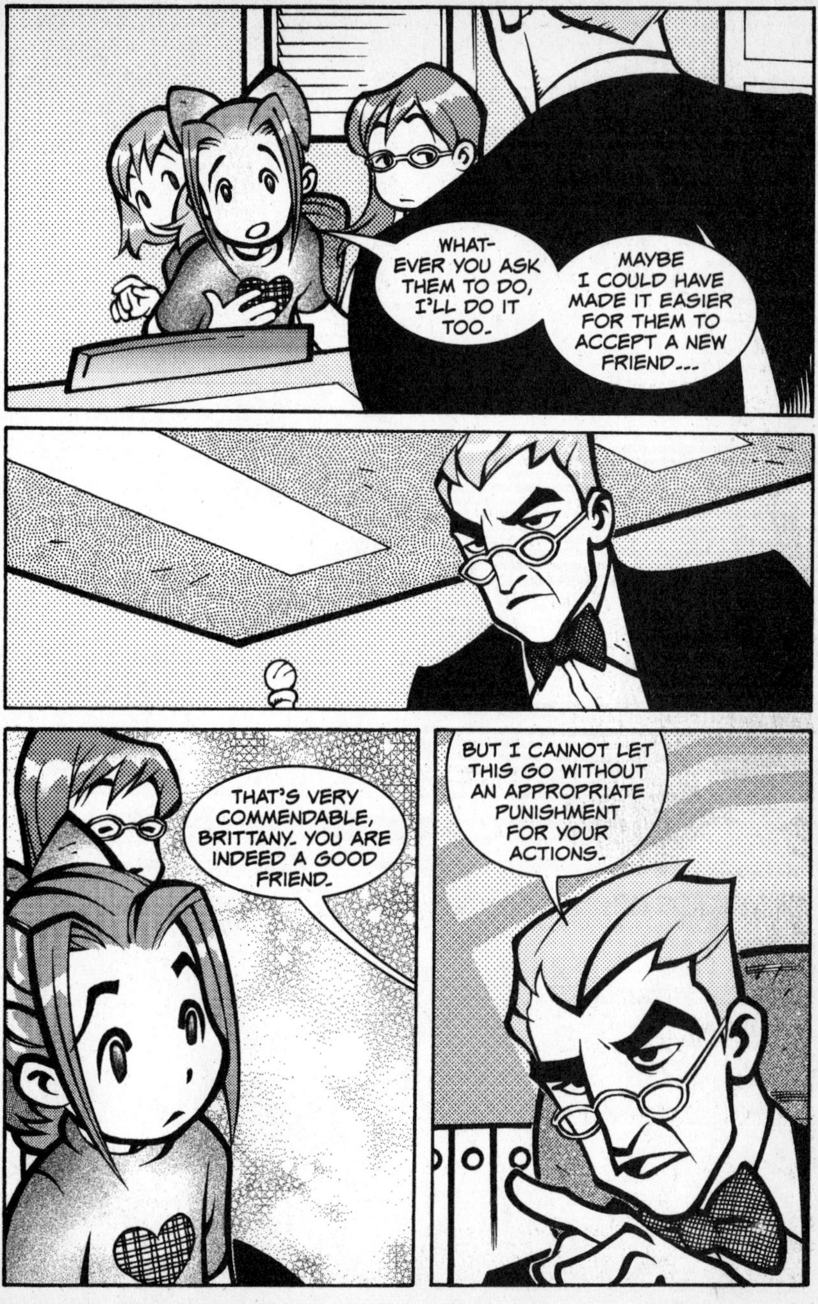
WHAT-EVER YOU ASK THEM TO DO, I'LL DO IT TOO.
MAYBE I COULD HAVE MADE IT EASIER FOR THEM TO ACCEPT A NEW FRIEND...
THAT'S VERY COMMENDABLE, BRITTANY. YOU ARE INDEED A GOOD FRIEND.
BUT I CANNOT LET THIS GO WITHOUT AN APPROPRIATE PUNISHMENT FOR YOUR ACTIONS.

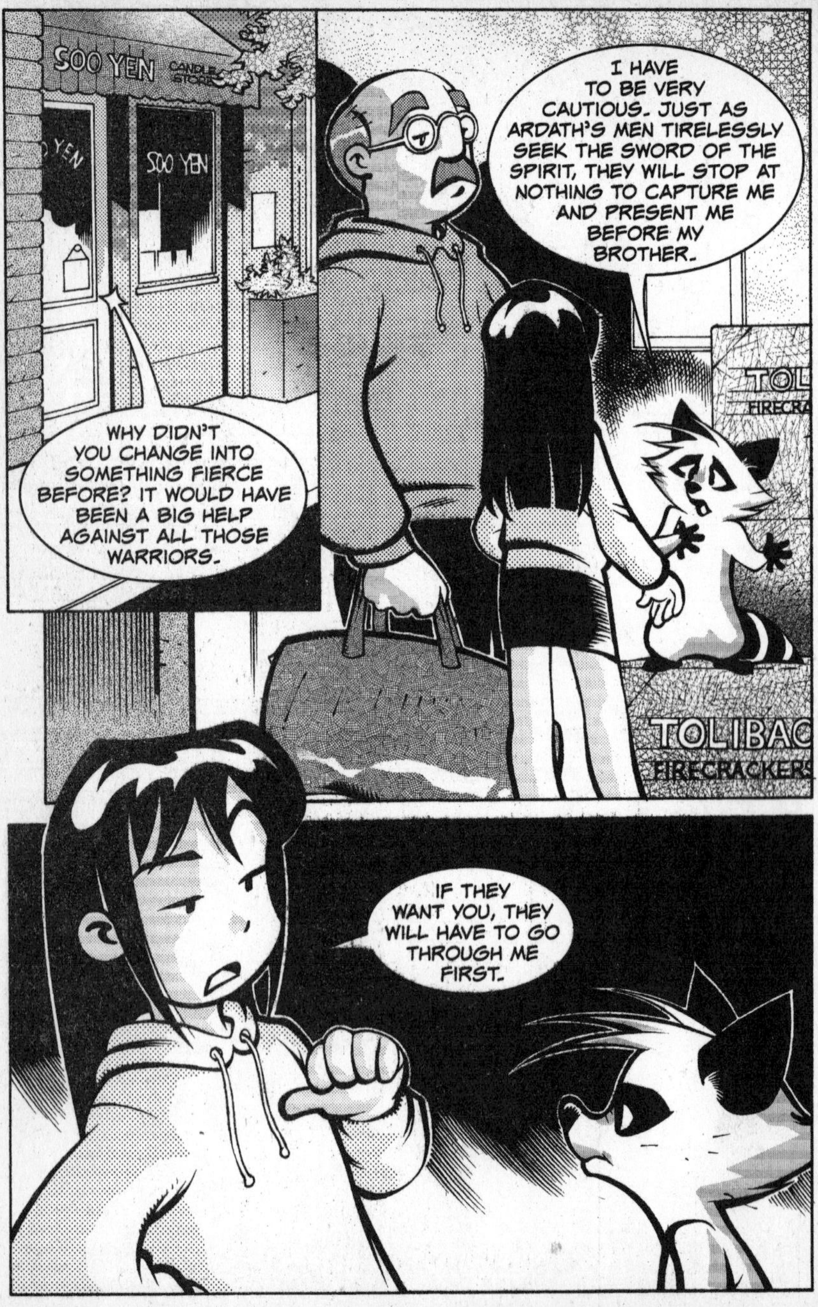
SOO YEN
WHY DIDN'T YOU CHANGE INTO SOMETHING FIERCE BEFORE? IT WOULD HAVE BEEN A BIG HELP AGAINST ALL THOSE WARRIORS.
I HAVE TO BE VERY CAUTIOUS. JUST AS ARDATH'S MEN TIRELESSLY SEEK THE SWORD OF THE SPIRIT, THEY WILL STOP AT NOTHING TO CAPTURE ME AND PRESENT ME BEFORE MY BROTHER.
FIRECRACKERS
IF THEY WANT YOU, THEY WILL HAVE TO GO THROUGH ME FIRST.

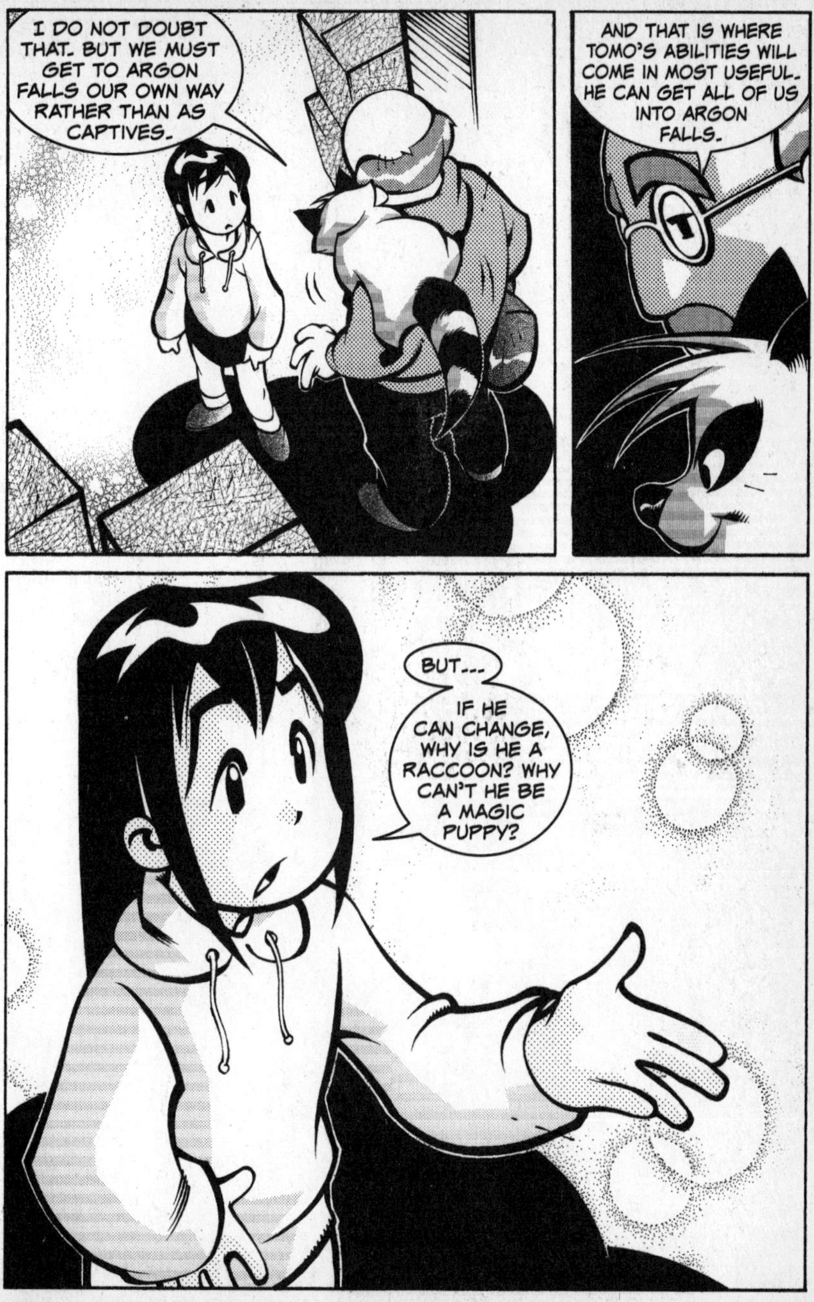
I DO NOT DOUBT THAT. BUT WE MUST GET TO ARGON FALLS OUR OWN WAY RATHER THAN AS CAPTIVES.
AND THAT IS WHERE TOMO'S ABILITIES WILL COME IN MOST USEFUL. HE CAN GET ALL OF US INTO ARGON FALLS.
BUT...
IF HE CAN CHANGE, WHY IS HE A RACCOON? WHY CAN'T HE BE A MAGIC PUPPY?

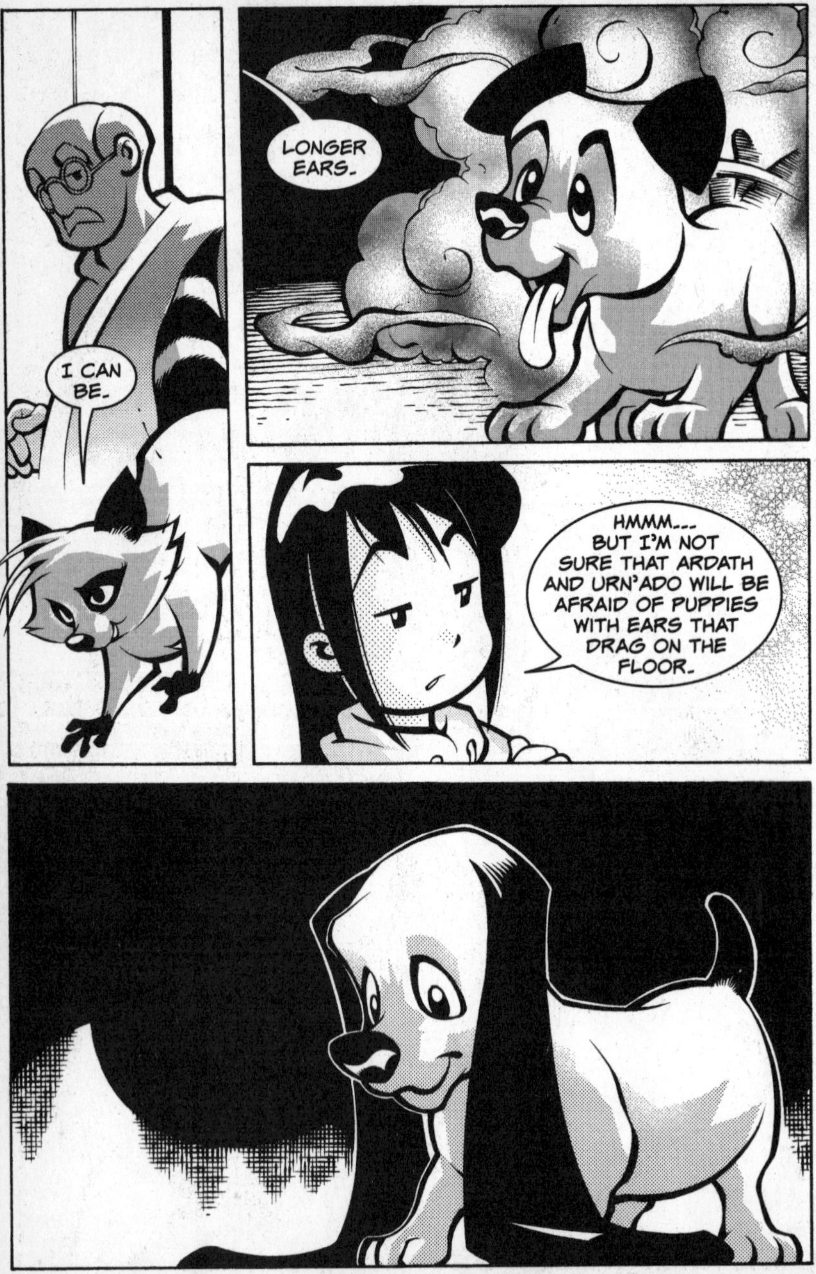
I CAN BE.
LONGER EARS.
HMMM... BUT I'M NOT SURE THAT ARDATH AND URN'ADO WILL BE AFRAID OF PUPPIES WITH EARS THAT DRAG ON THE FLOOR.

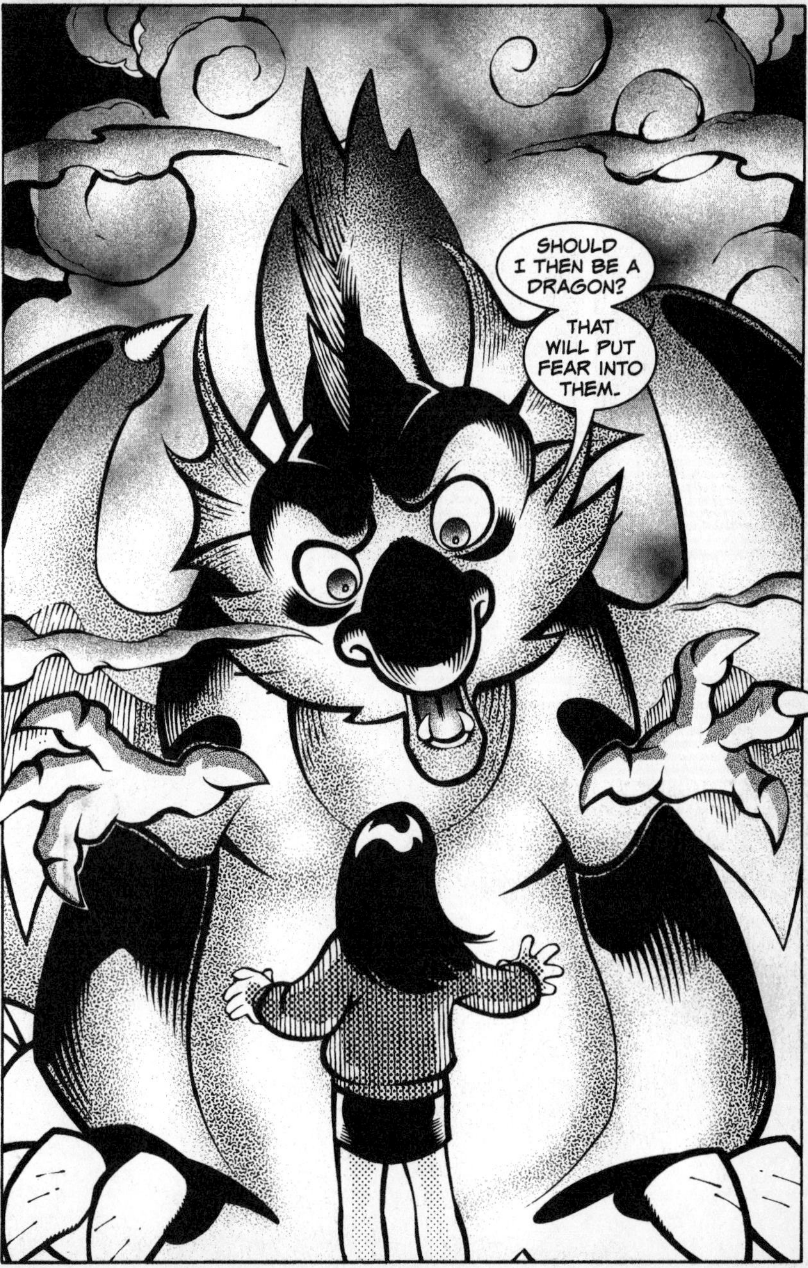
SHOULD I THEN BE A DRAGON?
THAT WILL PUT FEAR INTO THEM.

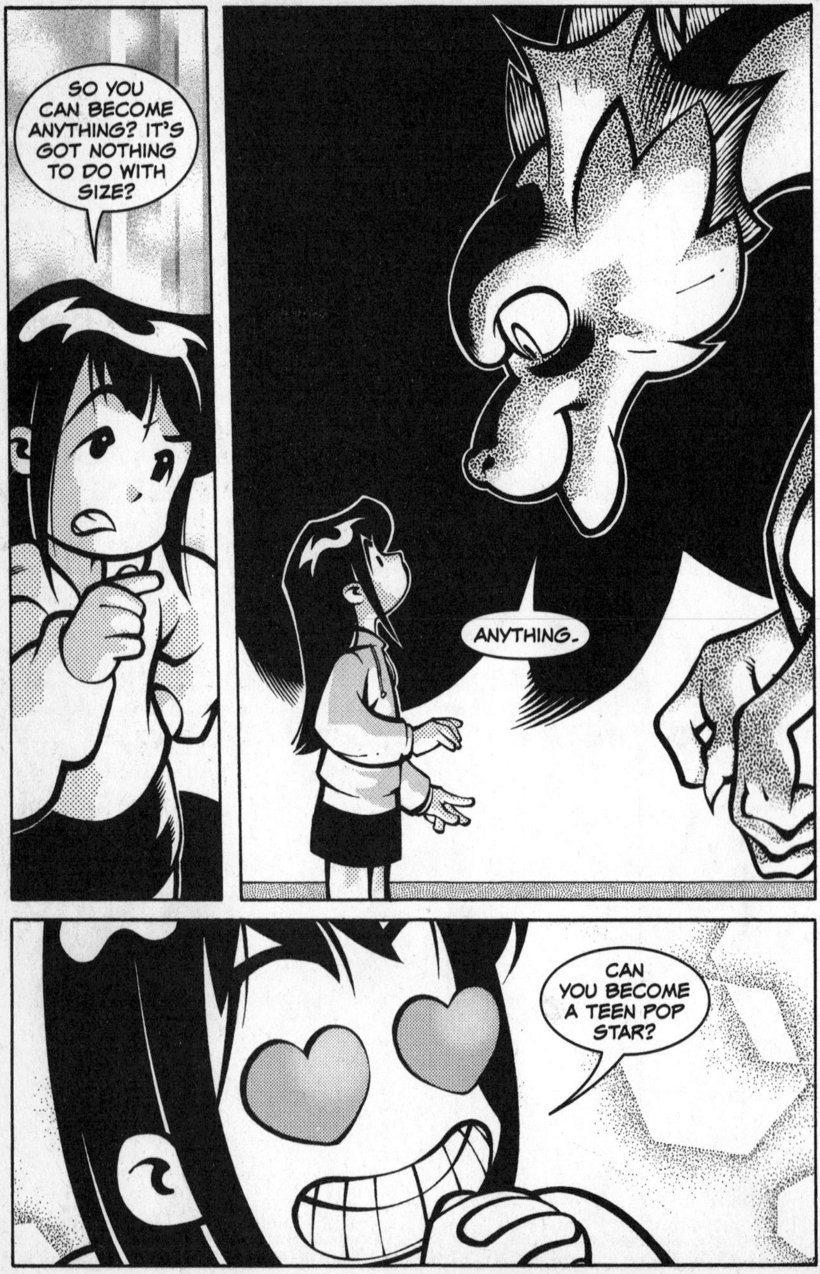
SO YOU CAN BECOME ANYTHING? IT'S GOT NOTHING TO DO WITH SIZE?
ANYTHING.
CAN YOU BECOME A TEEN POP STAR?

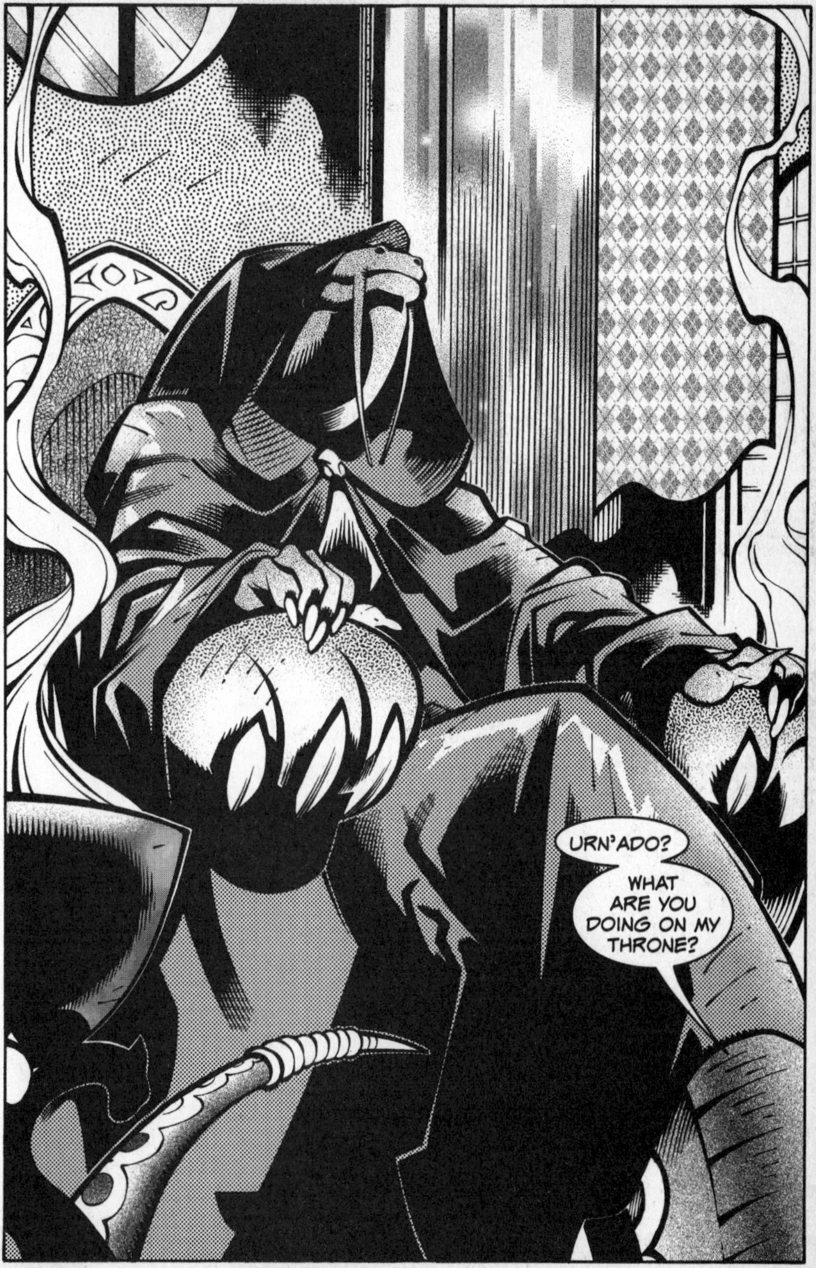
URN'ADO?
WHAT ARE YOU DOING ON MY THRONE?

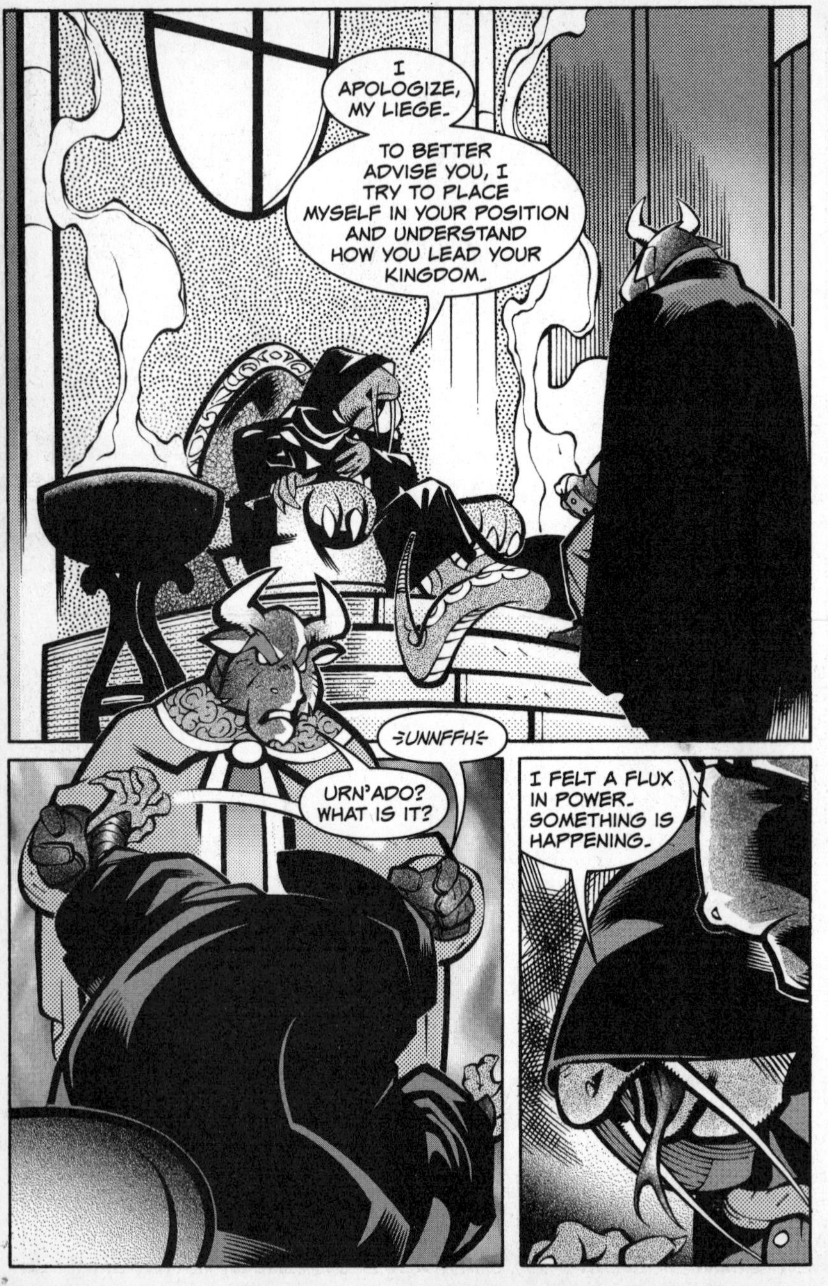
I APOLOGIZE, MY LIEGE.
TO BETTER ADVISE YOU, I TRY TO PLACE MYSELF IN YOUR POSITION AND UNDERSTAND HOW YOU LEAD YOUR KINGDOM.
UNNFFH
URN'ADO? WHAT IS IT?
I FELT A FLUX IN POWER. SOMETHING IS HAPPENING.

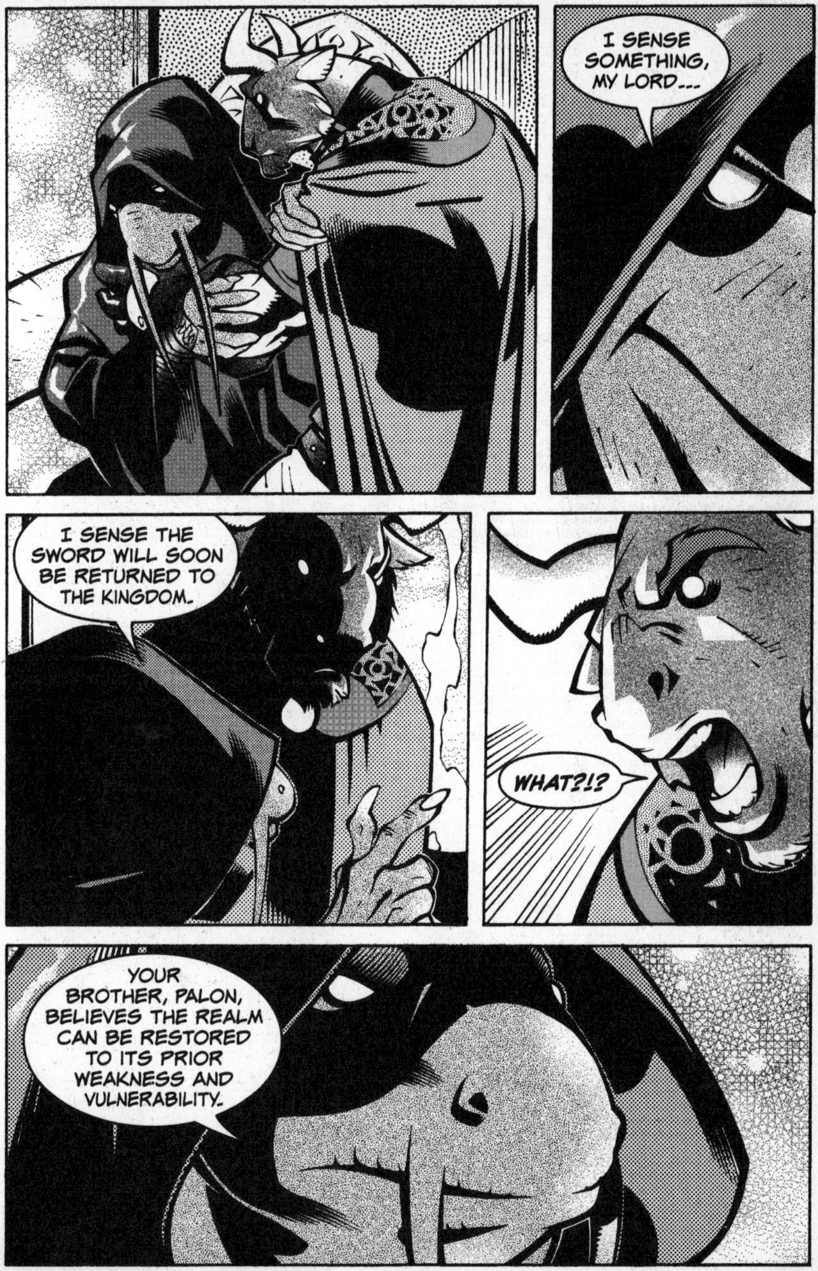
I SENSE SOMETHING, MY LORD...
I SENSE THE SWORD WILL SOON BE RETURNED TO THE KINGDOM.
WHAT?!?
YOUR BROTHER, PALON, BELIEVES THE REALM CAN BE RESTORED TO ITS PRIOR WEAKNESS AND VULNERABILITY.

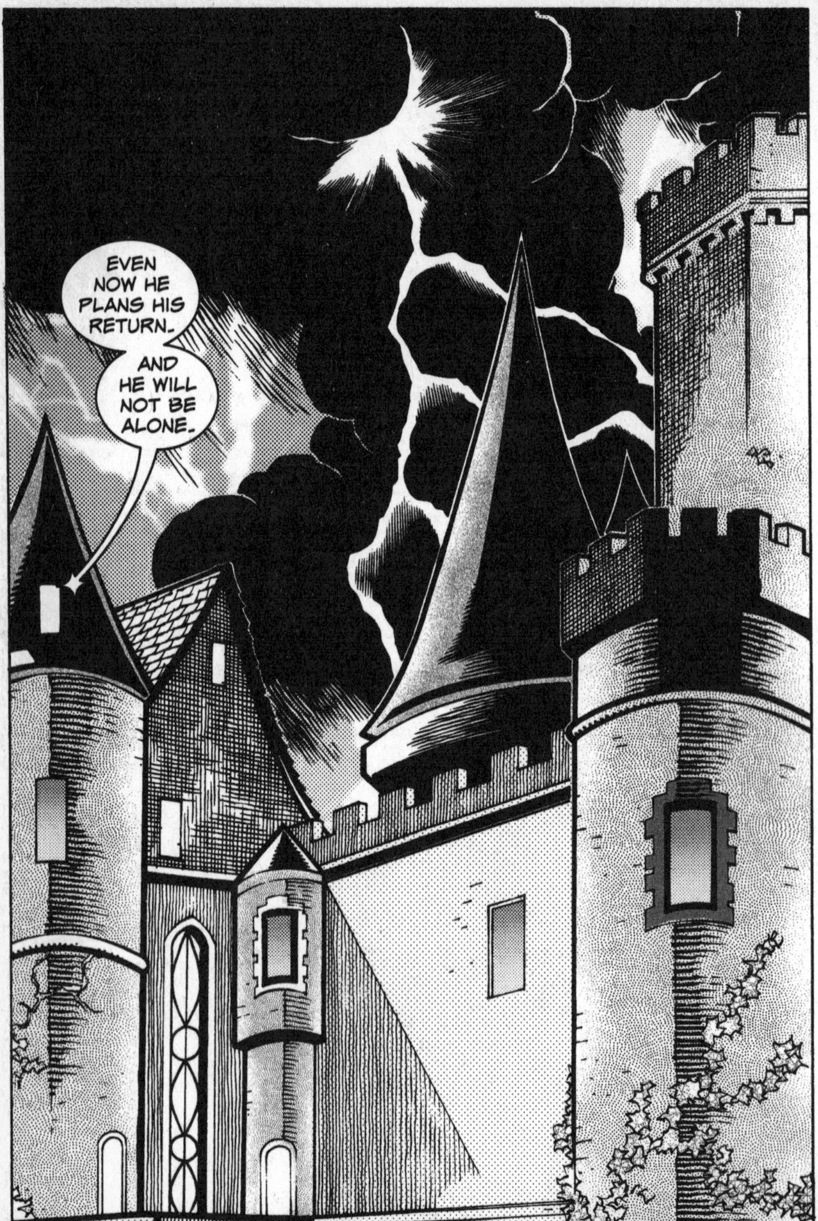
EVEN NOW HE PLANS HIS RETURN...
AND HE WILL NOT BE ALONE...

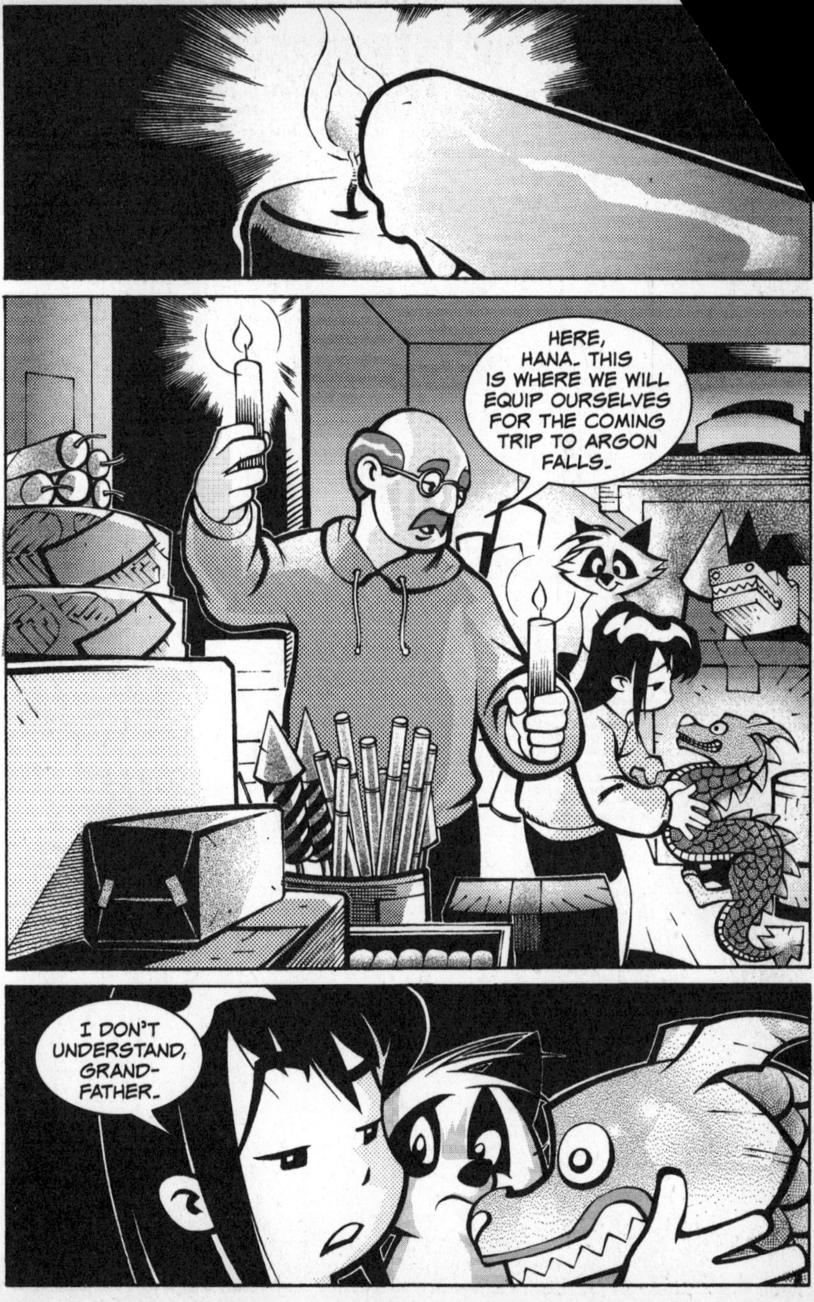
HERE, HANA. THIS IS WHERE WE WILL EQUIP OURSELVES FOR THE COMING TRIP TO ARGON FALLS.
I DON'T UNDERSTAND, GRAND-FATHER.

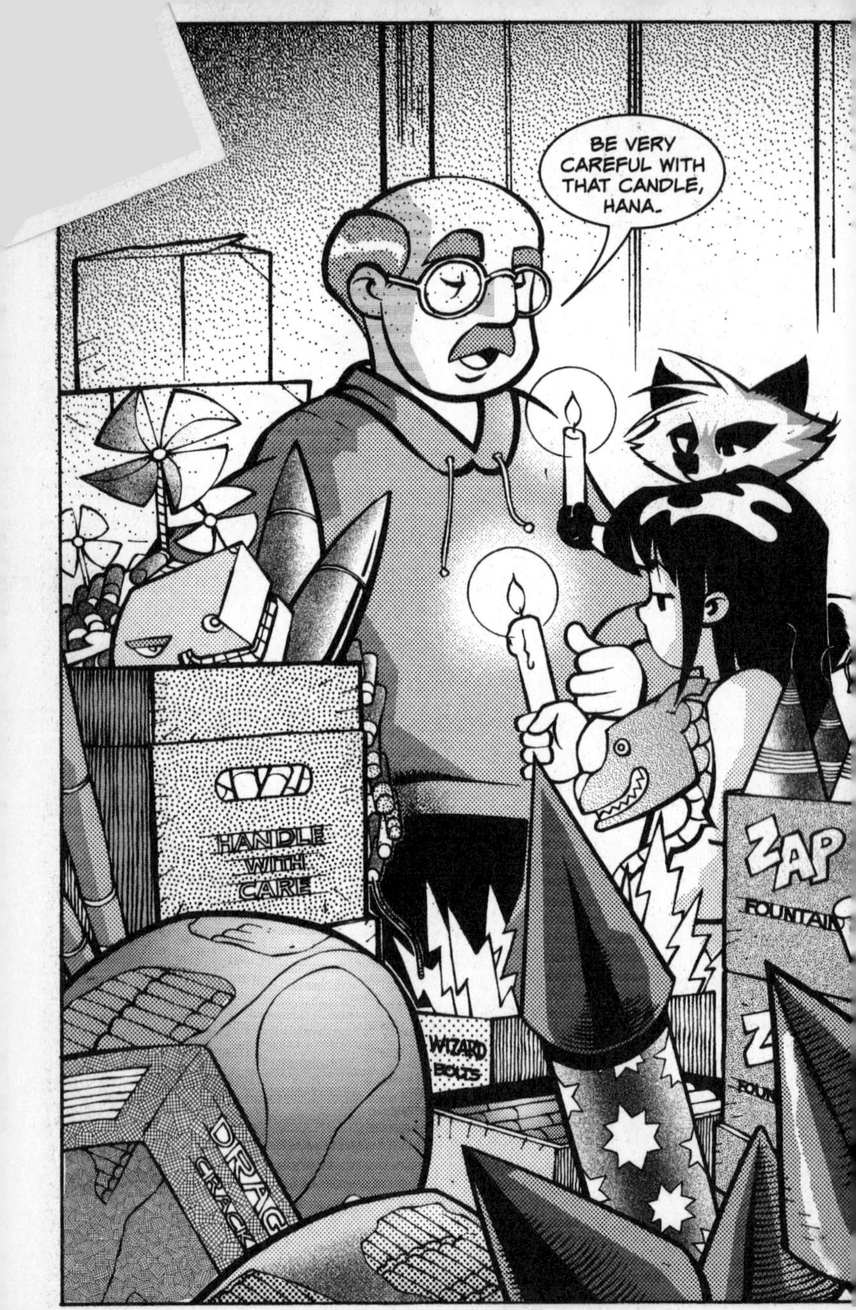
BE VERY CAREFUL WITH THAT CANDLE, HANA.
HANDLE WITH CARE
ZAP
FOUNTAIN
WIZARD BOLTS
DRAG
CRACK

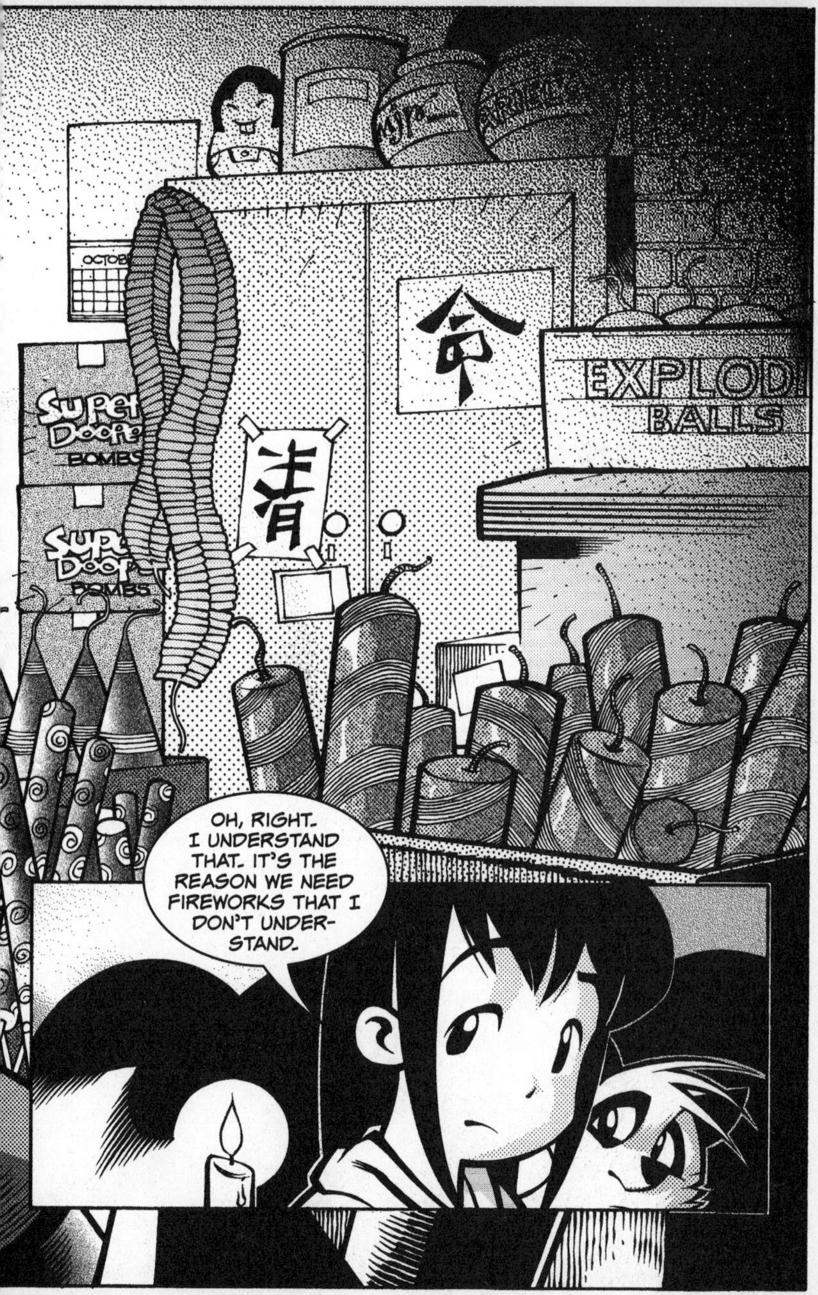
EXPLODI
BALLS
BOMBS
BOMBS
OH, RIGHT. I UNDERSTAND THAT. IT'S THE REASON WE NEED FIREWORKS THAT I DON'T UNDER-STAND.

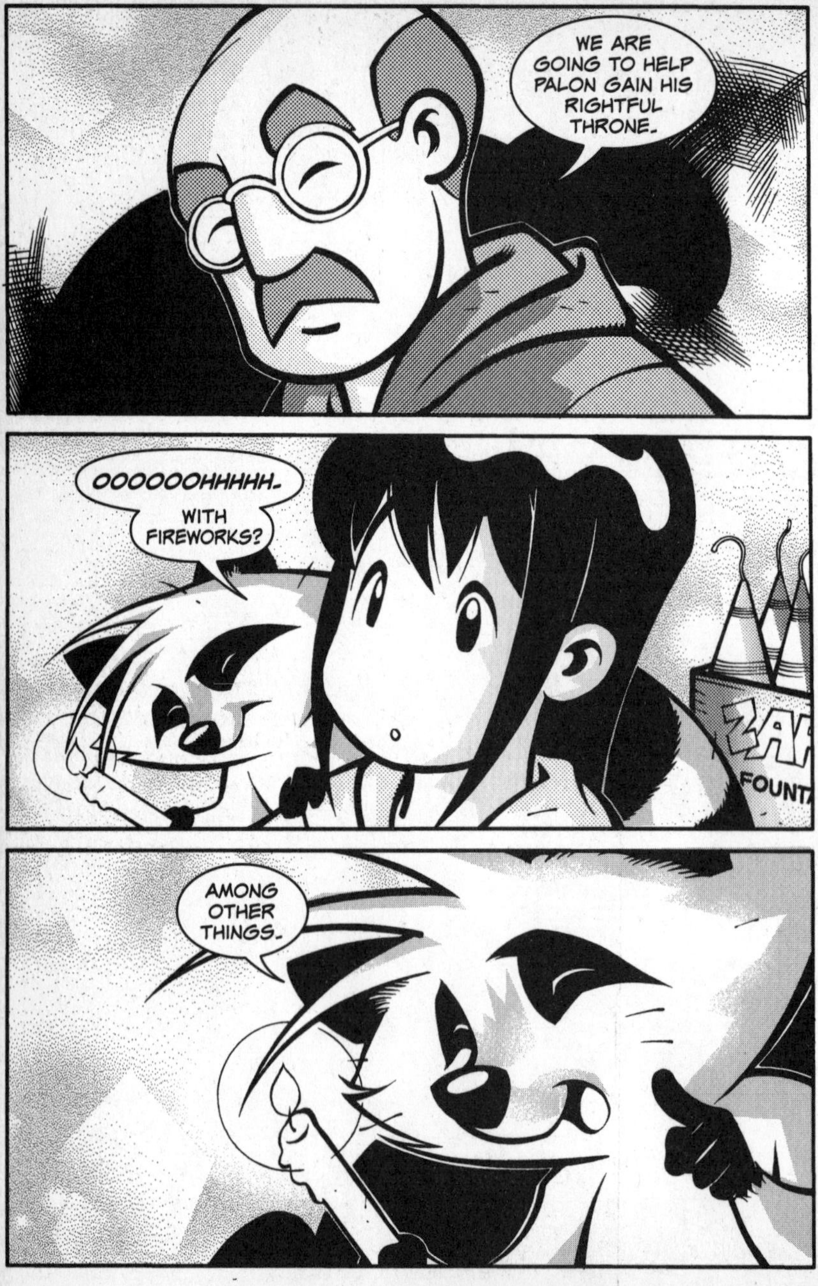
WE ARE GOING TO HELP PALON GAIN HIS RIGHTFUL THRONE.
OOOOOOHHHHH.
WITH FIREWORKS?
ZAP
FOUNT
AMONG OTHER THINGS.

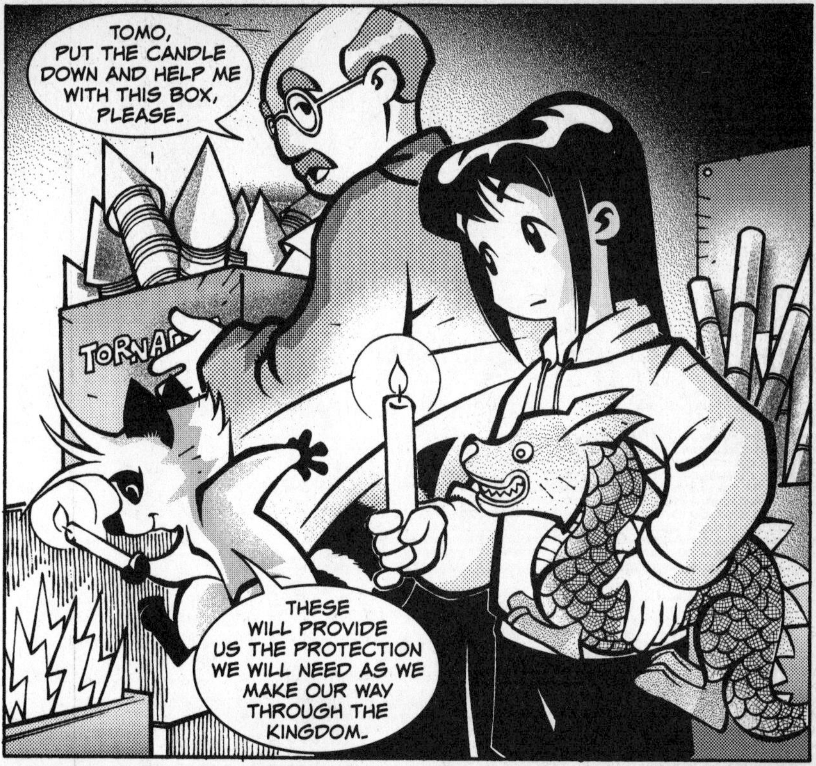
TOMO, PUT THE CANDLE DOWN AND HELP ME WITH THIS BOX, PLEASE.
TORNAD
THESE WILL PROVIDE US THE PROTECTION WE WILL NEED AS WE MAKE OUR WAY THROUGH THE KINGDOM.
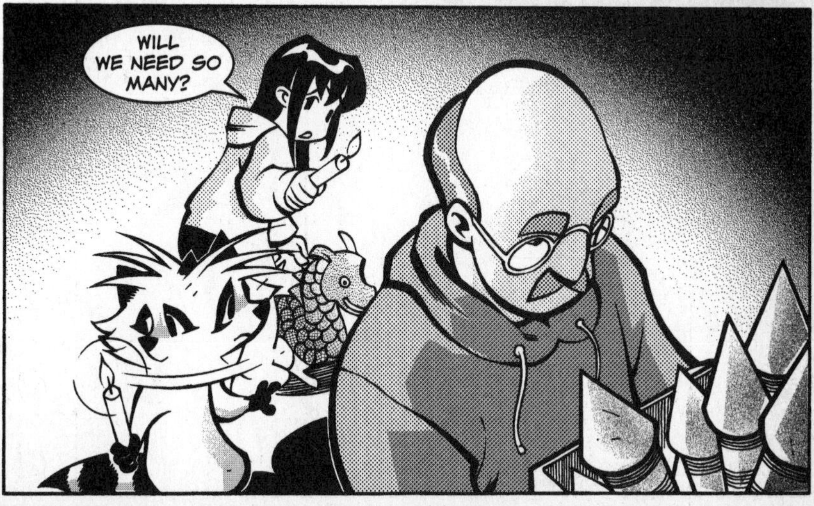
WILL WE NEED SO MANY?

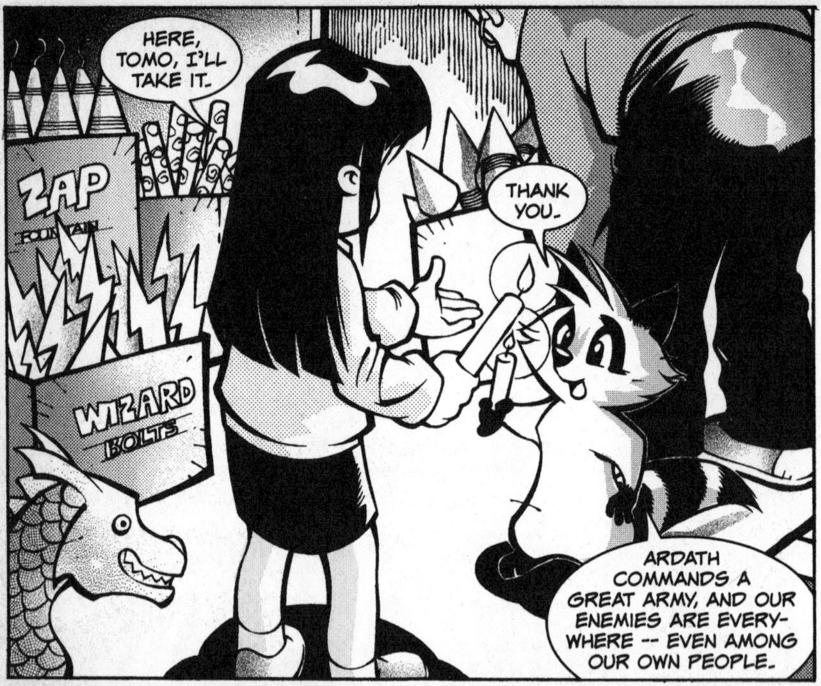
HERE, TOMO, I'LL TAKE IT.
ZAP
FOUNTAIN
THANK YOU.
WIZARD BOLTS
ARDATH COMMANDS A GREAT ARMY, AND OUR ENEMIES ARE EVERYWHERE -- EVEN AMONG OUR OWN PEOPLE.

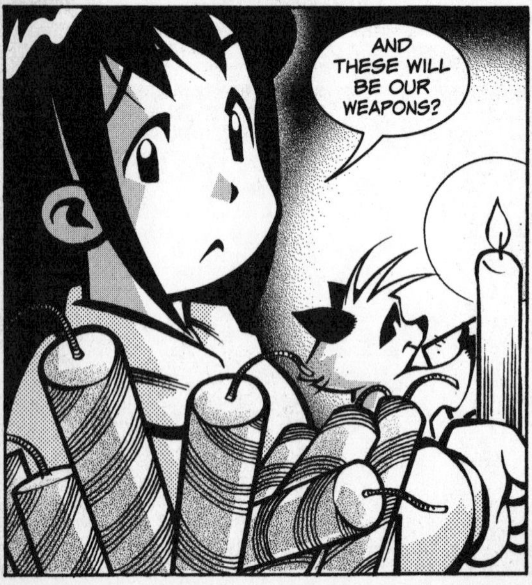
AND THESE WILL BE OUR WEAPONS?

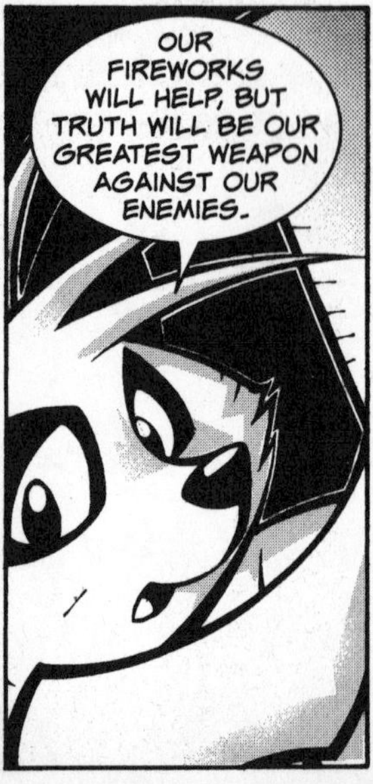
OUR FIREWORKS WILL HELP, BUT TRUTH WILL BE OUR GREATEST WEAPON AGAINST OUR ENEMIES.

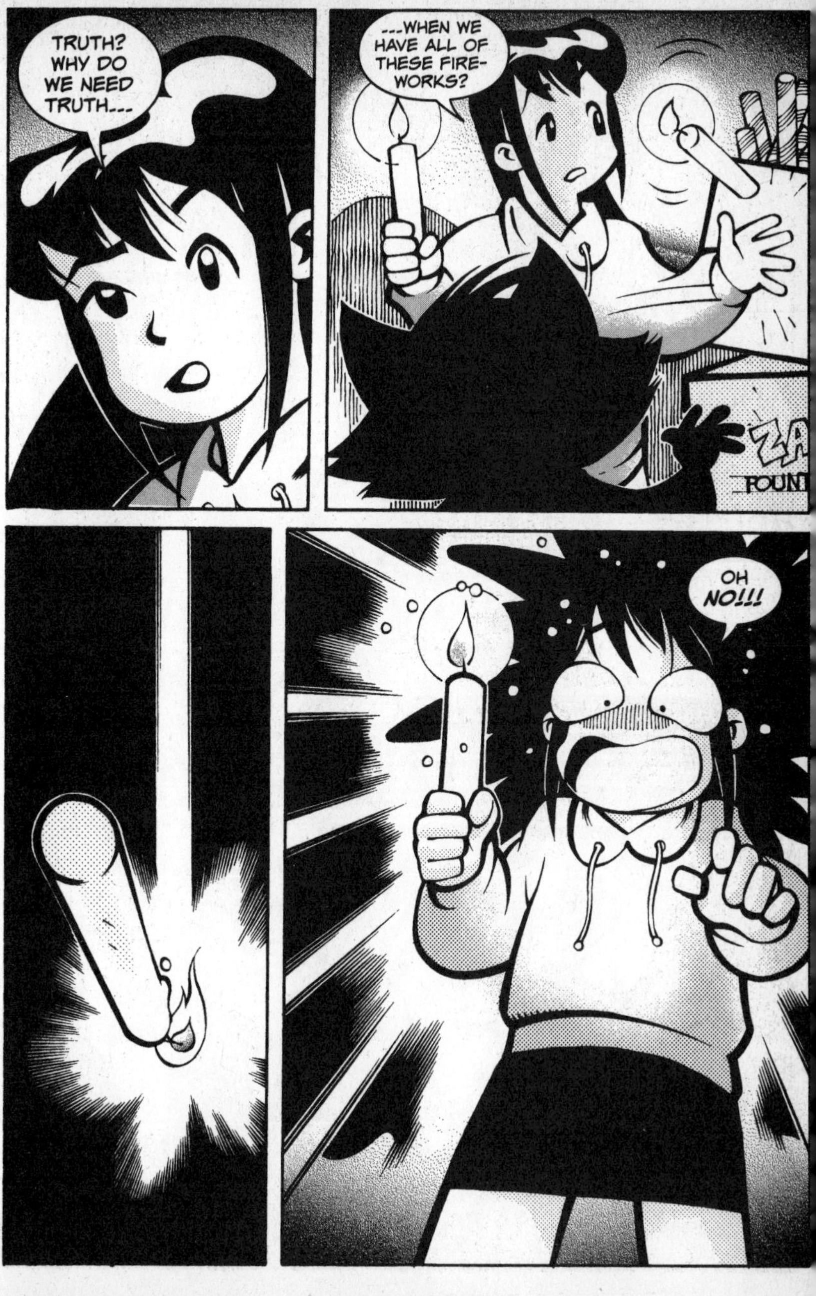
TRUTH? WHY DO WE NEED TRUTH...
...WHEN WE HAVE ALL OF THESE FIRE-WORKS?
ZA
FOUN
OH NO!!!

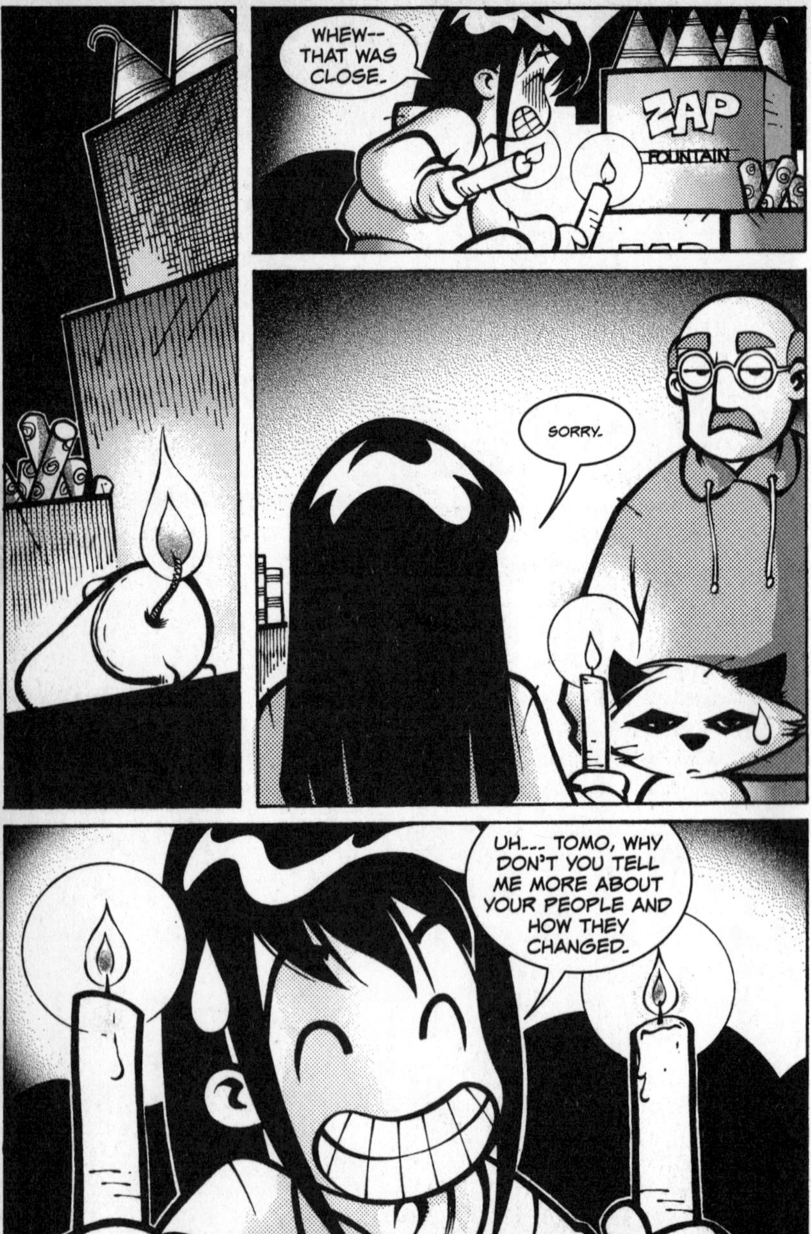
WHEW-- THAT WAS CLOSE.
ZAP
FOUNTAIN
SORRY.
UH... TOMO, WHY DON'T YOU TELL ME MORE ABOUT YOUR PEOPLE AND HOW THEY CHANGED.

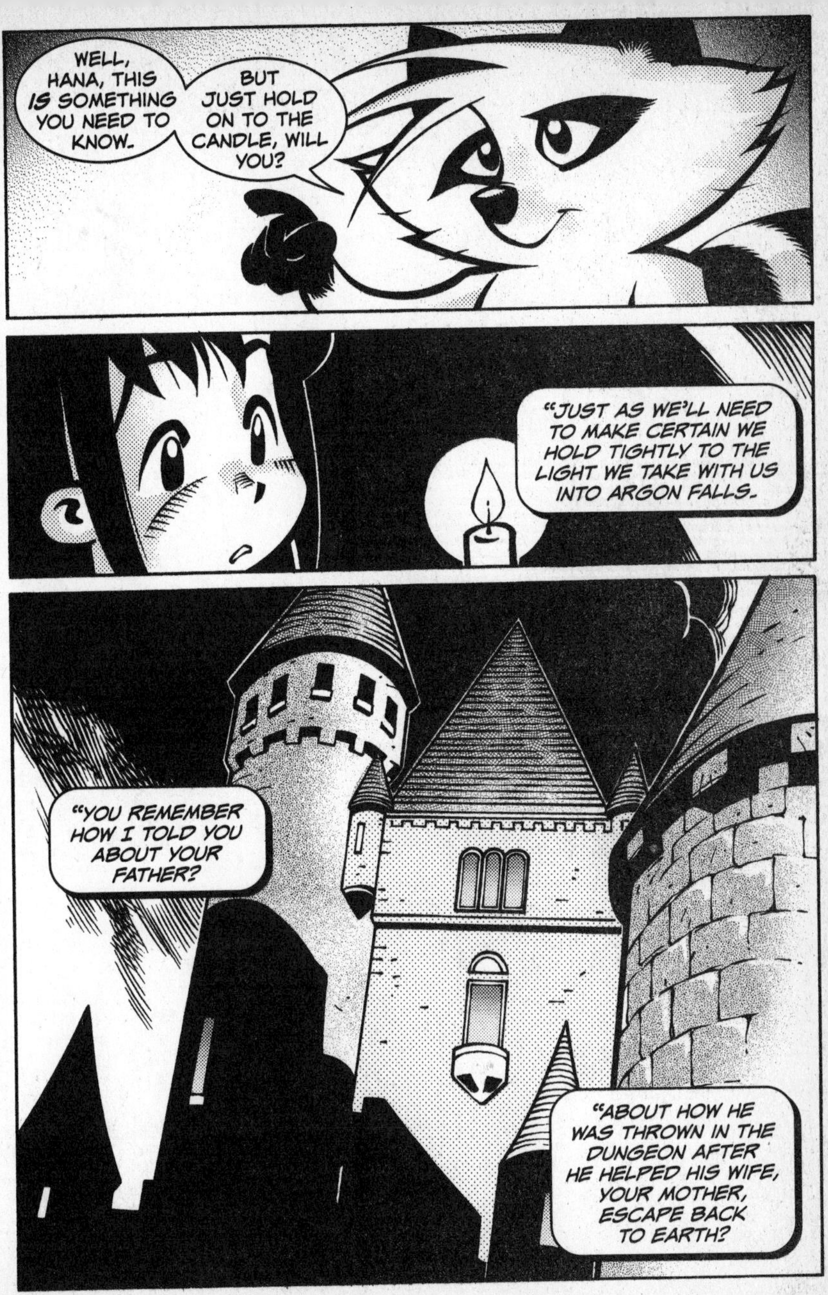
WELL, HANA, THIS *IS* SOMETHING YOU NEED TO KNOW.
BUT JUST HOLD ON TO THE CANDLE, WILL YOU?
"JUST AS WE'LL NEED TO MAKE CERTAIN WE HOLD TIGHTLY TO THE LIGHT WE TAKE WITH US INTO ARGON FALLS.
"YOU REMEMBER HOW I TOLD YOU ABOUT YOUR FATHER?
"ABOUT HOW HE WAS THROWN IN THE DUNGEON AFTER HE HELPED HIS WIFE, YOUR MOTHER, ESCAPE BACK TO EARTH?

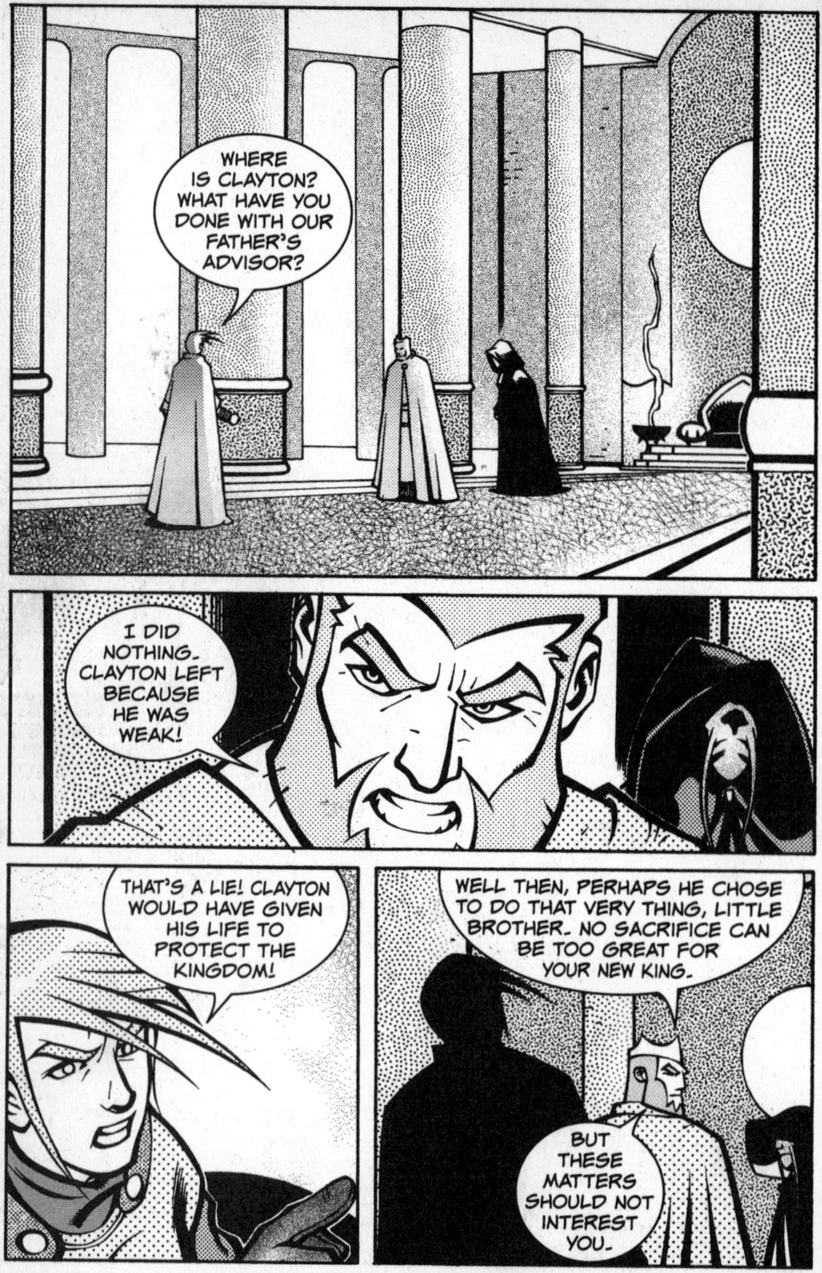
WHERE IS CLAYTON? WHAT HAVE YOU DONE WITH OUR FATHER'S ADVISOR?
I DID NOTHING. CLAYTON LEFT BECAUSE HE WAS WEAK!
THAT'S A LIE! CLAYTON WOULD HAVE GIVEN HIS LIFE TO PROTECT THE KINGDOM!
WELL THEN, PERHAPS HE CHOSE TO DO THAT VERY THING, LITTLE BROTHER. NO SACRIFICE CAN BE TOO GREAT FOR YOUR NEW KING.
BUT THESE MATTERS SHOULD NOT INTEREST YOU.

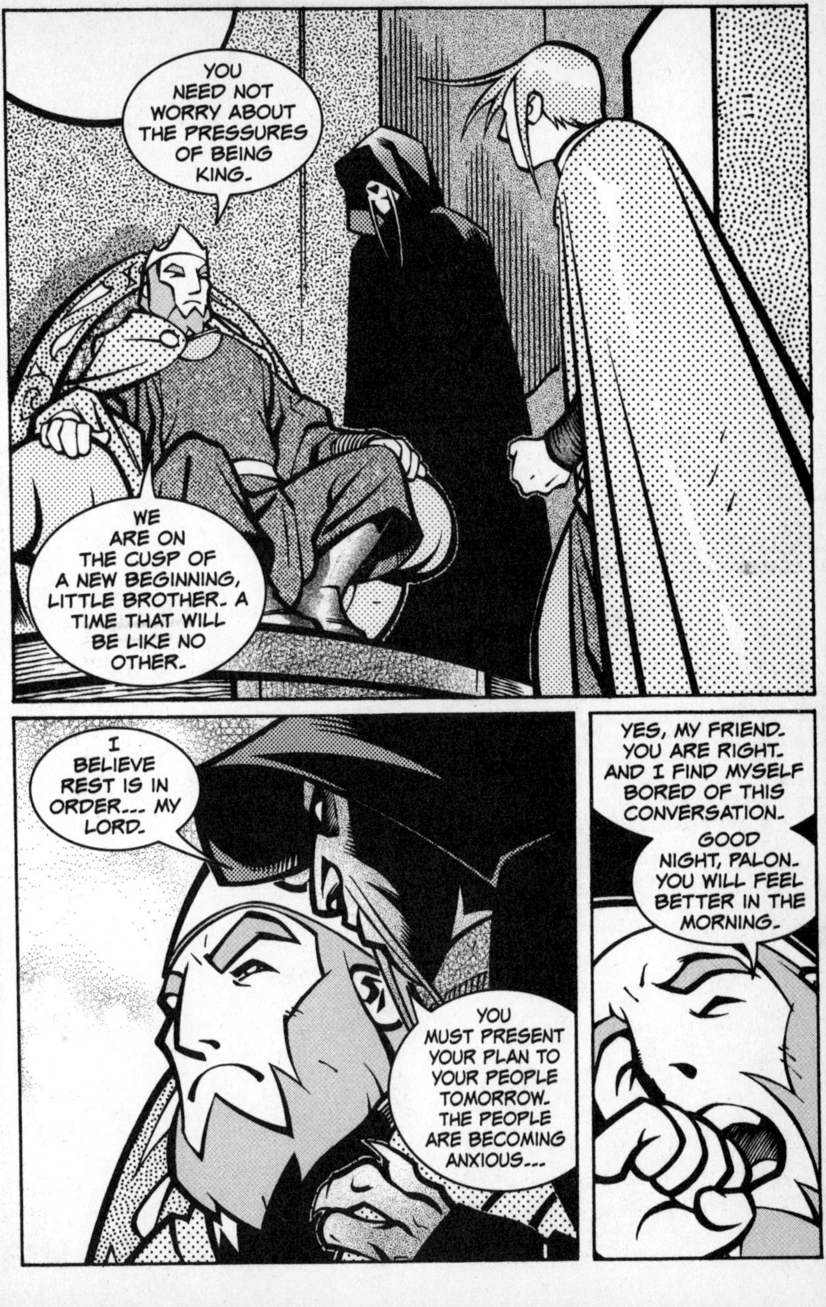
YOU NEED NOT WORRY ABOUT THE PRESSURES OF BEING KING.
WE ARE ON THE CUSP OF A NEW BEGINNING, LITTLE BROTHER. A TIME THAT WILL BE LIKE NO OTHER.
I BELIEVE REST IS IN ORDER... MY LORD.
YOU MUST PRESENT YOUR PLAN TO YOUR PEOPLE TOMORROW. THE PEOPLE ARE BECOMING ANXIOUS...
YES, MY FRIEND. YOU ARE RIGHT. AND I FIND MYSELF BORED OF THIS CONVERSATION.
GOOD NIGHT, PALON. YOU WILL FEEL BETTER IN THE MORNING.

"OF COURSE I DID NOT FEEL BETTER, HANA.
"THAT WAS A TERRIBLE NIGHT. I DID NOT SLEEP AT ALL.
"ALL HOPE FOR ARGON FALLS BEGAN TO FADE.
"ARDATH HAD CHANGED. I SCARCELY KNEW HIM AS MY BROTHER ANYMORE.
"I HAD NO IDEA WHAT TO DO. NO ONE WAS PREPARED FOR WHAT WE WERE FACING.

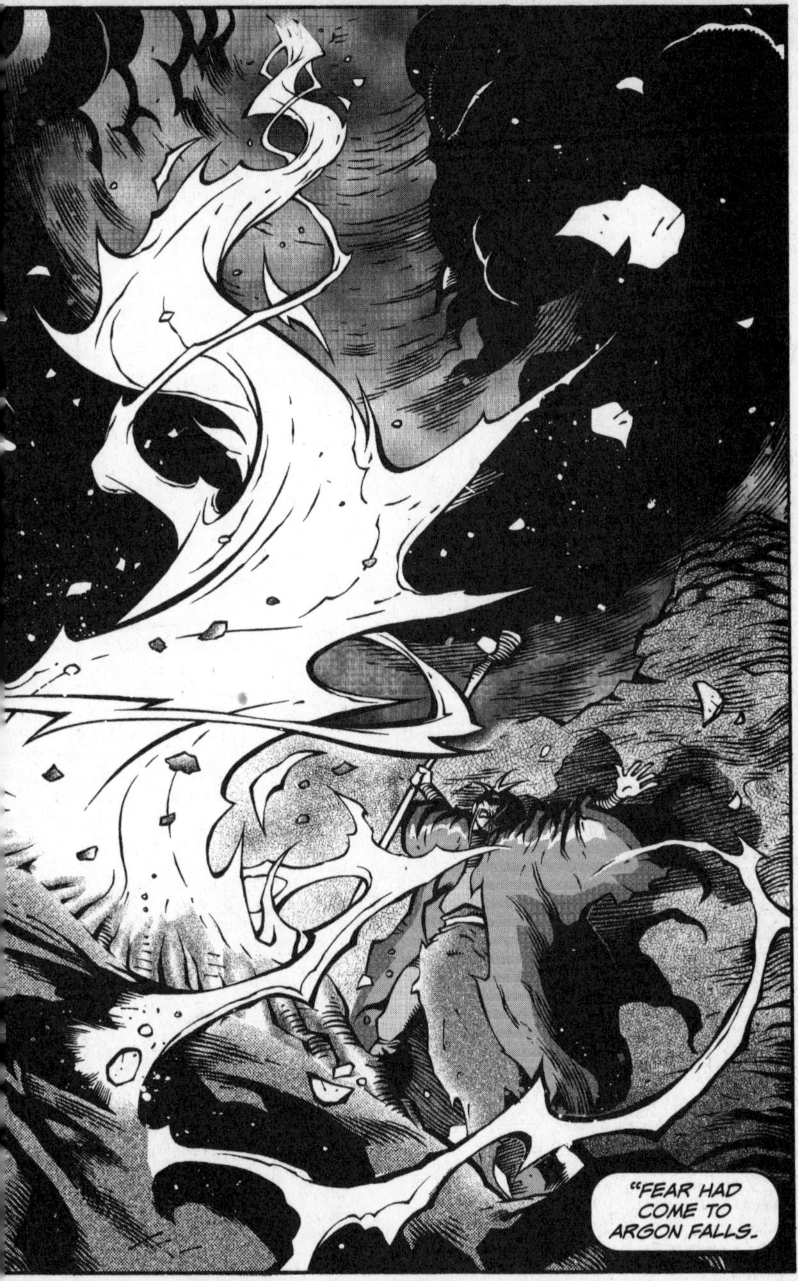
"FEAR HAD COME TO ARGON FALLS.

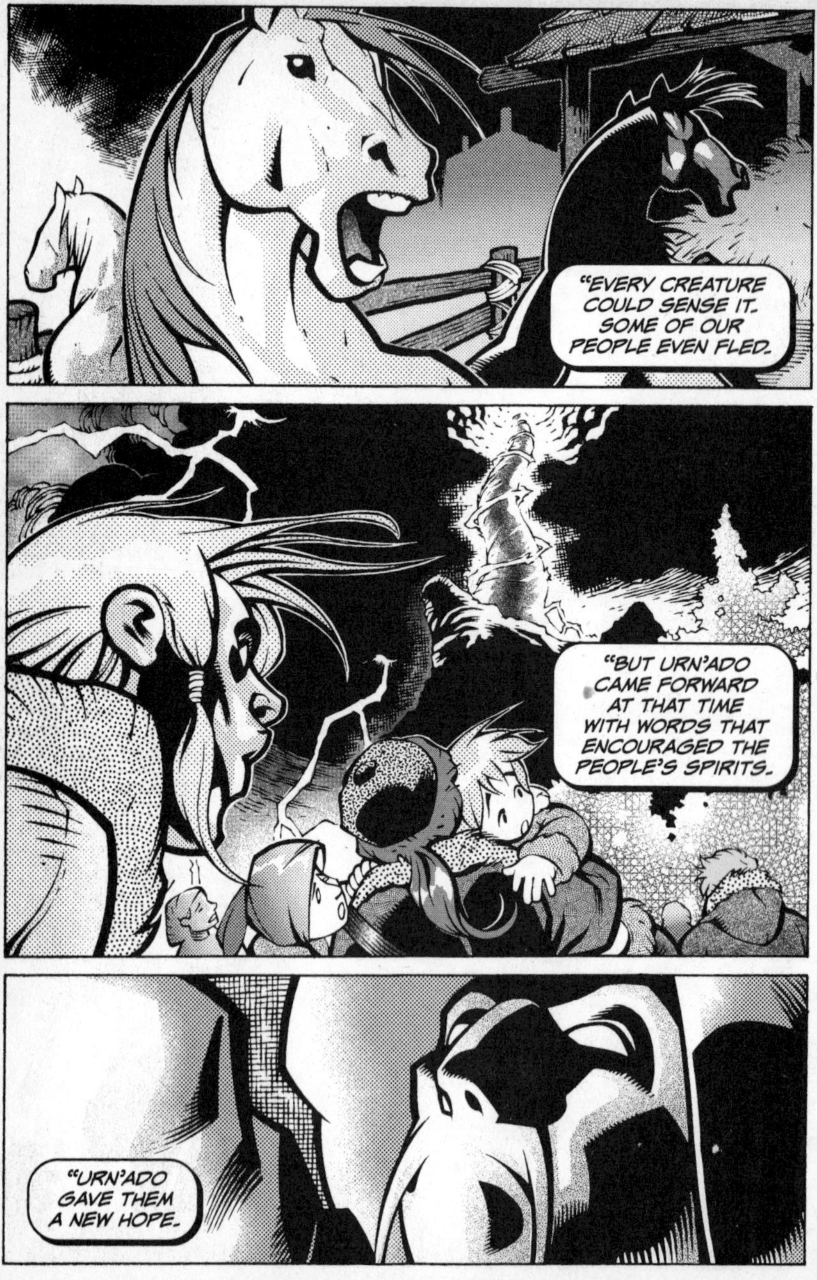
"EVERY CREATURE COULD SENSE IT. SOME OF OUR PEOPLE EVEN FLED.
"BUT URN'ADO CAME FORWARD AT THAT TIME WITH WORDS THAT ENCOURAGED THE PEOPLE'S SPIRITS.
"URN'ADO GAVE THEM A NEW HOPE.

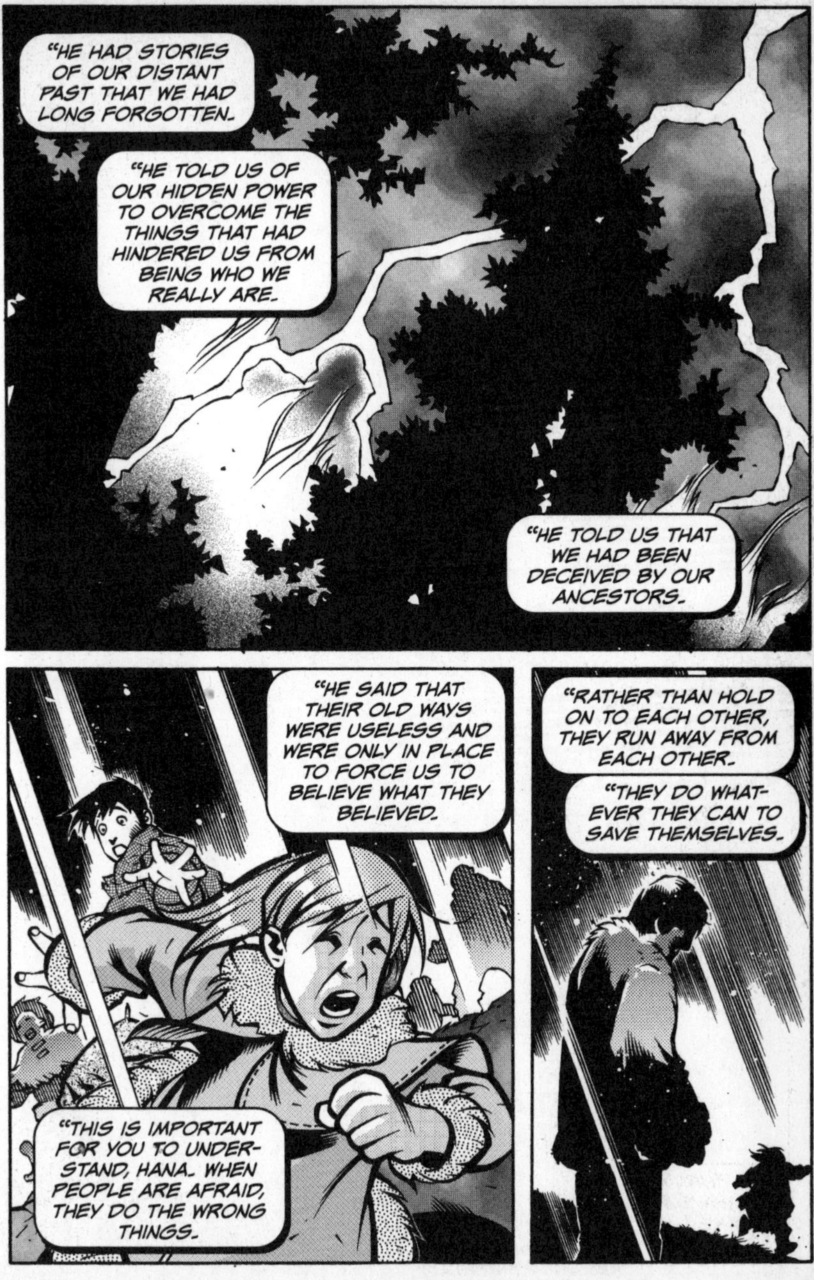
"HE HAD STORIES OF OUR DISTANT PAST THAT WE HAD LONG FORGOTTEN.
"HE TOLD US OF OUR HIDDEN POWER TO OVERCOME THE THINGS THAT HAD HINDERED US FROM BEING WHO WE REALLY ARE.
"HE TOLD US THAT WE HAD BEEN DECEIVED BY OUR ANCESTORS.
"HE SAID THAT THEIR OLD WAYS WERE USELESS AND WERE ONLY IN PLACE TO FORCE US TO BELIEVE WHAT THEY BELIEVED.
"THIS IS IMPORTANT FOR YOU TO UNDER-STAND, HANA. WHEN PEOPLE ARE AFRAID, THEY DO THE WRONG THINGS.
"RATHER THAN HOLD ON TO EACH OTHER, THEY RUN AWAY FROM EACH OTHER.
"THEY DO WHAT-EVER THEY CAN TO SAVE THEMSELVES.

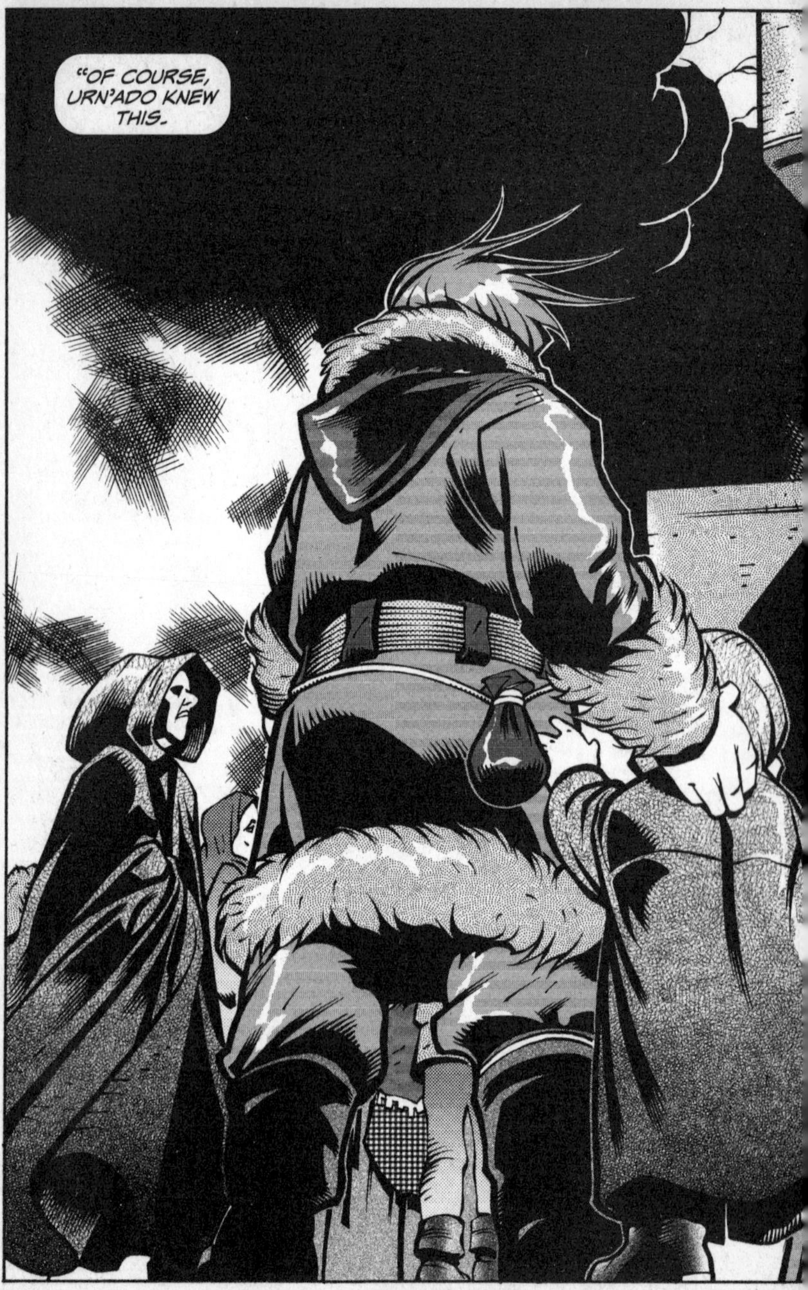
"OF COURSE, URN'ADO KNEW THIS.

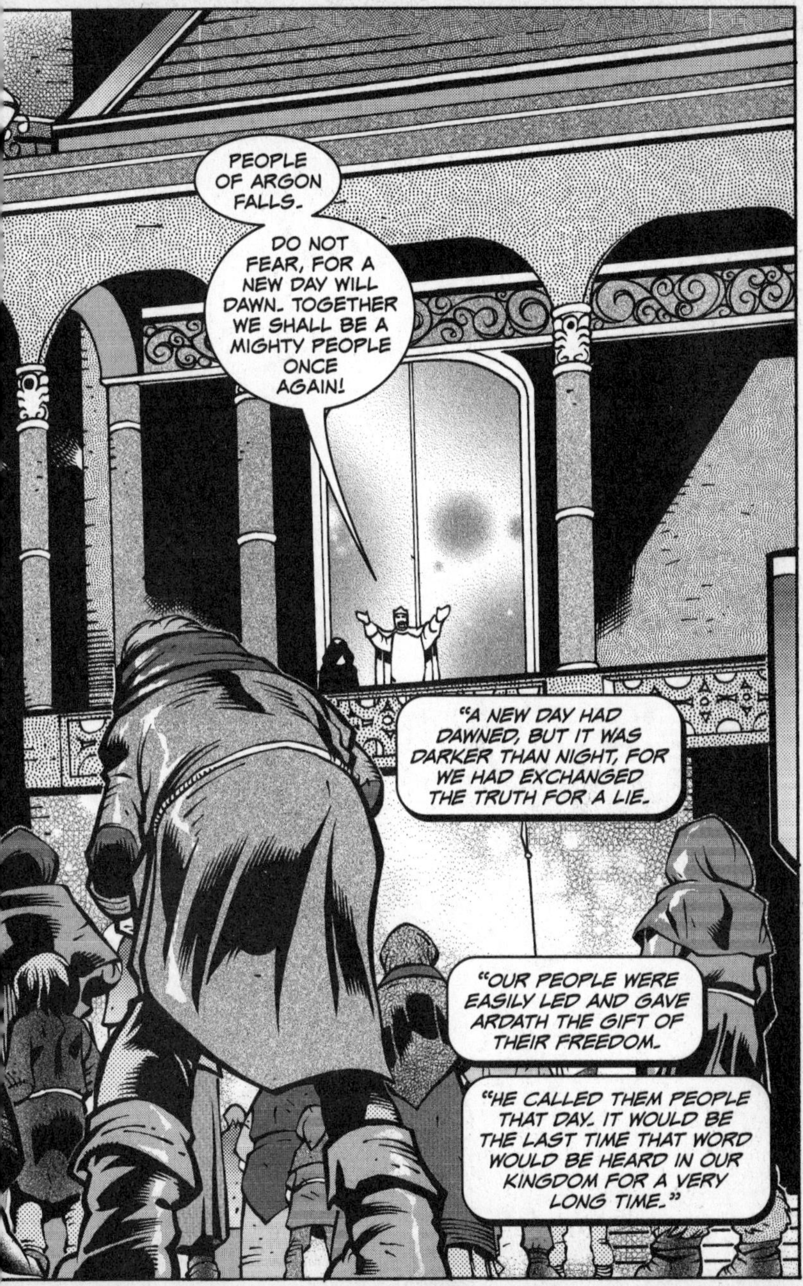
PEOPLE OF ARGON FALLS.
DO NOT FEAR, FOR A NEW DAY WILL DAWN. TOGETHER WE SHALL BE A MIGHTY PEOPLE ONCE AGAIN!
"A NEW DAY HAD DAWNED, BUT IT WAS DARKER THAN NIGHT, FOR WE HAD EXCHANGED THE TRUTH FOR A LIE.
"OUR PEOPLE WERE EASILY LED AND GAVE ARDATH THE GIFT OF THEIR FREEDOM.
"HE CALLED THEM PEOPLE THAT DAY. IT WOULD BE THE LAST TIME THAT WORD WOULD BE HEARD IN OUR KINGDOM FOR A VERY LONG TIME."

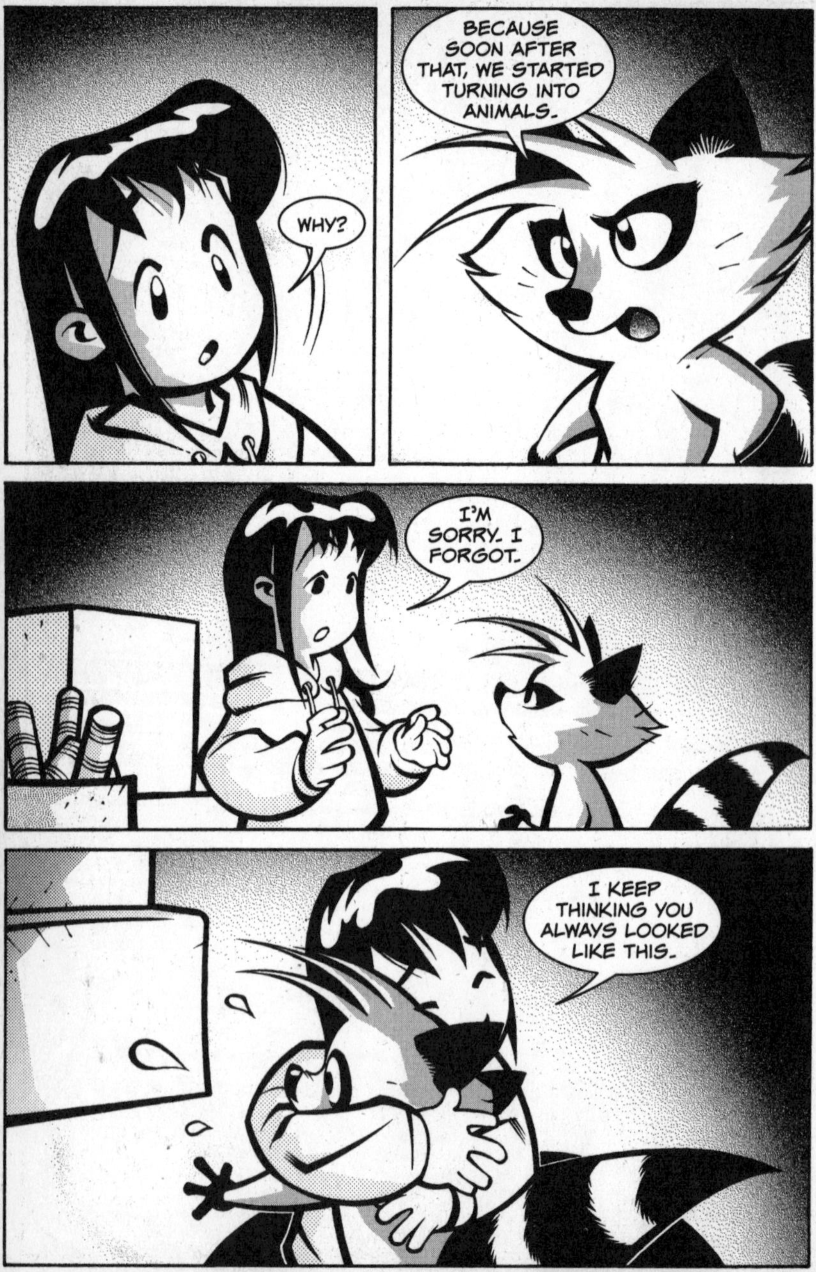
WHY?
BECAUSE SOON AFTER THAT, WE STARTED TURNING INTO ANIMALS.
I'M SORRY. I FORGOT.
I KEEP THINKING YOU ALWAYS LOOKED LIKE THIS.

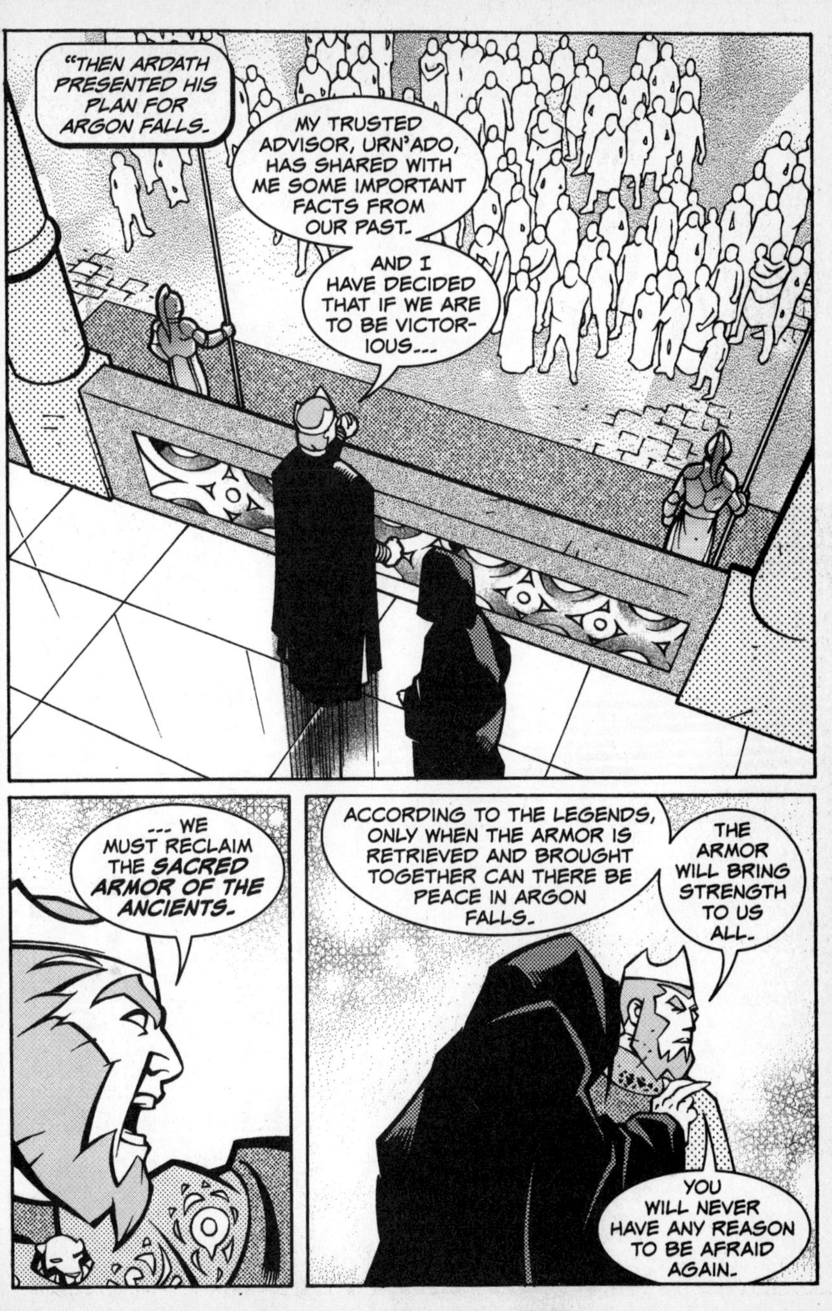
"THEN ARDATH PRESENTED HIS PLAN FOR ARGON FALLS.
MY TRUSTED ADVISOR, URN'ADO, HAS SHARED WITH ME SOME IMPORTANT FACTS FROM OUR PAST.
AND I HAVE DECIDED THAT IF WE ARE TO BE VICTORIOUS...
...WE MUST RECLAIM THE ***SACRED ARMOR OF THE ANCIENTS.***
ACCORDING TO THE LEGENDS, ONLY WHEN THE ARMOR IS RETRIEVED AND BROUGHT TOGETHER CAN THERE BE PEACE IN ARGON FALLS.
THE ARMOR WILL BRING STRENGTH TO US ALL.
YOU WILL NEVER HAVE ANY REASON TO BE AFRAID AGAIN.

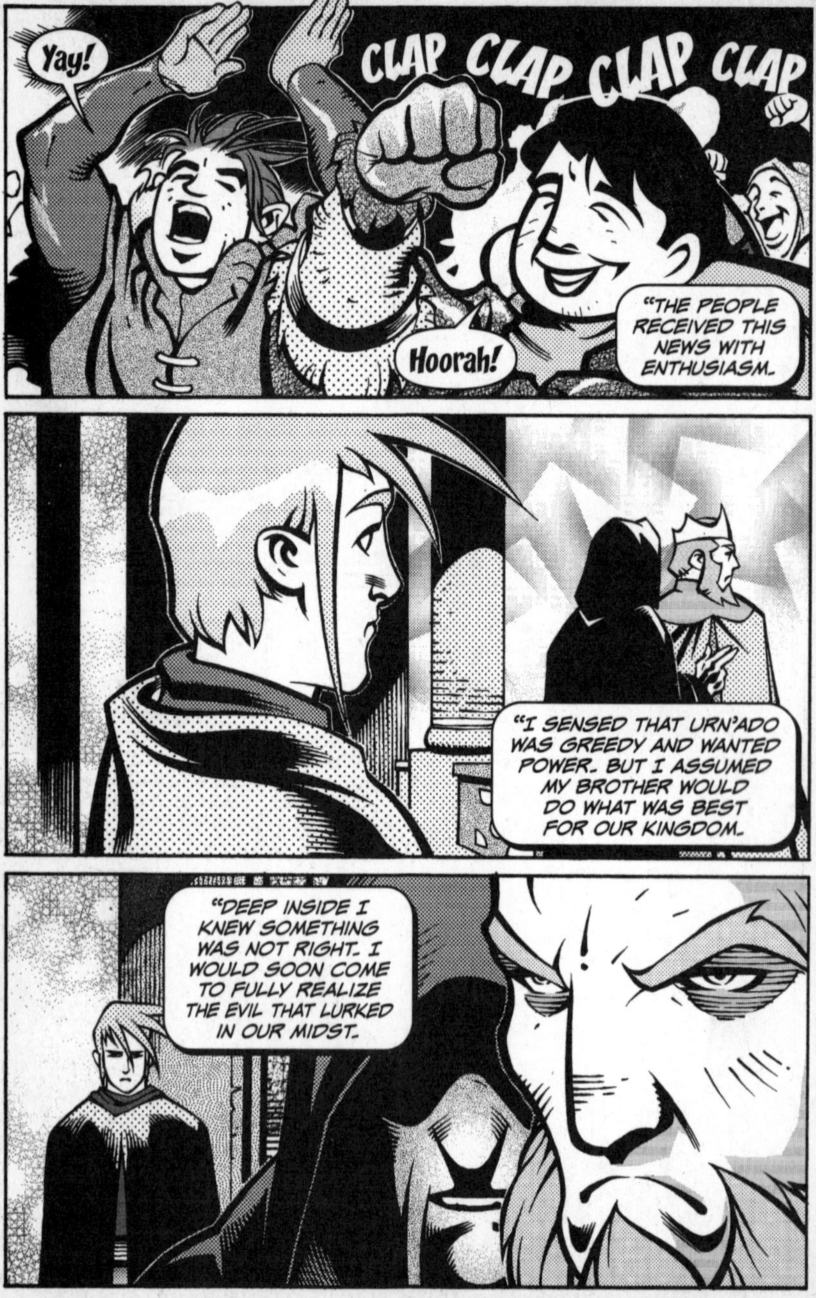
Yay!
CLAP CLAP CLAP CLAP
Hoorah!
"THE PEOPLE RECEIVED THIS NEWS WITH ENTHUSIASM.
"I SENSED THAT URN'ADO WAS GREEDY AND WANTED POWER. BUT I ASSUMED MY BROTHER WOULD DO WHAT WAS BEST FOR OUR KINGDOM.
"DEEP INSIDE I KNEW SOMETHING WAS NOT RIGHT. I WOULD SOON COME TO FULLY REALIZE THE EVIL THAT LURKED IN OUR MIDST.

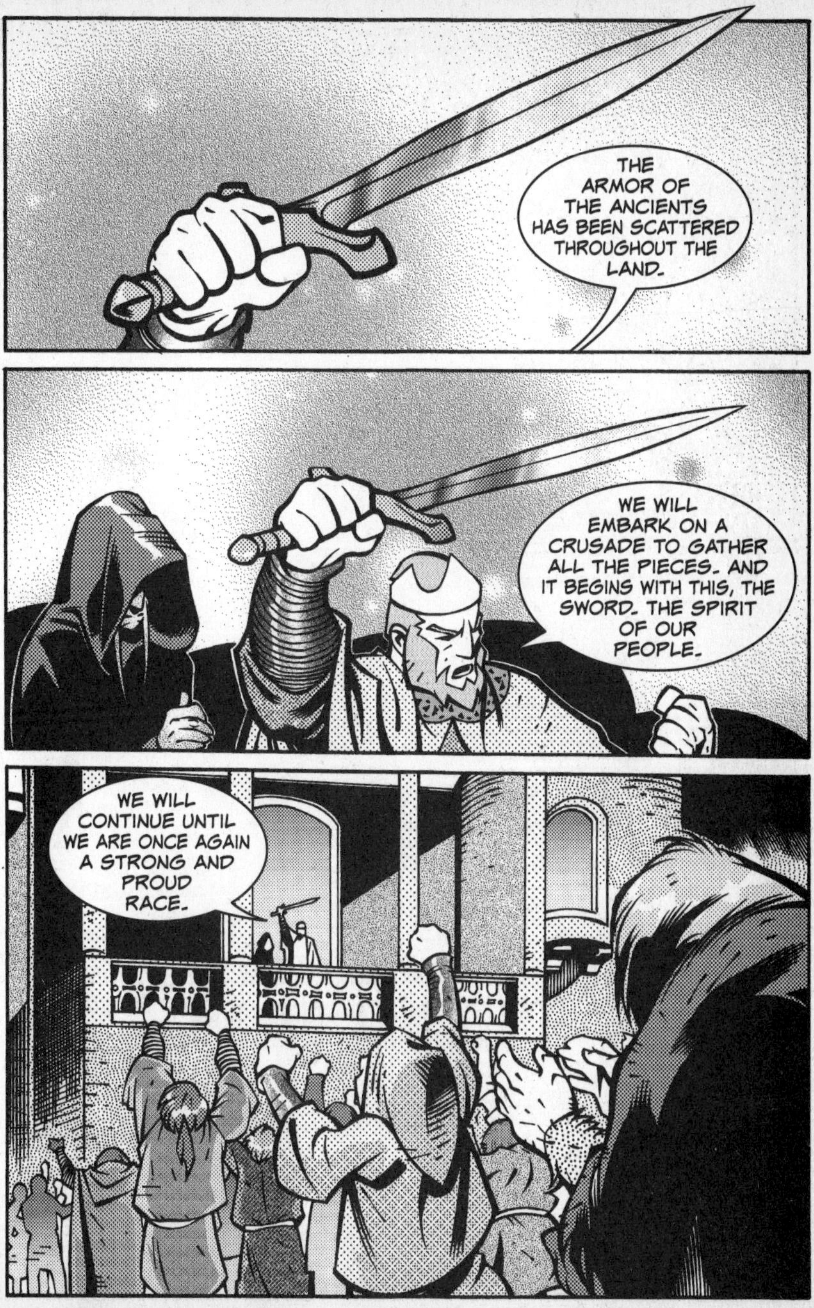
THE ARMOR OF THE ANCIENTS HAS BEEN SCATTERED THROUGHOUT THE LAND.
WE WILL EMBARK ON A CRUSADE TO GATHER ALL THE PIECES. AND IT BEGINS WITH THIS, THE SWORD. THE SPIRIT OF OUR PEOPLE.
WE WILL CONTINUE UNTIL WE ARE ONCE AGAIN A STRONG AND PROUD RACE.

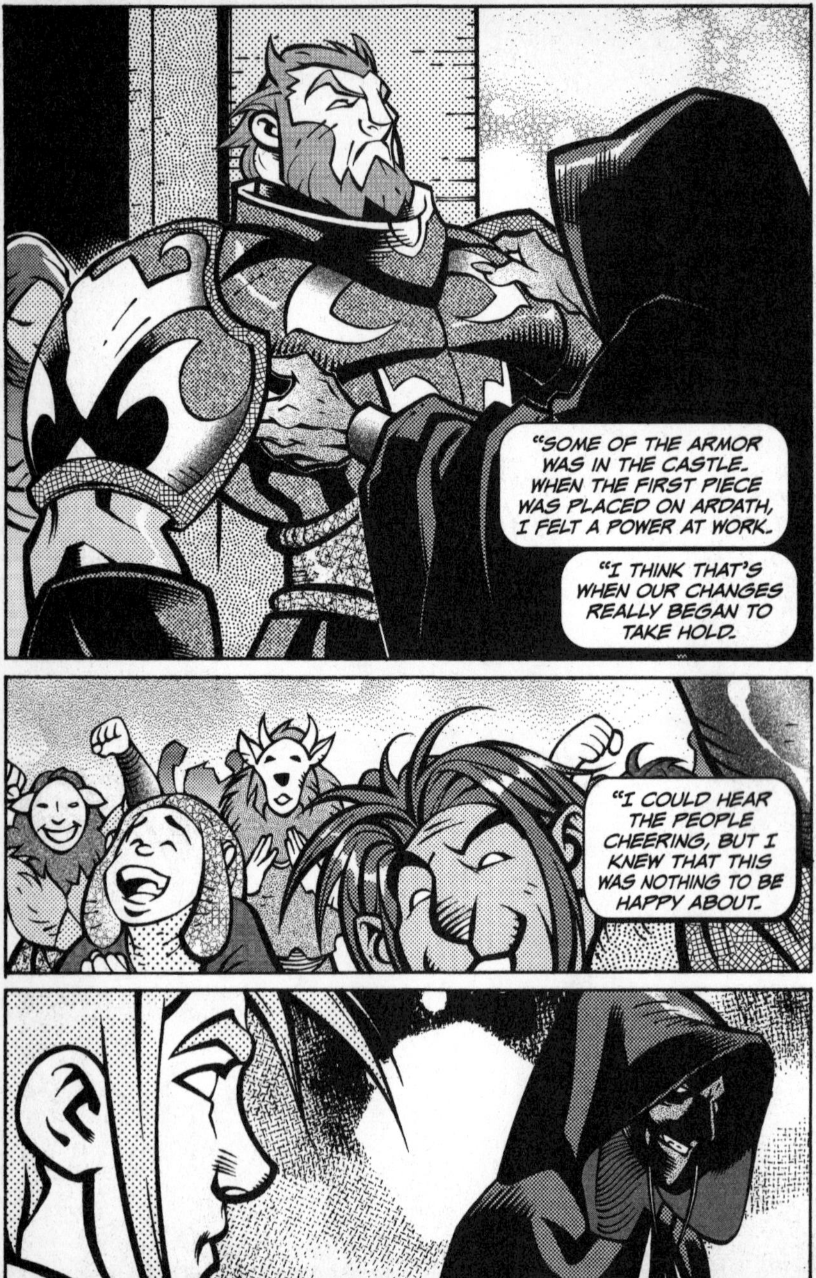
"SOME OF THE ARMOR WAS IN THE CASTLE. WHEN THE FIRST PIECE WAS PLACED ON ARDATH, I FELT A POWER AT WORK.
"I THINK THAT'S WHEN OUR CHANGES REALLY BEGAN TO TAKE HOLD.
"I COULD HEAR THE PEOPLE CHEERING, BUT I KNEW THAT THIS WAS NOTHING TO BE HAPPY ABOUT.

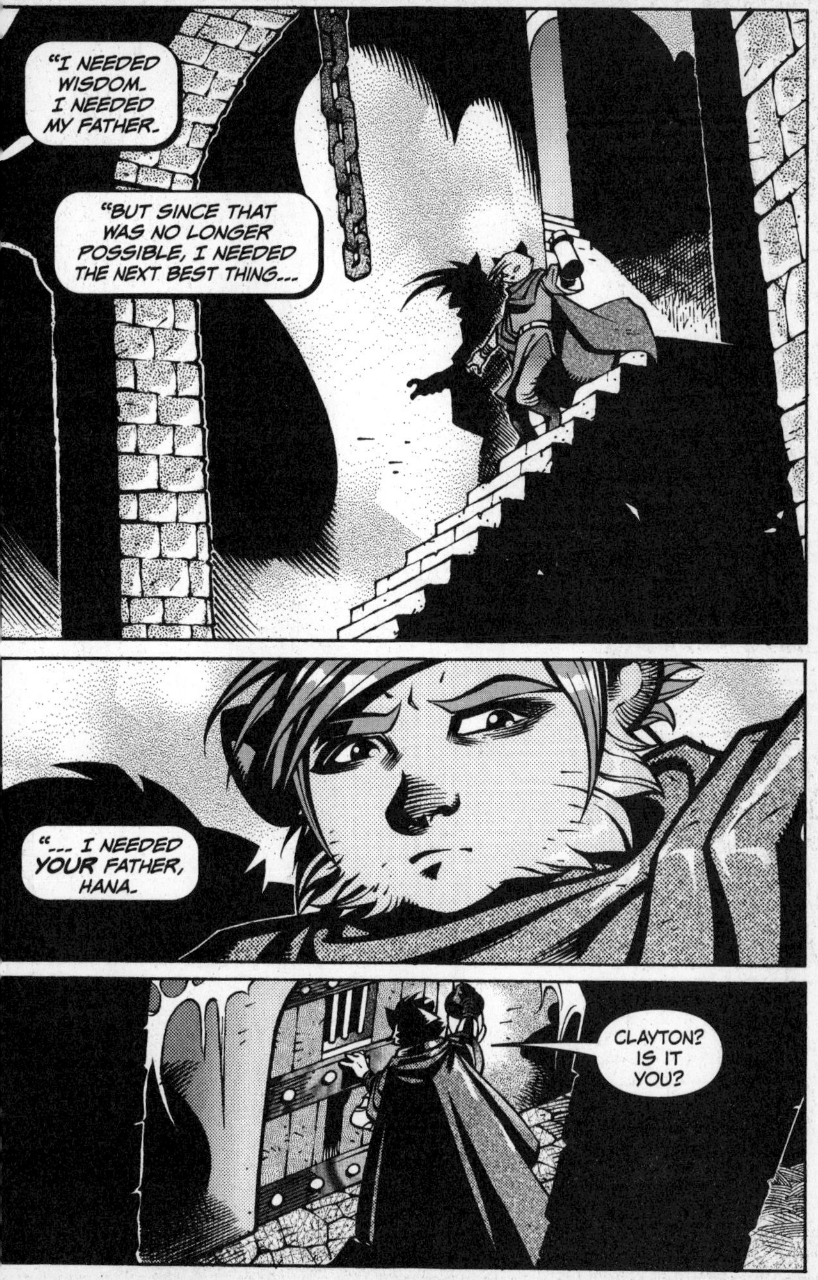
"I NEEDED WISDOM. I NEEDED MY FATHER.
"BUT SINCE THAT WAS NO LONGER POSSIBLE, I NEEDED THE NEXT BEST THING...
"... I NEEDED YOUR FATHER, HANA.
CLAYTON? IS IT YOU?

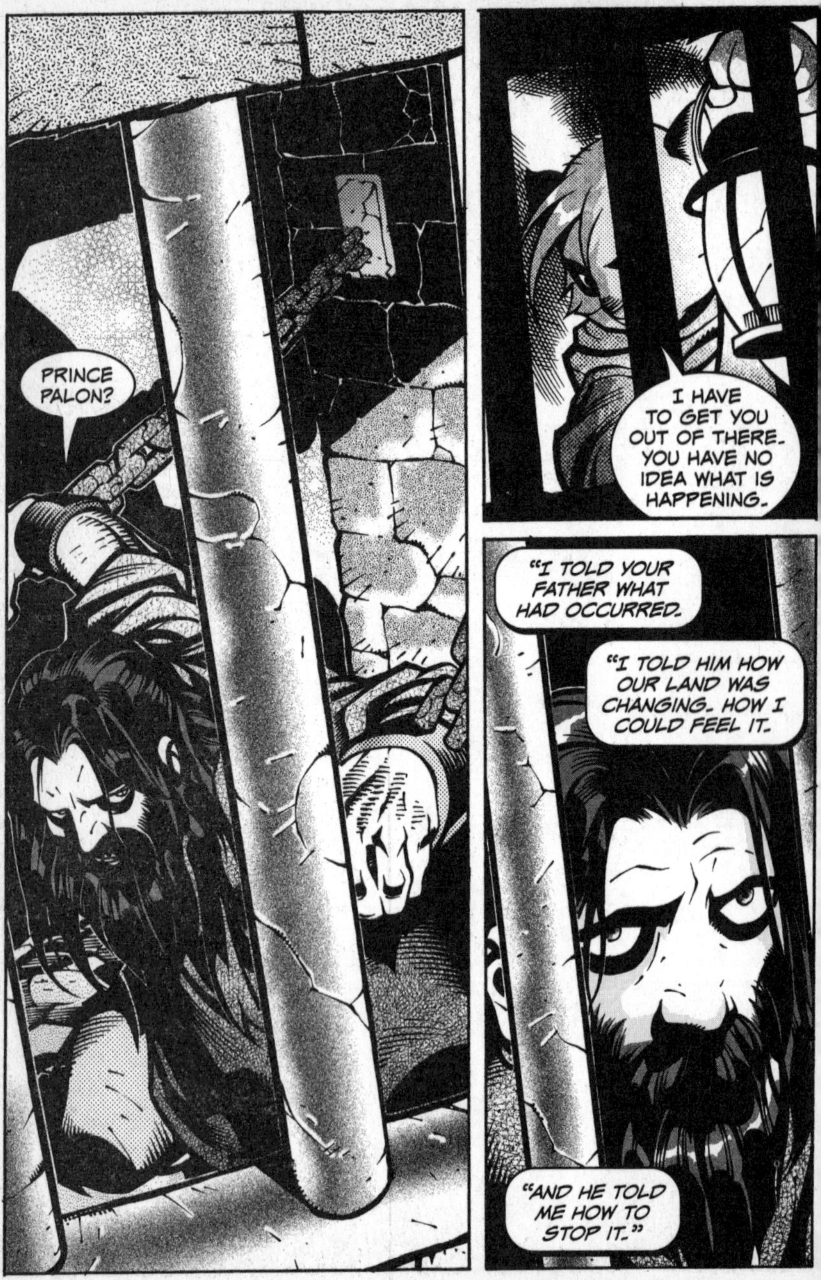
PRINCE PALON?
I HAVE TO GET YOU OUT OF THERE. YOU HAVE NO IDEA WHAT IS HAPPENING.
"I TOLD YOUR FATHER WHAT HAD OCCURRED.
"I TOLD HIM HOW OUR LAND WAS CHANGING. HOW I COULD FEEL IT.
"AND HE TOLD ME HOW TO STOP IT."

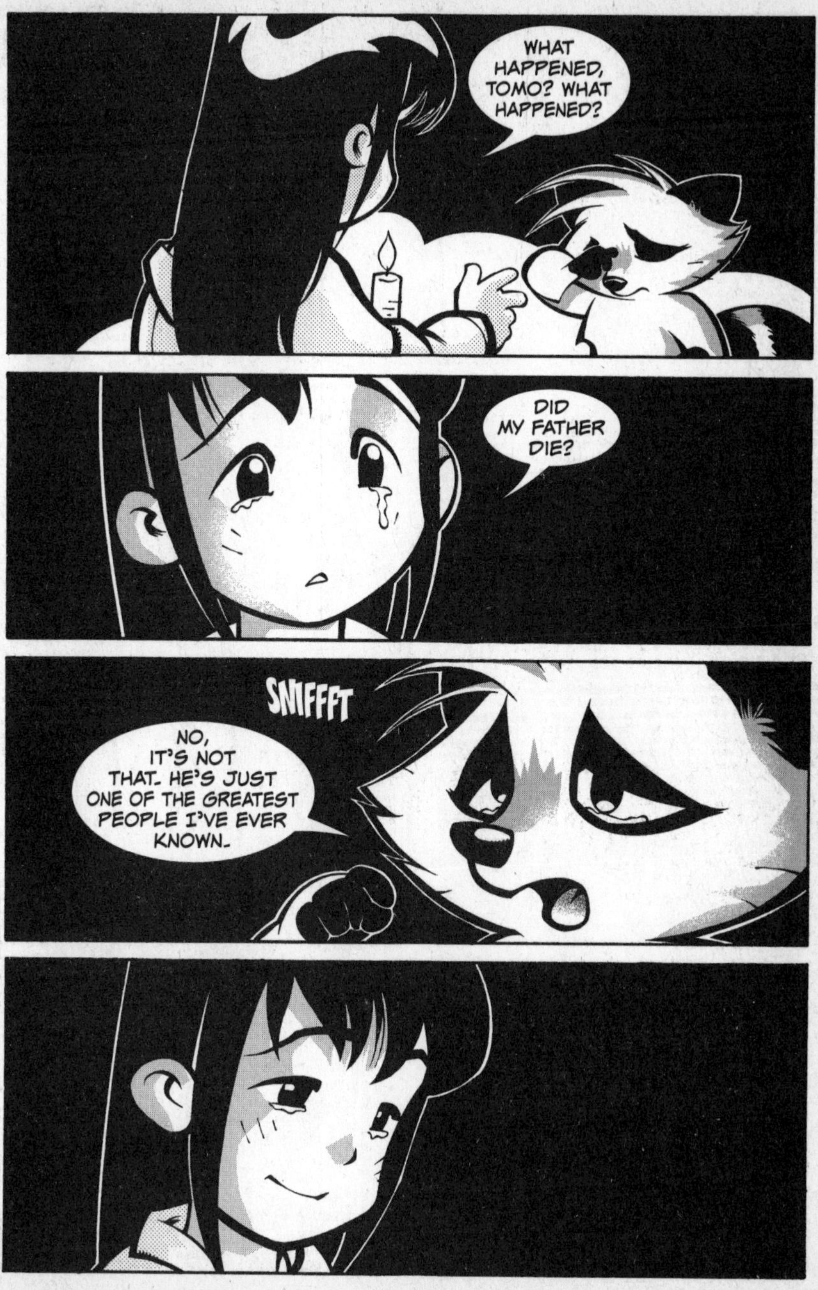
WHAT HAPPENED, TOMO? WHAT HAPPENED?
DID MY FATHER DIE?
SNIFFFT
NO, IT'S NOT THAT. HE'S JUST ONE OF THE GREATEST PEOPLE I'VE EVER KNOWN.

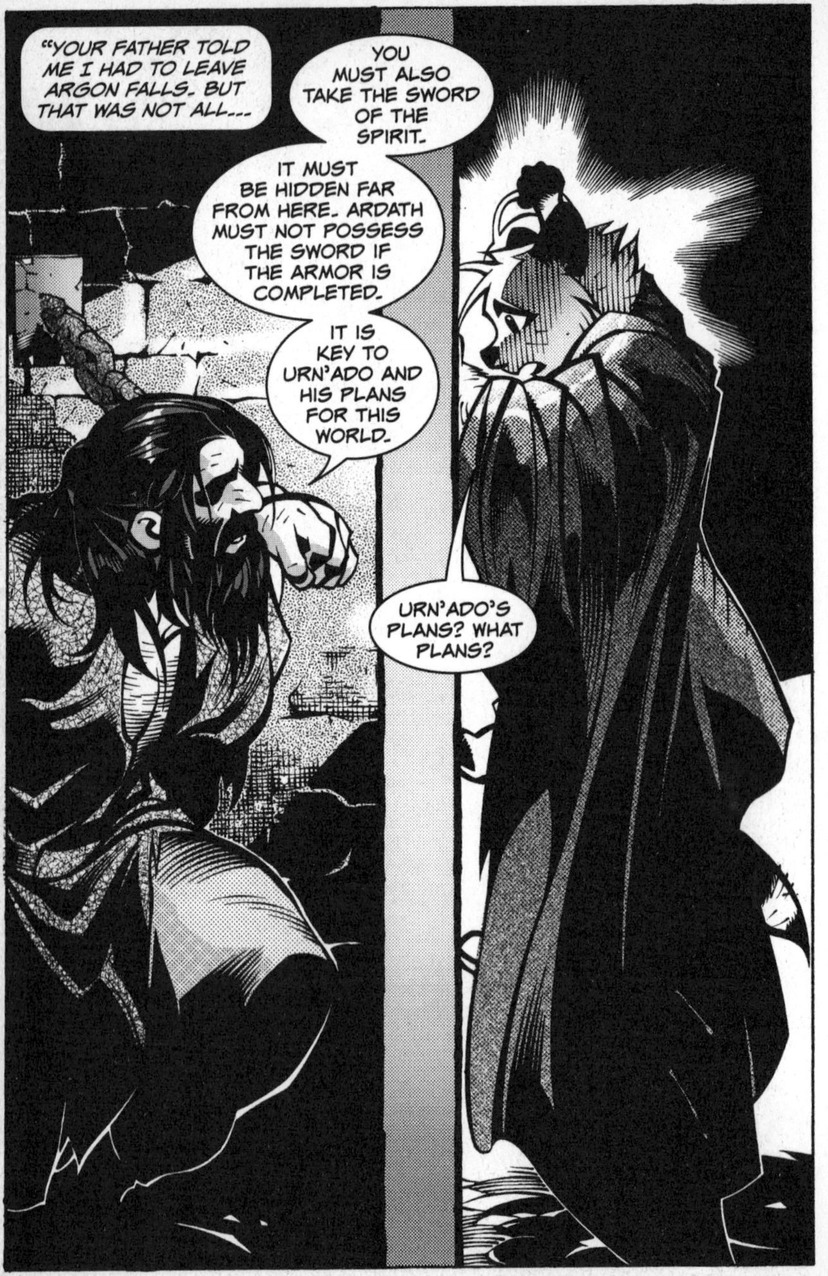
"YOUR FATHER TOLD ME I HAD TO LEAVE ARGON FALLS. BUT THAT WAS NOT ALL...
YOU MUST ALSO TAKE THE SWORD OF THE SPIRIT.
IT MUST BE HIDDEN FAR FROM HERE. ARDATH MUST NOT POSSESS THE SWORD IF THE ARMOR IS COMPLETED.
IT IS KEY TO URN'ADO AND HIS PLANS FOR THIS WORLD.
URN'ADO'S PLANS? WHAT PLANS?

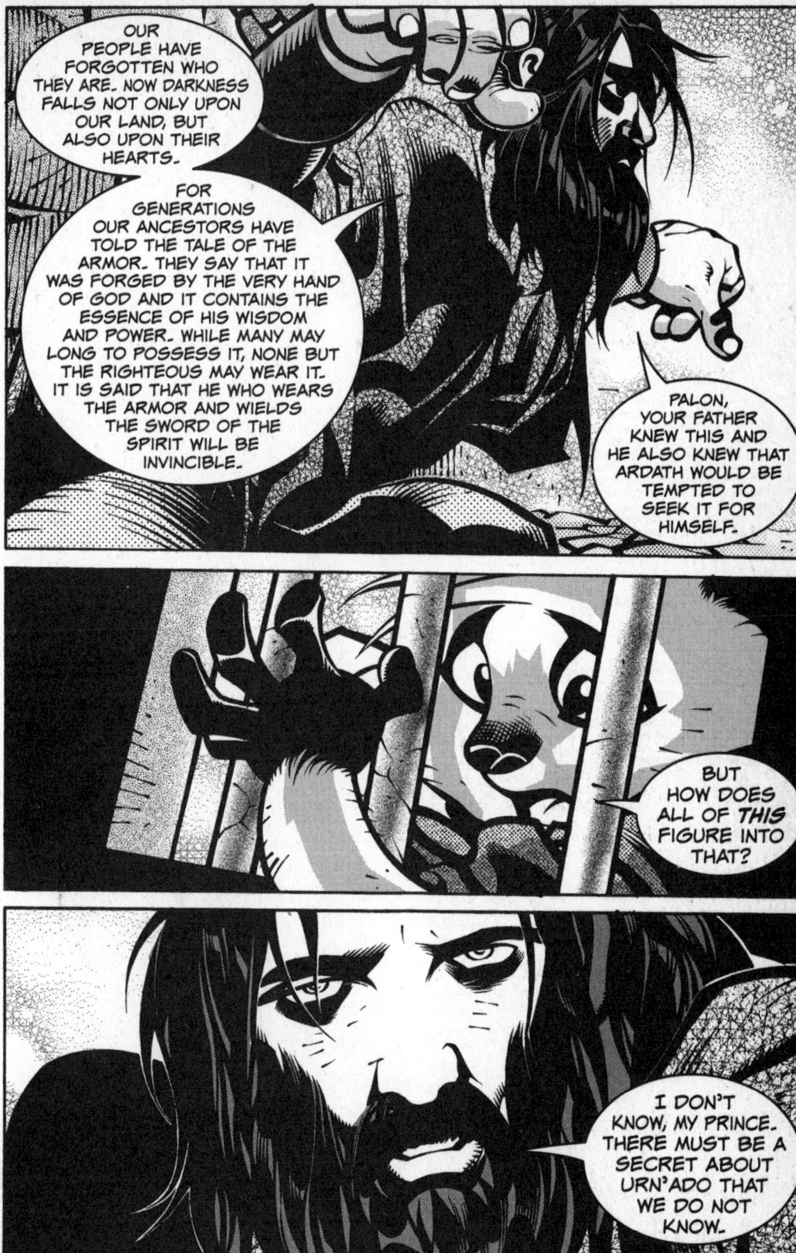
OUR PEOPLE HAVE FORGOTTEN WHO THEY ARE. NOW DARKNESS FALLS NOT ONLY UPON OUR LAND, BUT ALSO UPON THEIR HEARTS.
FOR GENERATIONS OUR ANCESTORS HAVE TOLD THE TALE OF THE ARMOR. THEY SAY THAT IT WAS FORGED BY THE VERY HAND OF GOD AND IT CONTAINS THE ESSENCE OF HIS WISDOM AND POWER. WHILE MANY MAY LONG TO POSSESS IT, NONE BUT THE RIGHTEOUS MAY WEAR IT. IT IS SAID THAT HE WHO WEARS THE ARMOR AND WIELDS THE SWORD OF THE SPIRIT WILL BE INVINCIBLE.
PALON, YOUR FATHER KNEW THIS AND HE ALSO KNEW THAT ARDATH WOULD BE TEMPTED TO SEEK IT FOR HIMSELF.
BUT HOW DOES ALL OF *THIS* FIGURE INTO THAT?
I DON'T KNOW, MY PRINCE. THERE MUST BE A SECRET ABOUT URN'ADO THAT WE DO NOT KNOW.

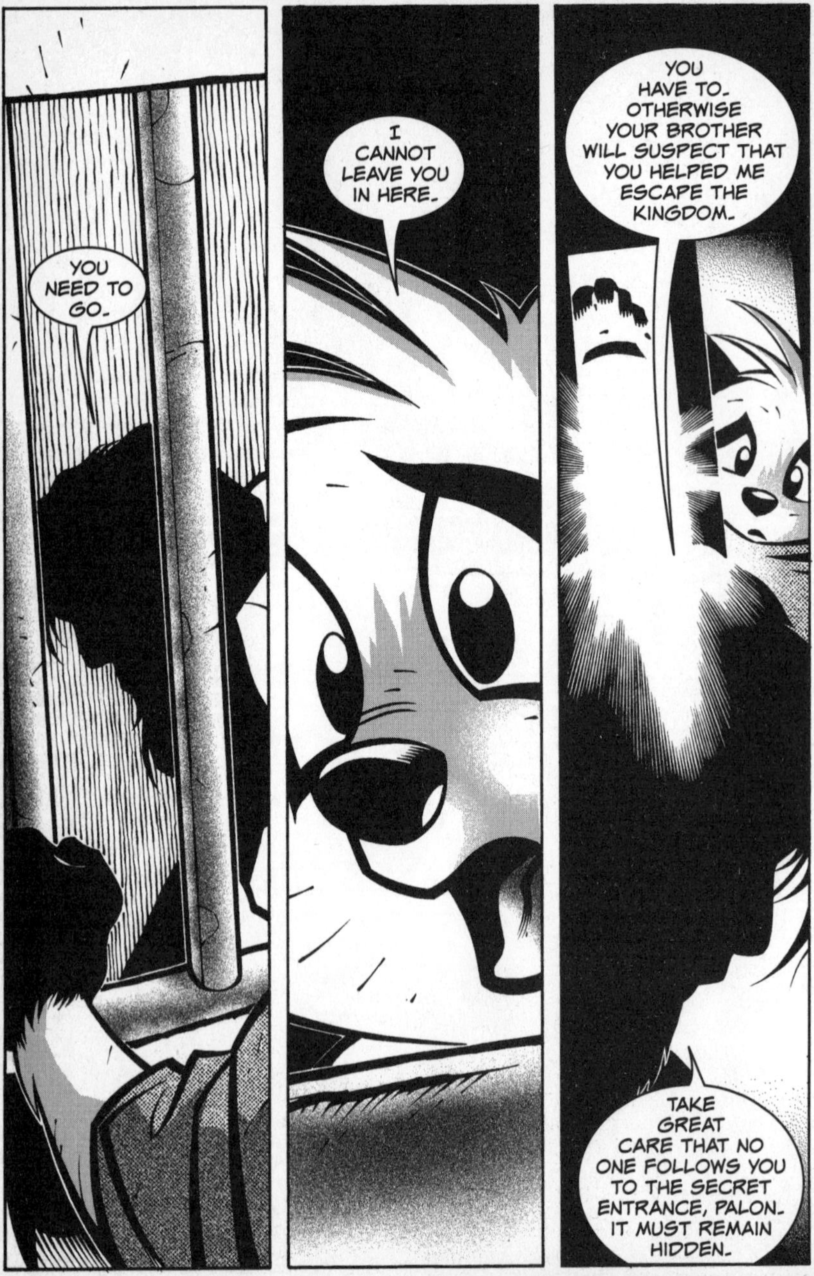
YOU NEED TO GO.
I CANNOT LEAVE YOU IN HERE.
YOU HAVE TO. OTHERWISE YOUR BROTHER WILL SUSPECT THAT YOU HELPED ME ESCAPE THE KINGDOM.
TAKE GREAT CARE THAT NO ONE FOLLOWS YOU TO THE SECRET ENTRANCE, PALON. IT MUST REMAIN HIDDEN.

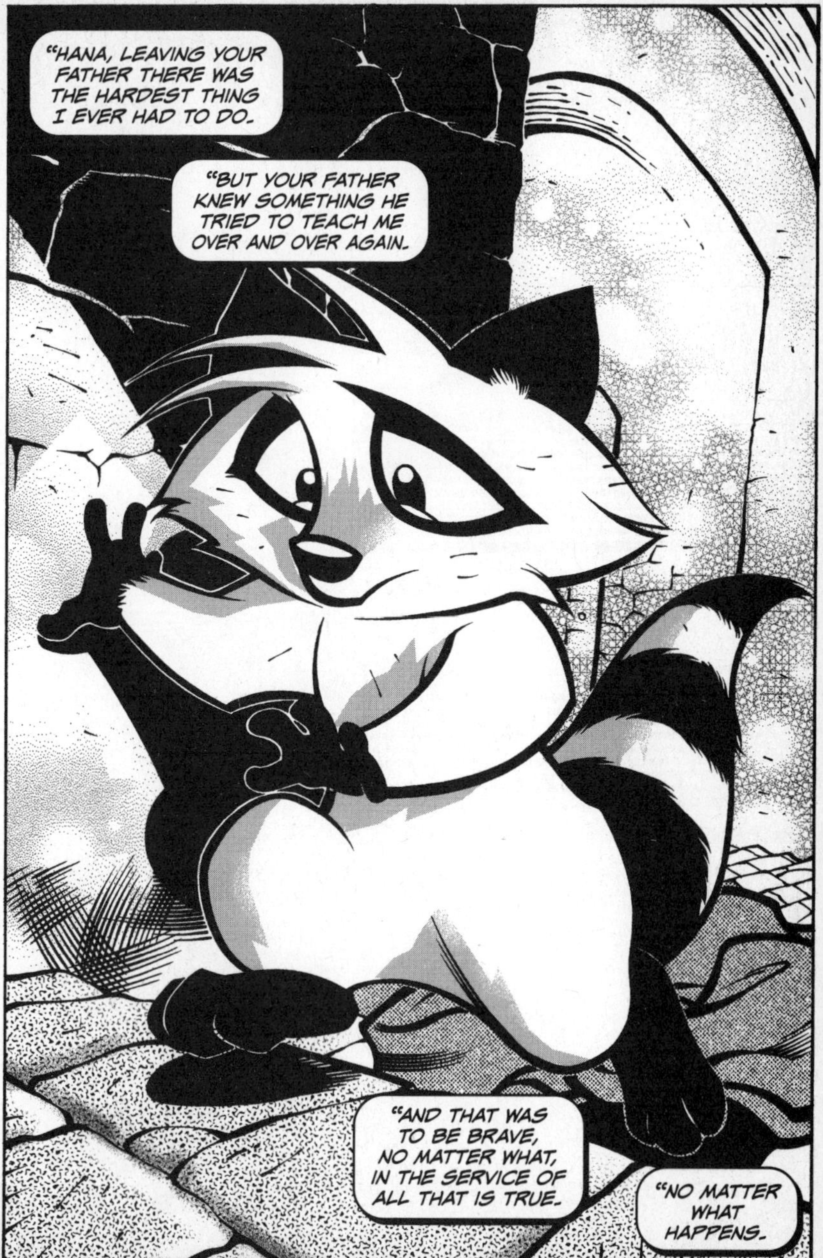
"HANA, LEAVING YOUR FATHER THERE WAS THE HARDEST THING I EVER HAD TO DO.
"BUT YOUR FATHER KNEW SOMETHING HE TRIED TO TEACH ME OVER AND OVER AGAIN.
"AND THAT WAS TO BE BRAVE, NO MATTER WHAT, IN THE SERVICE OF ALL THAT IS TRUE.
"NO MATTER WHAT HAPPENS.

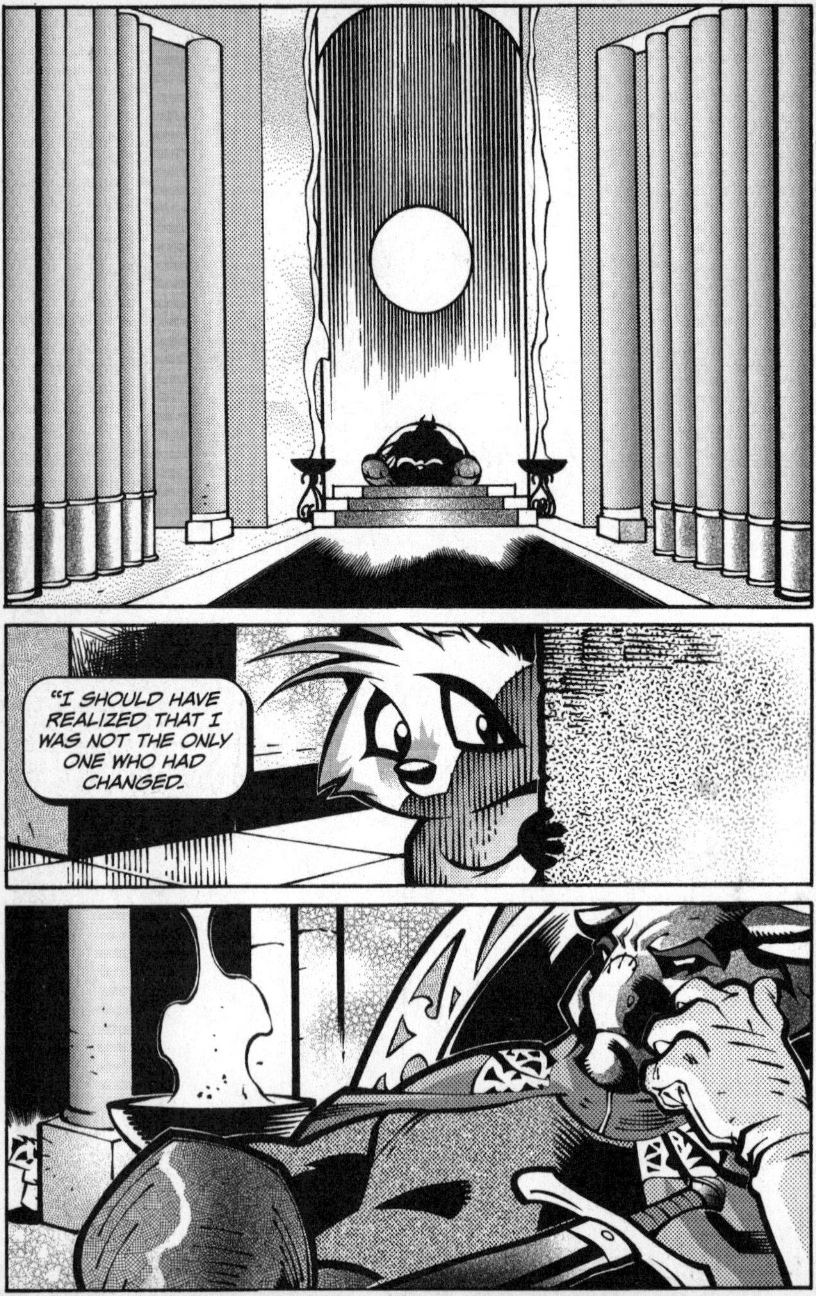
"I SHOULD HAVE REALIZED THAT I WAS NOT THE ONLY ONE WHO HAD CHANGED.

"MY BROTHER LOOKED TERRIBLE.

"IT WAS HARD, HANA, TO EVEN REMEMBER HIM AS HE WAS, WHEN WE BOTH LOVED FATHER, AND WHEN ARDATH WOULD LISTEN TO CLAYTON'S WISDOM.

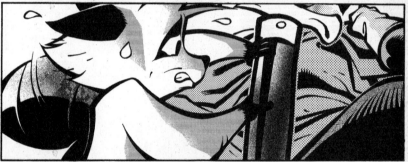

SNORE

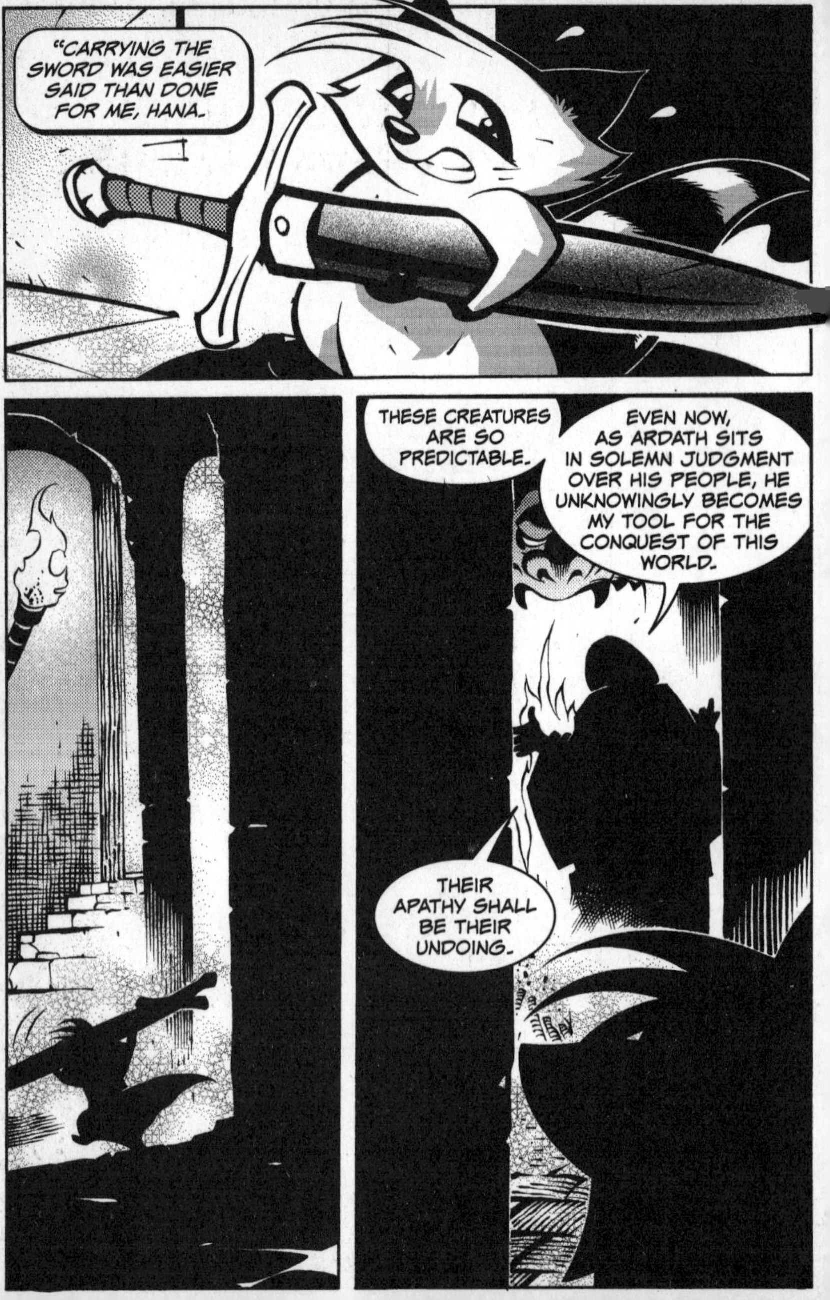
"CARRYING THE SWORD WAS EASIER SAID THAN DONE FOR ME, HANA.
THESE CREATURES ARE SO PREDICTABLE.
EVEN NOW, AS ARDATH SITS IN SOLEMN JUDGMENT OVER HIS PEOPLE, HE UNKNOWINGLY BECOMES MY TOOL FOR THE CONQUEST OF THIS WORLD.
THEIR APATHY SHALL BE THEIR UNDOING.

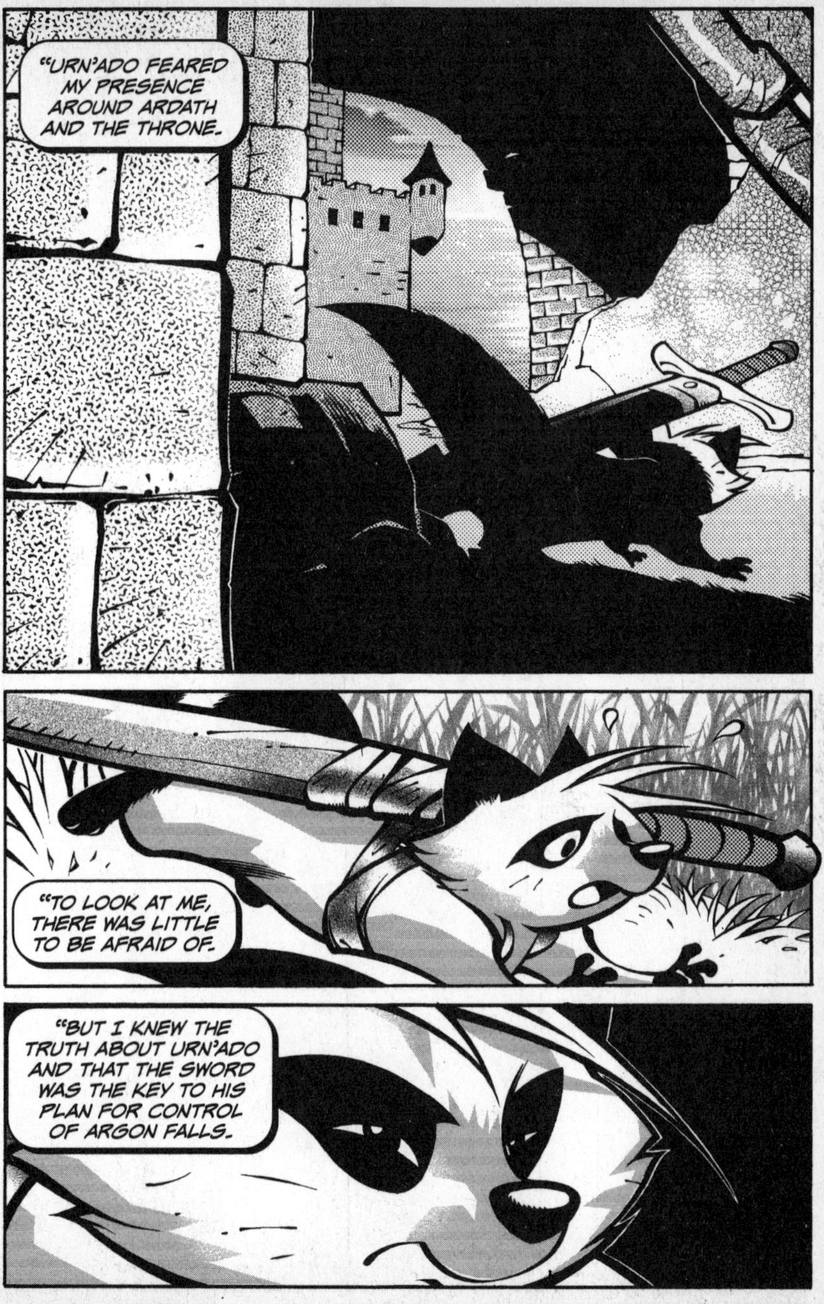
"URN'ADO FEARED MY PRESENCE AROUND ARDATH AND THE THRONE.
"TO LOOK AT ME, THERE WAS LITTLE TO BE AFRAID OF.
"BUT I KNEW THE TRUTH ABOUT URN'ADO AND THAT THE SWORD WAS THE KEY TO HIS PLAN FOR CONTROL OF ARGON FALLS.

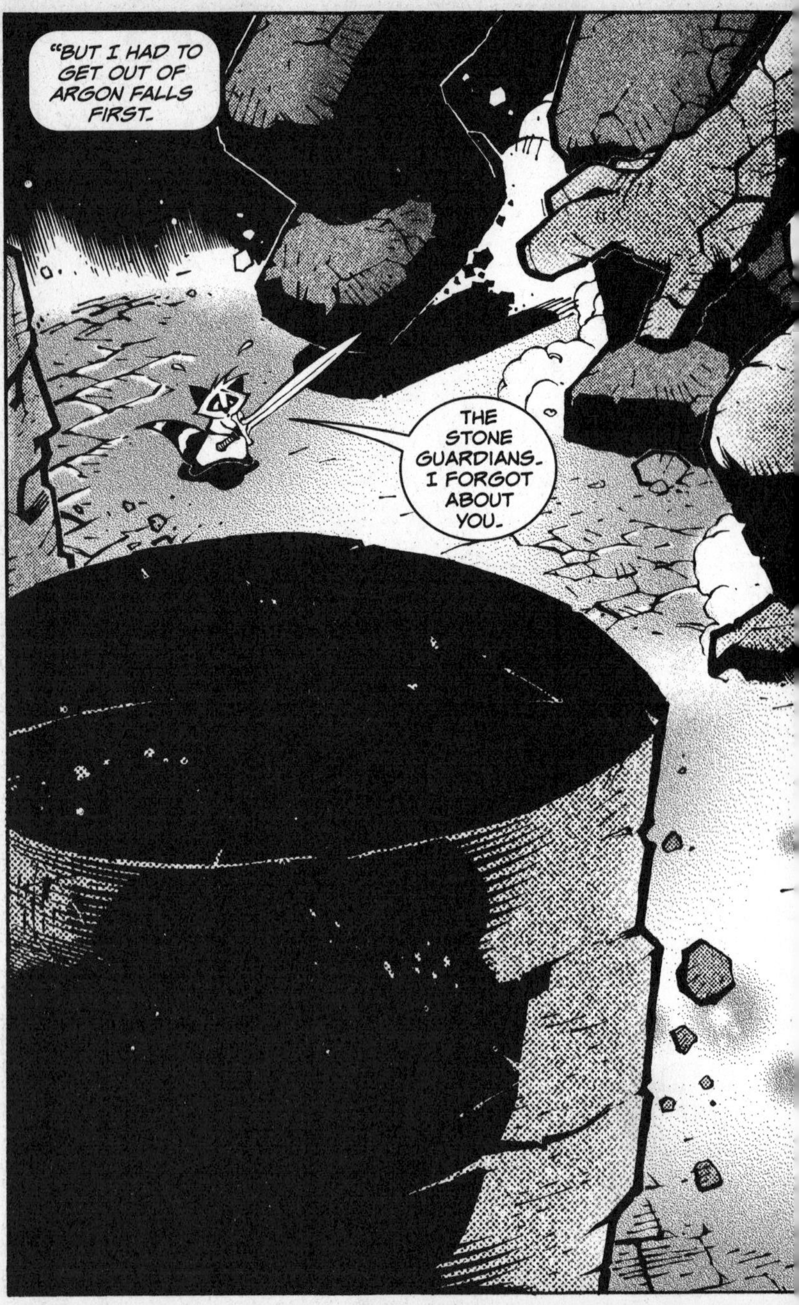
"BUT I HAD TO GET OUT OF ARGON FALLS FIRST...
THE STONE GUARDIANS... I FORGOT ABOUT YOU...

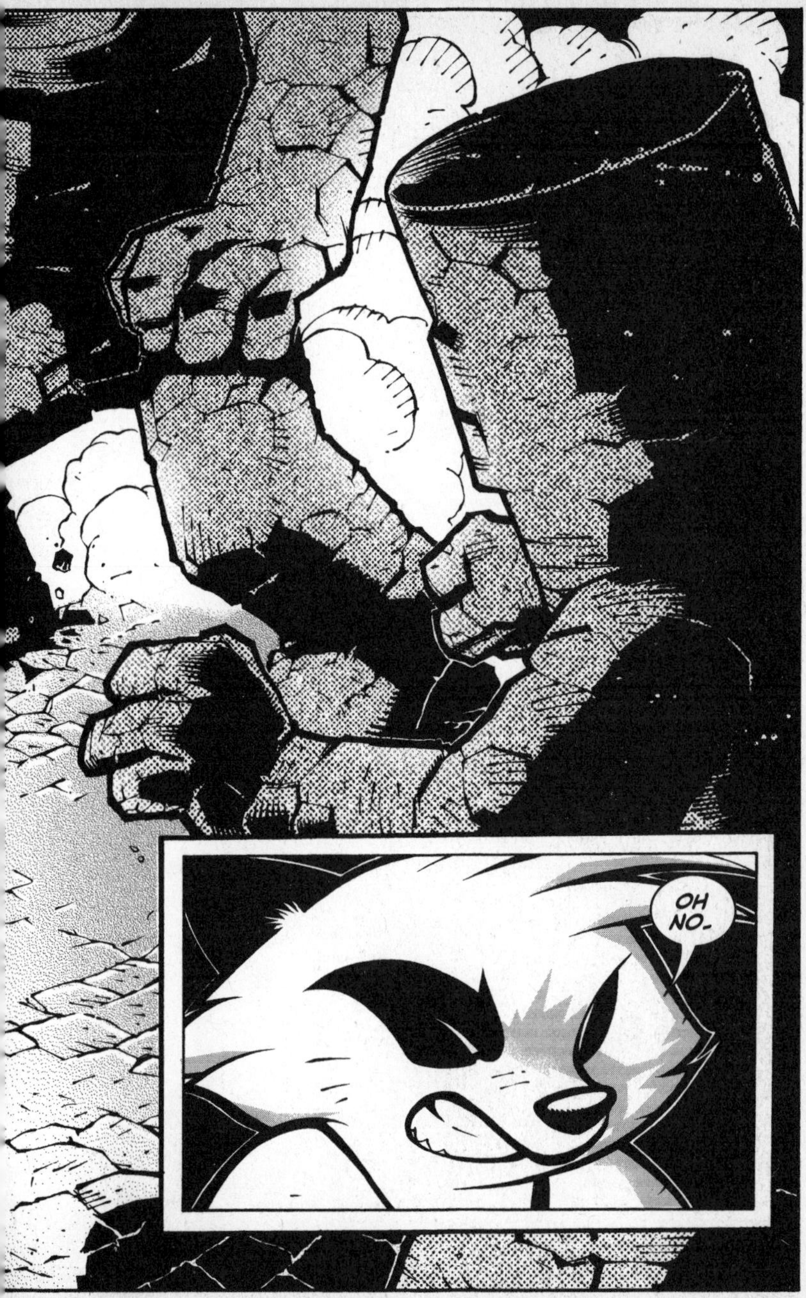
OH NO-

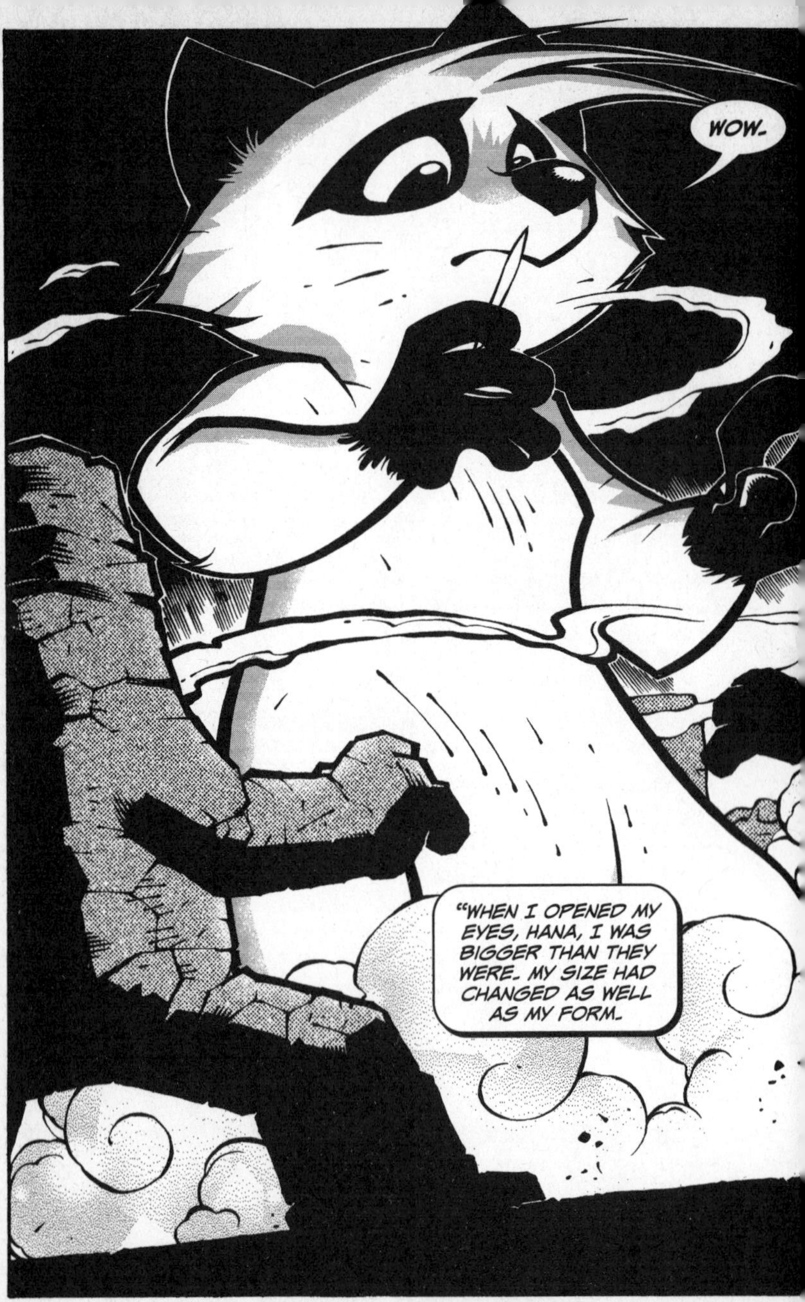
WOW.
"WHEN I OPENED MY EYES, HANA, I WAS BIGGER THAN THEY WERE. MY SIZE HAD CHANGED AS WELL AS MY FORM.

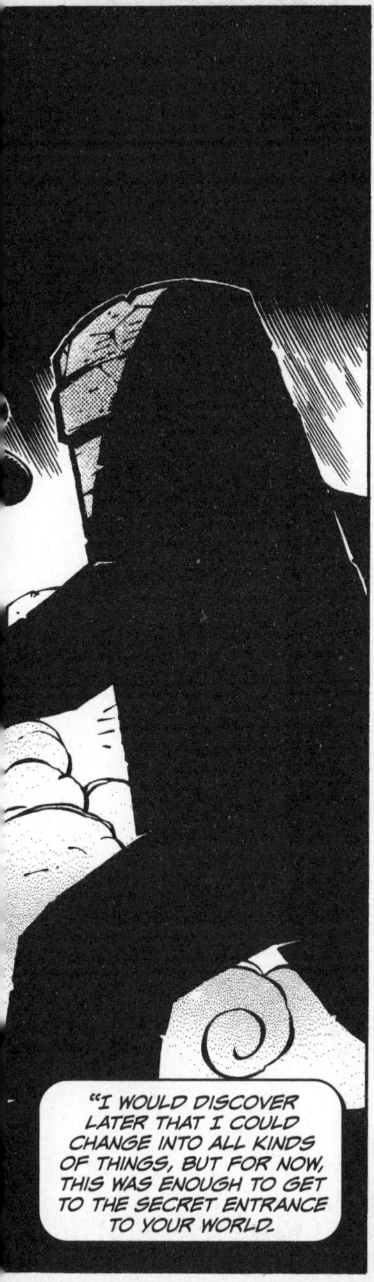
"I WOULD DISCOVER LATER THAT I COULD CHANGE INTO ALL KINDS OF THINGS, BUT FOR NOW, THIS WAS ENOUGH TO GET TO THE SECRET ENTRANCE TO YOUR WORLD.
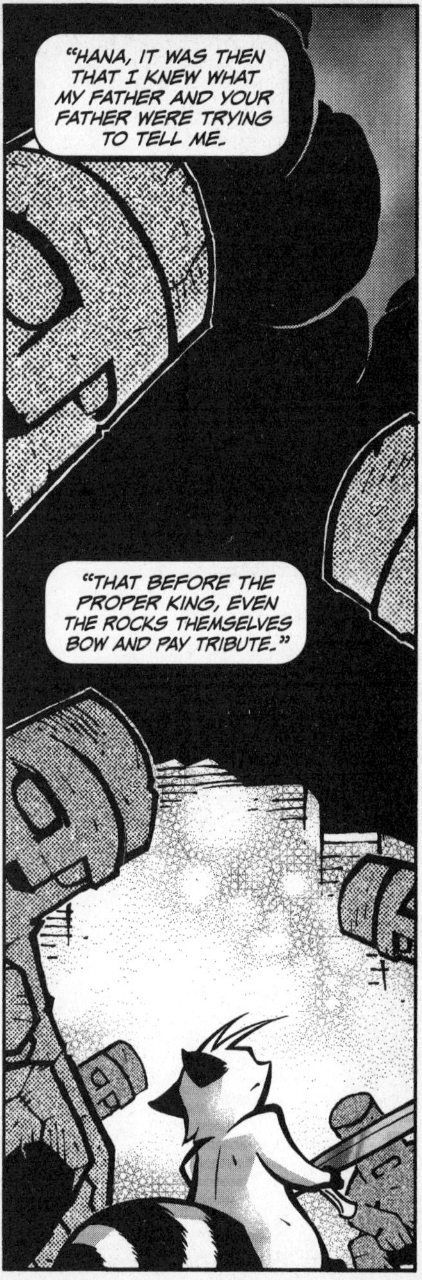
"HANA, IT WAS THEN THAT I KNEW WHAT MY FATHER AND YOUR FATHER WERE TRYING TO TELL ME.
"THAT BEFORE THE PROPER KING, EVEN THE ROCKS THEMSELVES BOW AND PAY TRIBUTE."

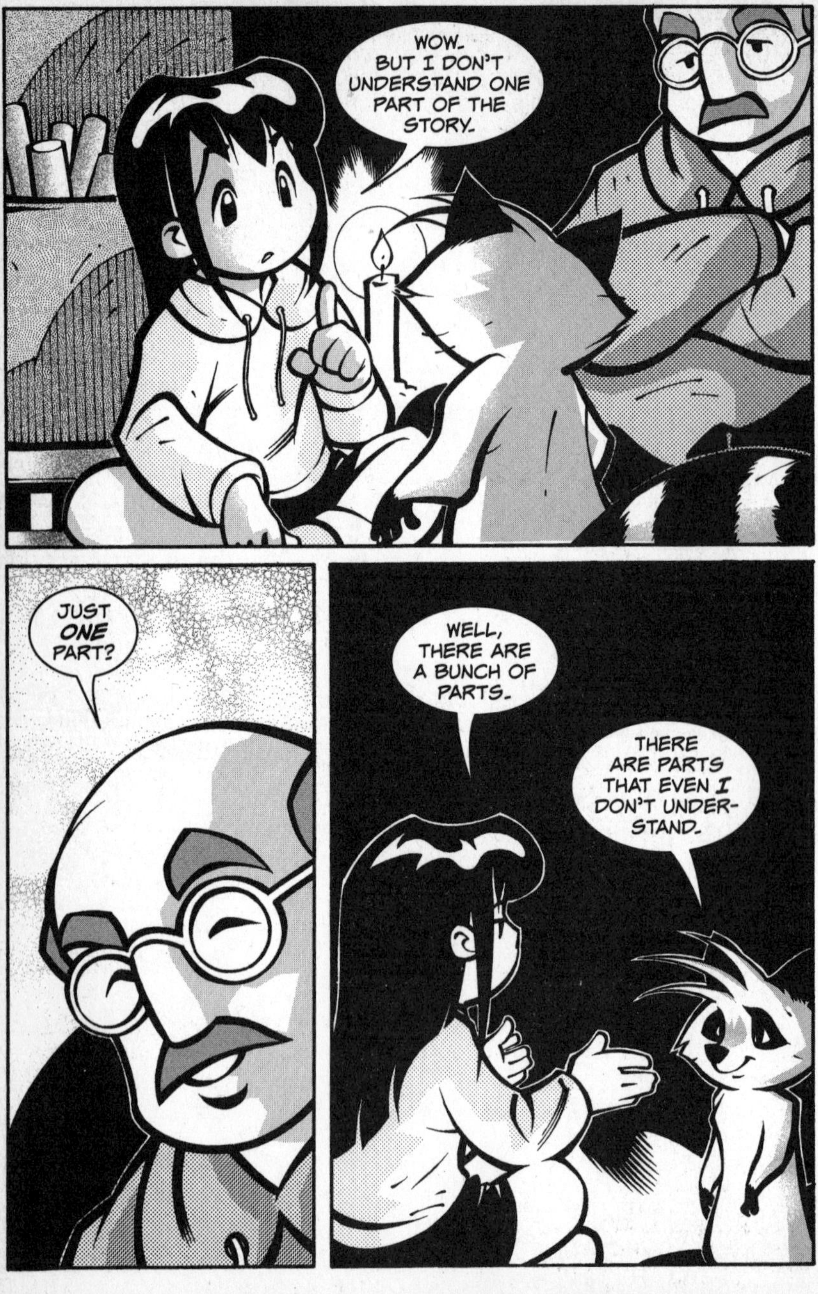
WOW. BUT I DON'T UNDERSTAND ONE PART OF THE STORY.
JUST *ONE* PART?
WELL, THERE ARE A BUNCH OF PARTS.
THERE ARE PARTS THAT EVEN *I* DON'T UNDER-STAND.

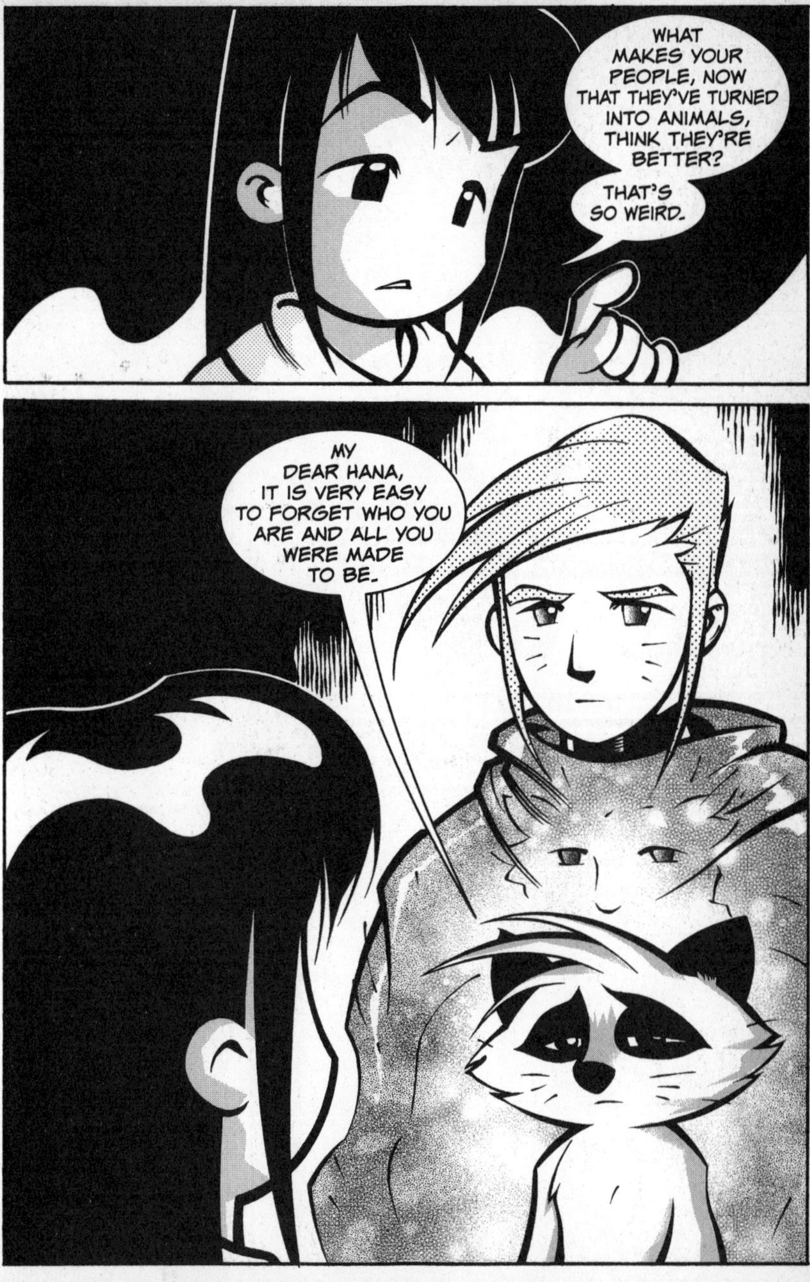
WHAT MAKES YOUR PEOPLE, NOW THAT THEY'VE TURNED INTO ANIMALS, THINK THEY'RE BETTER?
THAT'S SO WEIRD.
MY DEAR HANA, IT IS VERY EASY TO FORGET WHO YOU ARE AND ALL YOU WERE MADE TO BE.

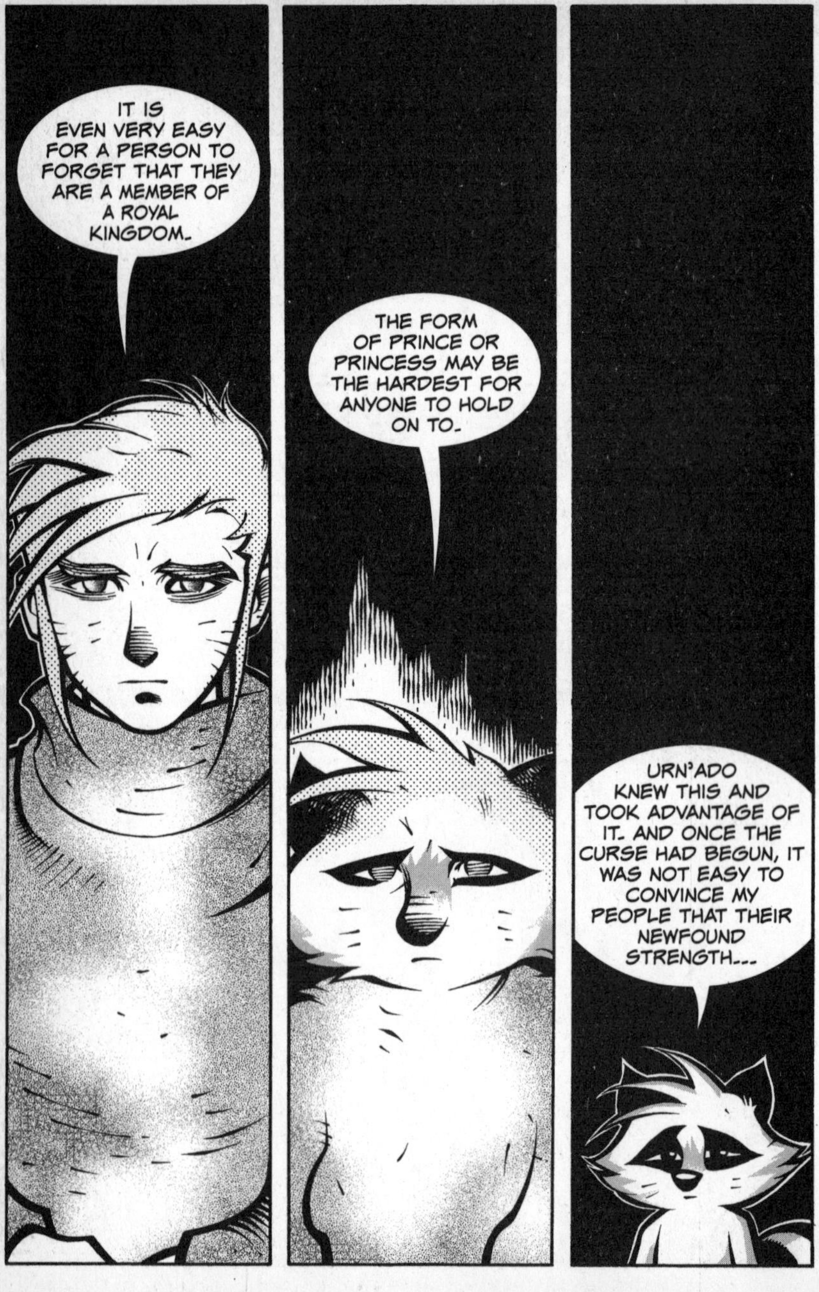
IT IS EVEN VERY EASY FOR A PERSON TO FORGET THAT THEY ARE A MEMBER OF A ROYAL KINGDOM.
THE FORM OF PRINCE OR PRINCESS MAY BE THE HARDEST FOR ANYONE TO HOLD ON TO.
URN'ADO KNEW THIS AND TOOK ADVANTAGE OF IT. AND ONCE THE CURSE HAD BEGUN, IT WAS NOT EASY TO CONVINCE MY PEOPLE THAT THEIR NEWFOUND STRENGTH...

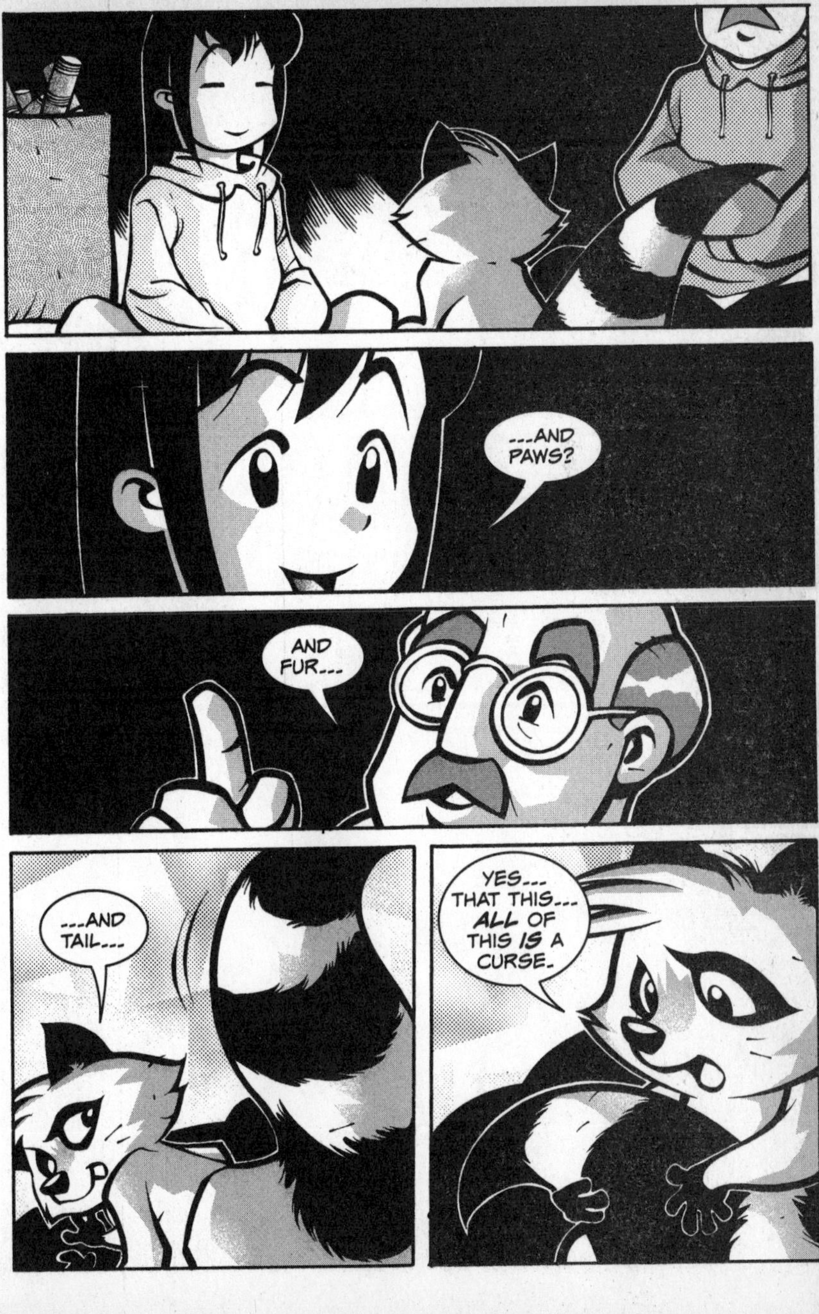
...AND
PAWS?
AND
FUR...
...AND
TAIL...
YES...
THAT THIS...
ALL OF
THIS IS A
CURSE.

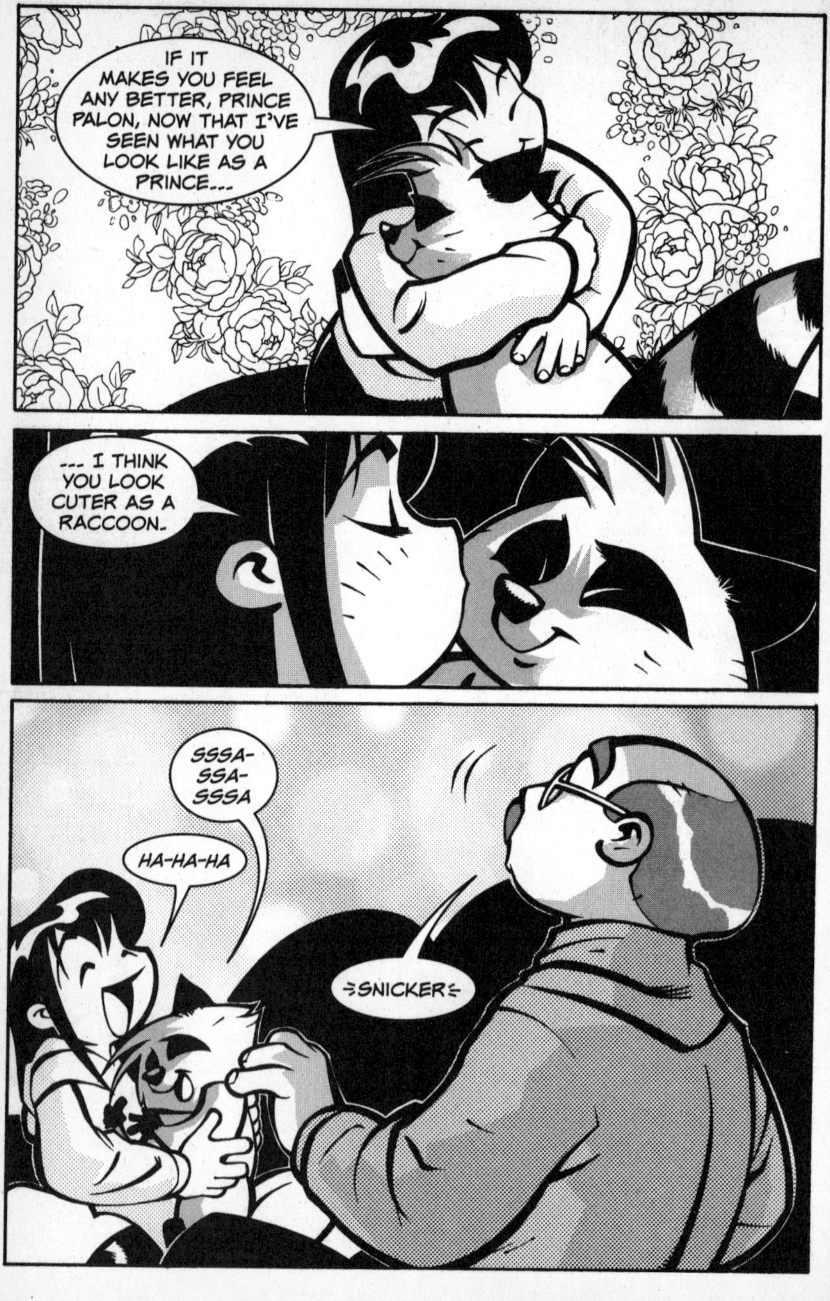
IF IT MAKES YOU FEEL ANY BETTER, PRINCE PALON, NOW THAT I'VE SEEN WHAT YOU LOOK LIKE AS A PRINCE...
... I THINK YOU LOOK CUTER AS A RACCOON.
SSSA-SSA-SSSA
HA-HA-HA
SNICKER

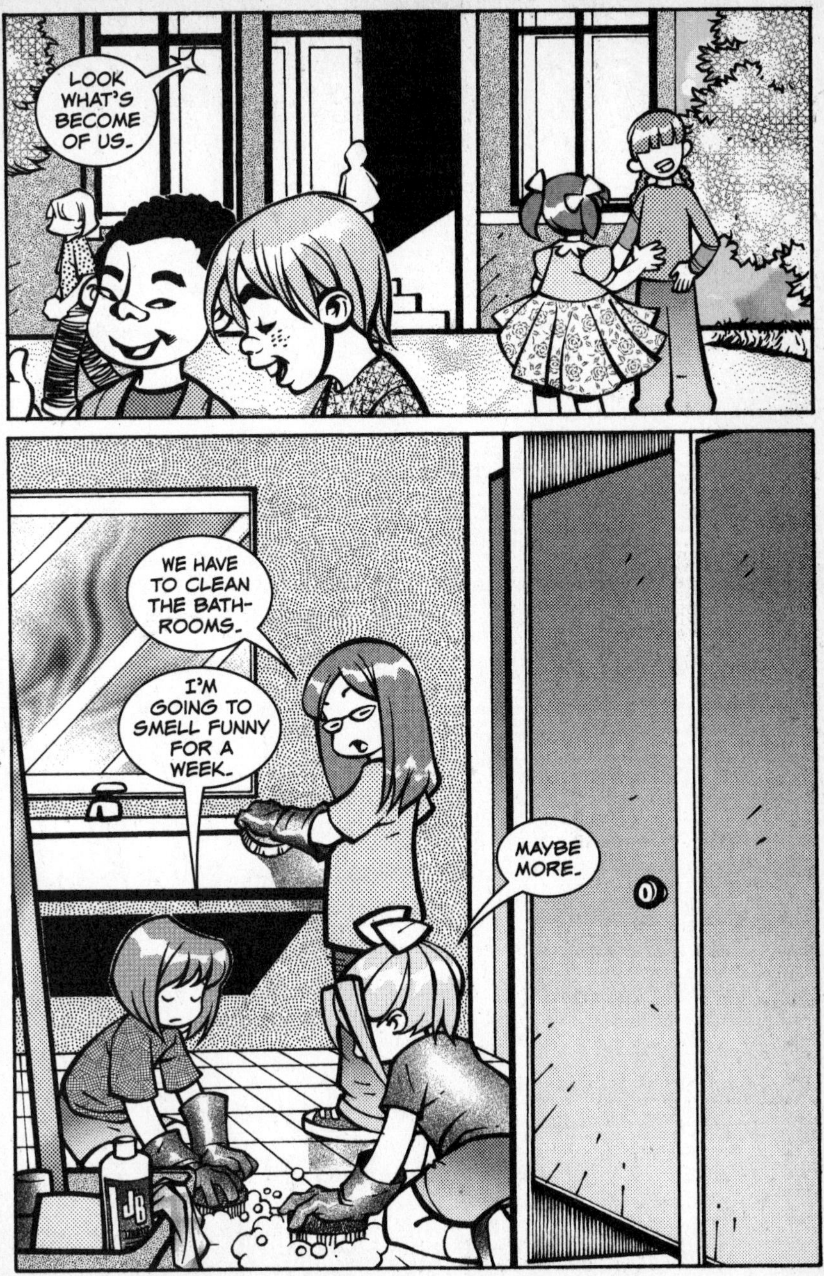
LOOK WHAT'S BECOME OF US.
WE HAVE TO CLEAN THE BATH-ROOMS.
I'M GOING TO SMELL FUNNY FOR A WEEK.
MAYBE MORE.
JB

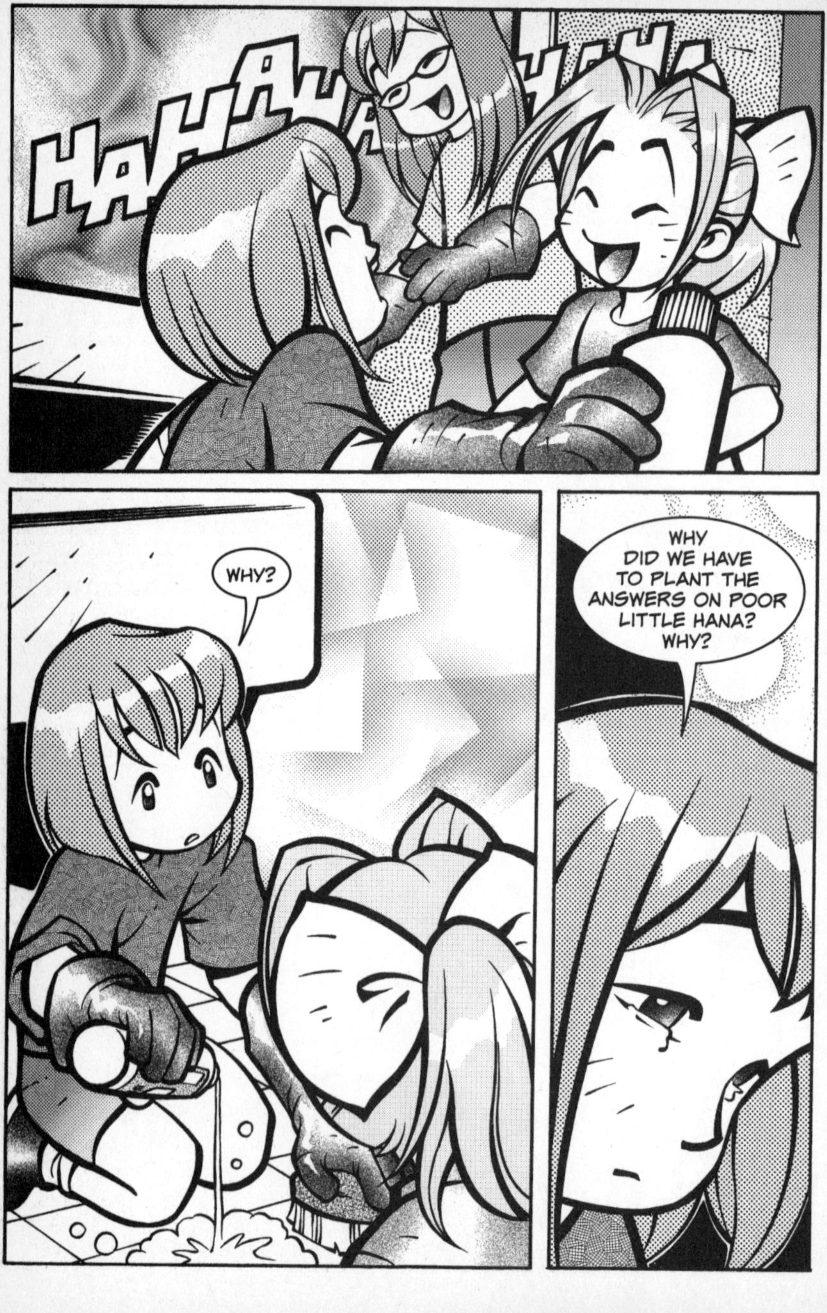
WHY?
WHY DID WE HAVE TO PLANT THE ANSWERS ON POOR LITTLE HANA? WHY?

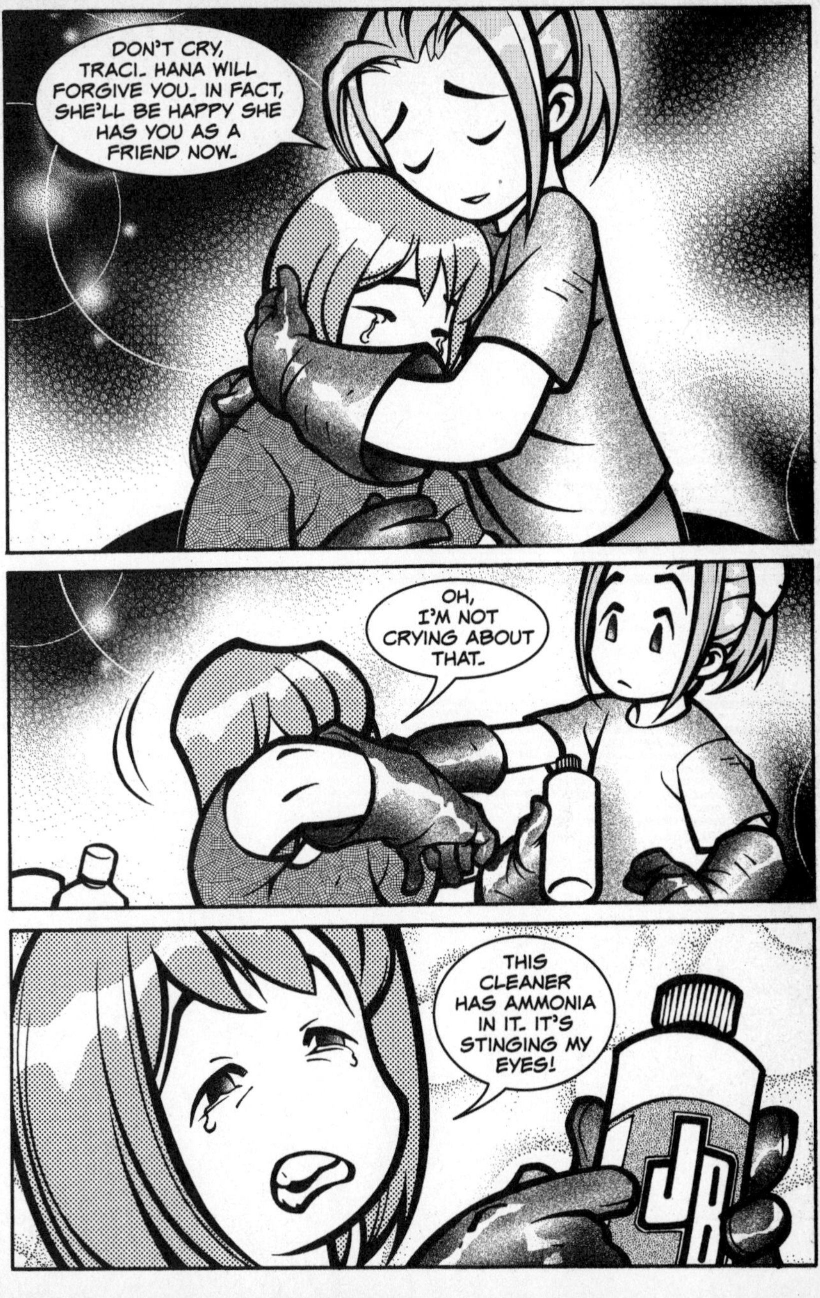
DON'T CRY, TRACI. HANA WILL FORGIVE YOU. IN FACT, SHE'LL BE HAPPY SHE HAS YOU AS A FRIEND NOW.
OH, I'M NOT CRYING ABOUT THAT.
THIS CLEANER HAS AMMONIA IN IT. IT'S STINGING MY EYES!

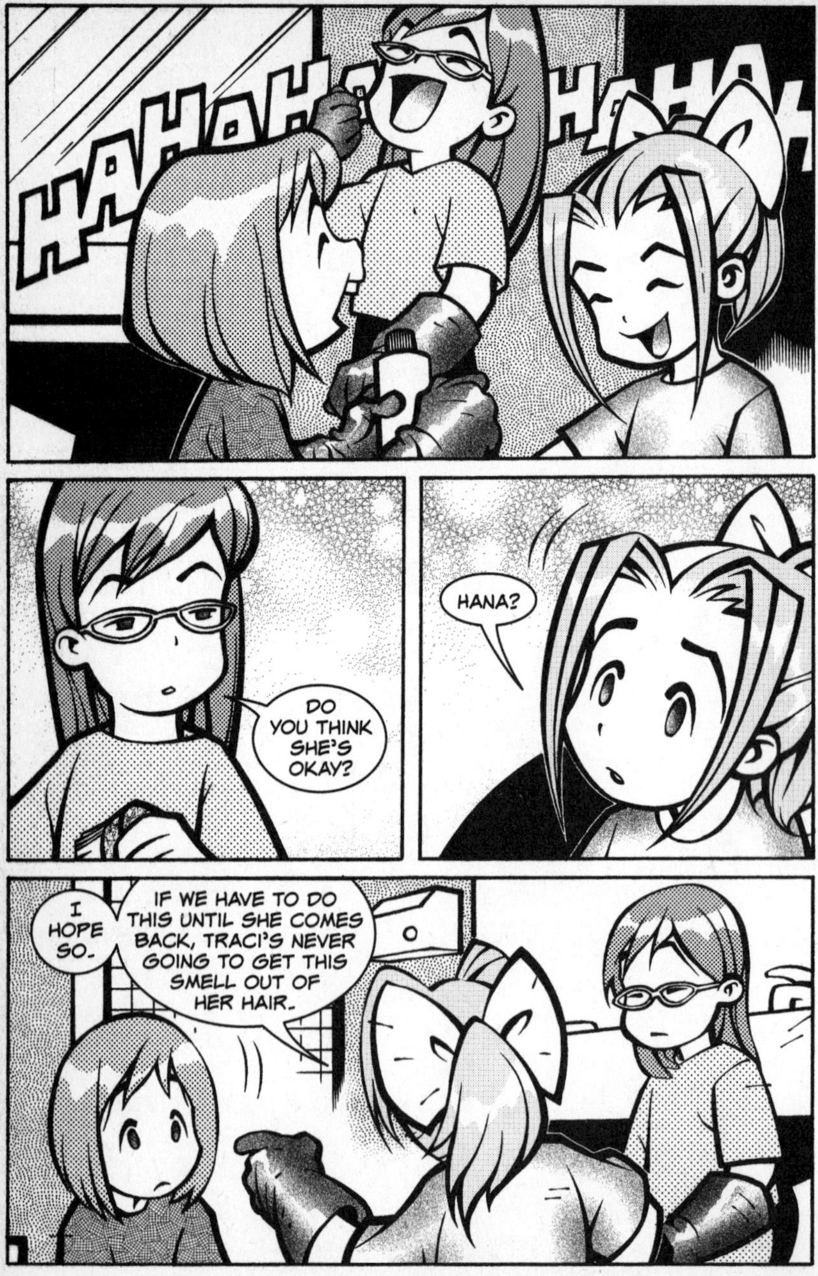
HAHAHAHA
HAHAHA
DO YOU THINK SHE'S OKAY?
HANA?
I HOPE SO.
IF WE HAVE TO DO THIS UNTIL SHE COMES BACK, TRACI'S NEVER GOING TO GET THIS SMELL OUT OF HER HAIR.

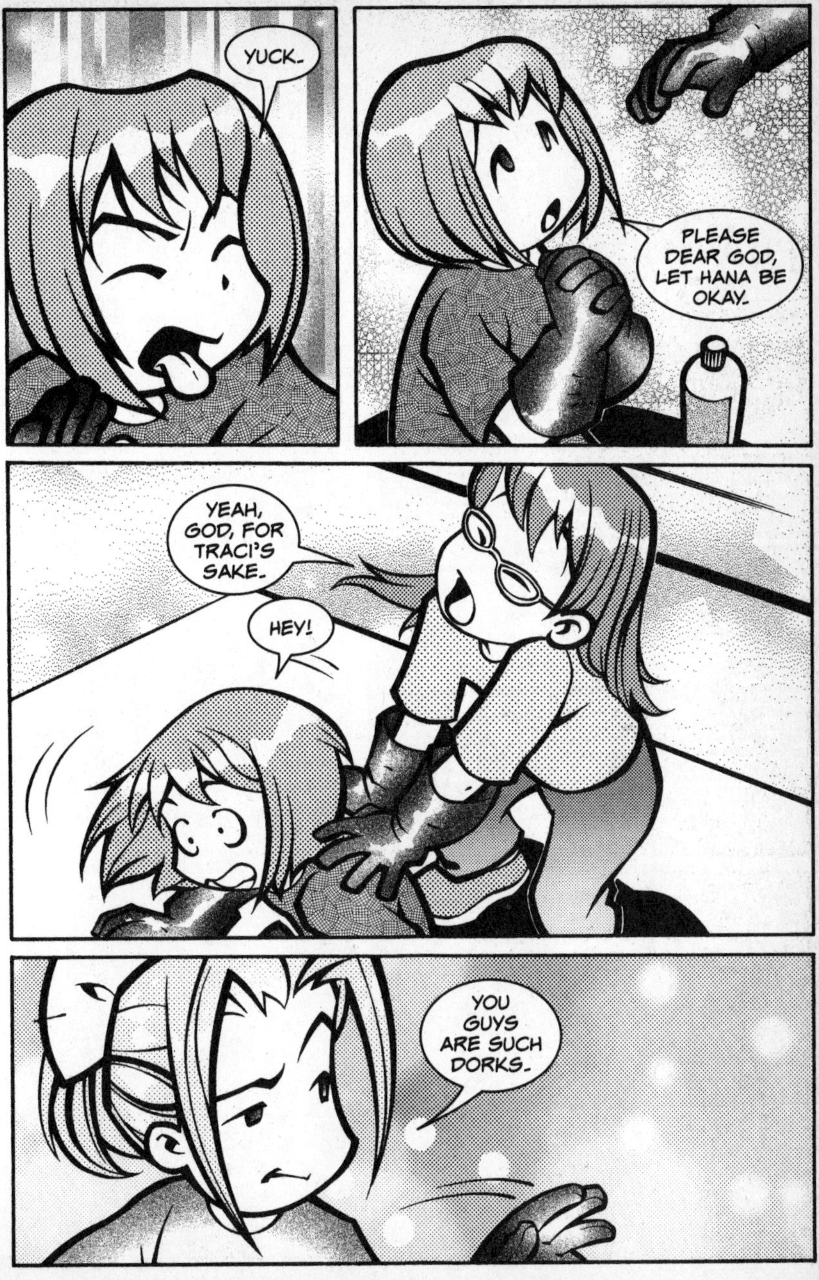
YUCK.
PLEASE DEAR GOD, LET HANA BE OKAY.
YEAH, GOD, FOR TRACI'S SAKE.
HEY!
YOU GUYS ARE SUCH DORKS.

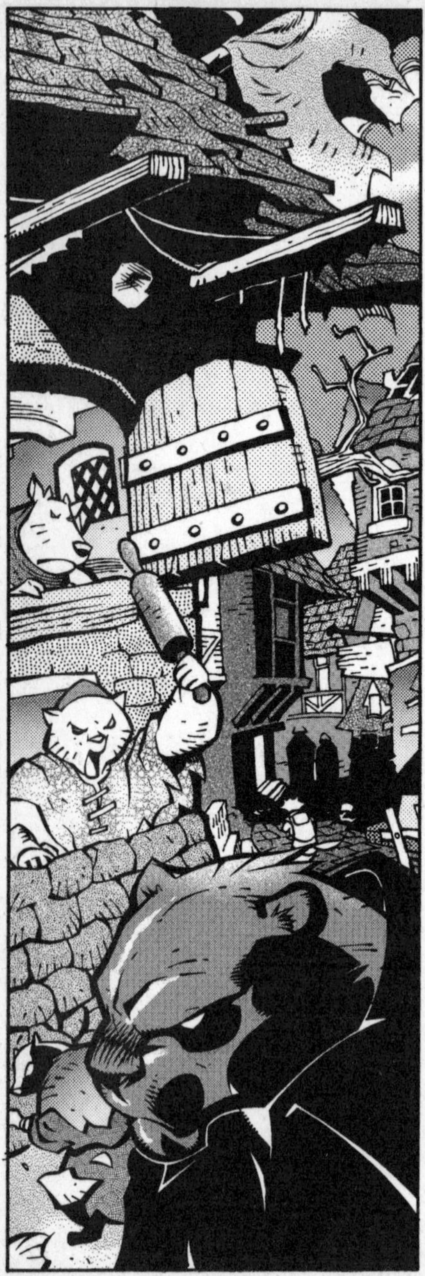

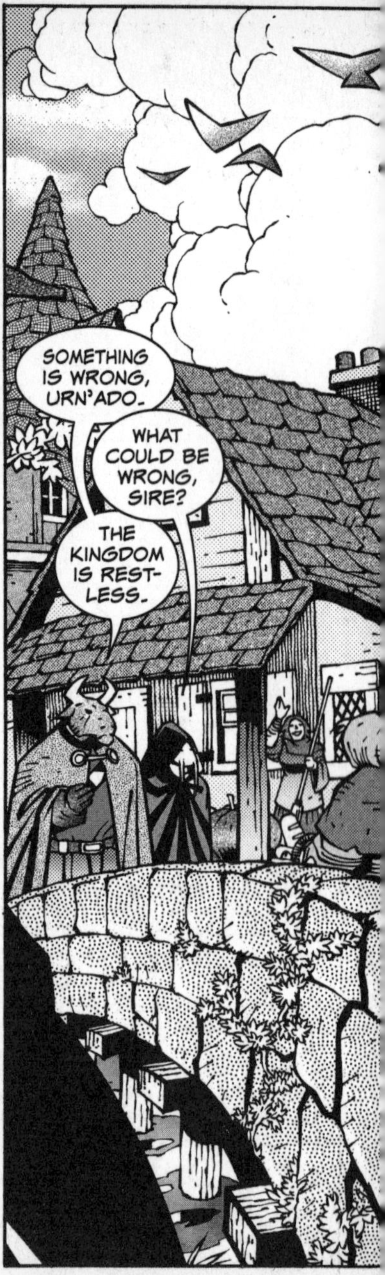

SOMETHING IS WRONG, URN'ADO.
WHAT COULD BE WRONG, SIRE?
THE KINGDOM IS REST-LESS.

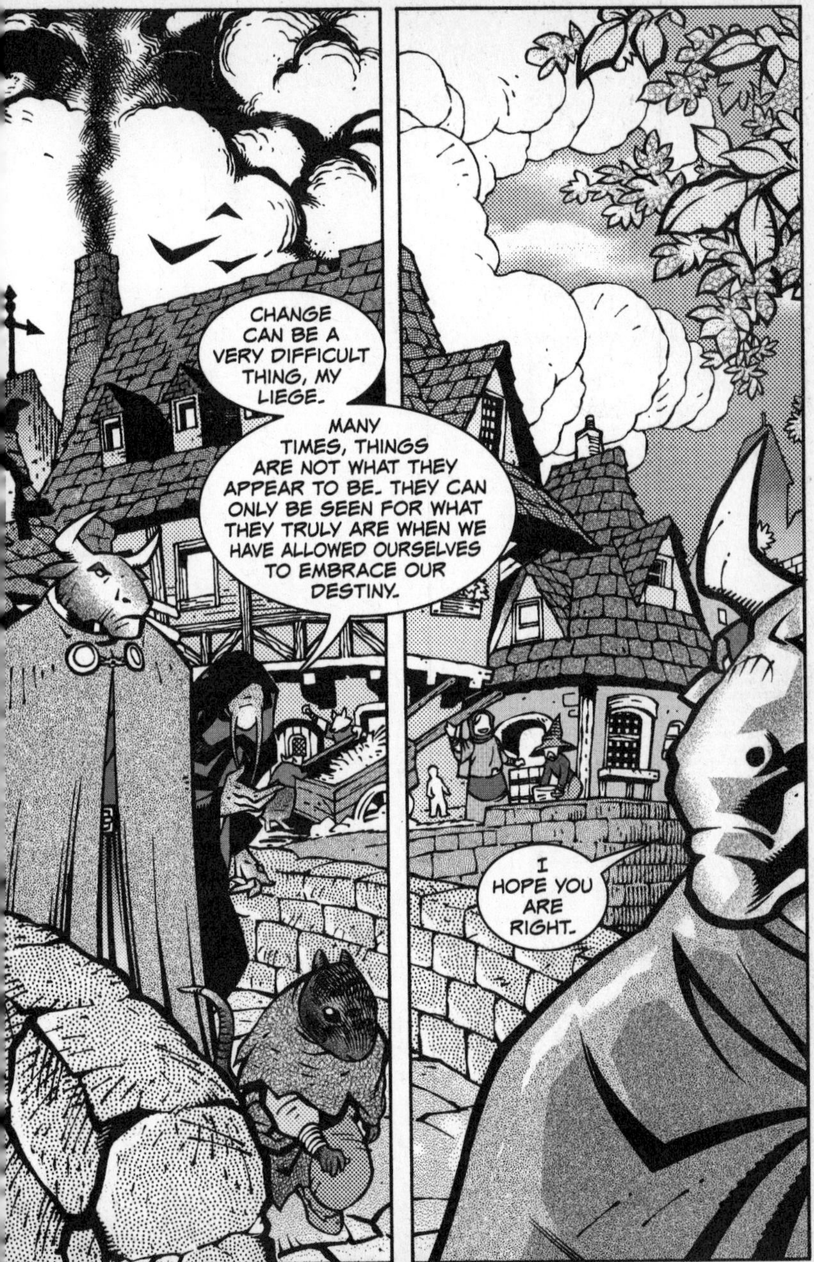
CHANGE CAN BE A VERY DIFFICULT THING, MY LIEGE.
MANY TIMES, THINGS ARE NOT WHAT THEY APPEAR TO BE. THEY CAN ONLY BE SEEN FOR WHAT THEY TRULY ARE WHEN WE HAVE ALLOWED OURSELVES TO EMBRACE OUR DESTINY.
I HOPE YOU ARE RIGHT.

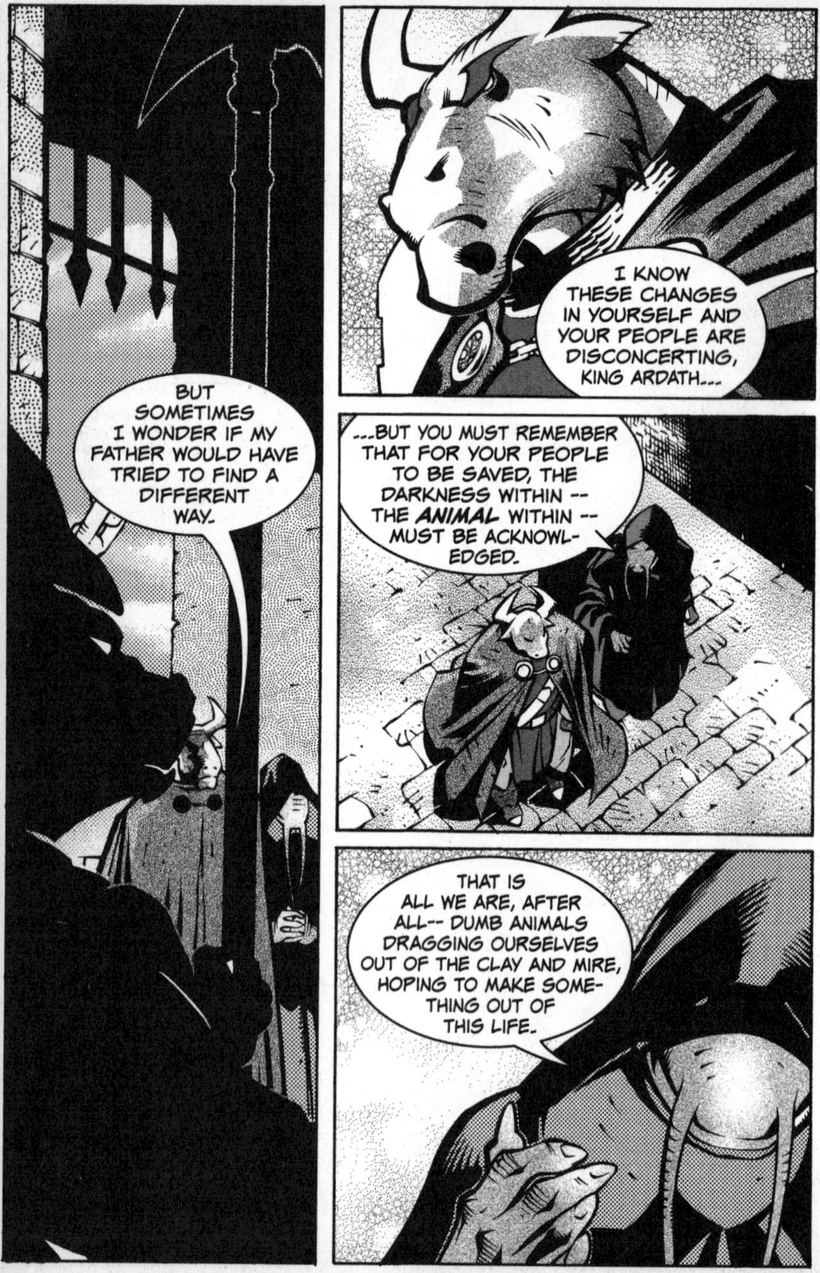
BUT SOMETIMES I WONDER IF MY FATHER WOULD HAVE TRIED TO FIND A DIFFERENT WAY.
I KNOW THESE CHANGES IN YOURSELF AND YOUR PEOPLE ARE DISCONCERTING, KING ARDATH...
...BUT YOU MUST REMEMBER THAT FOR YOUR PEOPLE TO BE SAVED, THE DARKNESS WITHIN -- THE *ANIMAL* WITHIN -- MUST BE ACKNOWLEDGED.
THAT IS ALL WE ARE, AFTER ALL-- DUMB ANIMALS DRAGGING OURSELVES OUT OF THE CLAY AND MIRE, HOPING TO MAKE SOMETHING OUT OF THIS LIFE.

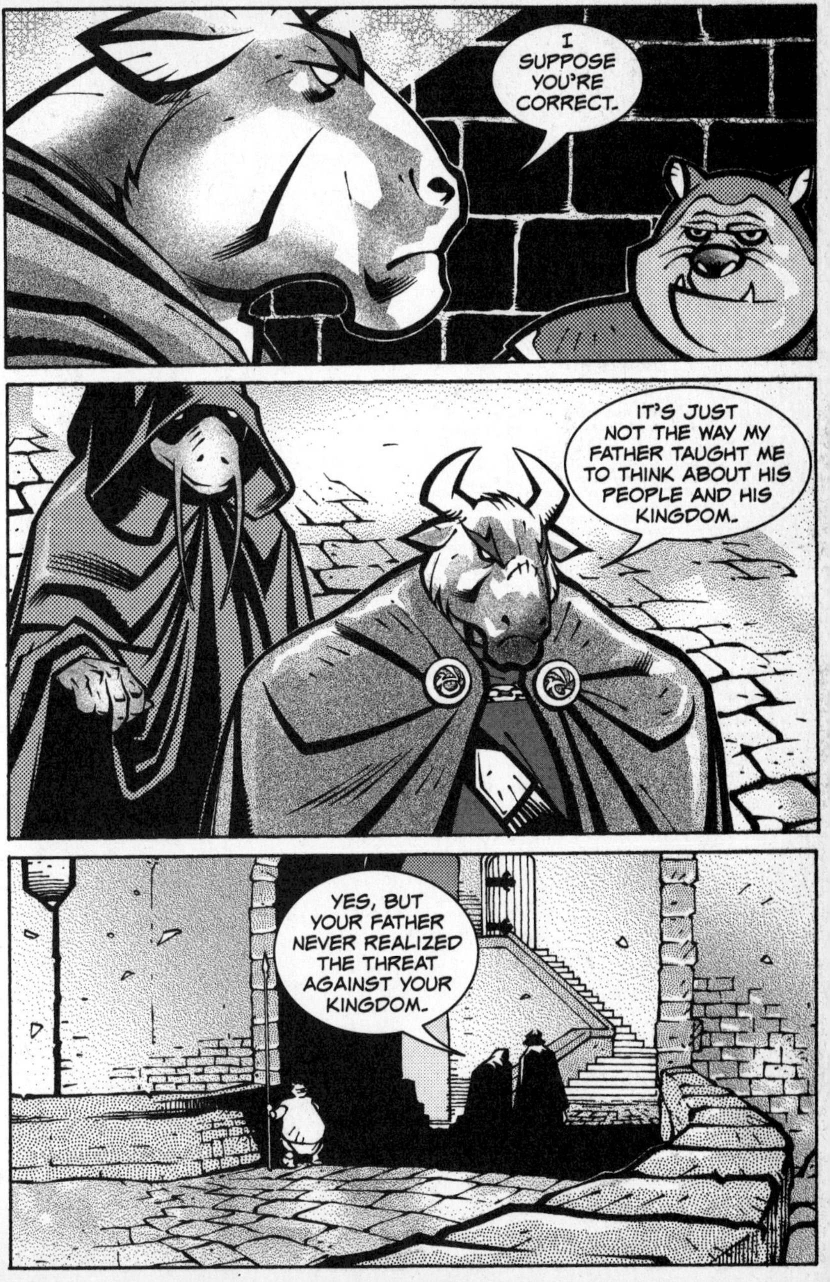
I SUPPOSE YOU'RE CORRECT.
IT'S JUST NOT THE WAY MY FATHER TAUGHT ME TO THINK ABOUT HIS PEOPLE AND HIS KINGDOM.
YES, BUT YOUR FATHER NEVER REALIZED THE THREAT AGAINST YOUR KINGDOM.

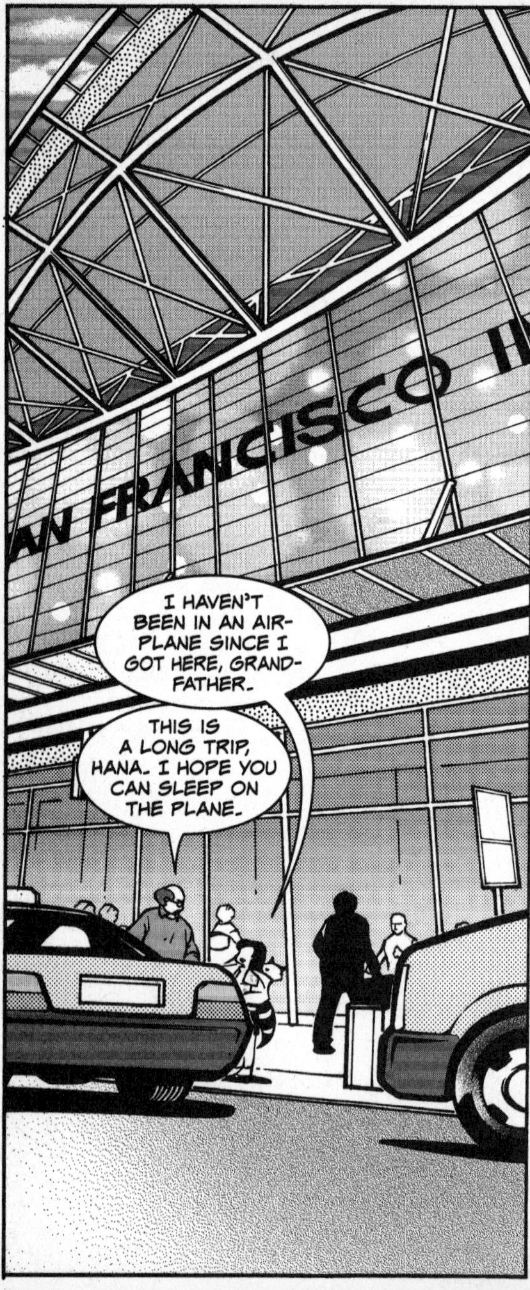

AN FRANCISCO I
I HAVEN'T BEEN IN AN AIR-PLANE SINCE I GOT HERE, GRAND-FATHER.
THIS IS A LONG TRIP, HANA. I HOPE YOU CAN SLEEP ON THE PLANE.

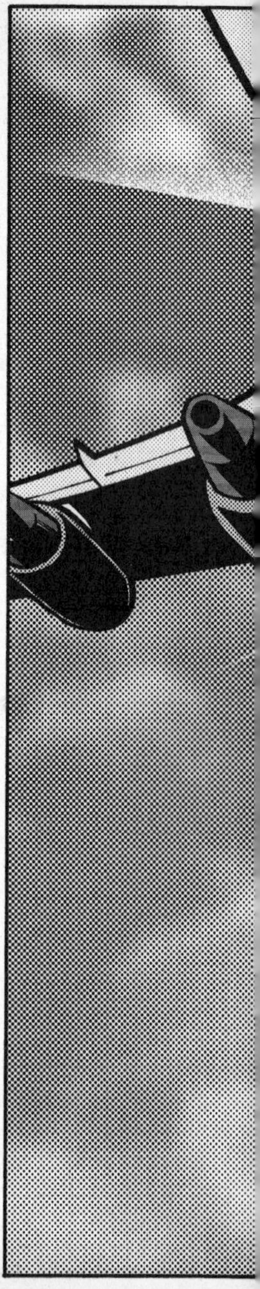

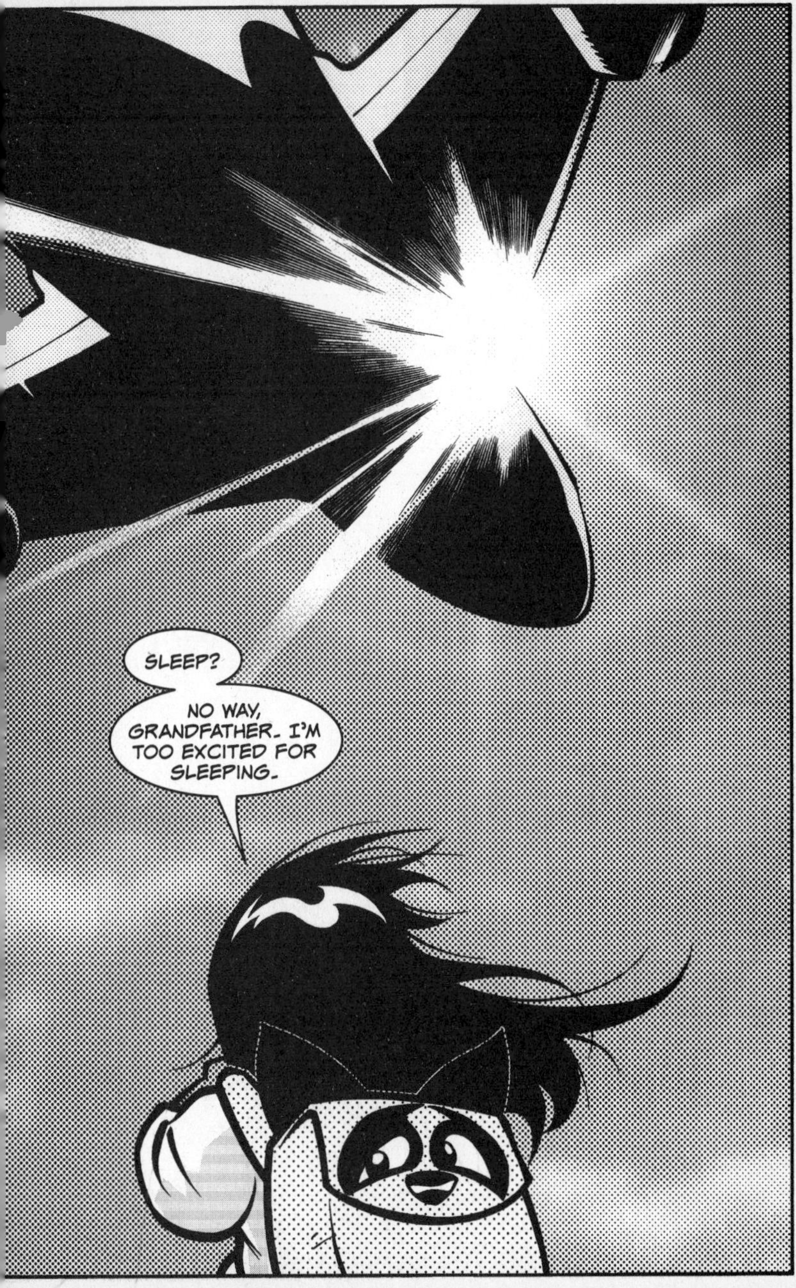
SLEEP?
NO WAY, GRANDFATHER. I'M TOO EXCITED FOR SLEEPING.

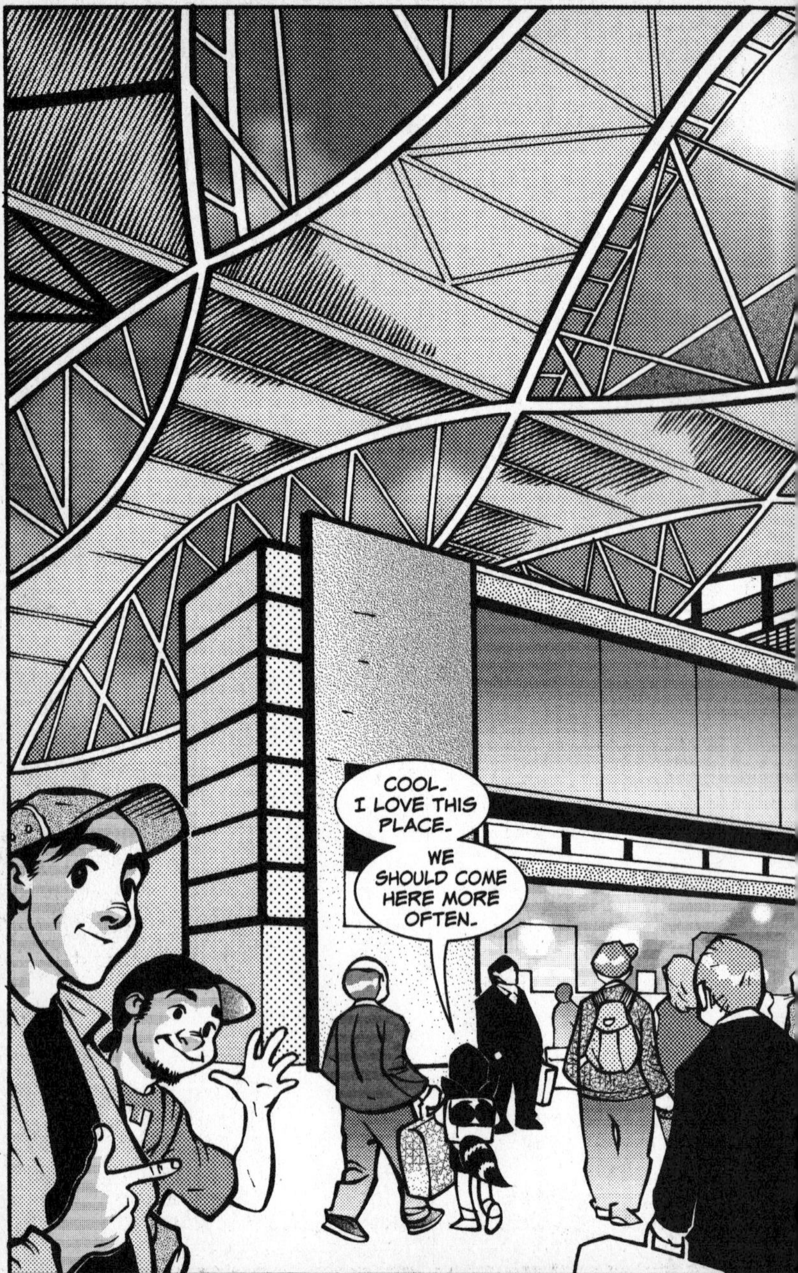
COOL. I LOVE THIS PLACE.
WE SHOULD COME HERE MORE OFTEN.

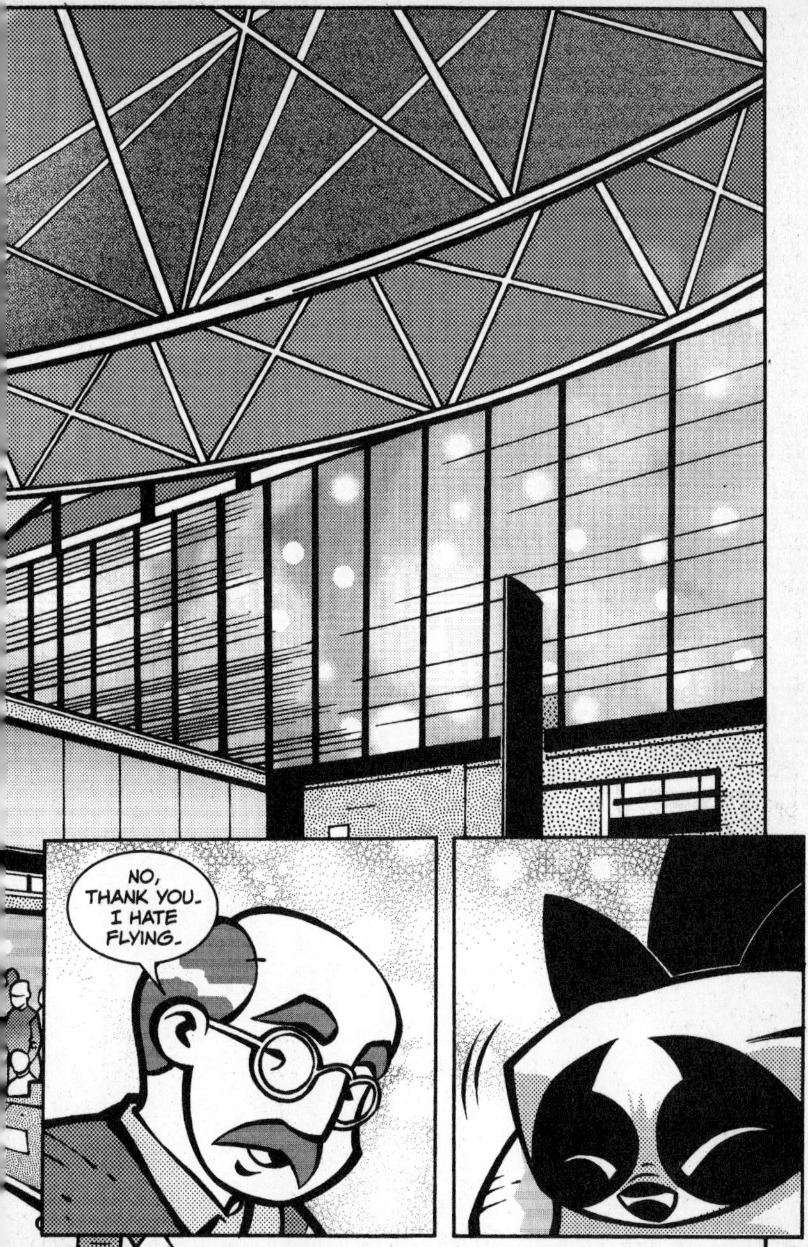
NO, THANK YOU. I HATE FLYING.

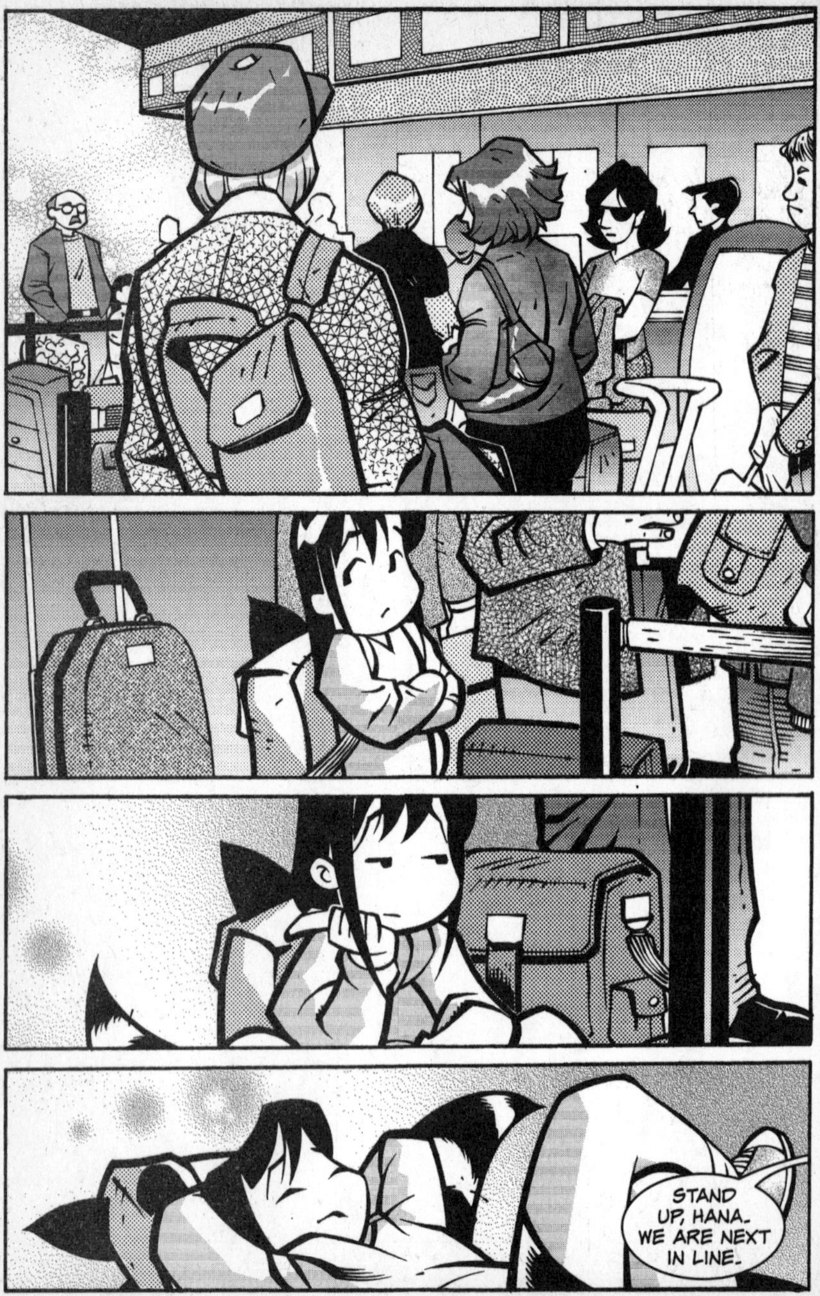
STAND UP, HANA. WE ARE NEXT IN LINE.

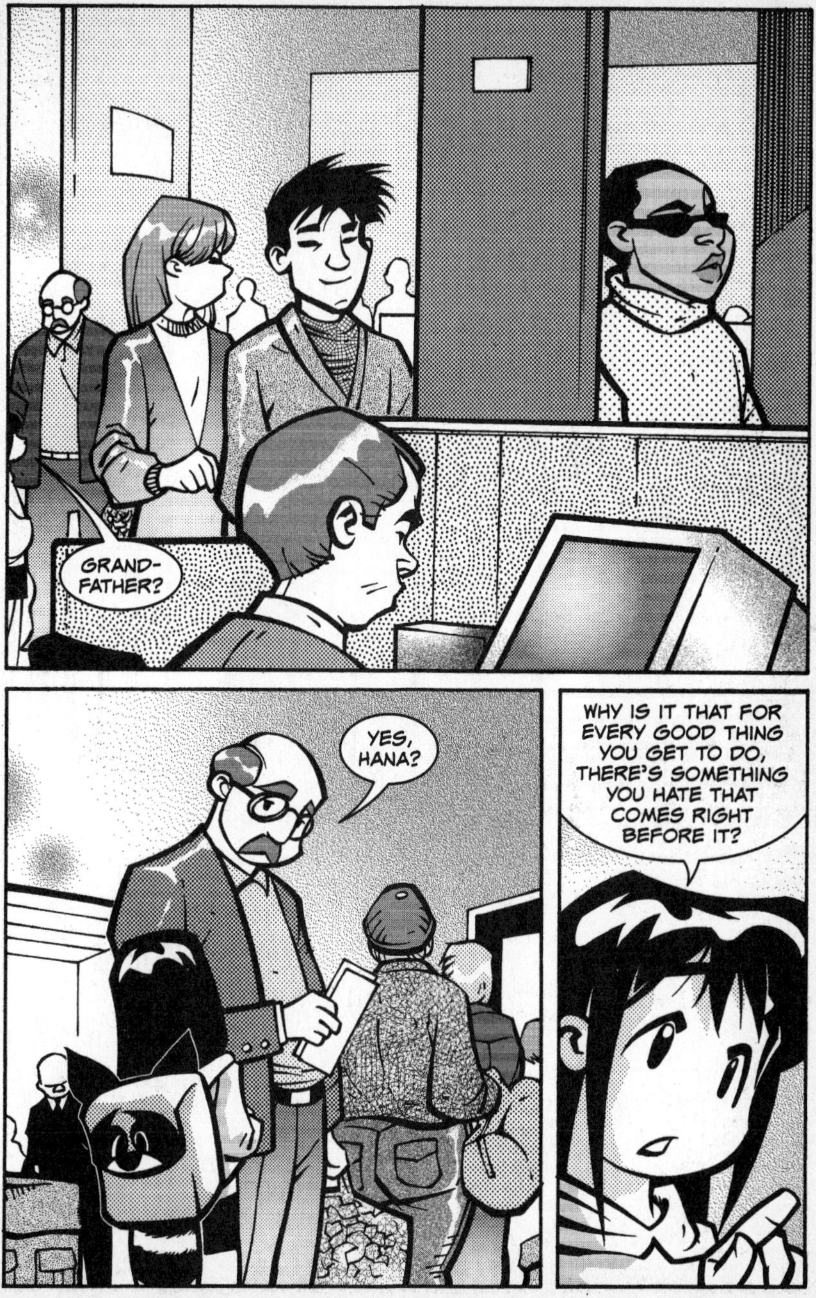
GRAND-FATHER?
YES, HANA?
WHY IS IT THAT FOR EVERY GOOD THING YOU GET TO DO, THERE'S SOMETHING YOU HATE THAT COMES RIGHT BEFORE IT?

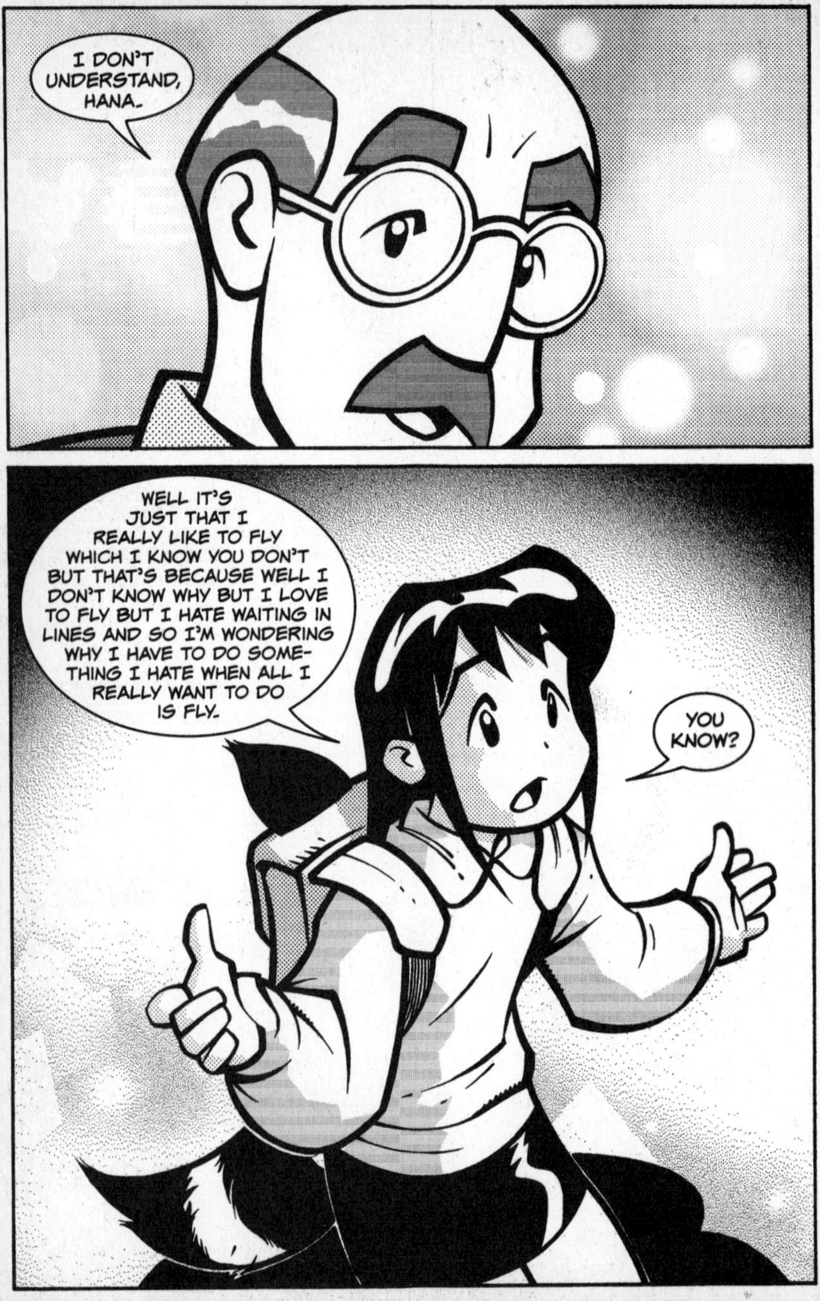
I DON'T UNDERSTAND, HANA...
WELL IT'S JUST THAT I REALLY LIKE TO FLY WHICH I KNOW YOU DON'T BUT THAT'S BECAUSE WELL I DON'T KNOW WHY BUT I LOVE TO FLY BUT I HATE WAITING IN LINES AND SO I'M WONDERING WHY I HAVE TO DO SOME-THING I HATE WHEN ALL I REALLY WANT TO DO IS FLY...
YOU KNOW?

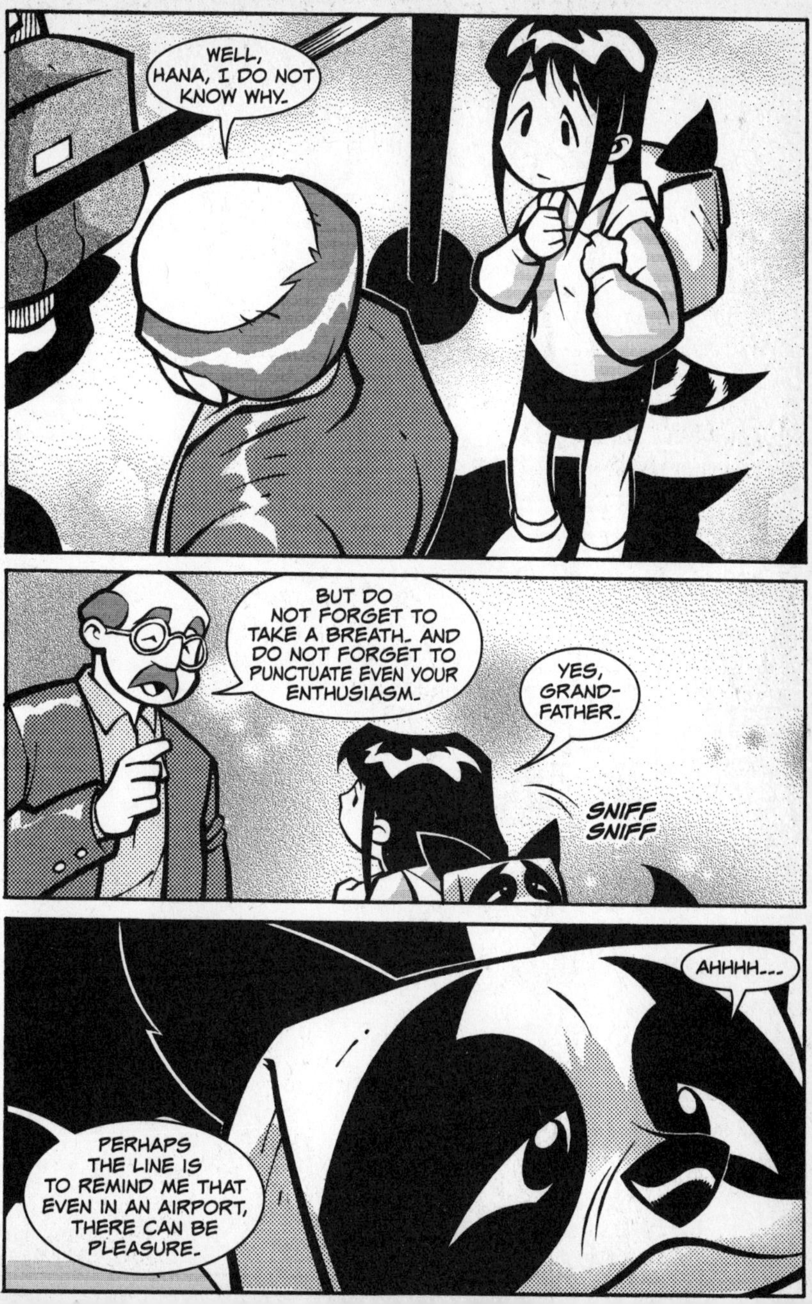
WELL, HANA, I DO NOT KNOW WHY.
BUT DO NOT FORGET TO TAKE A BREATH. AND DO NOT FORGET TO PUNCTUATE EVEN YOUR ENTHUSIASM.
YES, GRAND-FATHER.
SNIFF SNIFF
AHHHH...
PERHAPS THE LINE IS TO REMIND ME THAT EVEN IN AN AIRPORT, THERE CAN BE PLEASURE.

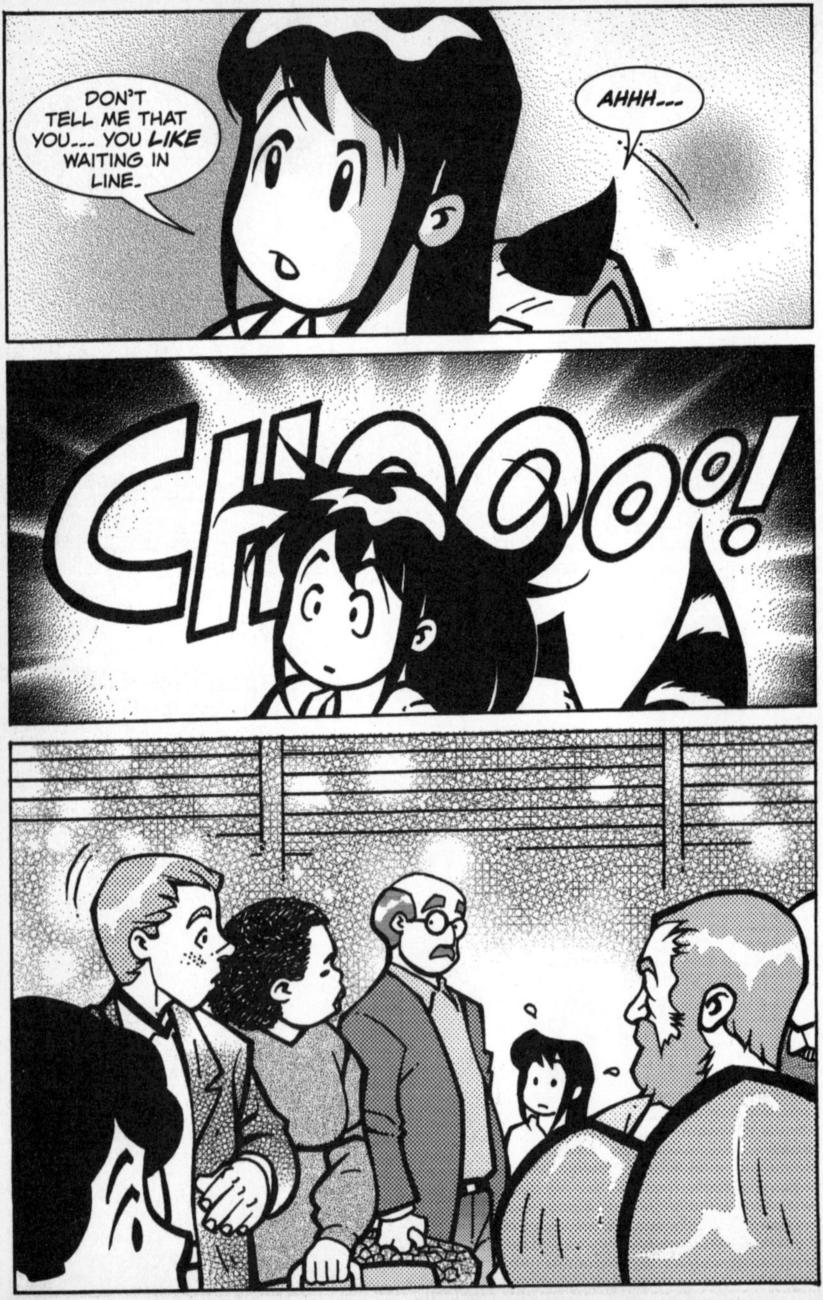
DON'T TELL ME THAT YOU... YOU **LIKE** WAITING IN LINE.
AHHH...
CHOOO!

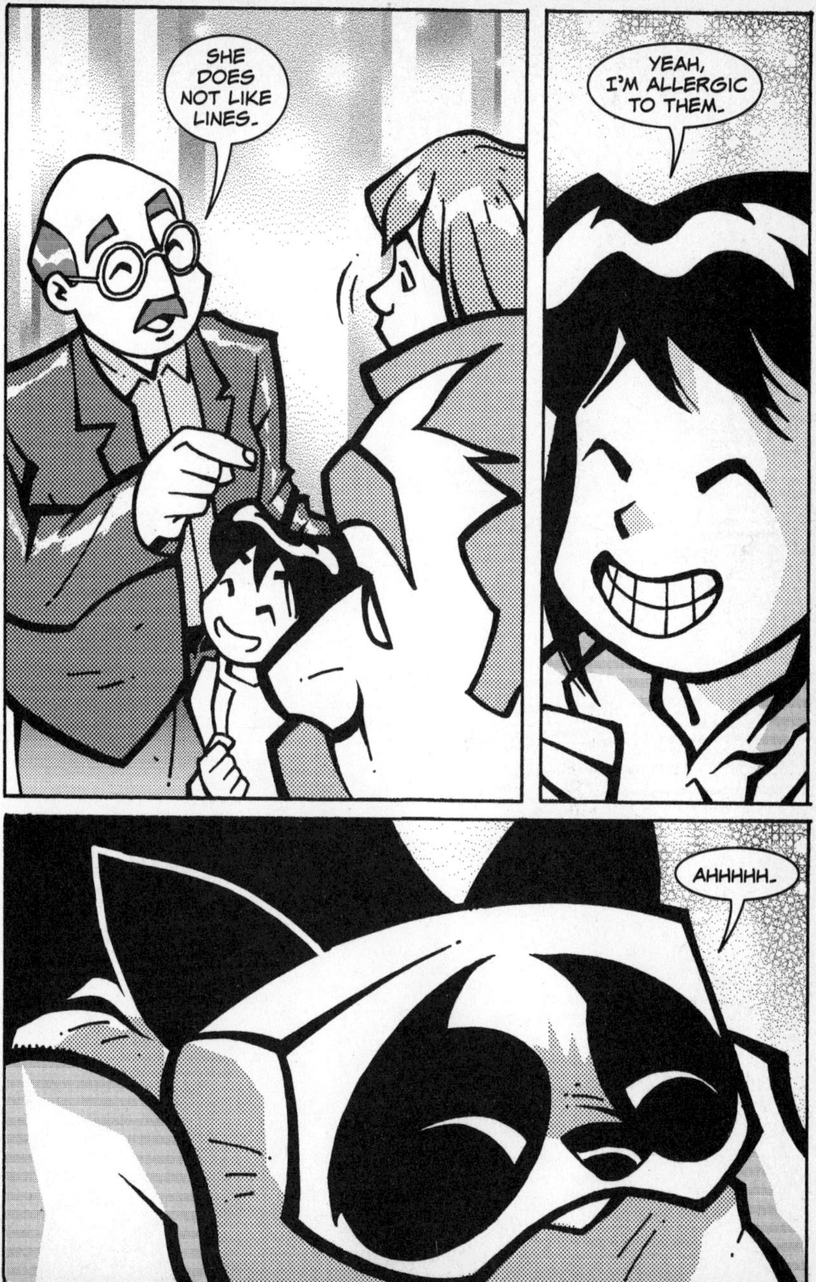
SHE DOES NOT LIKE LINES_
YEAH, I'M ALLERGIC TO THEM_
AHHHHH_

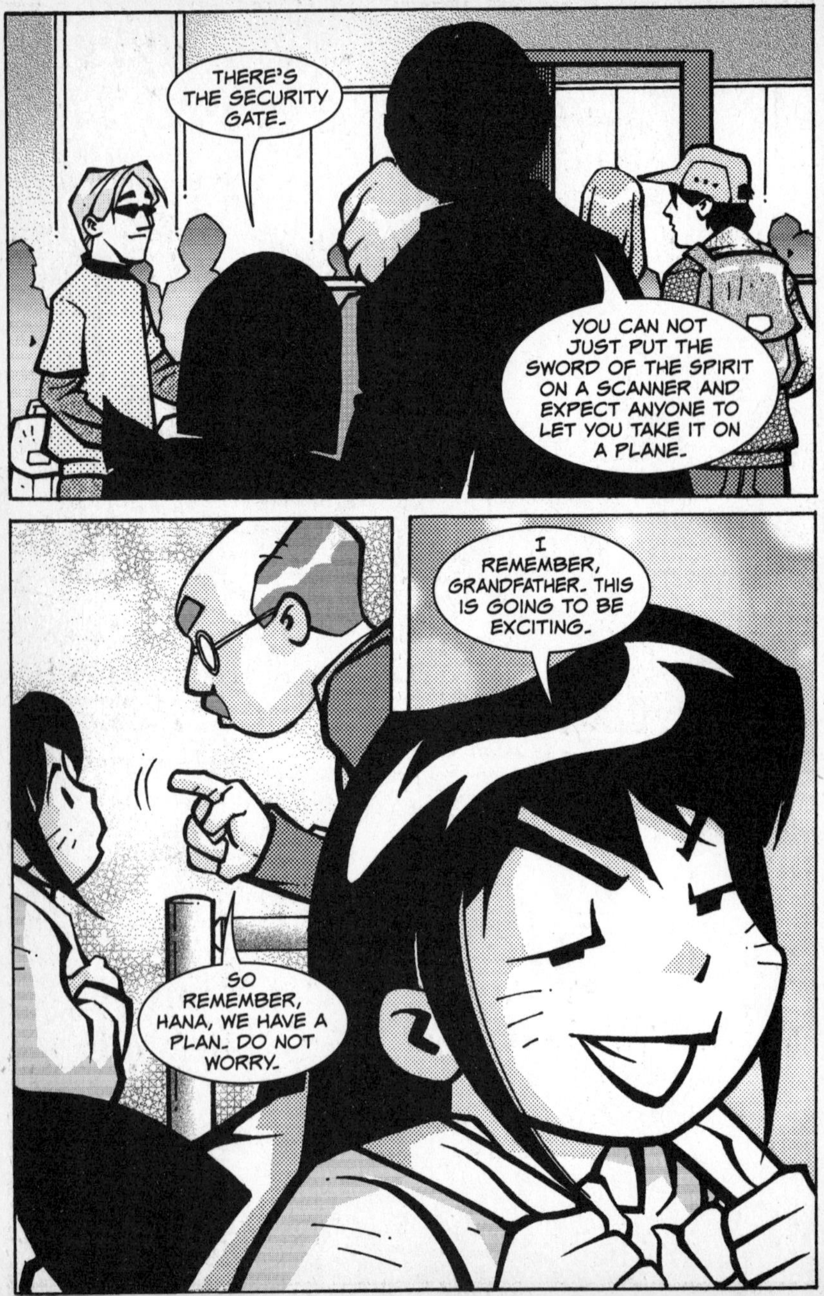
THERE'S THE SECURITY GATE.
YOU CAN NOT JUST PUT THE SWORD OF THE SPIRIT ON A SCANNER AND EXPECT ANYONE TO LET YOU TAKE IT ON A PLANE.
SO REMEMBER, HANA, WE HAVE A PLAN. DO NOT WORRY.
I REMEMBER, GRANDFATHER. THIS IS GOING TO BE EXCITING.

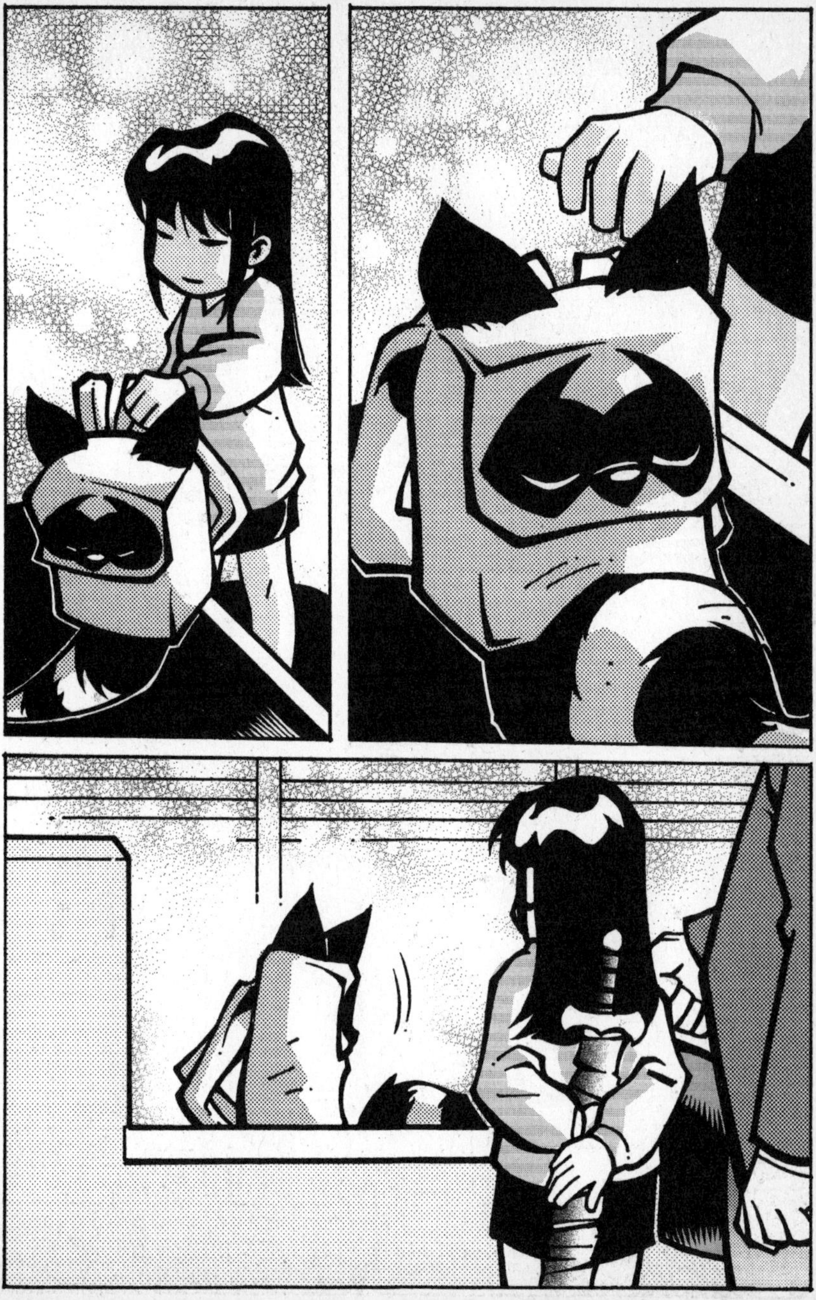

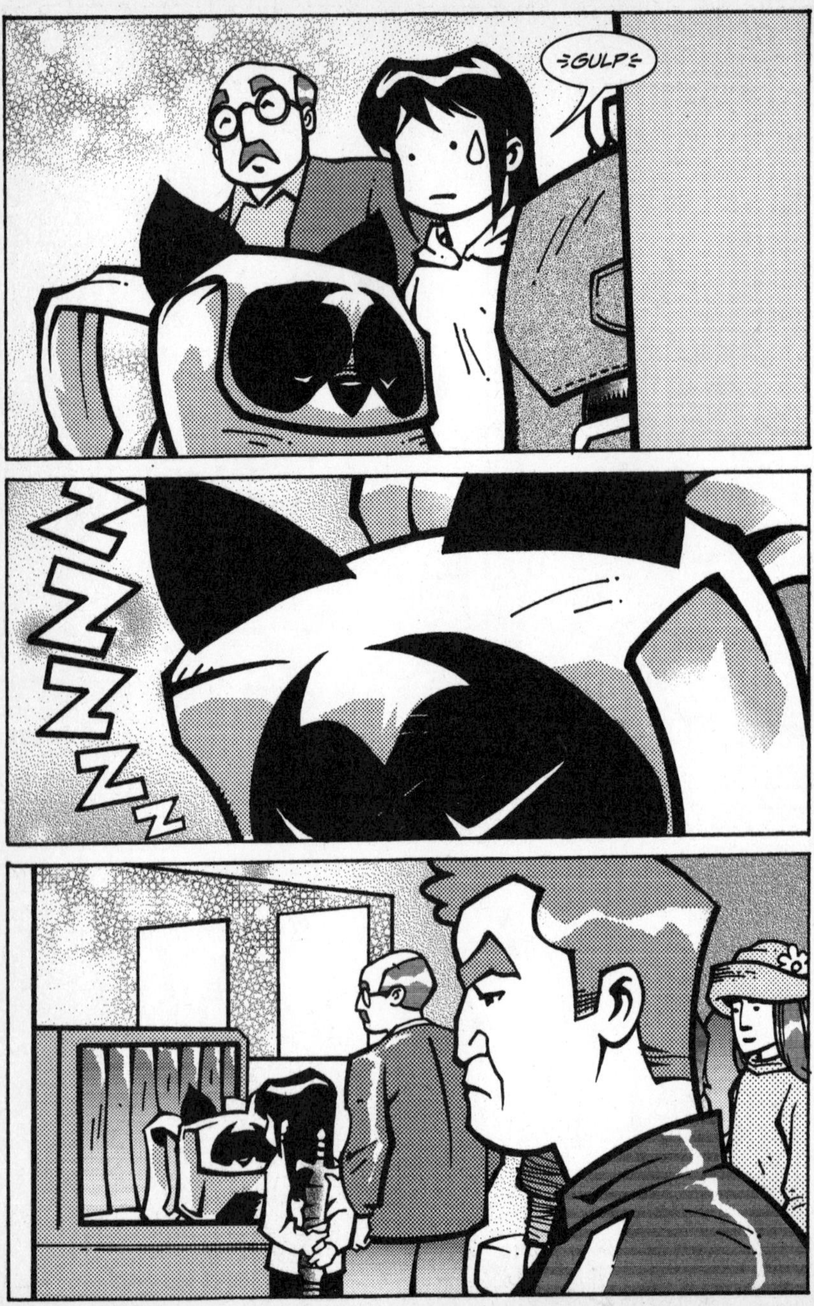
GULP
ZZZZZZ

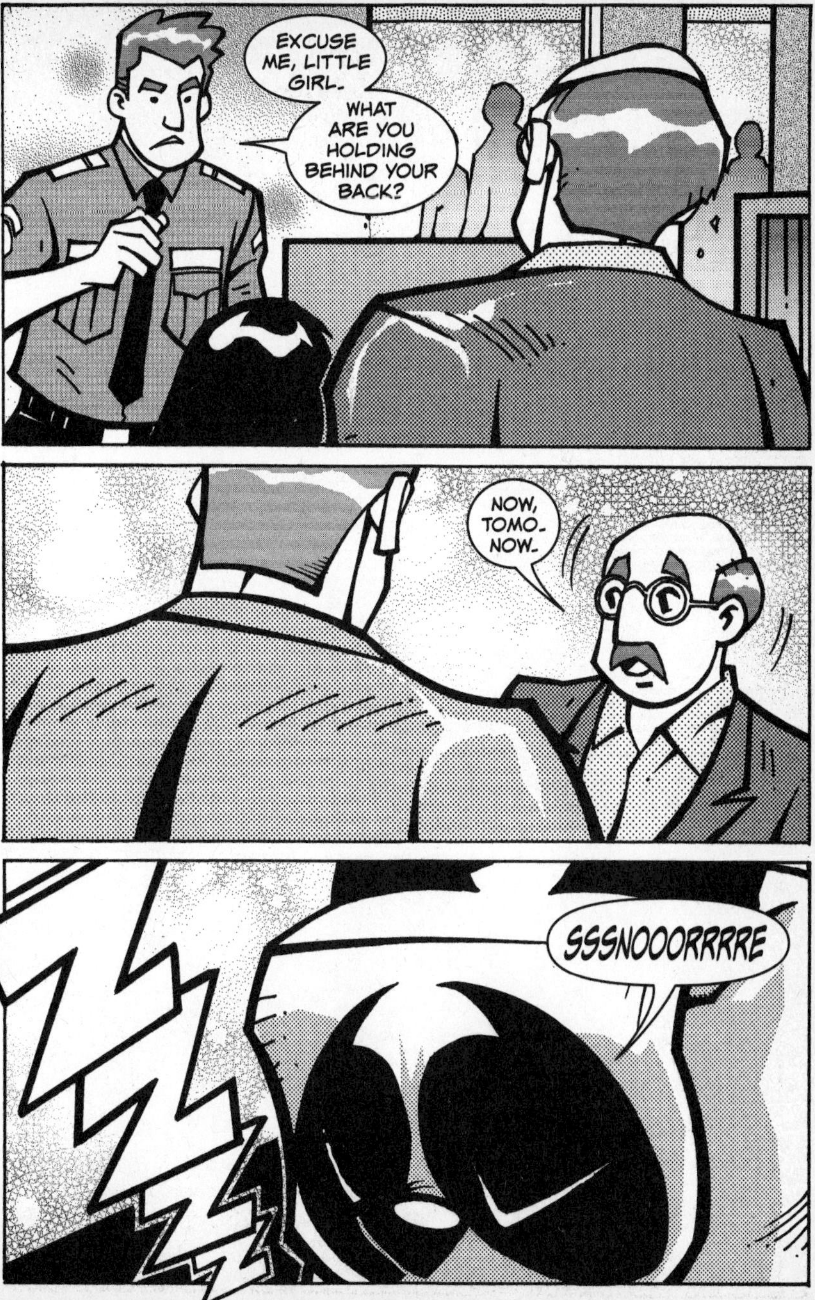
EXCUSE ME, LITTLE GIRL.
WHAT ARE YOU HOLDING BEHIND YOUR BACK?
NOW, TOMO. NOW.
SSSNOOORRRRE

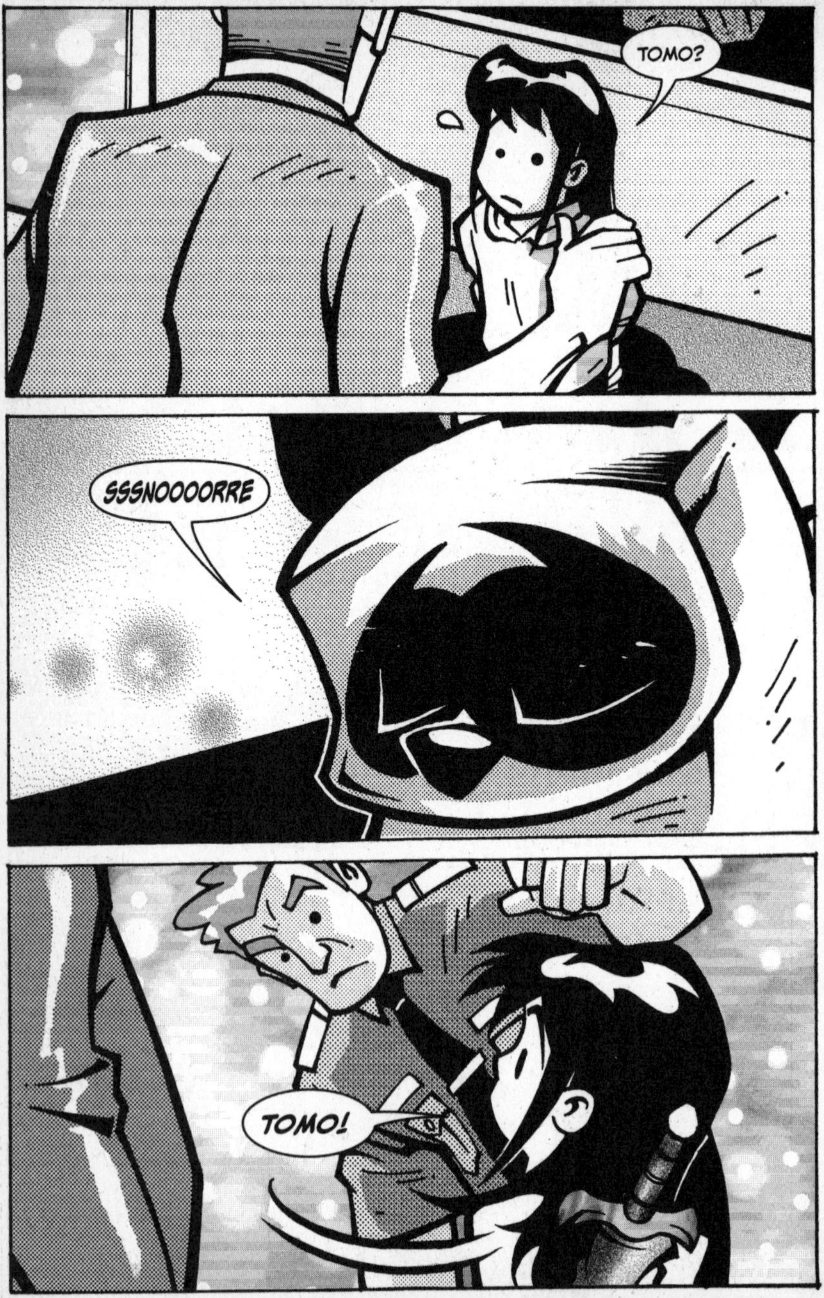
TOMO?
SSSNOOOORRE
TOMO!

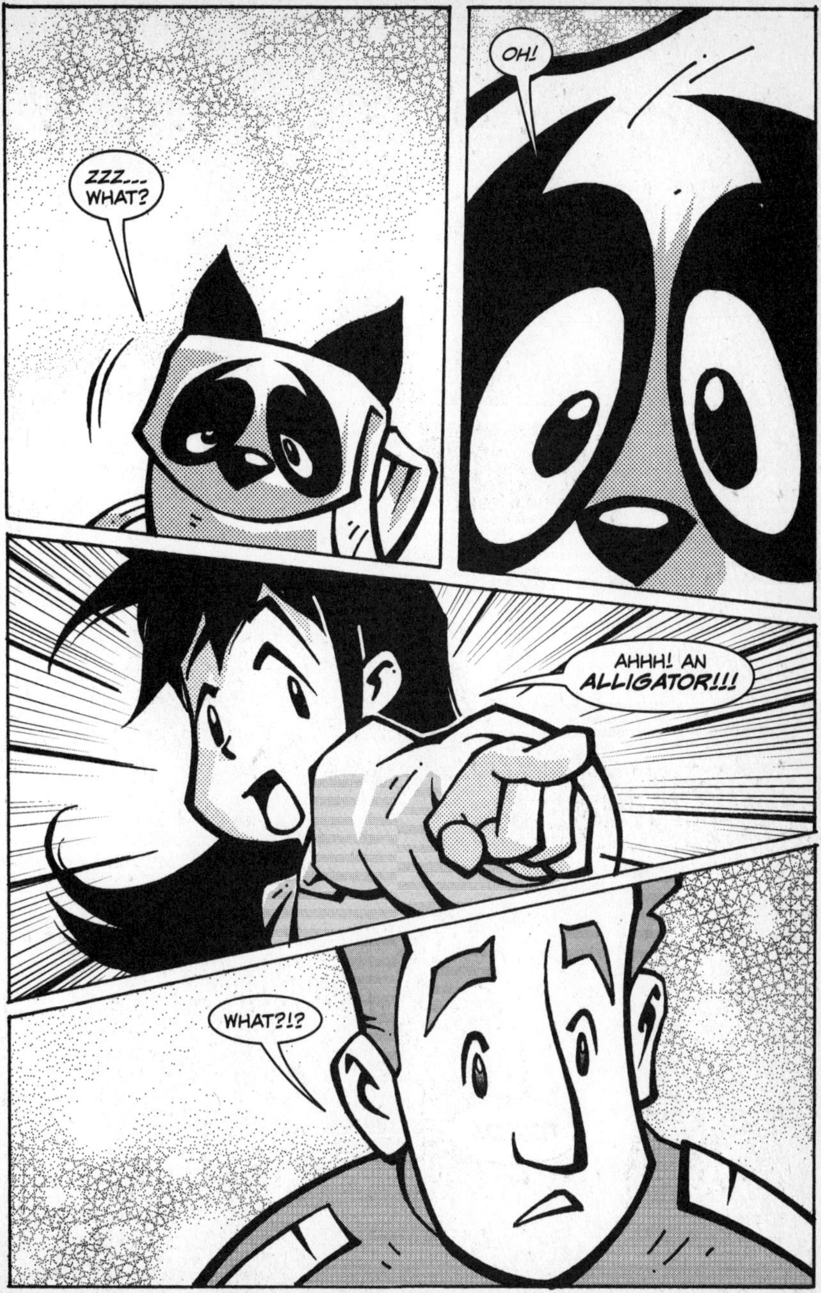
ZZZ...
WHAT?
OH!
AHHH! AN ALLIGATOR!!!
WHAT?!?

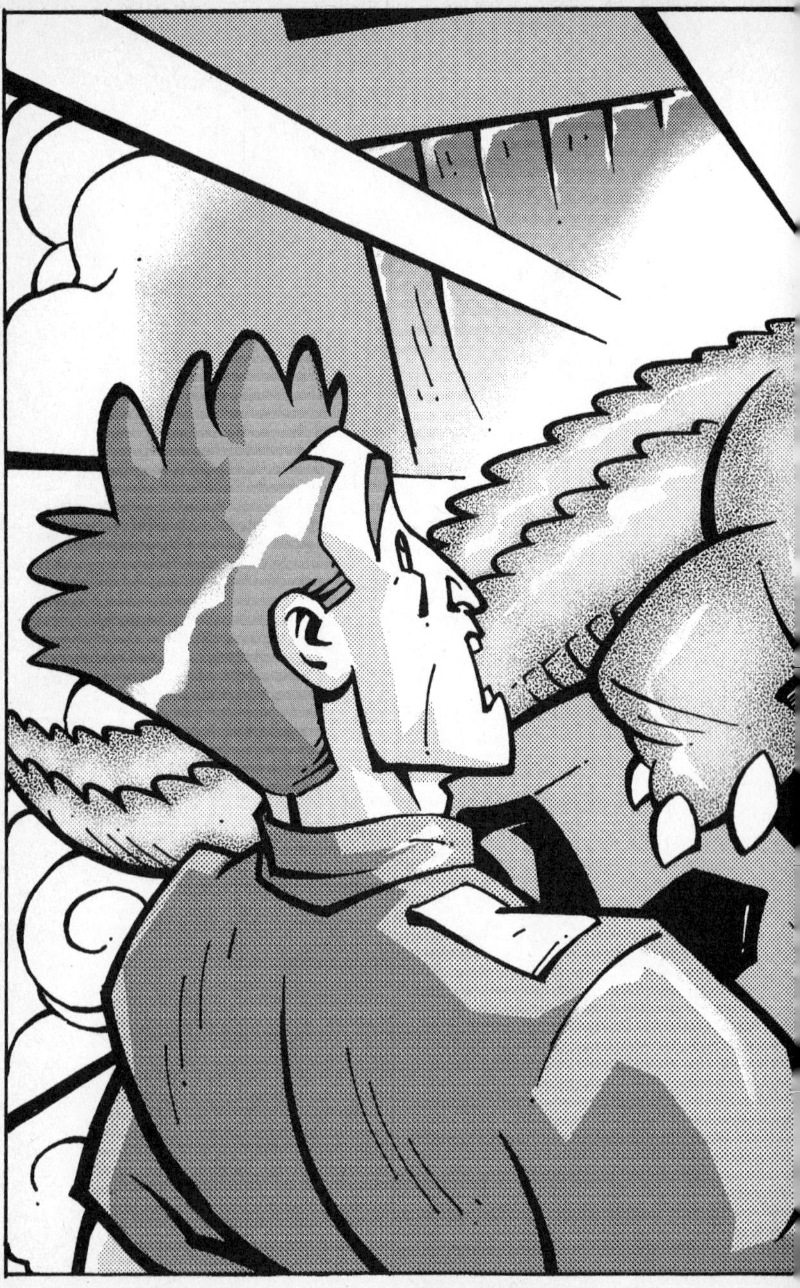

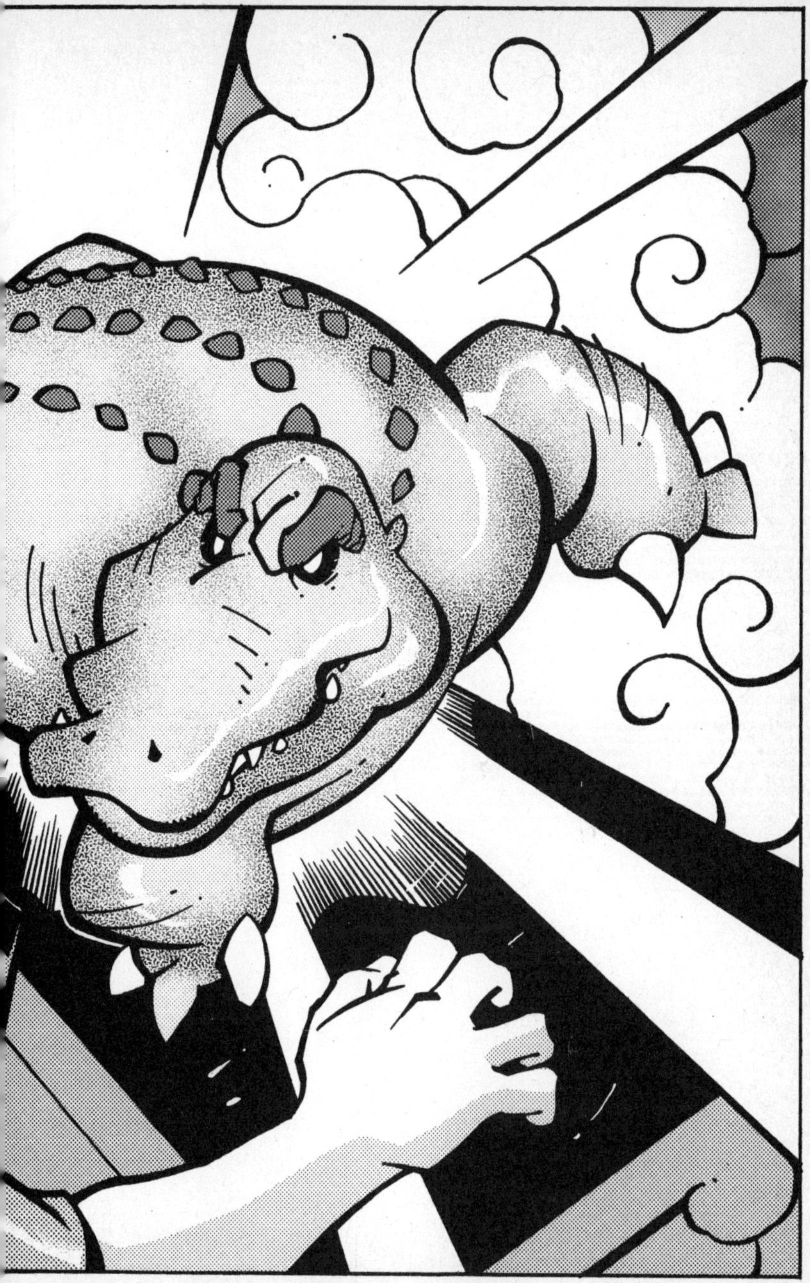

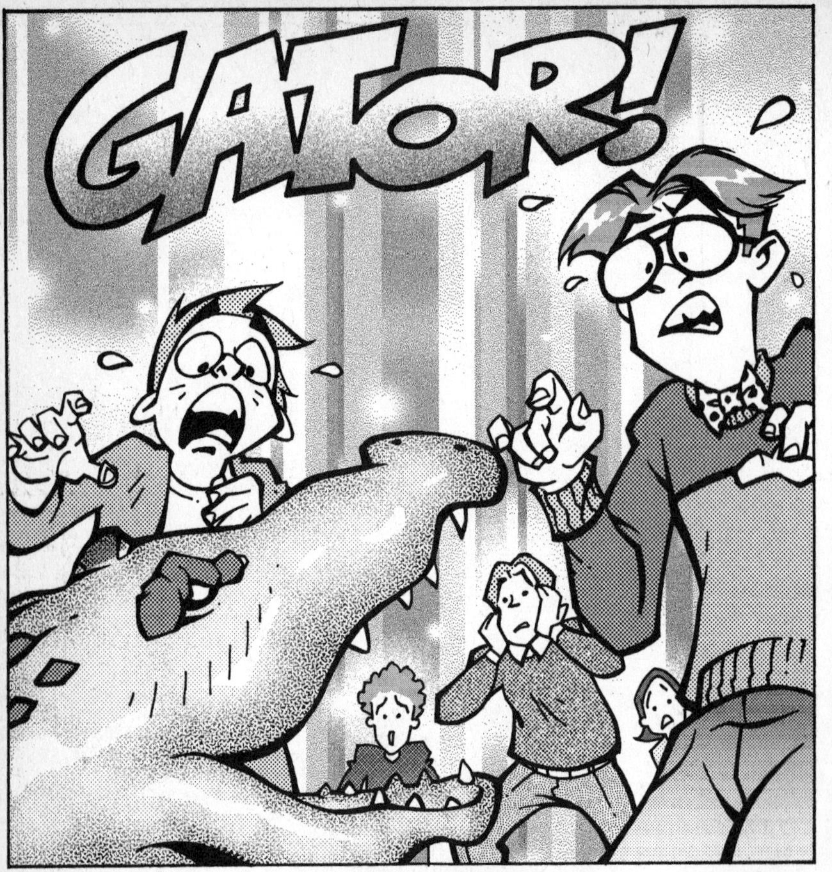
GATOR!

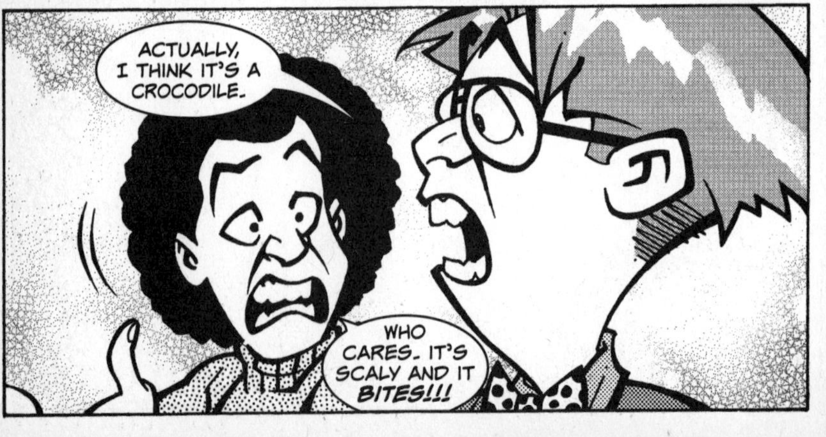
ACTUALLY, I THINK IT'S A CROCODILE.
WHO CARES. IT'S SCALY AND IT *BITES!!!*

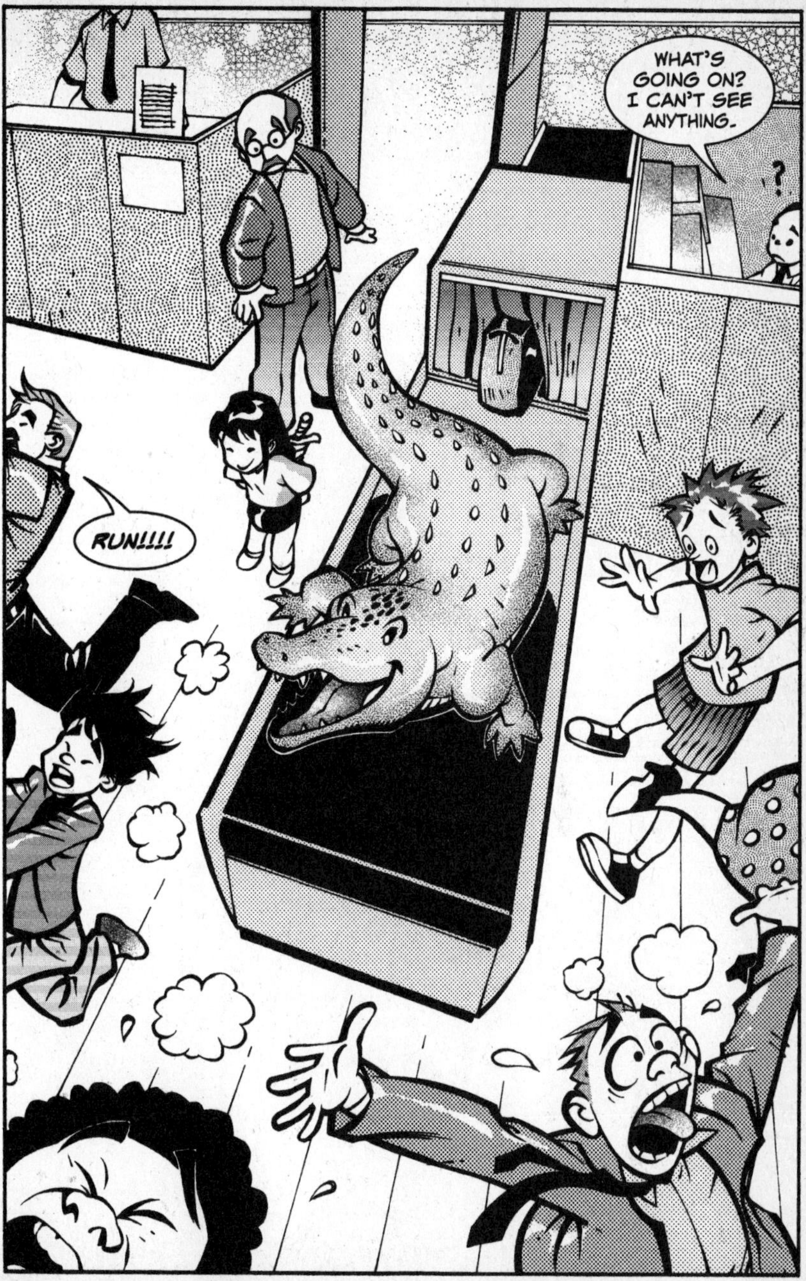
WHAT'S GOING ON? I CAN'T SEE ANYTHING.
?
RUN!!!!

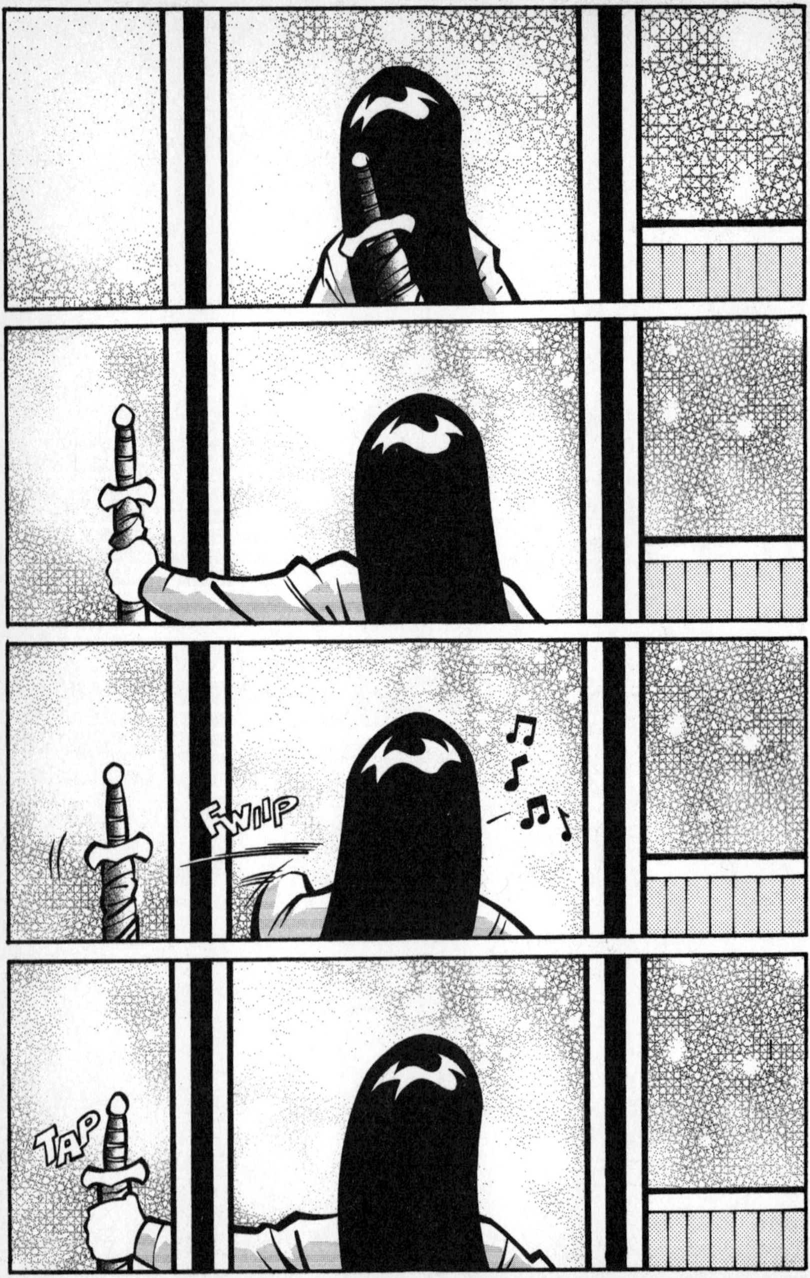
FWIP
TAP

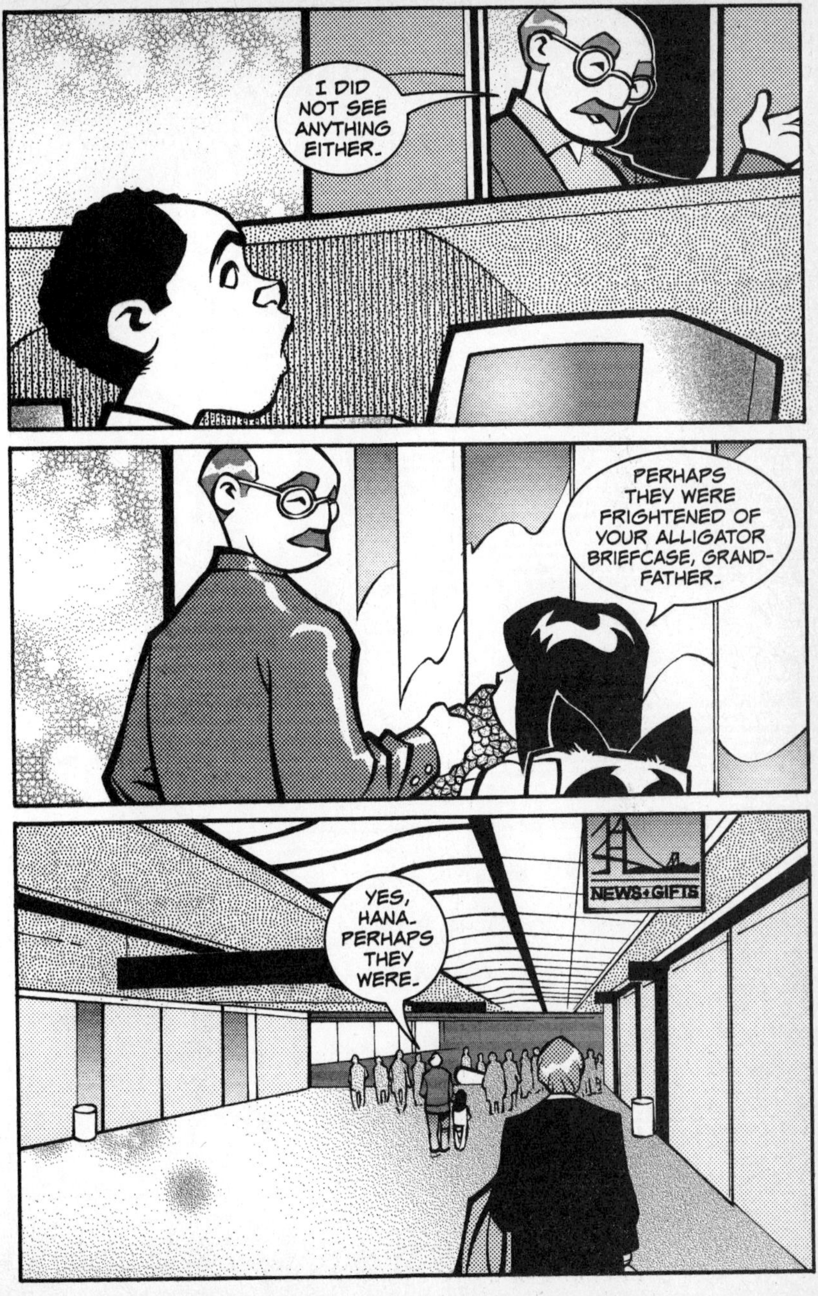
I DID NOT SEE ANYTHING EITHER.
PERHAPS THEY WERE FRIGHTENED OF YOUR ALLIGATOR BRIEFCASE, GRAND-FATHER.
NEWS+GIFTS
YES, HANA. PERHAPS THEY WERE.

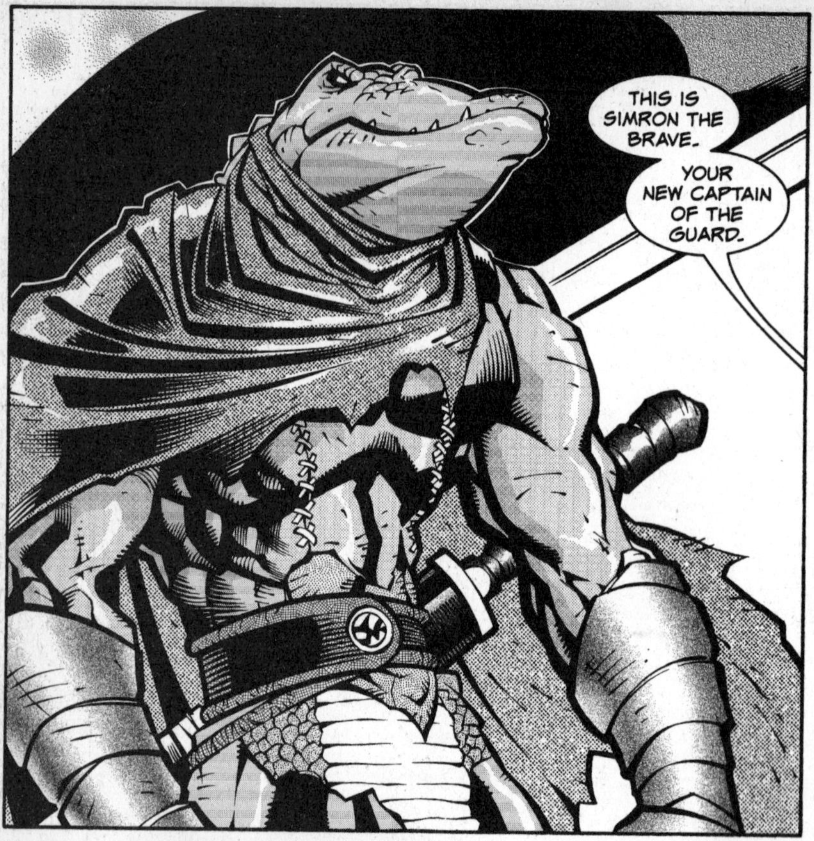
THIS IS SIMRON THE BRAVE.
YOUR NEW CAPTAIN OF THE GUARD.

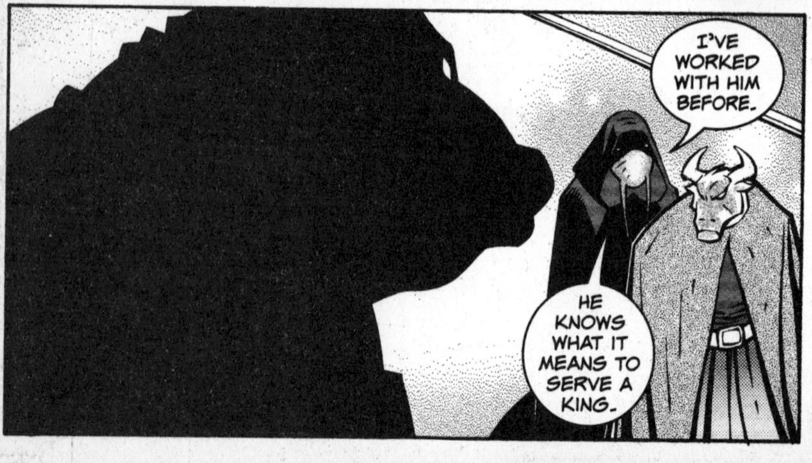
I'VE WORKED WITH HIM BEFORE.
HE KNOWS WHAT IT MEANS TO SERVE A KING.

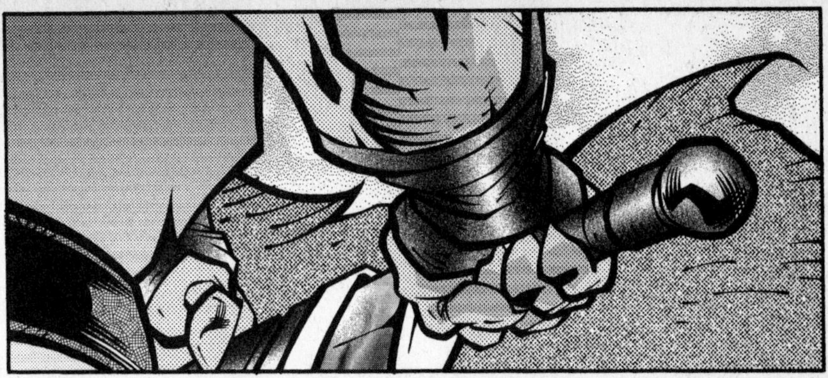
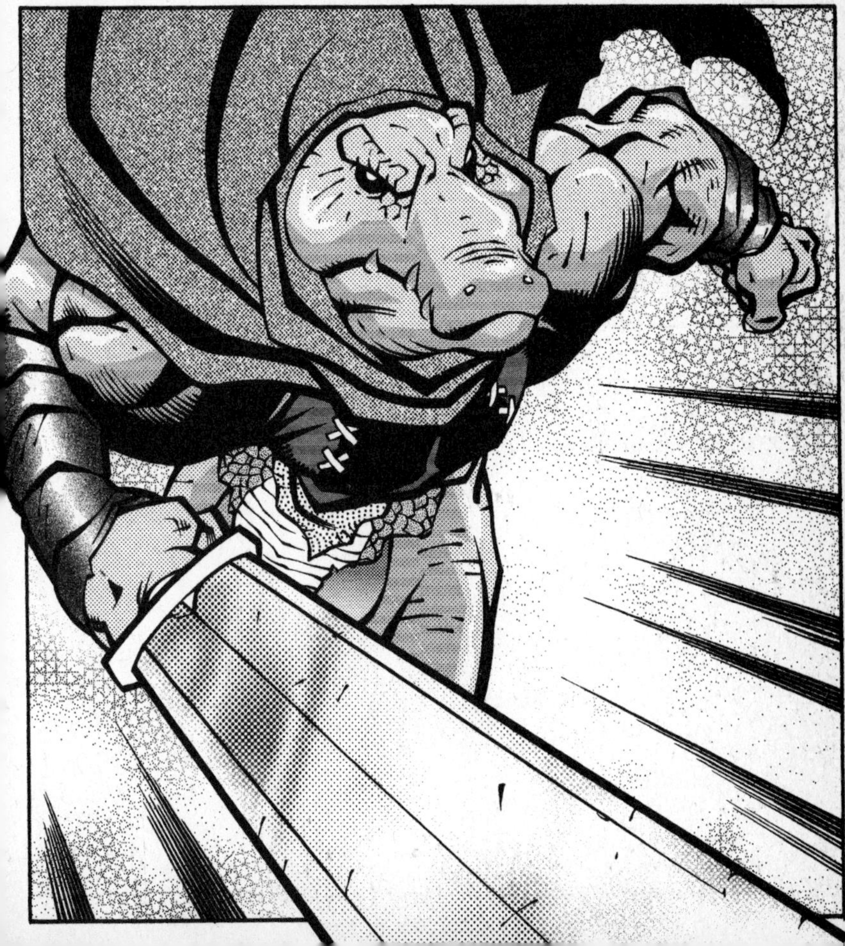

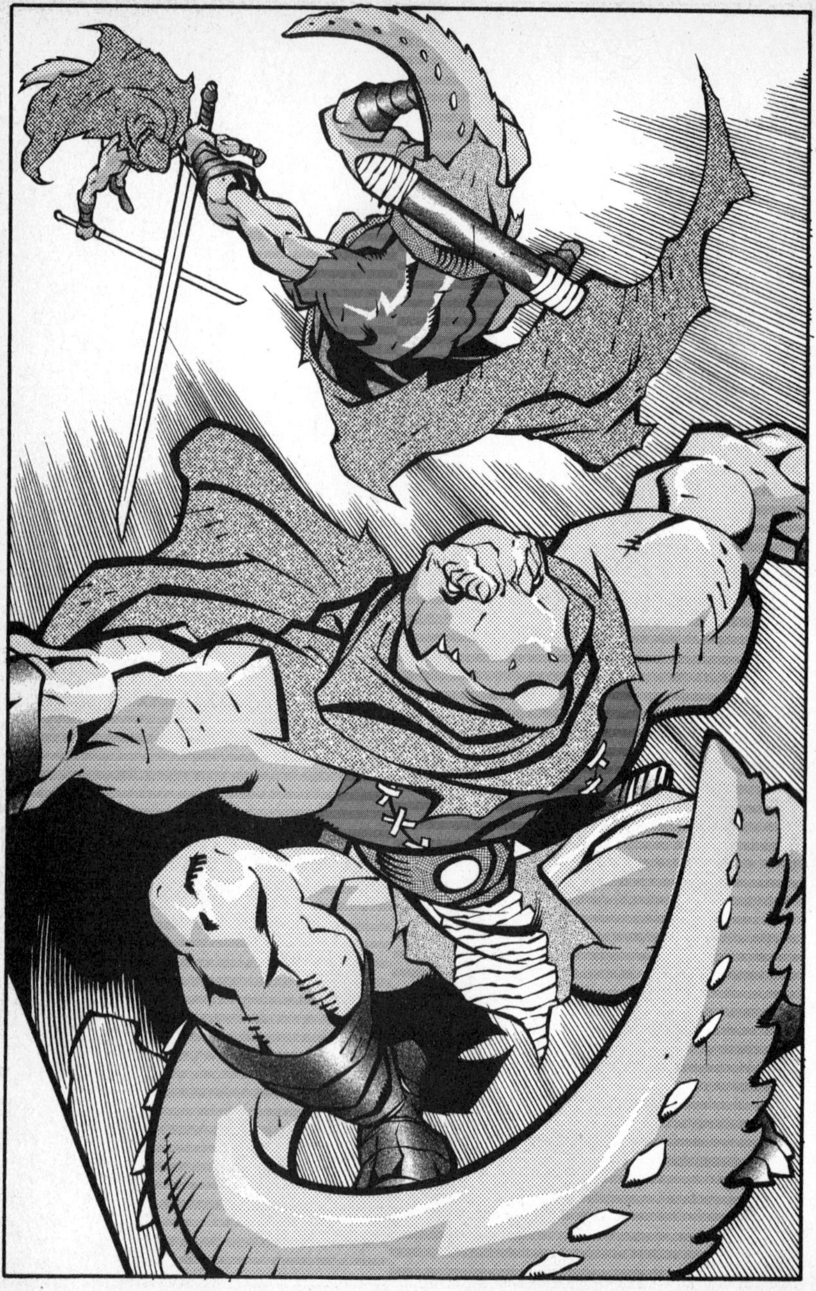

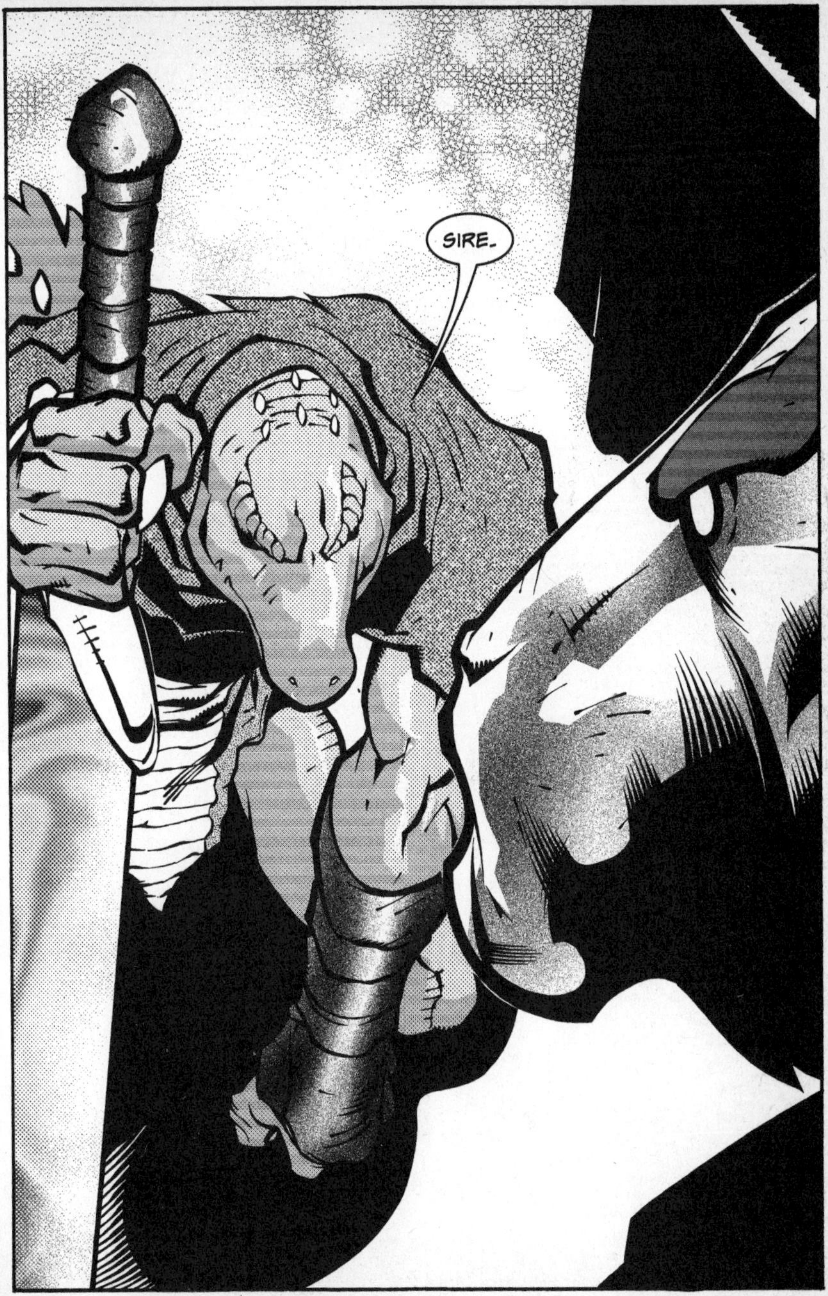
SIRE-

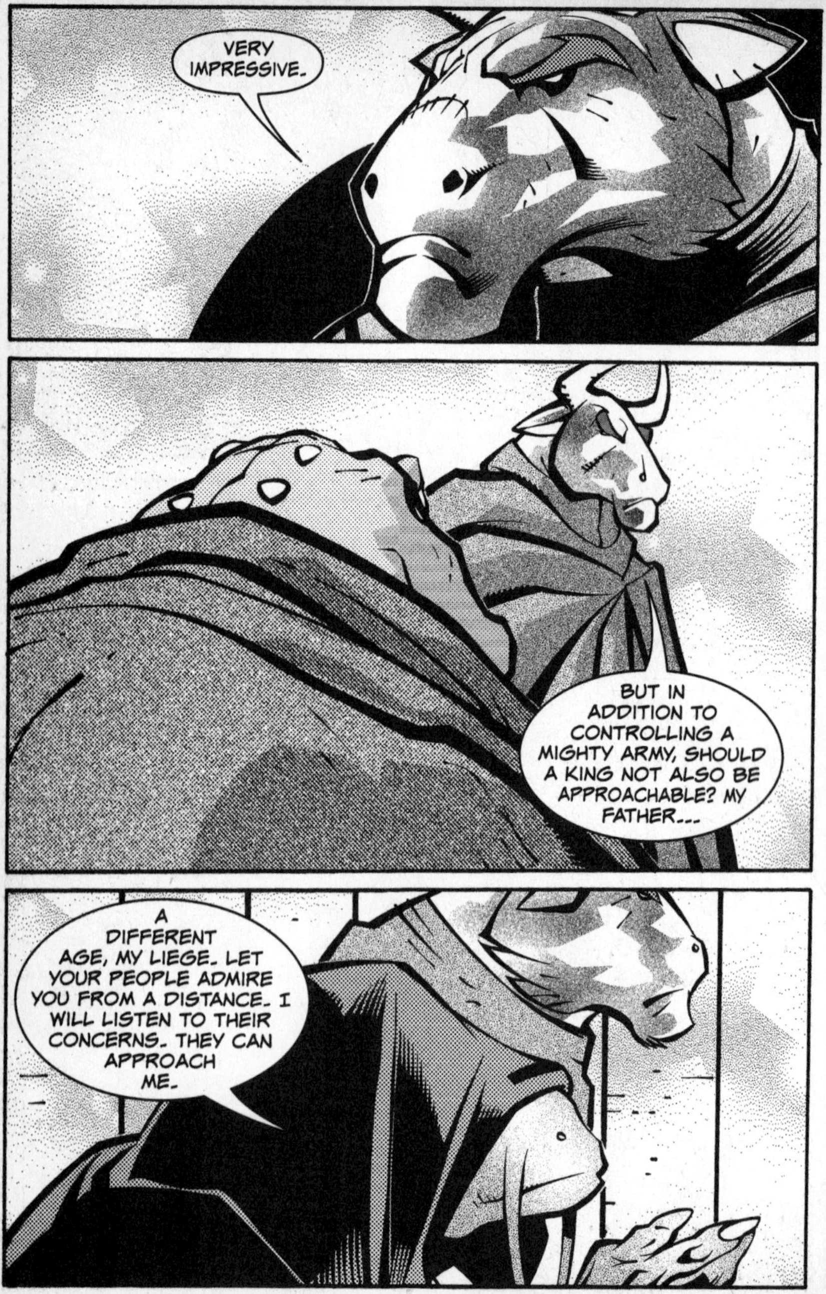
VERY IMPRESSIVE.
BUT IN ADDITION TO CONTROLLING A MIGHTY ARMY, SHOULD A KING NOT ALSO BE APPROACHABLE? MY FATHER...
A DIFFERENT AGE, MY LIEGE. LET YOUR PEOPLE ADMIRE YOU FROM A DISTANCE. I WILL LISTEN TO THEIR CONCERNS. THEY CAN APPROACH ME.

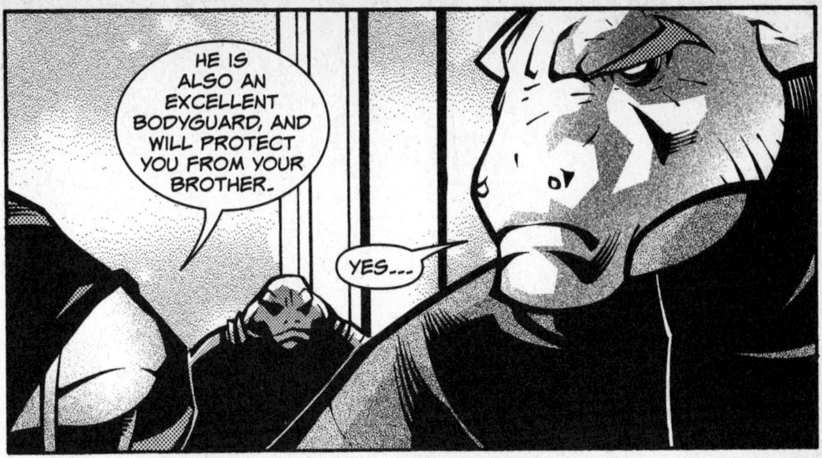
HE IS ALSO AN EXCELLENT BODYGUARD, AND WILL PROTECT YOU FROM YOUR BROTHER.
YES...

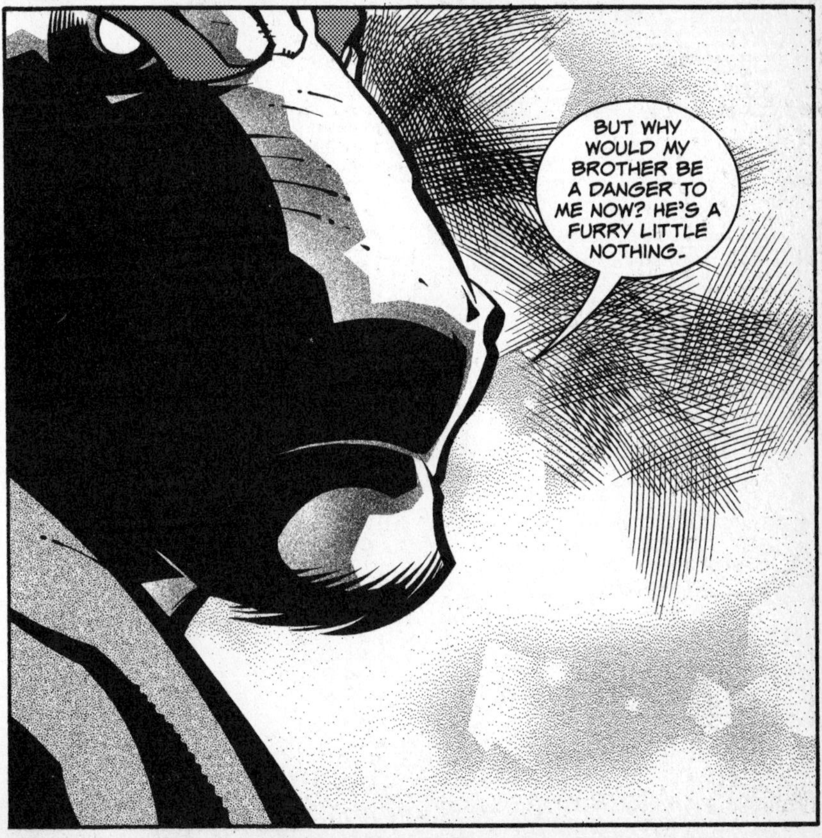
BUT WHY WOULD MY BROTHER BE A DANGER TO ME NOW? HE'S A FURRY LITTLE NOTHING.

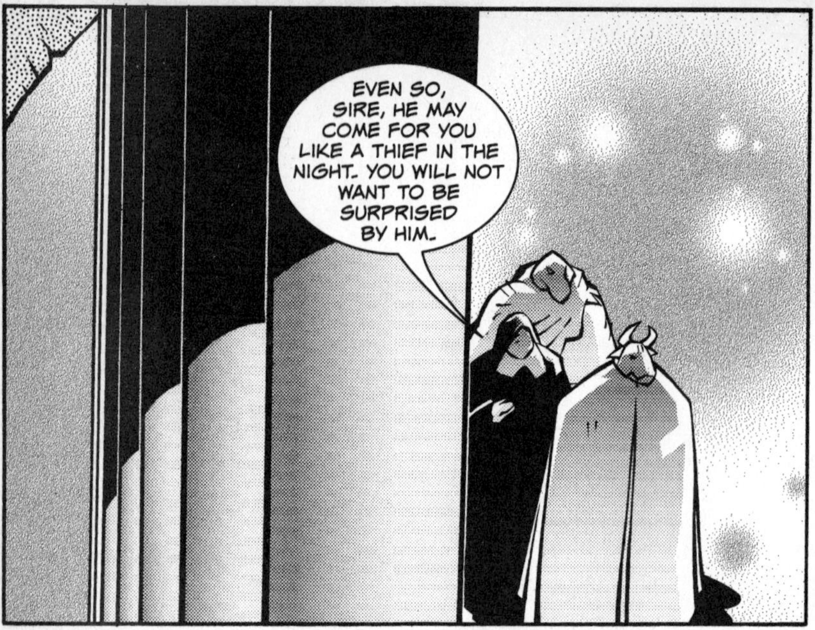
EVEN SO, SIRE, HE MAY COME FOR YOU LIKE A THIEF IN THE NIGHT. YOU WILL NOT WANT TO BE SURPRISED BY HIM.

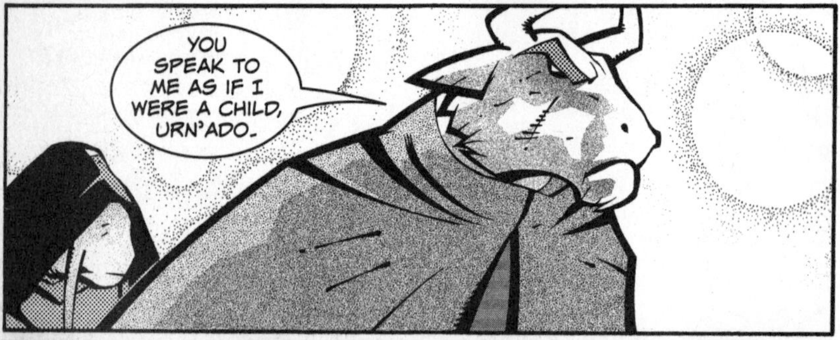
YOU SPEAK TO ME AS IF I WERE A CHILD, URN'ADO.

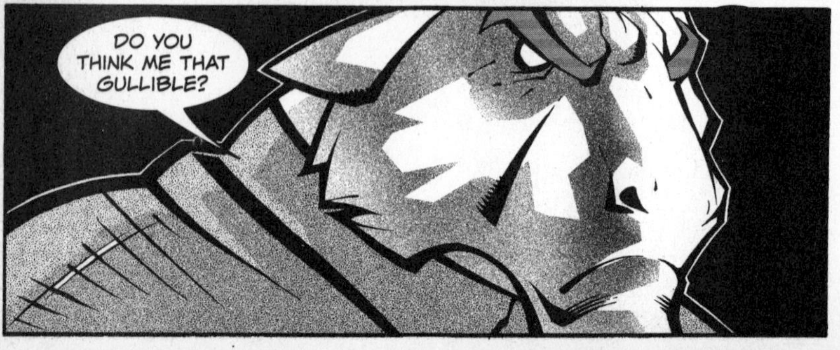
DO YOU THINK ME THAT GULLIBLE?

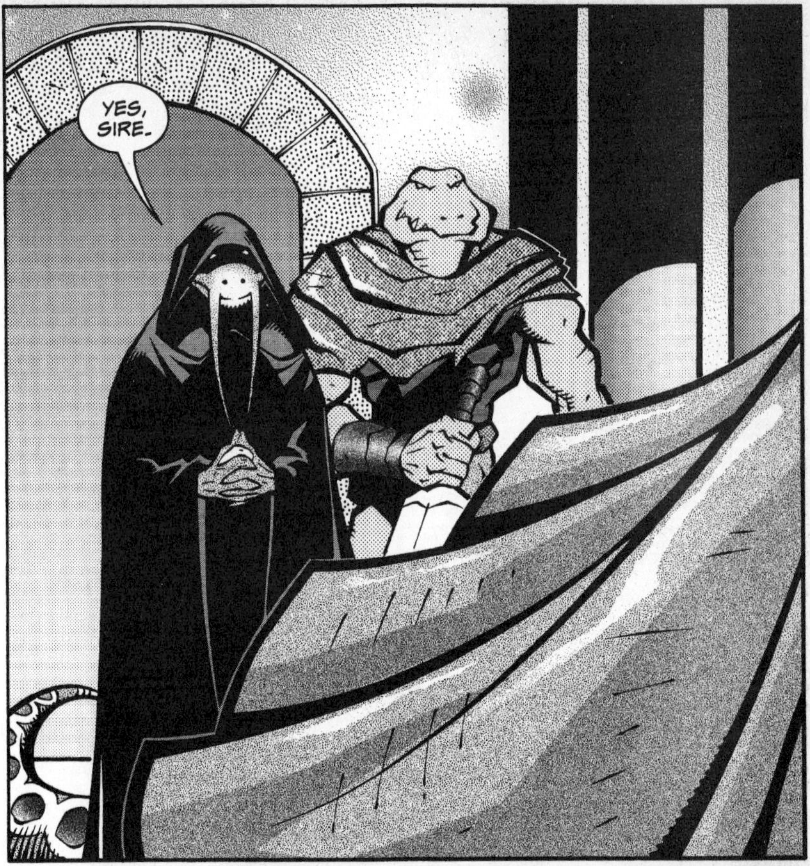
YES, SIRE.

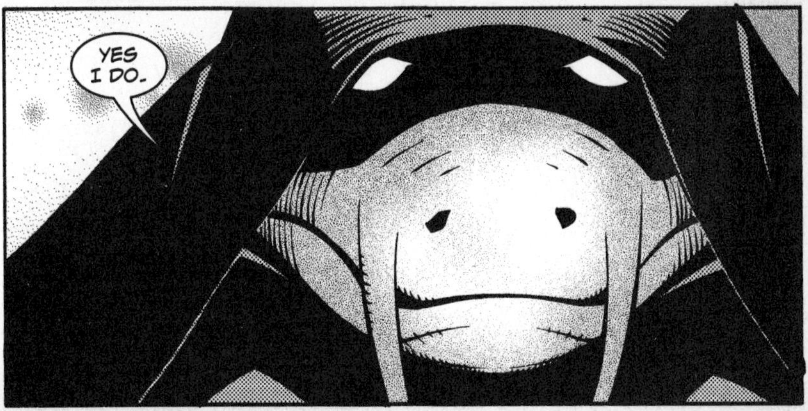
YES I DO.

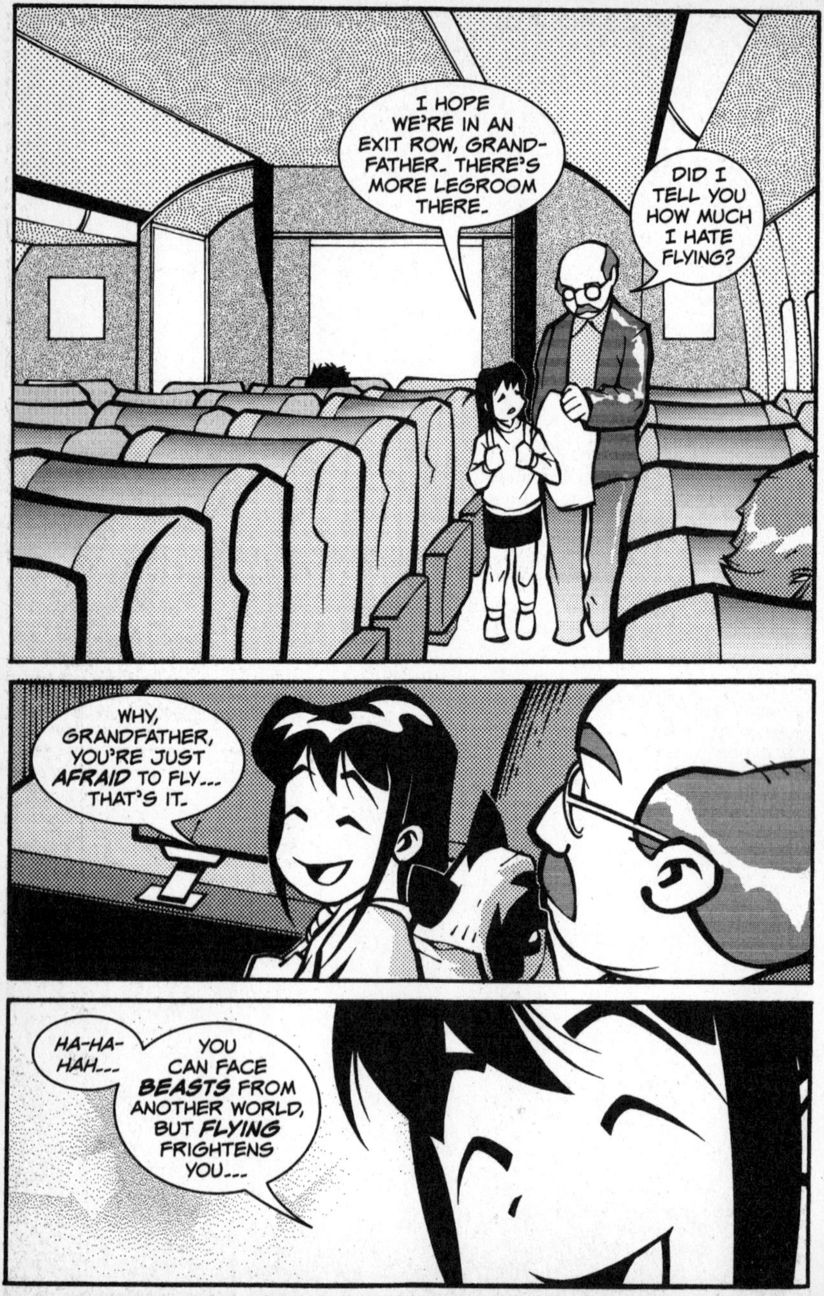
I HOPE WE'RE IN AN EXIT ROW, GRANDFATHER. THERE'S MORE LEGROOM THERE.
DID I TELL YOU HOW MUCH I HATE FLYING?
WHY, GRANDFATHER, YOU'RE JUST *AFRAID* TO FLY... THAT'S IT.
HA-HA-HAH...
YOU CAN FACE *BEASTS* FROM ANOTHER WORLD, BUT *FLYING* FRIGHTENS YOU...

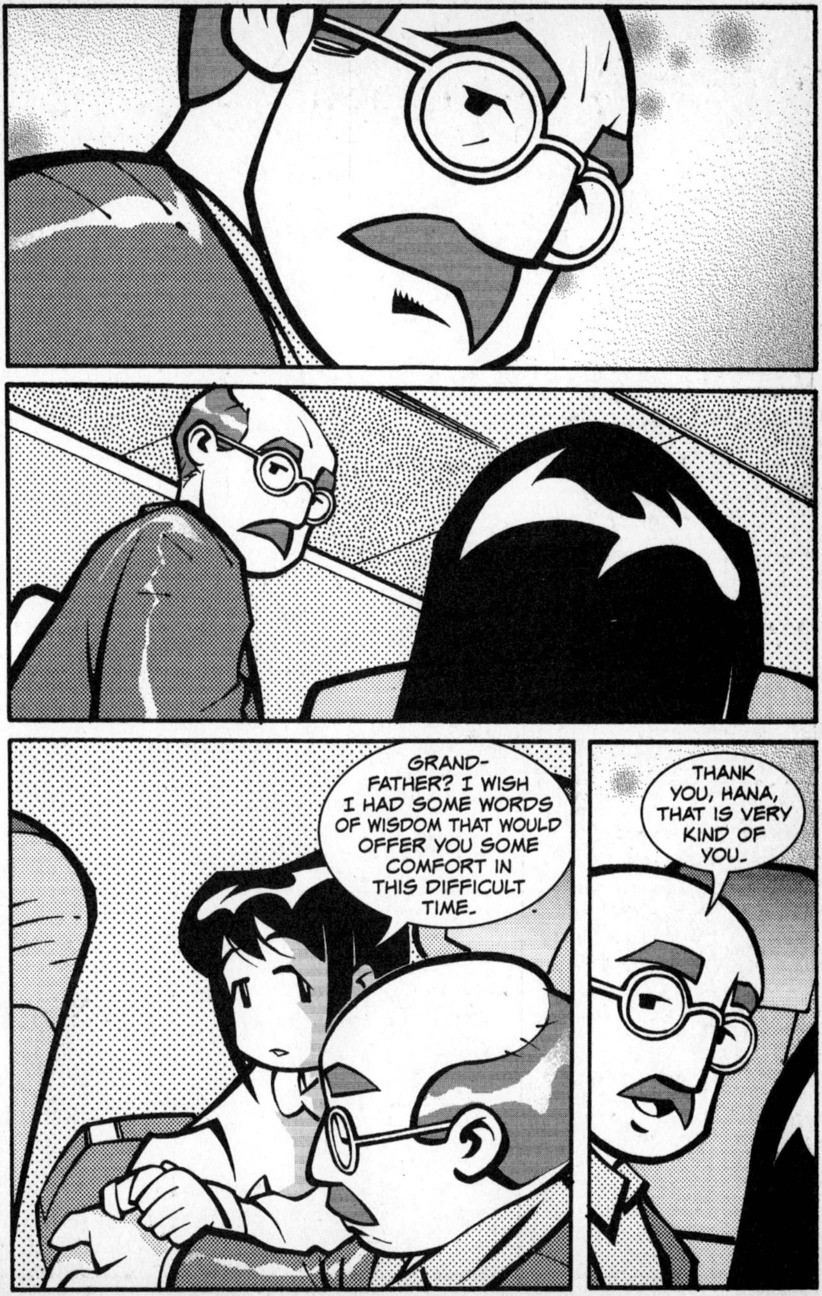
GRAND-FATHER? I WISH I HAD SOME WORDS OF WISDOM THAT WOULD OFFER YOU SOME COMFORT IN THIS DIFFICULT TIME.
THANK YOU, HANA, THAT IS VERY KIND OF YOU.

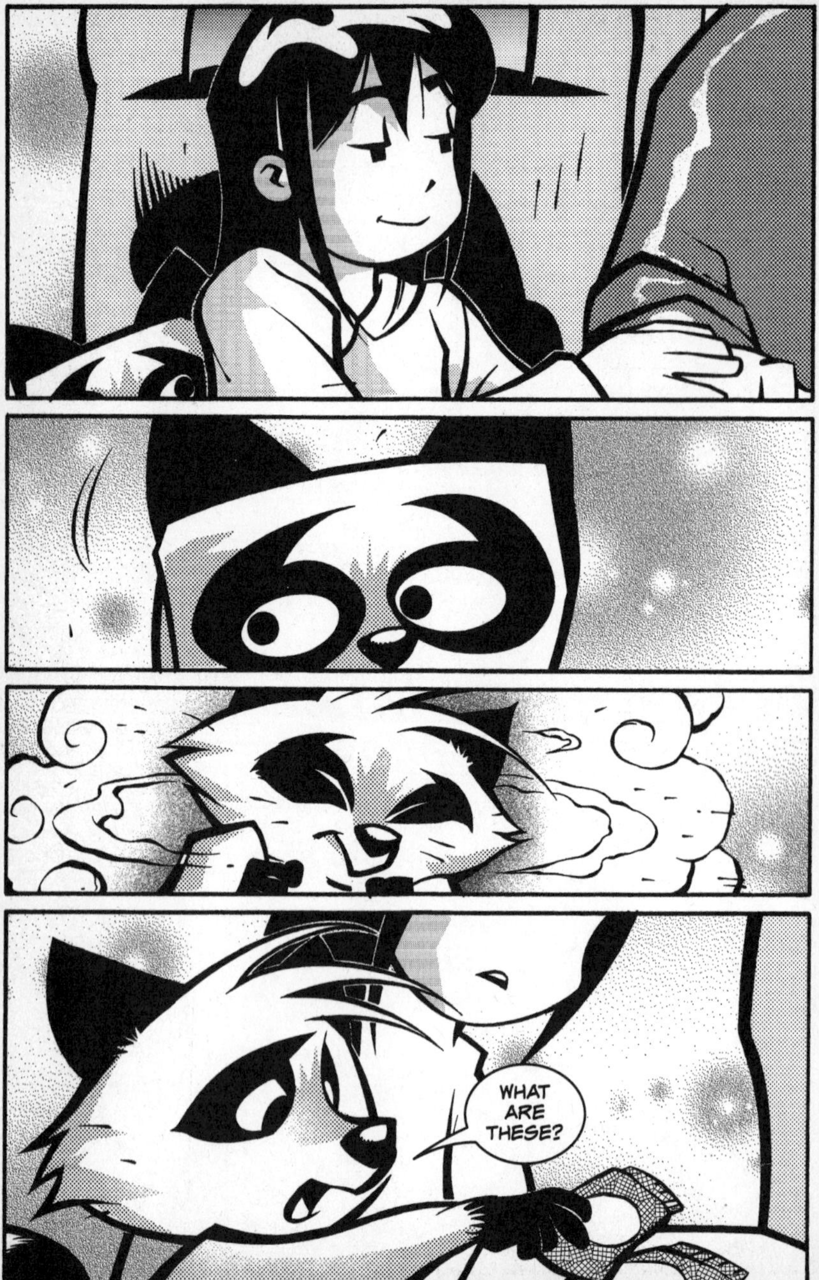
WHAT ARE THESE?

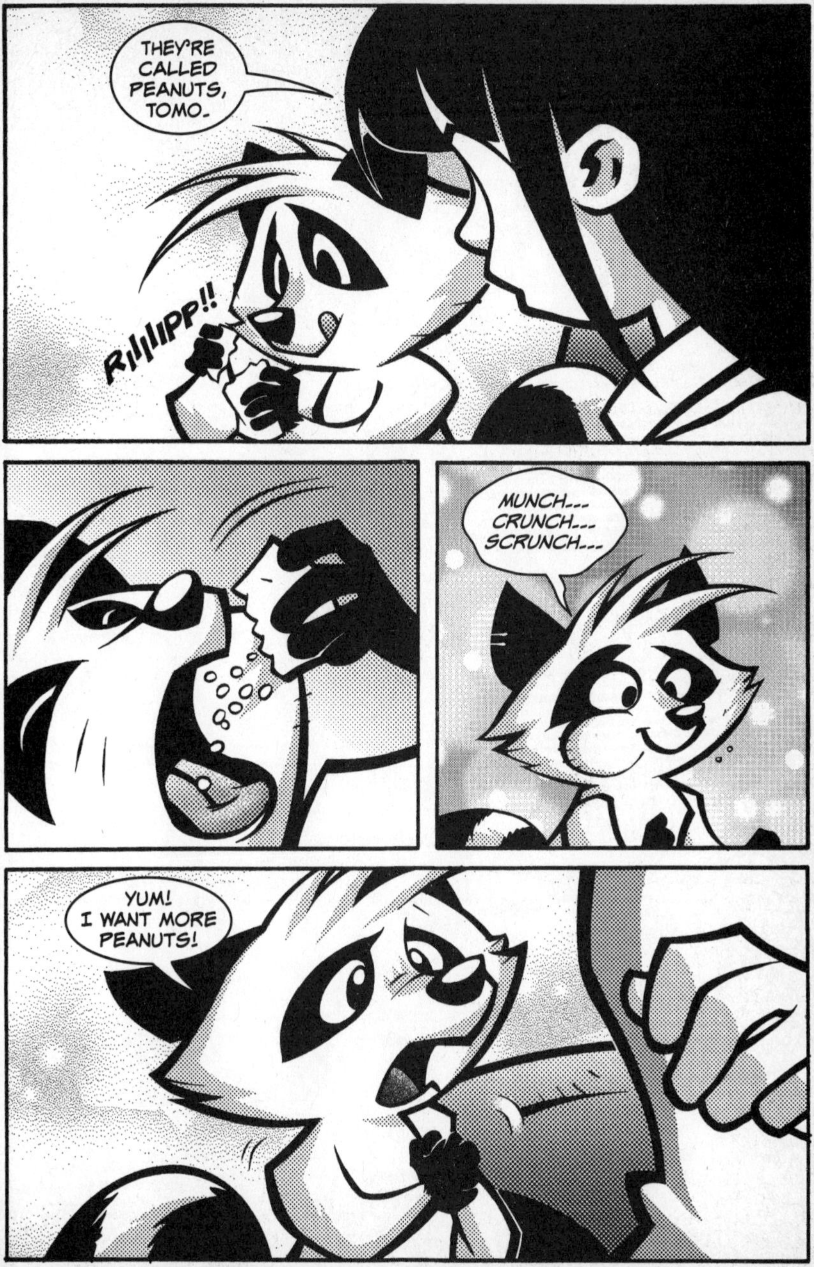
THEY'RE CALLED PEANUTS, TOMO.
RIIIIIPP!!
MUNCH... CRUNCH... SCRUNCH...
YUM! I WANT MORE PEANUTS!

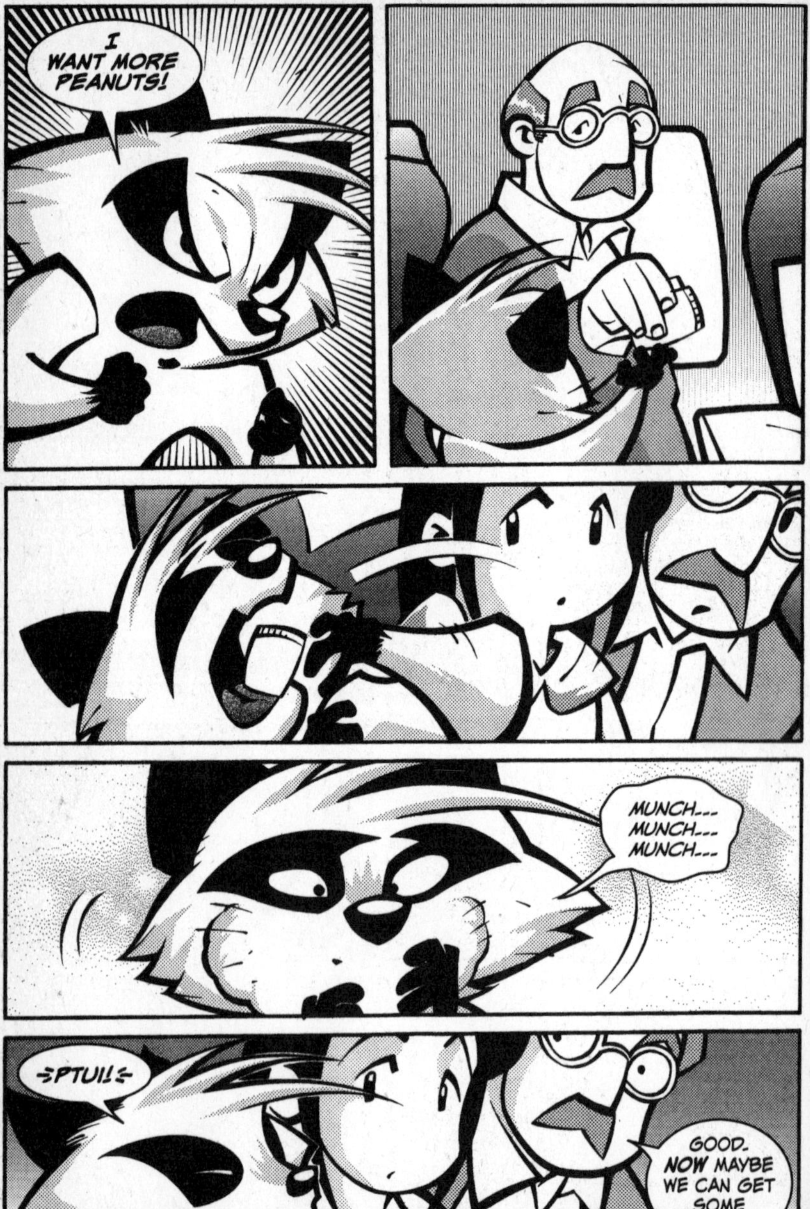
I WANT MORE PEANUTS!
MUNCH... MUNCH... MUNCH...
=PTUI!=
GOOD. NOW MAYBE WE CAN GET SOME SLEEP.

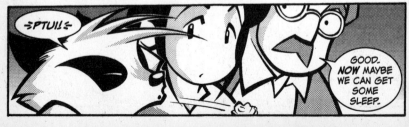

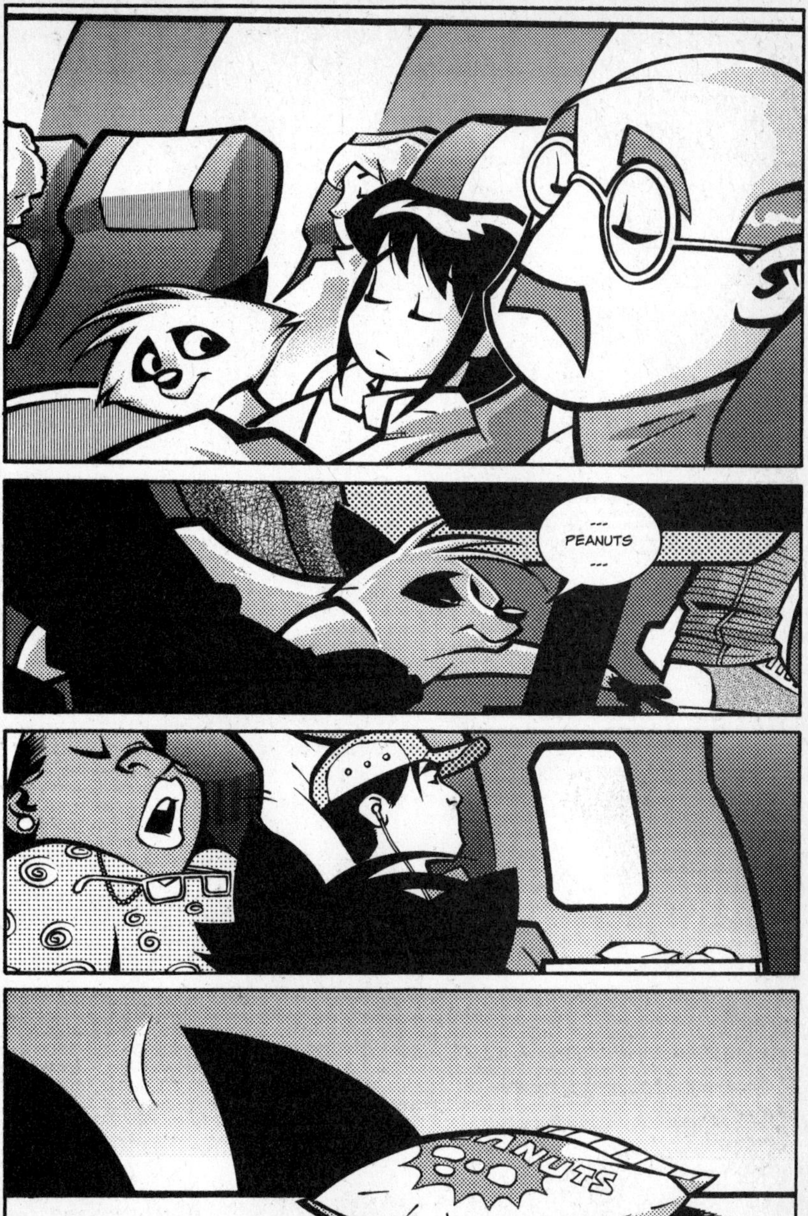
--- PEANUTS ---
ANUTS

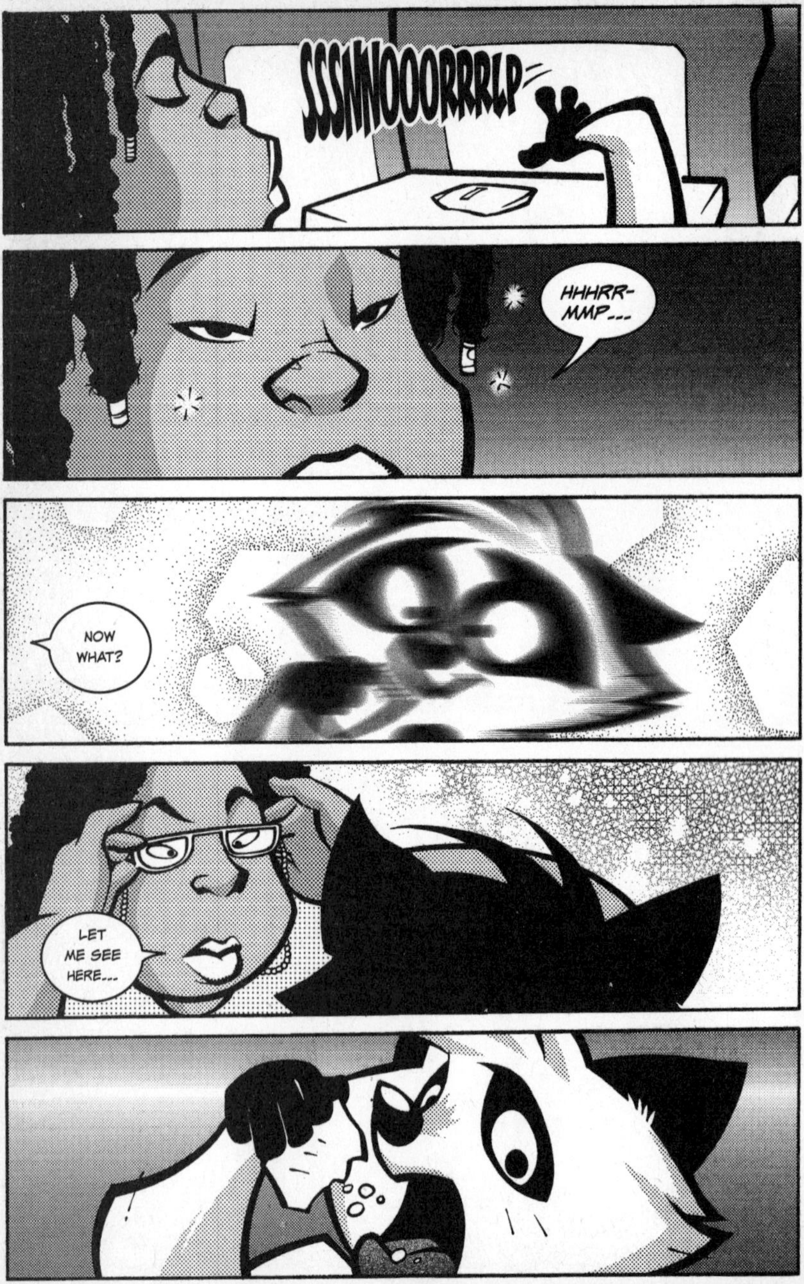
SSSNNOOORRRRLP
HHHRR-MMP---
NOW WHAT?
LET ME SEE HERE---

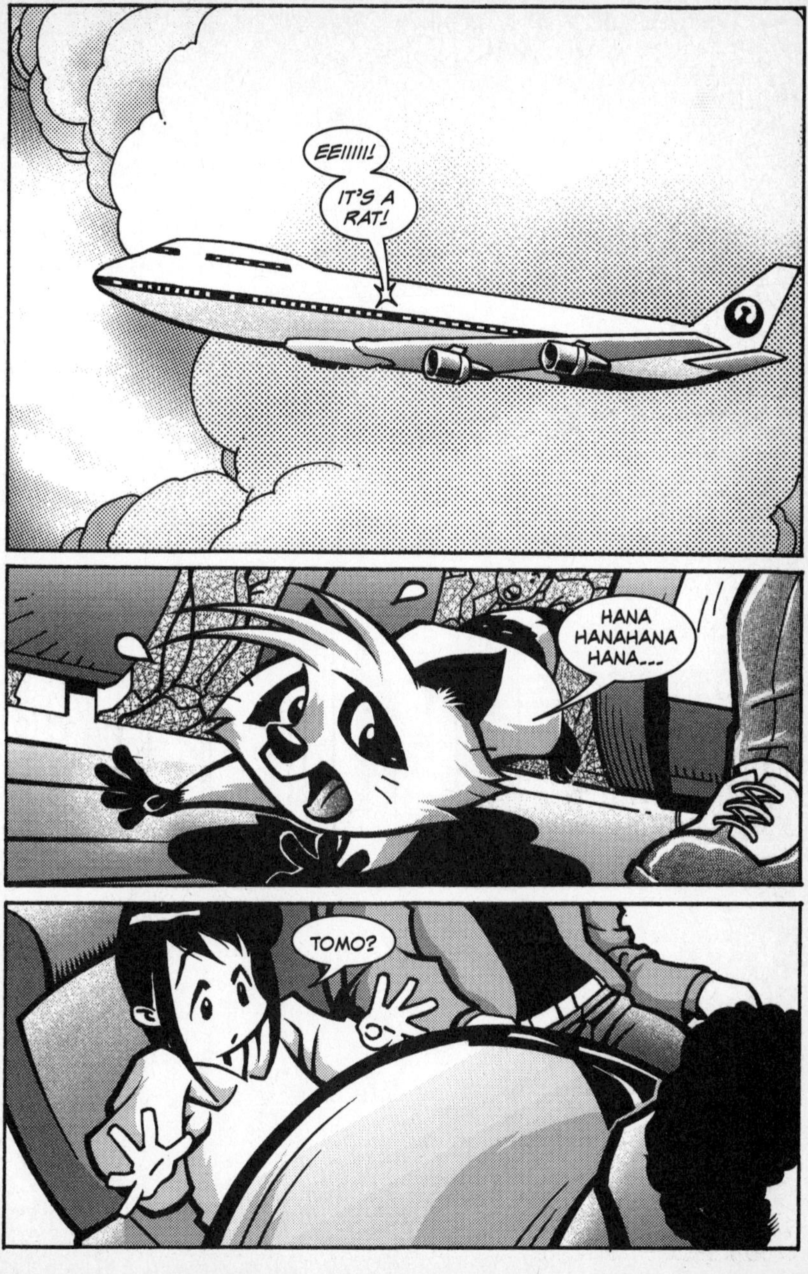
EEIIIII!
IT'S A RAT!
HANA HANAHANA HANA...
TOMO?

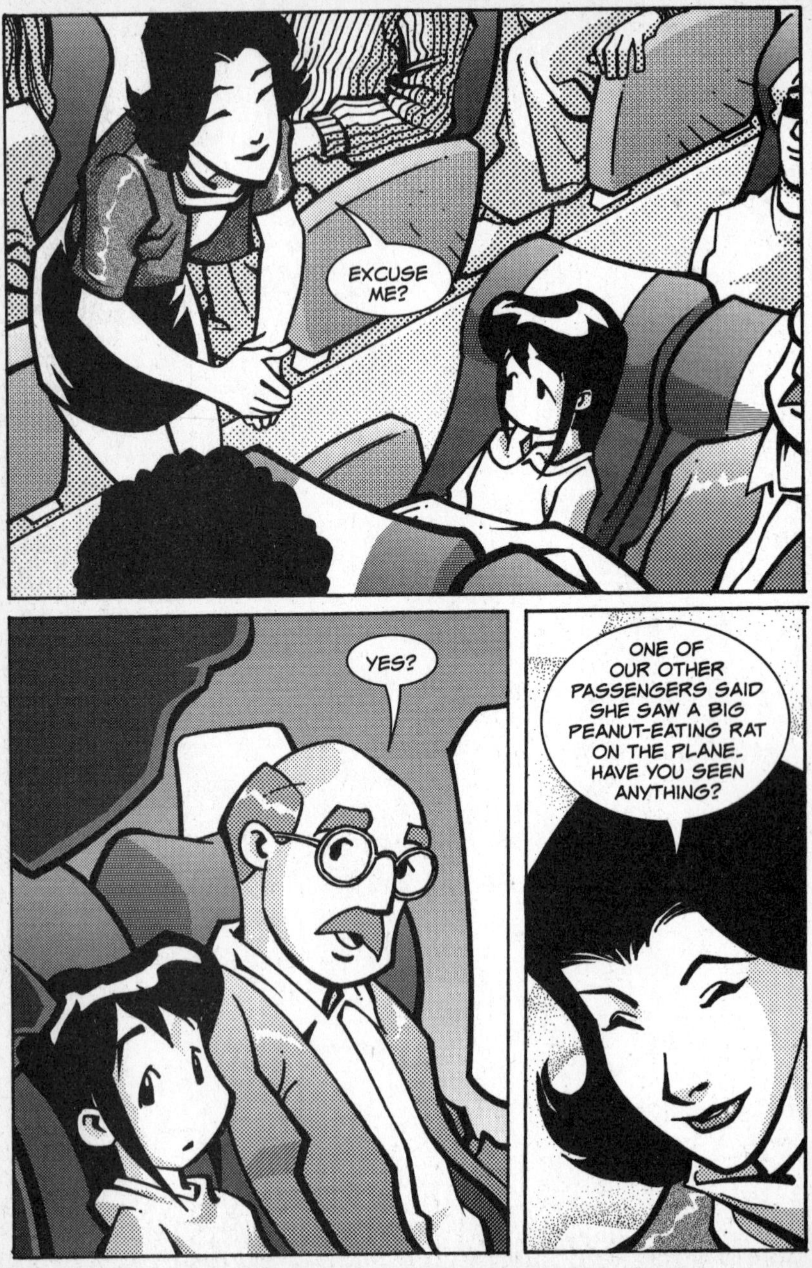
EXCUSE ME?
YES?
ONE OF OUR OTHER PASSENGERS SAID SHE SAW A BIG PEANUT-EATING RAT ON THE PLANE. HAVE YOU SEEN ANYTHING?

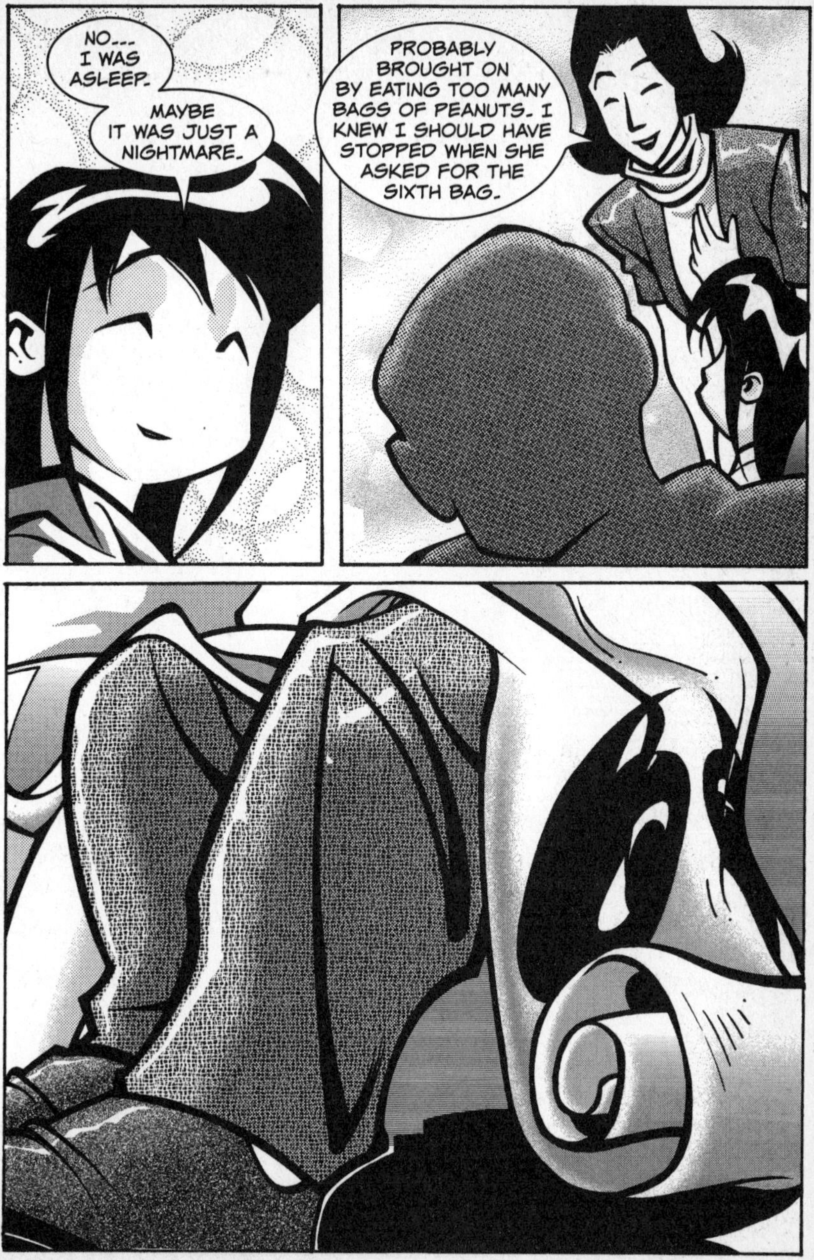
NO...
I WAS
ASLEEP.
MAYBE
IT WAS JUST A
NIGHTMARE.
PROBABLY
BROUGHT ON
BY EATING TOO MANY
BAGS OF PEANUTS. I
KNEW I SHOULD HAVE
STOPPED WHEN SHE
ASKED FOR THE
SIXTH BAG.

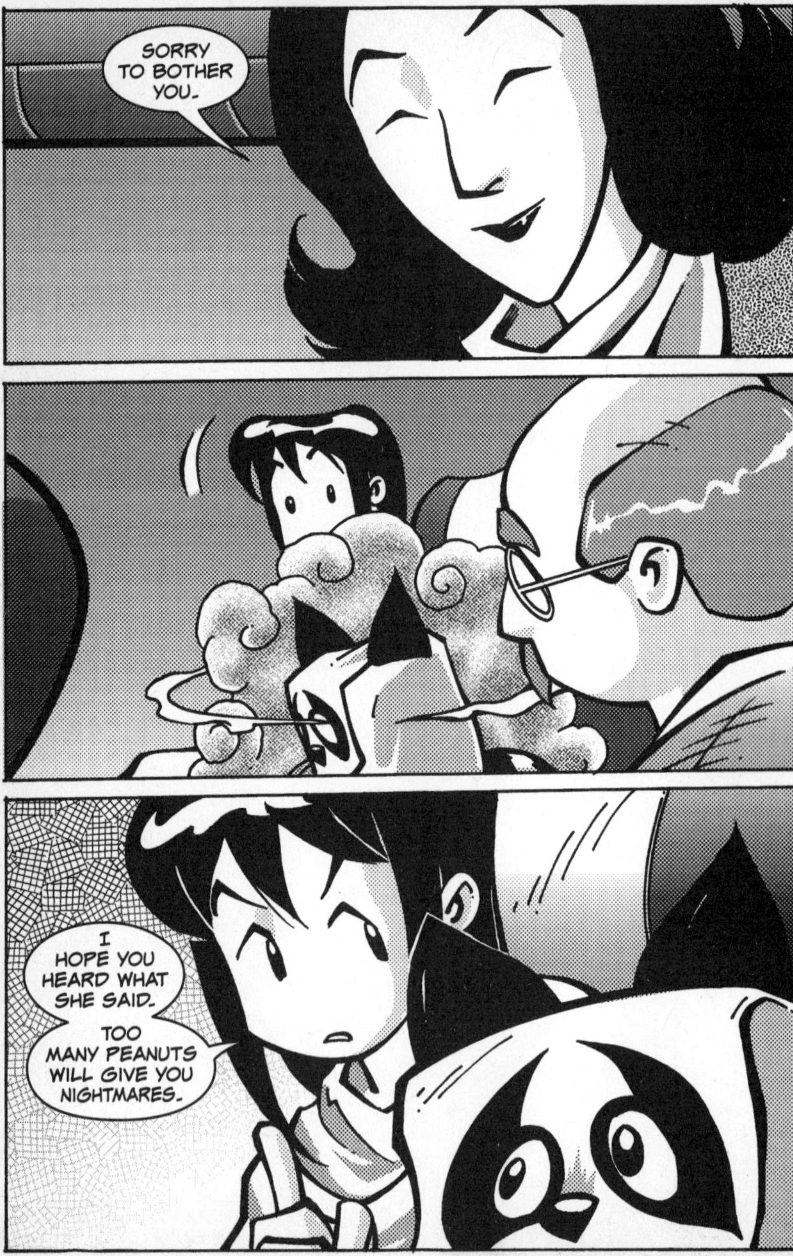
SORRY TO BOTHER YOU.
I HOPE YOU HEARD WHAT SHE SAID.
TOO MANY PEANUTS WILL GIVE YOU NIGHTMARES.

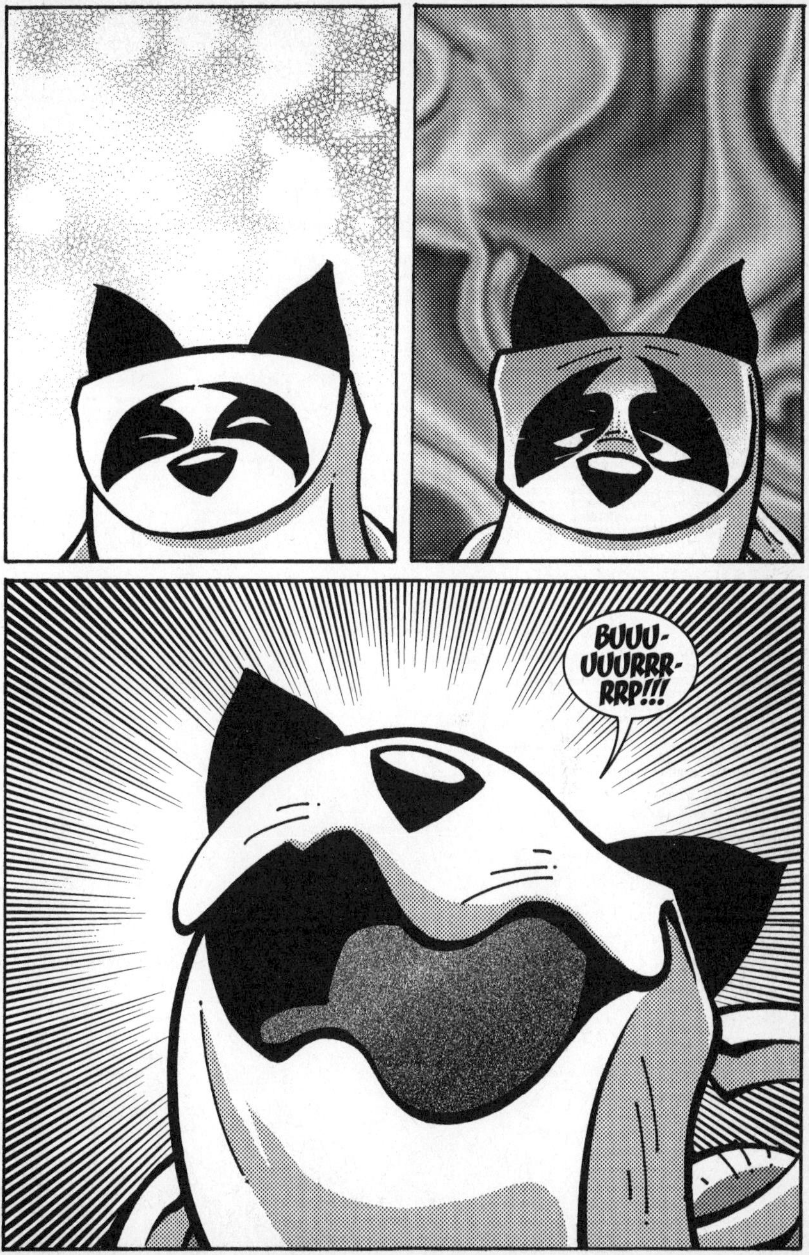
BUUU-UUURRR-RRP!!!

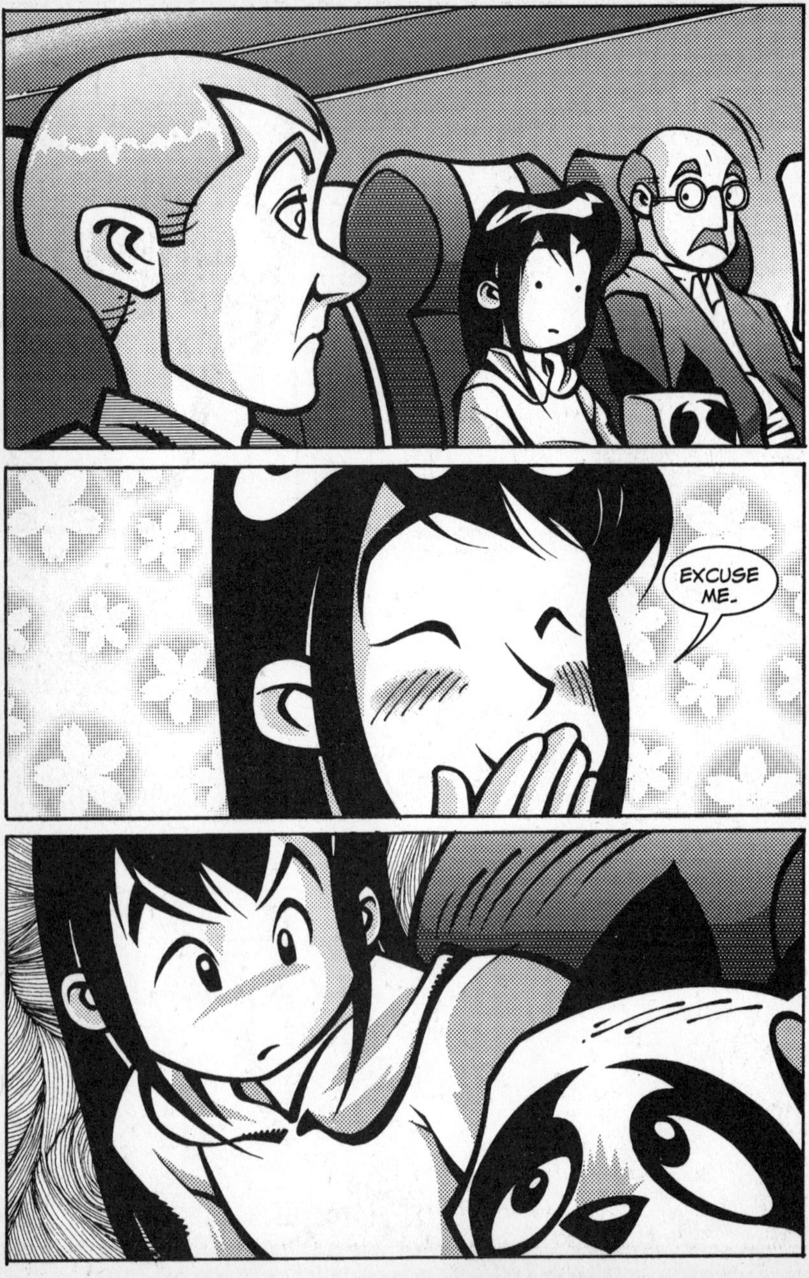
EXCUSE ME_

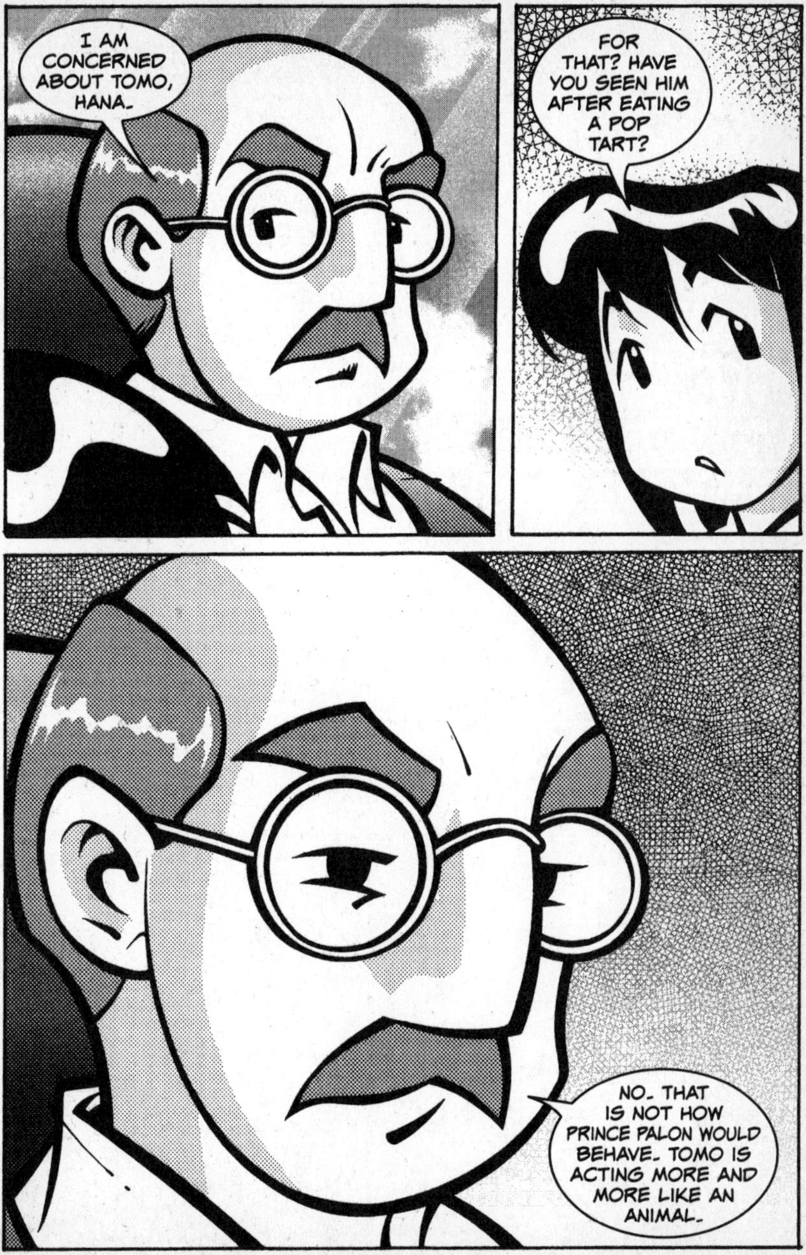
I AM CONCERNED ABOUT TOMO, HANA.
FOR THAT? HAVE YOU SEEN HIM AFTER EATING A POP TART?
NO. THAT IS NOT HOW PRINCE PALON WOULD BEHAVE. TOMO IS ACTING MORE AND MORE LIKE AN ANIMAL.

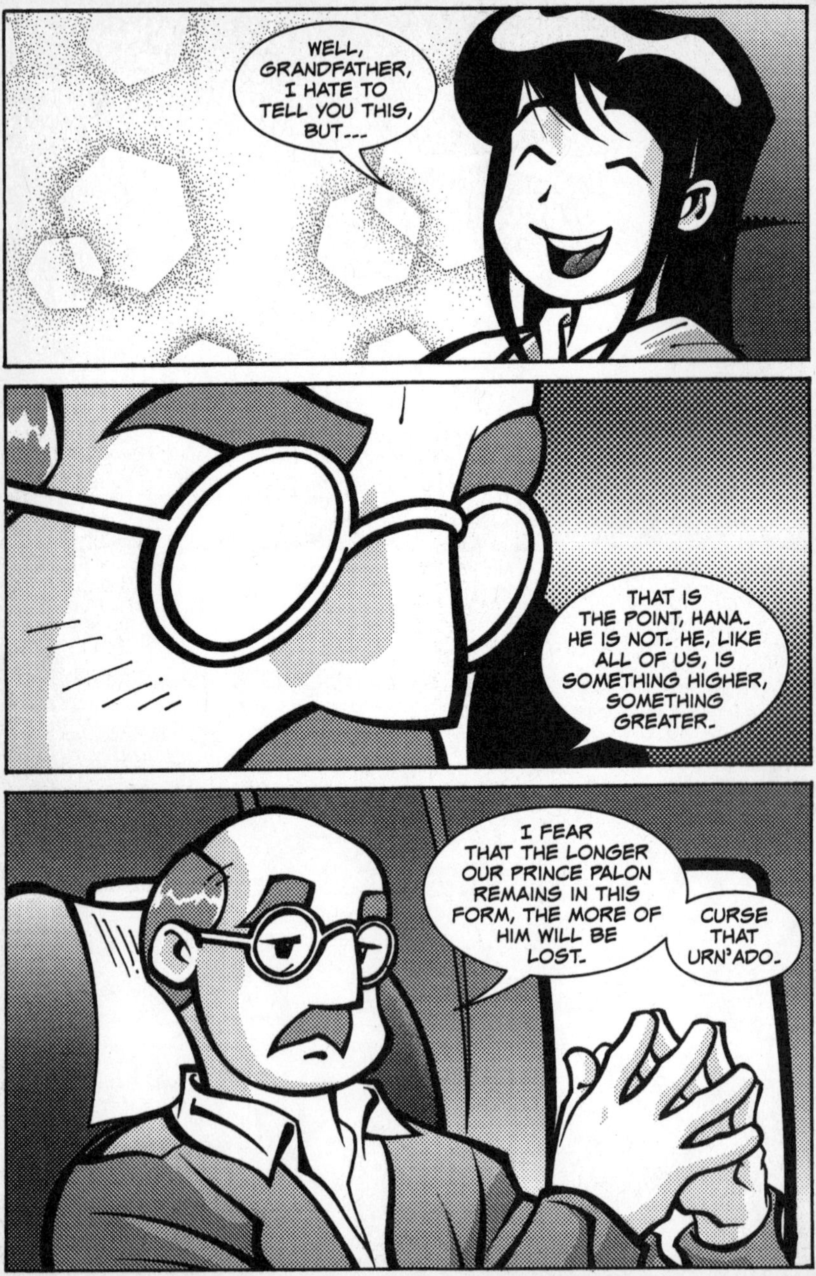
WELL, GRANDFATHER, I HATE TO TELL YOU THIS, BUT...
THAT IS THE POINT, HANA. HE IS NOT. HE, LIKE ALL OF US, IS SOMETHING HIGHER, SOMETHING GREATER.
I FEAR THAT THE LONGER OUR PRINCE PALON REMAINS IN THIS FORM, THE MORE OF HIM WILL BE LOST.
CURSE THAT URN'ADO.

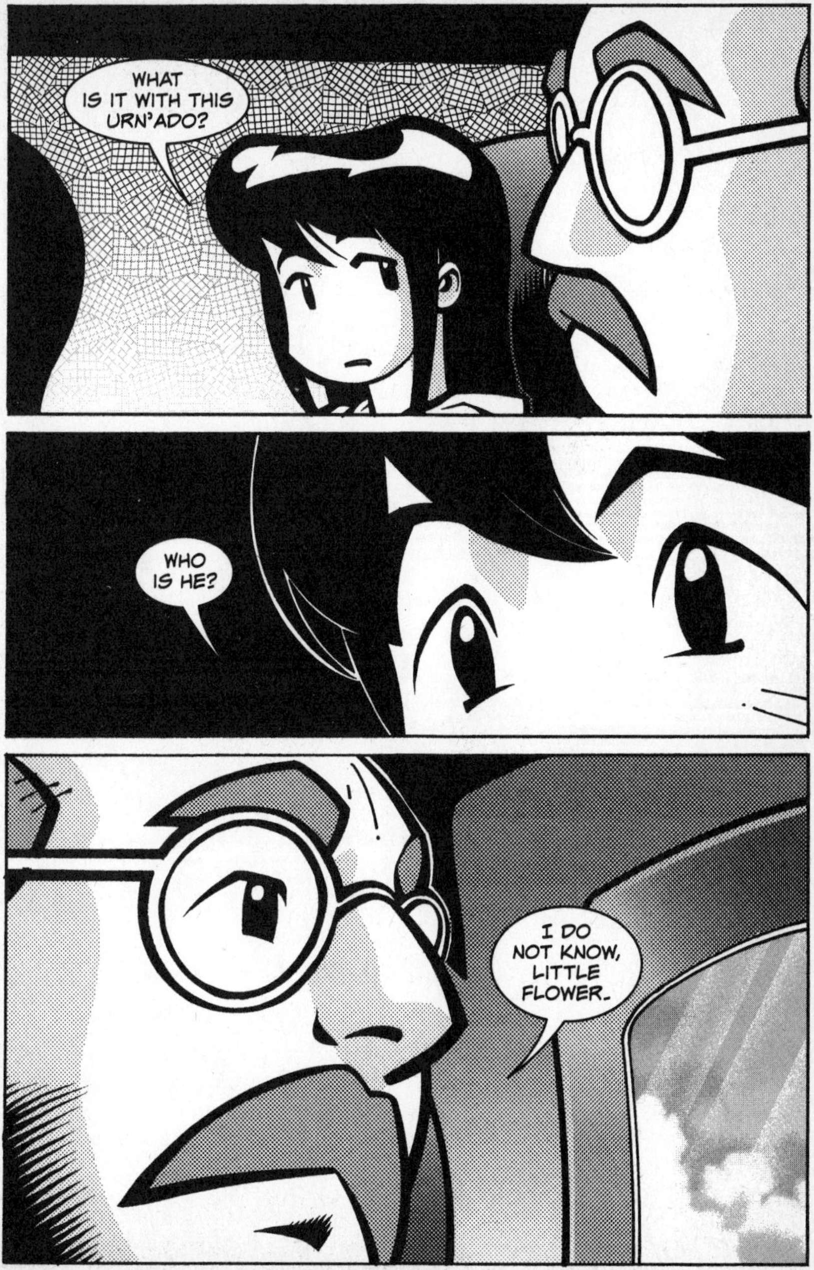
WHAT IS IT WITH THIS URN'ADO?
WHO IS HE?
I DO NOT KNOW, LITTLE FLOWER.

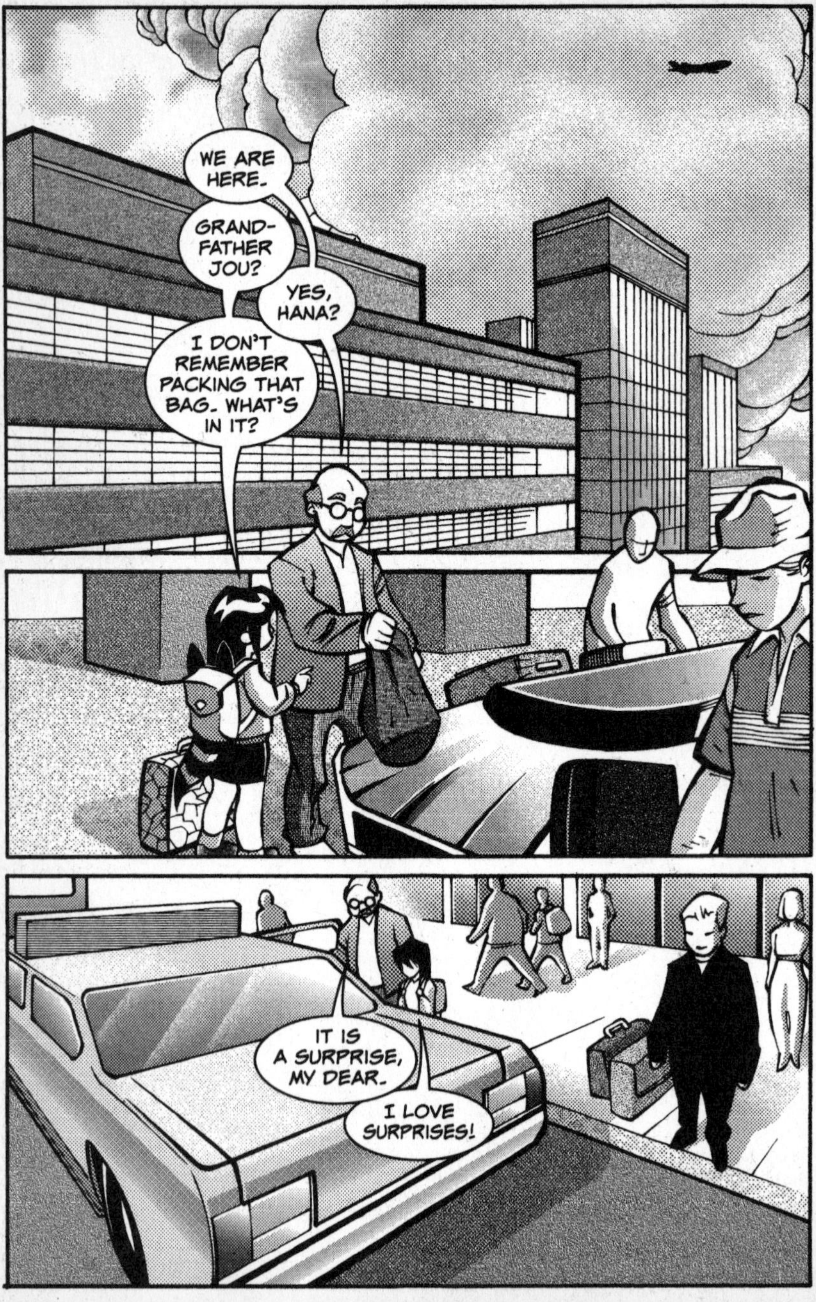
WE ARE HERE.
GRAND-FATHER JOU?
YES, HANA?
I DON'T REMEMBER PACKING THAT BAG. WHAT'S IN IT?
IT IS A SURPRISE, MY DEAR.
I LOVE SURPRISES!

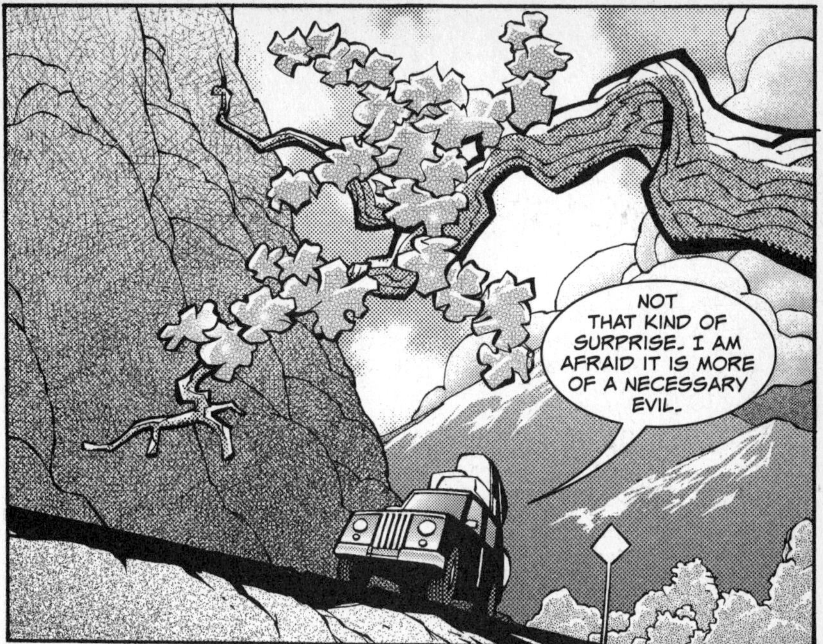
NOT THAT KIND OF SURPRISE. I AM AFRAID IT IS MORE OF A NECESSARY EVIL.

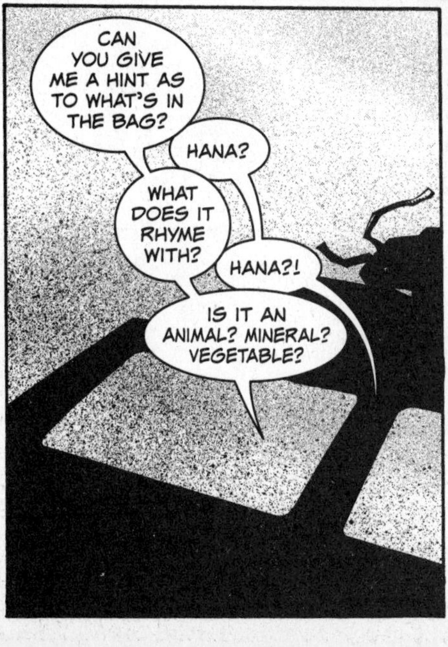
CAN YOU GIVE ME A HINT AS TO WHAT'S IN THE BAG?
HANA?
WHAT DOES IT RHYME WITH?
HANA?!
IS IT AN ANIMAL? MINERAL? VEGETABLE?

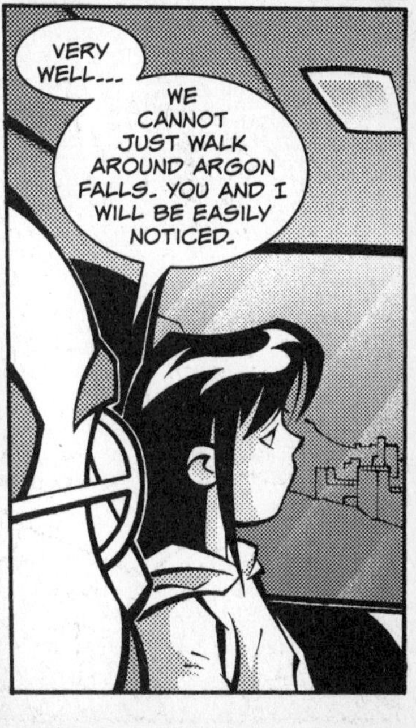
VERY WELL...
WE CANNOT JUST WALK AROUND ARGON FALLS. YOU AND I WILL BE EASILY NOTICED.

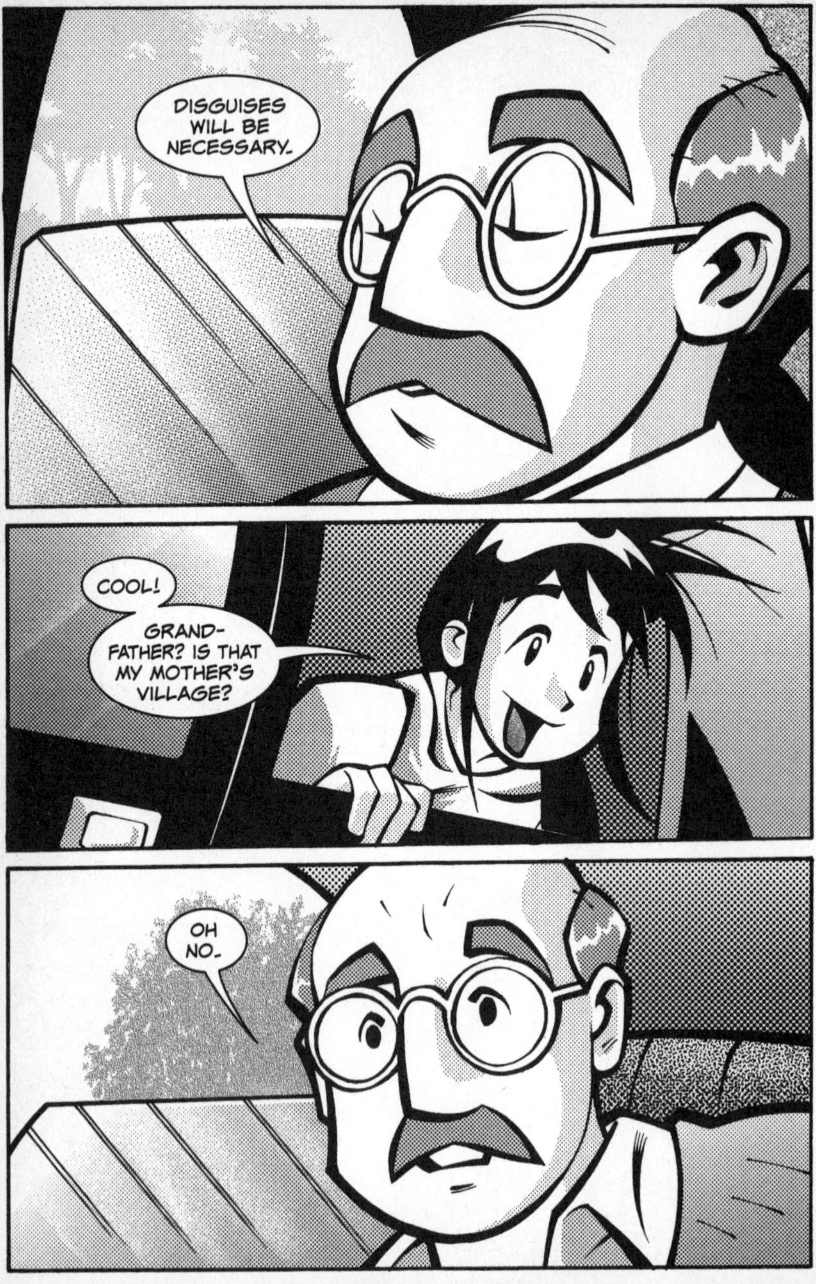
DISGUISES WILL BE NECESSARY.
COOL!
GRANDFATHER? IS THAT MY MOTHER'S VILLAGE?
OH NO.

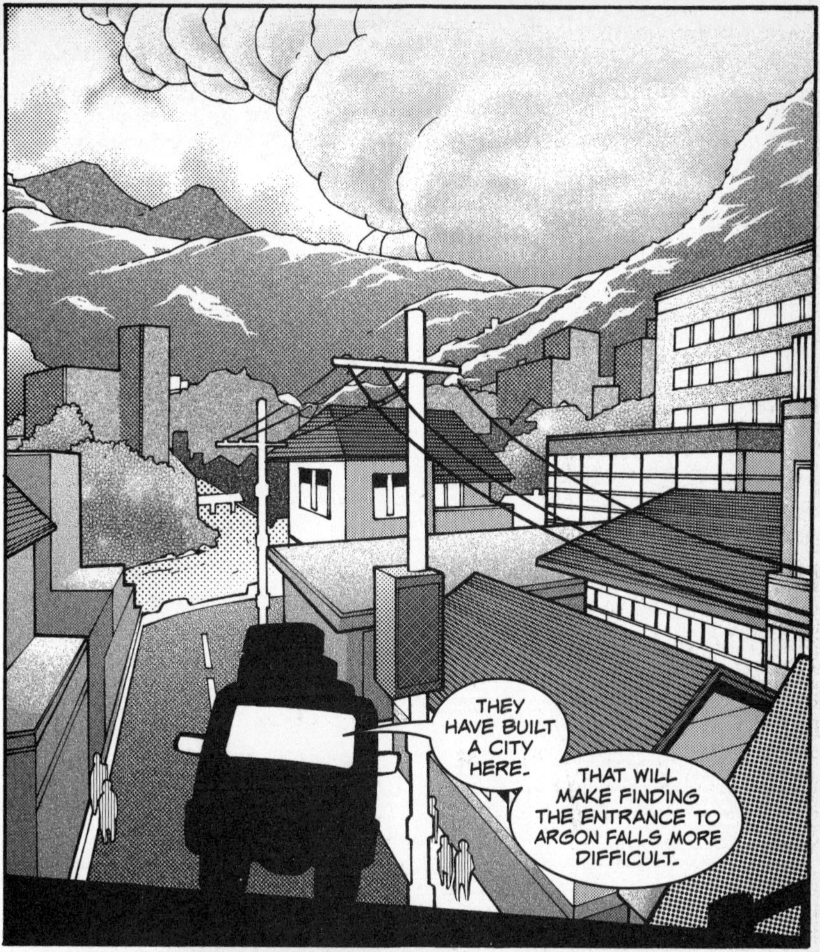
THEY HAVE BUILT A CITY HERE.
THAT WILL MAKE FINDING THE ENTRANCE TO ARGON FALLS MORE DIFFICULT.

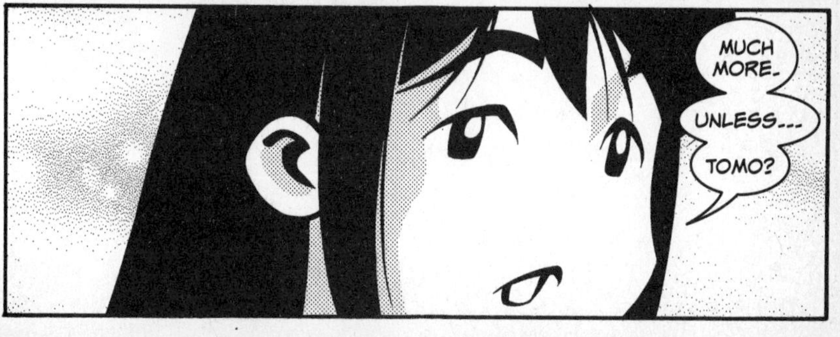
MUCH MORE.
UNLESS...
TOMO?

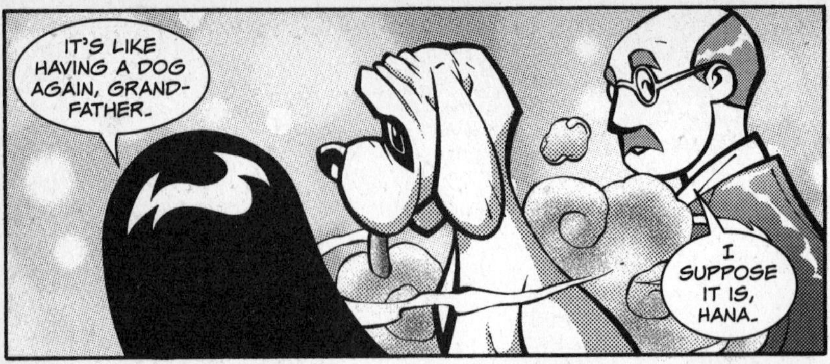
IT'S LIKE HAVING A DOG AGAIN, GRAND-FATHER.
I SUPPOSE IT IS, HANA.

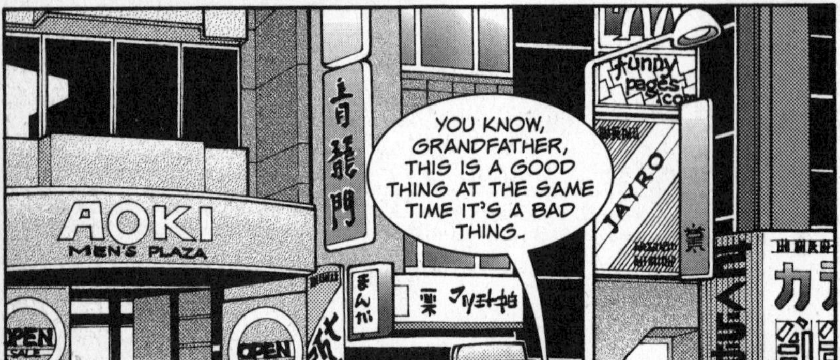
AOKI
MEN'S PLAZA
OPEN SALE
OPEN SALE
まんが
funny pages .com
JAYRO
YOU KNOW, GRANDFATHER, THIS IS A GOOD THING AT THE SAME TIME IT'S A BAD THING.

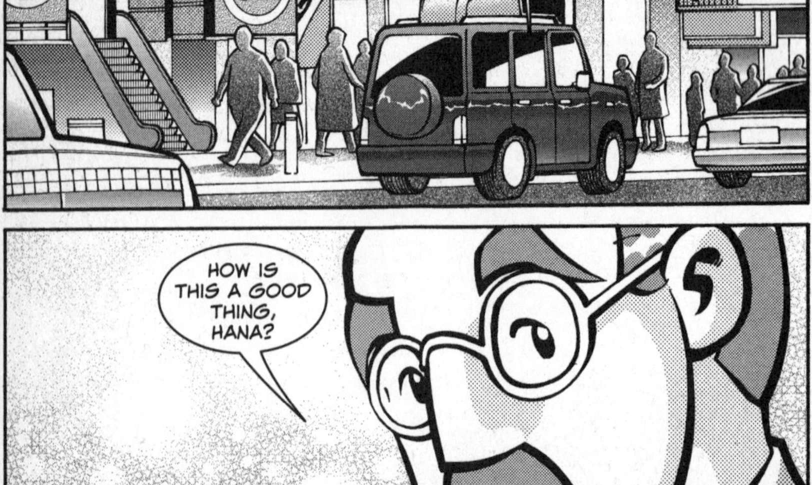
HOW IS THIS A GOOD THING, HANA?

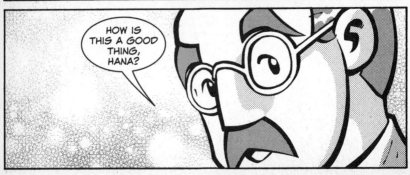

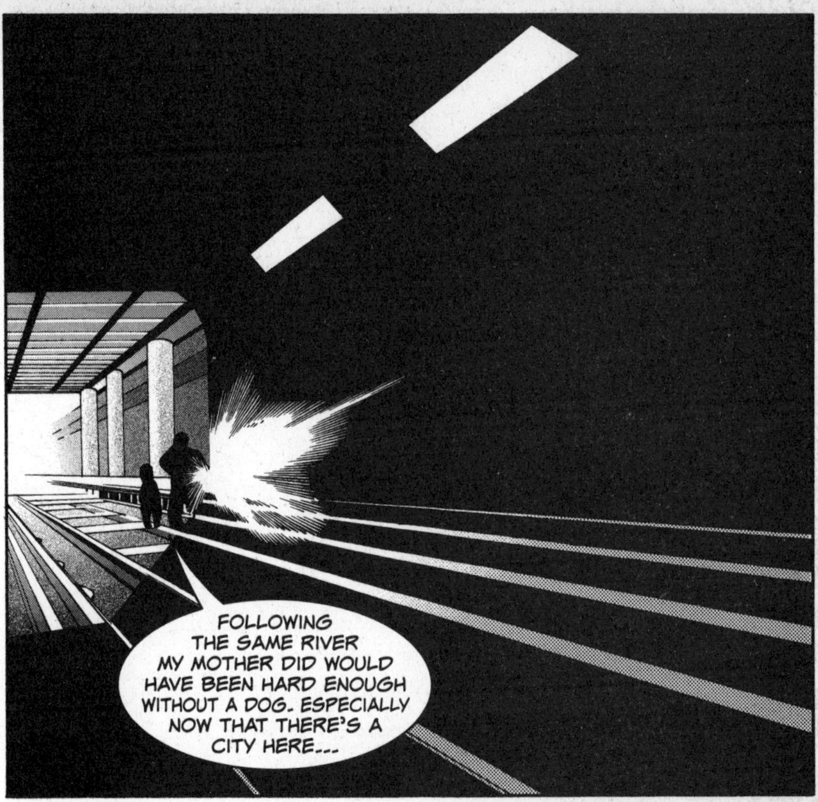
FOLLOWING THE SAME RIVER MY MOTHER DID WOULD HAVE BEEN HARD ENOUGH WITHOUT A DOG. ESPECIALLY NOW THAT THERE'S A CITY HERE...
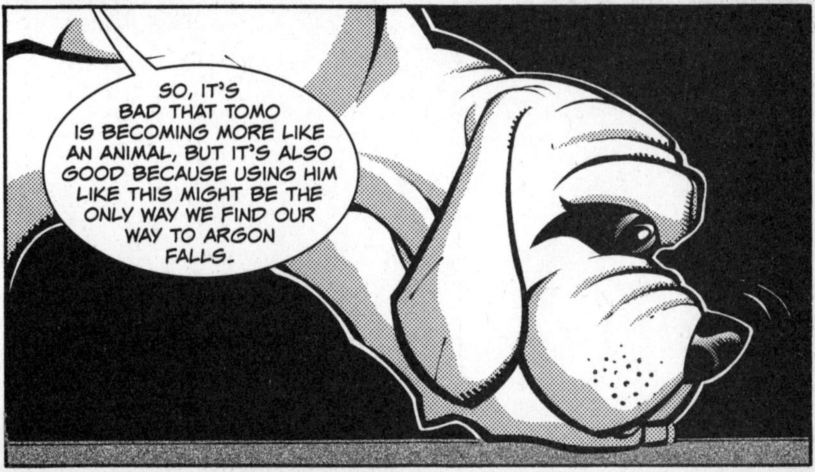
SO, IT'S BAD THAT TOMO IS BECOMING MORE LIKE AN ANIMAL, BUT IT'S ALSO GOOD BECAUSE USING HIM LIKE THIS MIGHT BE THE ONLY WAY WE FIND OUR WAY TO ARGON FALLS.

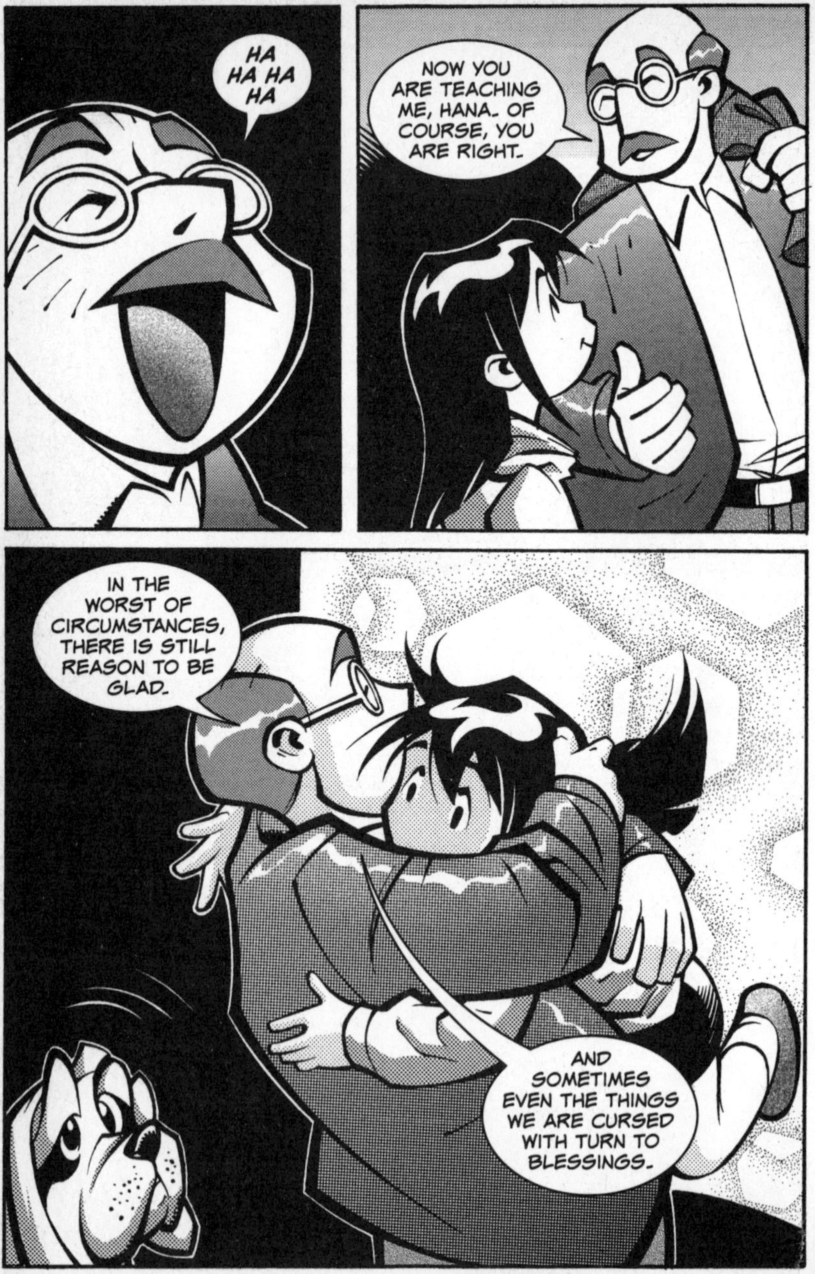
HA HA HA HA HA
NOW YOU ARE TEACHING ME, HANA. OF COURSE, YOU ARE RIGHT.
IN THE WORST OF CIRCUMSTANCES, THERE IS STILL REASON TO BE GLAD.
AND SOMETIMES EVEN THE THINGS WE ARE CURSED WITH TURN TO BLESSINGS.

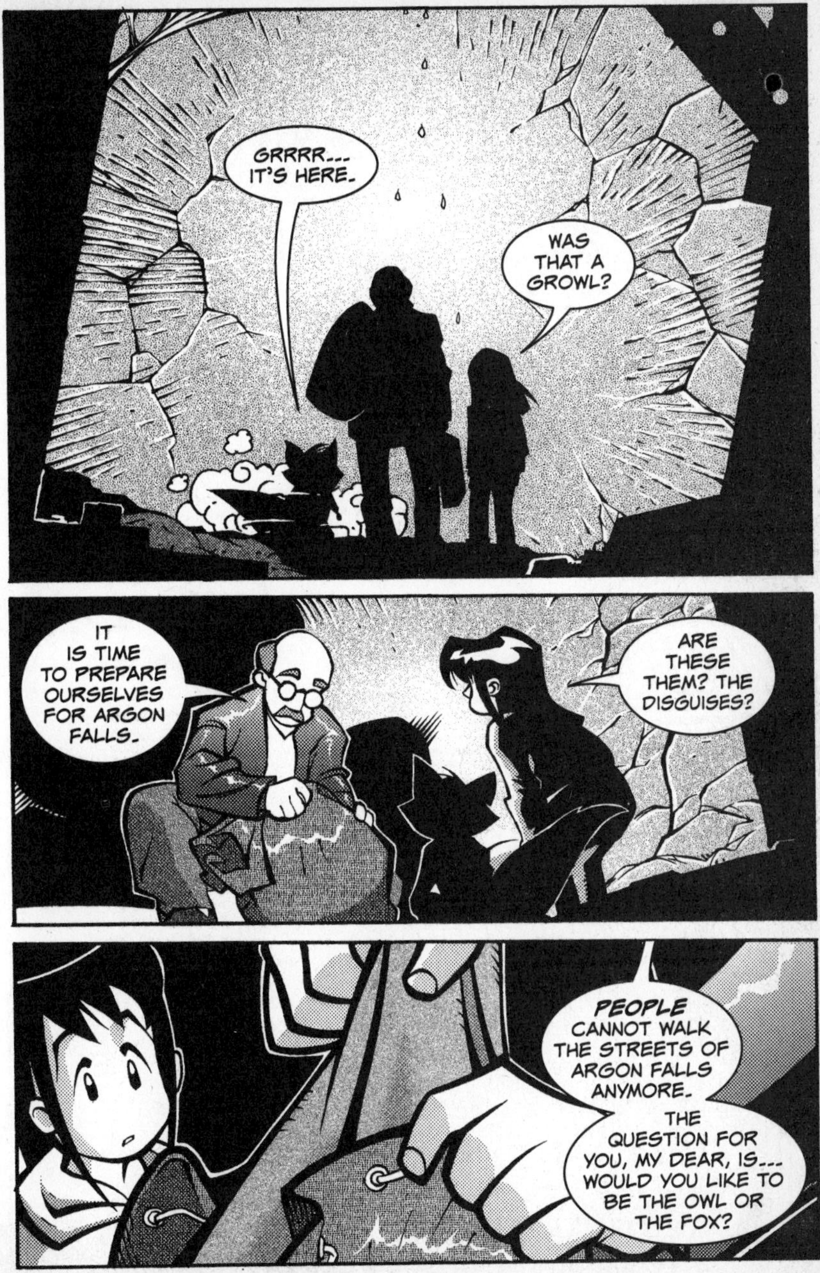
GRRRR... IT'S HERE.
WAS THAT A GROWL?
IT IS TIME TO PREPARE OURSELVES FOR ARGON FALLS.
ARE THESE THEM? THE DISGUISES?
PEOPLE CANNOT WALK THE STREETS OF ARGON FALLS ANYMORE.
THE QUESTION FOR YOU, MY DEAR, IS... WOULD YOU LIKE TO BE THE OWL OR THE FOX?

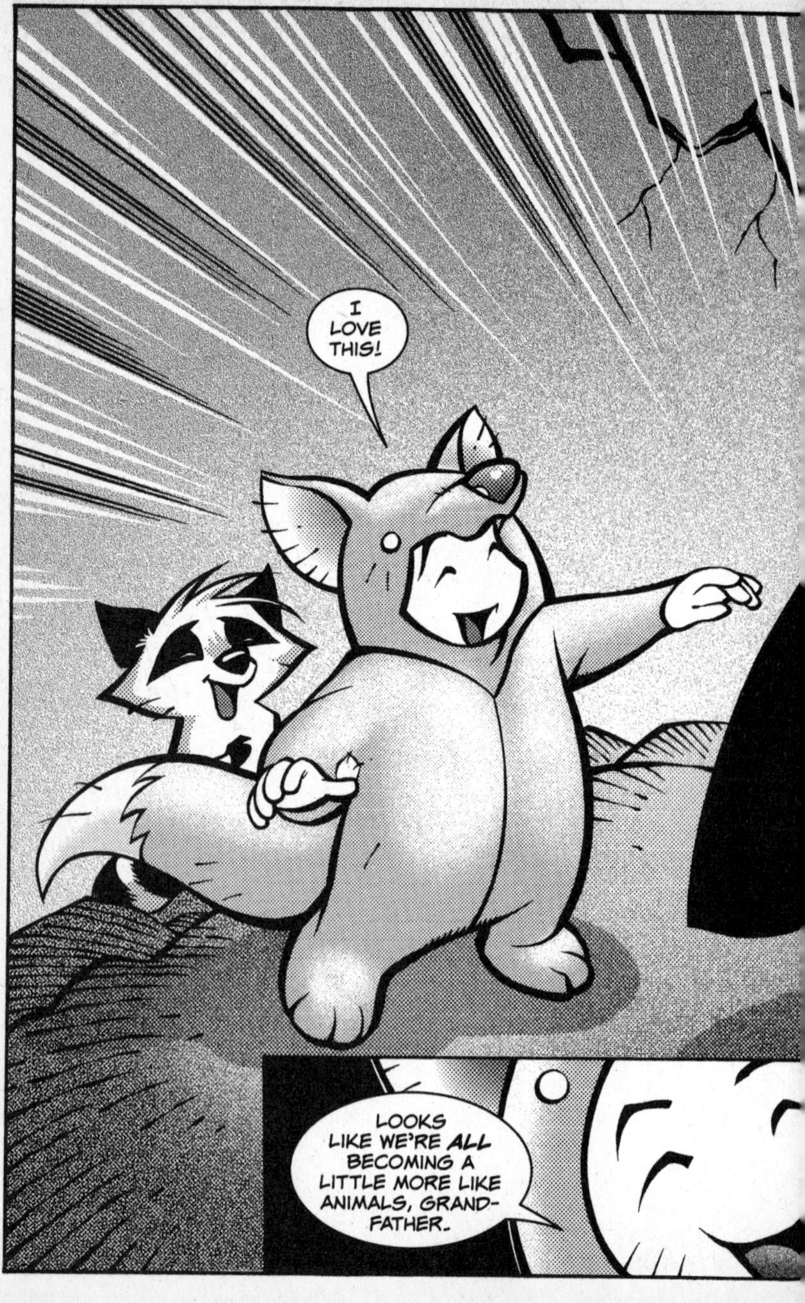
I LOVE THIS!
LOOKS LIKE WE'RE *ALL* BECOMING A LITTLE MORE LIKE ANIMALS, GRAND-FATHER.

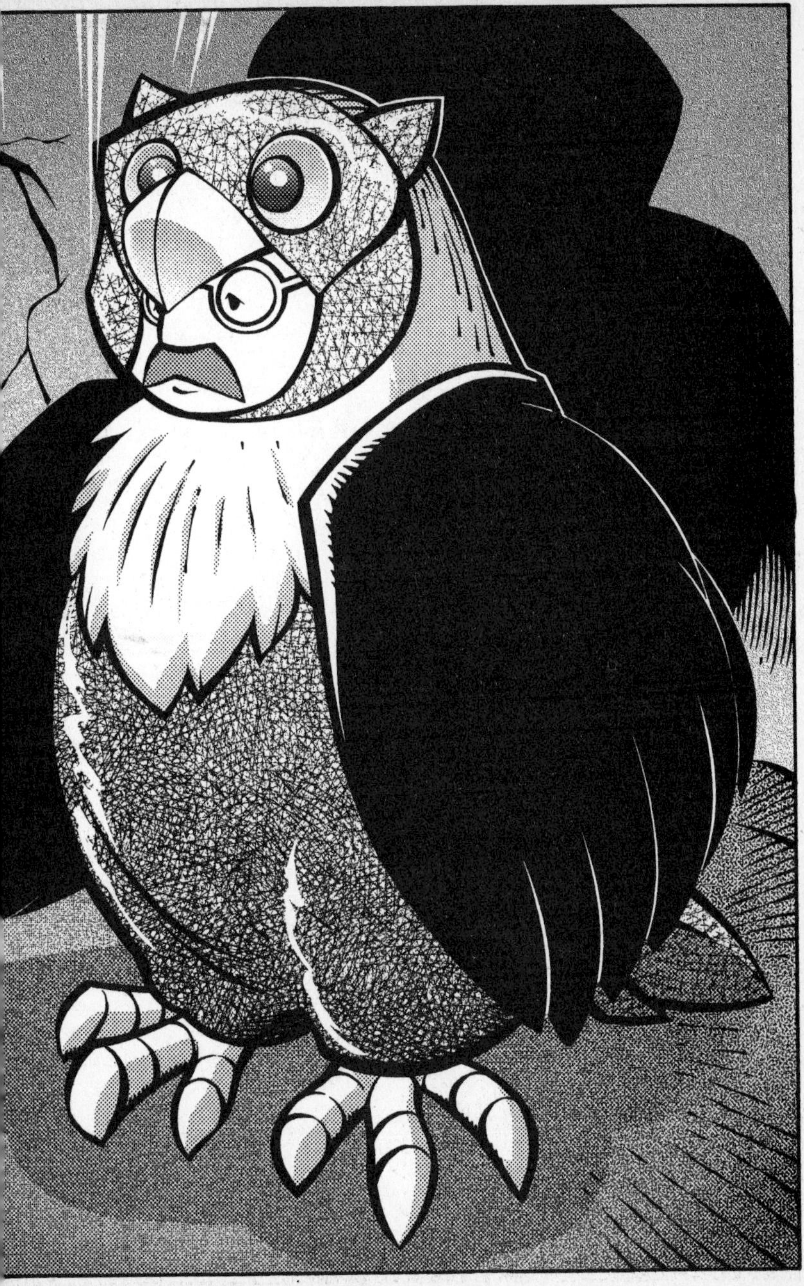

THIS IS JUST HOW YOUR MOTHER DESCRIBED THIS PLACE, HANA.

OF COURSE, THINNER COSTUMES WOULD HAVE FIT BETTER.

I AM SORRY, BUT THE LATEST TEENAGE FASHIONS WOULD NOT WORK IN ARGON FALLS.

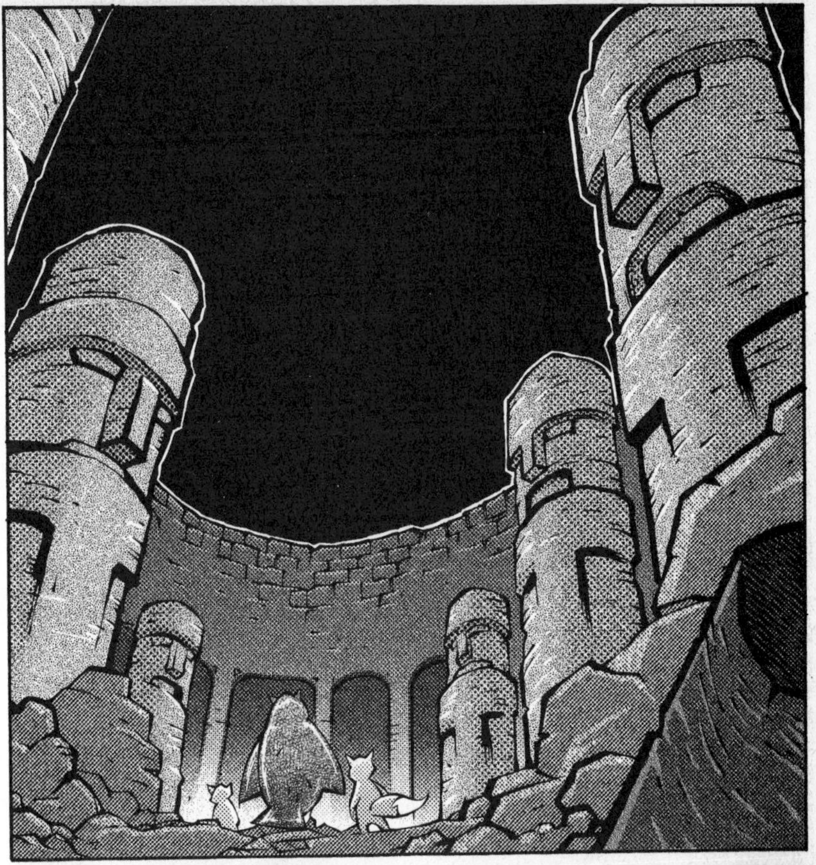

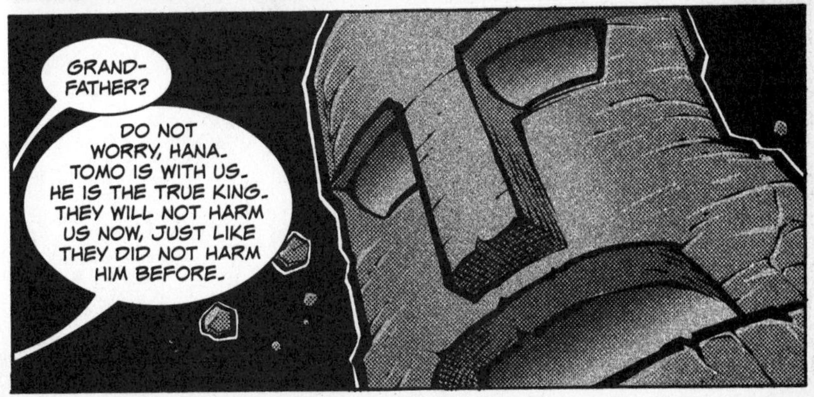
GRAND-FATHER?
DO NOT WORRY, HANA. TOMO IS WITH US. HE IS THE TRUE KING. THEY WILL NOT HARM US NOW, JUST LIKE THEY DID NOT HARM HIM BEFORE.

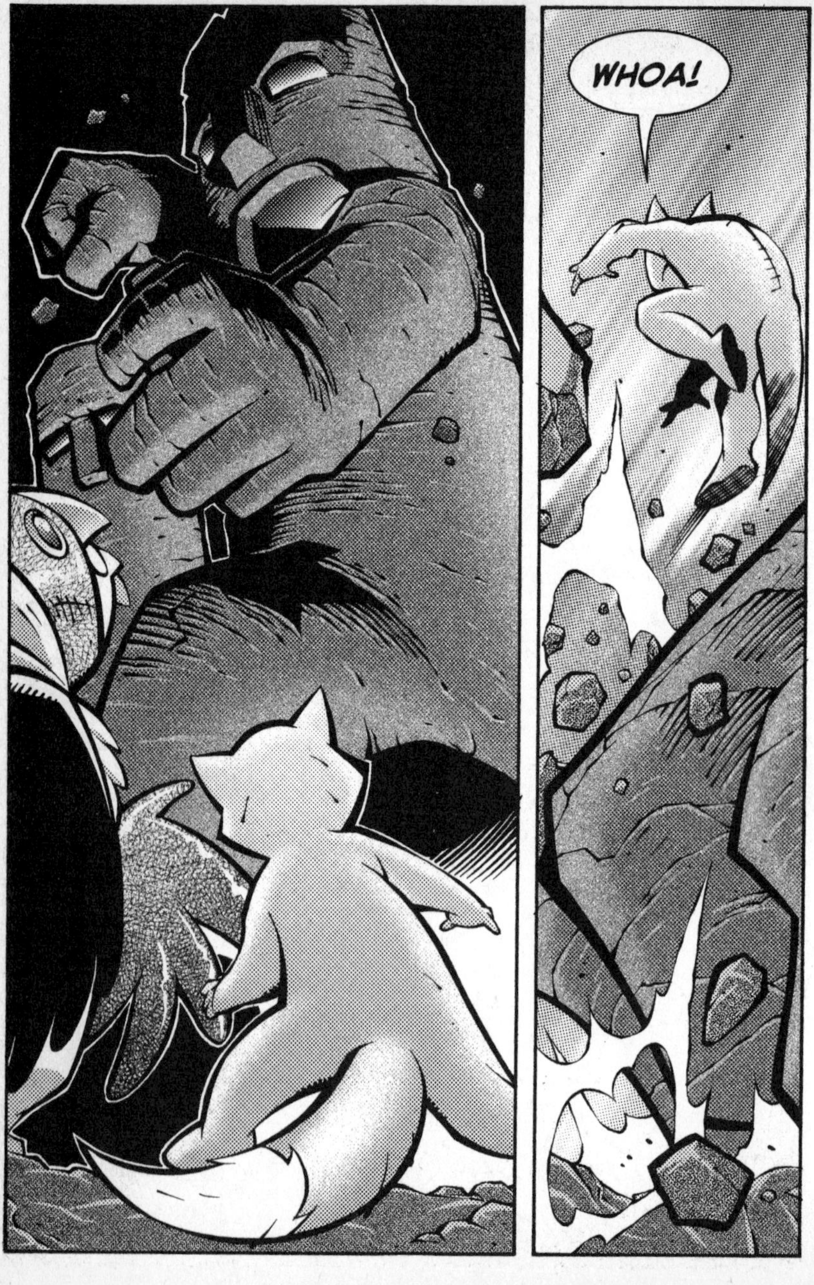
WHOA!

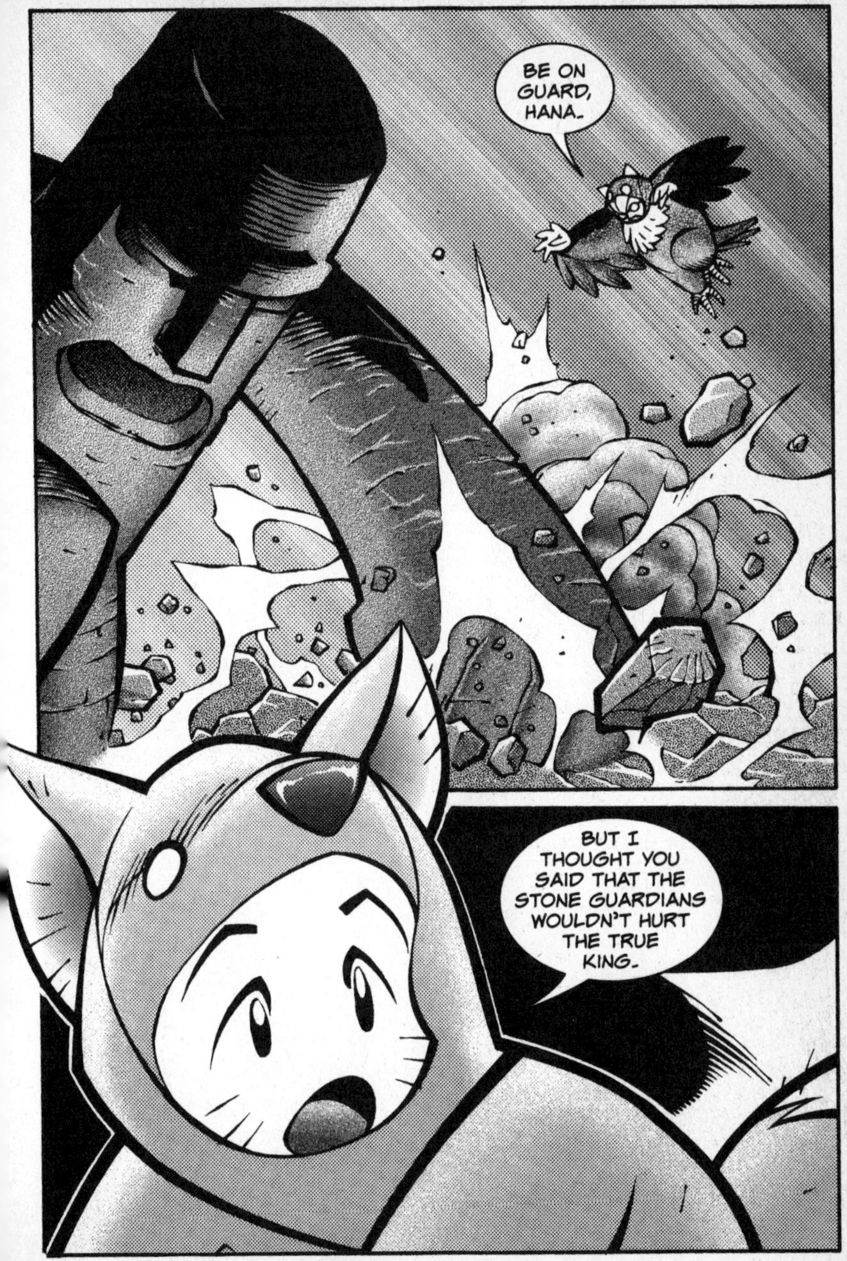
BE ON GUARD, HANA.
BUT I THOUGHT YOU SAID THAT THE STONE GUARDIANS WOULDN'T HURT THE TRUE KING.

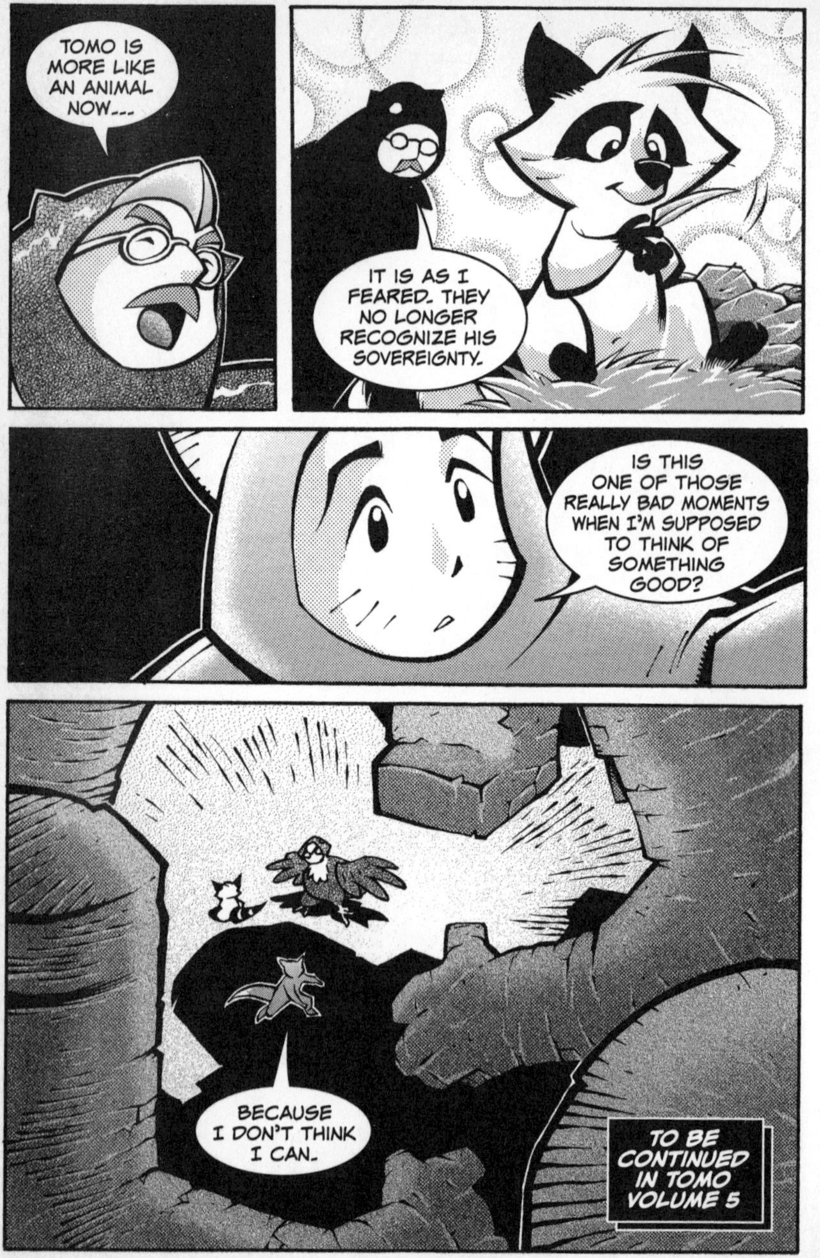
TOMO IS MORE LIKE AN ANIMAL NOW...
IT IS AS I FEARED. THEY NO LONGER RECOGNIZE HIS SOVEREIGNTY.
IS THIS ONE OF THOSE REALLY BAD MOMENTS WHEN I'M SUPPOSED TO THINK OF SOMETHING GOOD?
BECAUSE I DON'T THINK I CAN.
TO BE CONTINUED IN TOMO VOLUME 5

 ZONDERVAN®

We want to hear from you. Please send your comments
about this book to us in care of zreview@zondervan.com. Thank you.

Grand Rapids, MI 49530
www.zonderkidz.com

ZONDERVAN.com/
AUTHORTRACKER
follow your favorite authors